CONTROLLED FLIGHT

CONTROLLED FLIGHT

MIKE VAN HORN

Controlled Flight

ISBN: 978-1-7339293-3-2

Cover by Lauren Reneau
Some images from Pixabay.com

"I am an enthusiast, but not a crank in the sense that I have some pet theories as to the proper construction of a flying machine."

> —Wilbur Wright, in a letter written to the Smithsonian Institution on May 30, 1899.

"When this one feature has been worked out, the age of flying machines will have arrived, for all other difficulties are of minor importance."

> —Wilbur Wright, on establishing control of a flying machine's balance and steering. Statement made during his speech to the Western Society of Engineers, Chicago, Illinois on September 18, 1901.

CHAPTER ONE

WEDNESDAY

It all began so innocently.

Things spun out of control in a hurry, that couldn't be argued. But in the very beginning there was no urgency, no danger. No hint of anything out of the ordinary.

Paul Hull sat behind the wheel of his wife's Jeep Grand Cherokee, humming absentmindedly as he negotiated the gently curving asphalt of Indiana's State Route 36. It was just past seven on a pleasant August evening. He'd set the cruise control at fifty-seven miles per hour, a speed that ordinarily would've driven him batshit crazy, but he was in a state of mind that could best be described as *satisfied*.

He ran a hand through his curly black hair. Once jet-black, it now showed flecks of grey. Paul was 50 years old. Some days he felt every one of those years. The ache in his leg, the emotional baggage.

But today he felt satisfied.

Paul thought of himself as an average guy. Not average in the way it was defined by the general public. To most Americans the average guy was middle-aged, smarter than many, not as much as others, still retained a fair percentage of his athletic prowess—at least in his own mind—had enough money to do some of the things on his bucket list, and could navigate the hell out of his iPhone. Well, at least the five or six features he used most often.

No, Paul thought of himself as the sum of his experiences. There was quite a range. On one side of the ledger was a childhood that was perfectly happy while at the same time being astoundingly uneventful. There were B-minuses on grade reports, long minutes on the bench during ballgames, and thousands of blank-minded steps while pushing a mower across his parents' yard.

There were mind-numbing menial jobs, long discussions in the military with his buddies where he didn't seem to have many interesting stories to add, and bland MREs to eat. Lots of bland MREs.

Paul seemed to have more than his share of low flying life events in his footlocker.

But Paul had a whole other set of experiences in his background, and these tilted the balance of his life back to the average category.

Paul was an Air Force Combat Controller.

Well he had been, at least. Up until a couple years ago.

Paul saw heroism nearly every day during his twelve combat deployments to Afghanistan and Iraq. Most Americans, he supposed, had never seen an act their entire lives that fit into that category.

He saw gunfights, horrifying injuries, and unfortunately, more than his share of funerals for men he idolized.

Paul weighed his experiences and came to the conclusion that the bland, combined with the exceptional, equaled *average*.

Very few people that knew him well thought of Paul as average.

Paul felt satisfied because he and his wife Lauren had just spent an enjoyable few days with old friends. Glancing to his right he was assured that Lauren was feeling the same. She was wearing her customary car trip earbuds. Lauren, 45, had spent twenty-three-years in the Air Force. After completing basic training, she qualified as a Medical Laboratory Technician. She moved up the enlisted ranks and, twelve years into her career "went warrant," becoming a WO1 Warrant Officer and assuming greater responsibility. She still took every opportunity to further her education by listening to lectures by leading healthcare experts. She typically wore a look of concentration while driving or riding in a vehicle. Now, though, her lips curled in a smile. Still listening to a lecture, but smiling.

"Catching up on some Bill Burr?" teased Paul.

Lauren paused her phone, turned to him and asked "What?" A fraction of a second later his comment ran its way through her brain and she frowned.

Paul loved the irreverent comedian with Boston roots. So did all of his old Spec Ops buddies. Lauren had repeatedly said she detested his material. Secretly she admitted a fair percentage of it was damn funny. It was sometimes all she could do to keep a grin from burning through her frown when Paul had a Burr special up on Netflix.

"Not Burr, but something almost as appealing, a clinical study on how to better preserve human stool samples."

A half smile came to Paul's lips.

"No, seriously, looked like you were pretty content."

She responded, "Yeah, I guess I was only half listening to the recording. I was thinking of how nice it was to catch up with Ronnie and Deena."

The weather had been mild that week for August in the Midwest, highs in the mid-eighties with bearable humidity. Paul and Ronnie played a couple rounds of golf, Lauren and Deena shopped and lounged near the backyard pool, and they all enjoyed some easy summer evening meals with the Indianapolis couple's two high school daughters, Brinley and Shay, and their friends.

Ronnie Beaseley was a retired Army Ranger Lieutenant Colonel. He now worked for an investment firm in Indianapolis. Deena taught second grade. Ronnie and Paul first met in 2012 in Central Afghanistan. Ronnie was a Captain at the time with the 3rd Battalion, 75th Ranger Regiment. Paul was a Combat Controller attached to the Navy's SEAL Team Six. Shit happened. Ronnie was an officer, Paul was enlisted, they were in different branches of the service, and it didn't matter a damn bit.

The four of them all grew up in different states. They were thrown together by the military and that was that.

3

Deena grew up outside of Atlanta and met Ronnie, a native Californian, when he was stationed at Fort Benning. She was the only one of the four that had not been a member of the military, but by association had done her time in the Global War On Terror just the same. It was no picnic being married to a Ranger out on the tip of the spear.

That was all behind them now. They'd paid their dues and were making the best of their place in a slower world.

"We were overdue for some R&D time, was great seeing them," Paul said. Then, before Lauren could expand on the subject, he added, "So... I was thinking about a quick stop."

Lauren eyed him, realizing that they were basically in the middle of nowhere.

"Let me guess, there's some kind of historical site around here?"

Paul tried to keep his face blank for a few seconds, then his grin widened.

"Wait, wait, wait," she held up a hand. "OK, it's not the Air Force Pararescue Memorial Highway. We went out of our way to see that the last time we went to Indy....Hmmmm, couldn't be Annie Oakley's grave, that was right at the end of COVID......How about something to do with the Wright brothers?"

Paul's lips parted but nothing came out as he stared at her for three full seconds.

"Eyes on the road, Master Sergeant." She smiled.

Paul turned back to his view of State Route 36.

"Was it the books?" he asked. It came out with a hint of embarrassment.

"Sometimes you are easier to read than they are."

Her intelligent brown eyes sparkled as she tilted her head. Lauren tended to do this when she was trying to make a point. Her hair, also brown, fought to stay in place when she did this. Paul noticed the idiosyncrasy every time she did it. It was, after all, directed at him most of the time.

Paul slowly shook his head, a wry look on his face. They had just passed through the small farming community of Sulphur

4

Springs. Another village, Mt. Summit, was coming into view to the east.

"I guess there *have* been books about them laying all over the house lately," Paul admitted.

"Uh, your office desk and floor, on the island in the kitchen, next to our bed......not to mention the electronic versions of books on your phone downloaded from the library and the podcasts you're constantly listening to."

Paul didn't realize it had been *that* obvious.

"It's okay, I don't mind. Looks like the Wright brothers are your new obsession."

Lauren's head was upright now. She'd had her fun. Left unsaid was the understanding by both of them that Paul needed something in his life to occupy his mind. Three years before separating from the Air Force he'd suffered a devastating injury in a parachute jump.

It happened in training, not while downrange during a combat deployment. Ronnie had been there, down at Fort Bragg, North Carolina. He hadn't been in the field so didn't see Paul's compound-fractured left femur protruding through his fatigues. But he was at Womack Army Medical Center before Paul woke up after surgery.

This began a long period of recovery and rehabilitation. That was the physical part. The mental component was a bigger issue. Paul was still dealing with this. He missed subsequent deployments. Americans would be lost in that time, including a couple close friends. He would never stop wondering if he could've done something to prevent this.

Eventually the injury led to Paul's return to civilian life. The leg would probably always bother him. He limped a bit. He was back to running but the overcompensation in his gait often led to hip and lower back issues. All this *could* go away.

The mental part of the injury, Paul feared, would always be with him.

He now had time on his hands. Lots and lots of time. He had struggled some with alcohol, as a great many GWOT vets had, but fortunately had avoided the worst of those demons. He was able to have a few drinks and knew when to call it

5

quits. PTSD was a part of him now, a component of his being. It was the curse of his military generation, at least for the "tip of the spear" personnel. Paul didn't like it, but accepted it.

He exercised daily. Rather than subjecting his leg to the stress of running, he often cycled on the extensive network of bike paths that crisscrossed the area near their Troy, Ohio house. He also worked out in their home gym several times a week. It wasn't elaborate, but contained all the equipment the couple needed.

It was the mental aspect of Paul's situation that was more problematic. He needed something to occupy his mind. Lauren often worked long hours at Kettering Health in downtown Troy. Paul thought about taking a part time job or volunteering at a local historic site. There were several in the area. He'd even considered looking into options with the Air Force at Wright-Patterson Air Force Base near Dayton.

He wasn't quite there yet.

What *did* seem to grab him, seemingly randomly, were deep dives into various subjects. For a few months it had been cooking. Next came landscaping, an activity that provided the same distraction to Paul in retirement as it had after graduating from high school with no set plan. Then, a couple years ago, a near-obsession with Neil Armstrong seized him.

The Hulls now had a kitchen that a small city fire department would be proud to call their own. Their yard and garden were the envy of the neighborhood, and Paul owned a number of books on Armstrong and the Apollo 11 mission.

But he always needed something else.

Enter the Wright brothers.

Paul had been scrolling through random sites on his phone a few weeks earlier when he came across *Find a Grave*, a website dedicated to exactly what it sounds like. He employed one of the filters to search for famous people interred nearby. The Wright family site in Woodland Cemetery in Dayton popped up. Both Wilbur and Orville were buried there along with several family members. A memory was triggered.

Paul had actually been to the site.

In 2003 he and his unit were at Wright-Patterson Air Force Base for several weeks. They spent a good portion of their off time in the bars near the University of Dayton. Flanagan's Pub on Stewart Street was a favorite. Woodland Cemetery was a short distance away. After seeing the odd site of a Wright Flyer replica pass overhead, they decided to walk over and see what all the commotion was about. Paul would have rather ordered another Bloody Mary, but he was the junior man present and went along. It turns out there was a celebration marking the 100th anniversary of the first flight in Kitty Hawk. Paul, ironically a member of the Air Force, had no clue.

Dayton's "Centennial Celebration of Flight" included a number of special dates throughout 2003. None, though, were more significant than this day, July 20. It was the thirty-fourth anniversary of the Apollo 11 moon landing. Neil Armstrong himself spoke at the gravesite. He was introduced by John Glenn, the first American in Space.

Armstrong laid a wreath of red and white carnations next to Orville's grave. Glenn did the same for Wilbur.

Paul was flabbergasted. He had no idea the First Man On The Moon was in the area. Neither did any of his teammates. If it had been advertised, none of them had seen it. Paul was sure that this was the event that formed the basis for his interest in these pioneers. He was just too engaged to act upon it until his retirement.

Staring at the *Find a Grave* site years later, the interest sparked.

The hook was set.

Soon the books began to accumulate in the house.

His favorites, so far, were David McCullough's *The Wright Brothers*, William Hazelgrove's *Wright Brothers, Wrong Story*, and a fantastic compilation of photos titled *Gentleman Amateurs*, by Mark Bernstein. This last book was produced by the Dayton Daily News.

A squirrel darted from the right side of the road up ahead. It crossed the centerline, seemed to sense the approach of their vehicle, and froze. After turning in their direction for a beat it reversed course and scurried all the way back across their lane before disappearing in a small stand of trees.

Paul gently swerved and asked "So you're good with stopping up here for a few minutes?"

"Sure," Lauren answered, "but what is 'up here?'"

They had just passed through Mt. Summit. Paul squinted ahead and pointed.

Lauren turned her head and saw a brown sign coming into view. It featured an arrow pointing to the right, the icon of an old airplane, and the words "WILBUR WRIGHT BIRTHPLACE."

CHAPTER TWO

Smithson and Biggs pushed through the inner door of the old farmhouse. Biggs had worked at picking the lock for what seemed to Smithson an inordinate length of time.

Wasn't this guy supposed to be good at this shit?

While Biggs tinkered, Smithson stood behind him, holding open the outer screen door and checking nervously to his left and right. He'd used Grey to disable the cameras so he had no worries about being discovered electronically. Once the schedule had been agreed upon he'd known the only danger might come from a random discovery. Some farmer blundering onto the scene, a kid passing by in a four-wheeler, or whatever the hell these hayseeds in flyover country called their toys.

It was still light out and would be for another hour or so. But their prep work on this target led them to conclude that mid-week would be the best time to execute. Traffic analysis by Grey indicated that a strange car on this road during daylight hours was not completely abnormal and little notice would be paid by the few locals. The facility, if you could call it that, closed at 5 p.m. The two or three staffers locked up a few minutes later and returned to their homes, which, he was confident, almost certainly smelled of some kind of manure.

There was a caretaker. He actually lived in a room inside the Welcome Center. Grey discovered he used his Visa card for groceries every Wednesday night at a Kroger in New Castle, a few miles to the west. Once he departed, usually around the same time as the other staffers, the site was deserted.

They did not want to wait until dark. There was a higher probability that their vehicle would be noticed. They'd theorized that they could try to navigate these roads with headlights switched off. Smithson, of course, owned a set of night vision goggles. The NVG's were cutting edge, the same model some of the top military units used. Smithson had to admit to himself that he hadn't actually practiced much with them. They were cool though. How did the shooters in the military describe cool gear? *High speed.*

Another consideration was that farmers were known to get up and start their workday at ungodly hours. So that ruled out most of the morning.

They needed to hit the place sometime between 6 p.m. and sundown. Once inside they should only need a few minutes to accomplish their task.

The pair moved into the narrow hallway. Smithson closed both doors behind them. The only sounds were their own quickened breathing and the creaking of the dark brown plank floor. It was not the original house. That had been razed in 1955. The current structure had been built in 1973 but here, now, it had the spooky feel of age.

Biggs was visibly nervous. Smithson had built the entire operation around Biggs' work, but he sensed the man was rapidly losing the drive to implement it. Biggs had twice dropped one of his lock picking tools while working on the inner door. It was as if he had never worked with these instruments while wearing gloves. He was sweating profusely.

Smithson had never before worked with a partner. He first began to wonder about Biggs as they eased their vehicle doors open after pulling off the narrow county road. They 'd driven up from the south and Smithson had eased his Audi S8 into a gap in the cornfield on the east side of the road, several hundred feet south of the Wright location.

Biggs had asked, "Are you sure you want to go through with this? We could leave now and do more research... come back later."

Smithson's eyes had narrowed. He'd put some steel into his voice, "Look goddammit, we've spent six months setting this up. You were sure about your part. I paid for every piece of antique crap you asked for. I drove all the way out here to meet you. We're in the middle of nowhere standing in a fucking cornfield. Now is the time!"

He'd said this in a low tone but got his point across. Biggs, Smithson realized, looked terrible. He was thinner than he'd been in their only other meeting. Although still significantly overweight, he was somehow edging toward gaunt. Instead of improving his appearance, the weight loss seemed to give him a sallow look.

Biggs was in his early sixties. He was balding and had apparently decided to let the remaining locks grow without restriction. It was mostly grey now, a few dark streaks still visible. At 5'11" and in the vicinity of 250 pounds Biggs was still not near his optimum body weight. Smithson wondered if his "partner" had developed a serious health problem or if the man was having second thoughts about the operation.

Biggs had swallowed, nodded, and with his toolkit followed Smithson to the edge of the cornfield. Smithson scanned the north and south using his Steiner Military-Marine binoculars, another piece of high speed gear that the Australian Army uses....at least that's what the internet said. All clear. The road was Indiana County Road 750 East. Smithson would've called it a lane. He could not remember when he'd seen a less impressive stretch of asphalt.

Smithson stowed the binos, gripped the small zippered binder that contained the letter, and crossed the road. Biggs followed as sweat began to appear on his brow.

They had crossed the road and reached a ragged line of trees a few feet beyond, then turned north. It was only a couple hundred yards to the farmhouse but neither man was in great physical condition and both were feeling the effects of the late day heat. Smithson was accustomed to the lower humidity of the Western United States and was having second thoughts about wearing his trademark dark hoodie. The site had two parking lots. The one on the south end of the property was to their left. They then passed a full sized jet fighter, also on their left. It was propped up on concrete pedestals. Smithson had seen the jet in Google Earth views of the site. He thought it was a weird thing to have at an old Wright brothers memorial.

Smithson slowed his pace as he reached the shade of a hawthorn tree. When he turned to check on Biggs he adjusted his course slightly and a thorny branch raked across his right cheek, drawing blood.

"Goddammit!!!" he hissed.

He turned and glared at the branch. He then remembered that these trees were added to the property to honor the Wright brothers. They had lived on Hawthorn Street in Dayton when working on their flying machines. They built a mansion in Dayton years later when they had money, and named it *Hawthorn Hill.* Now the damn thorny trees were in Smithson's way out here in the sticks.

"Move your ass, Biggs!"

The older man picked up the pace a bit. They neared the back of the house and Smithson stepped up to the door. A small chrome hook and eye mechanism held the screen door shut. Smithson removed the hook with his gloved hand and twisted the doorknob. As soon as he'd pulled the door back Biggs dropped to his knees and went to work on the inner door lock.

Now they were in and moving through the house. They were looking for an antique pump organ, of all things. Biggs had identified it as the one authentic piece of furniture at the site that was actually owned by the Wright family and was constructed in such a way to allow them to place the letter inside.

There were other items at the site that were positively linked to the brothers. None of the others featured small hidden spaces that could hide a letter, one that could be discovered 120-plus years after the First Flight.

There were many pieces of antique furniture at the site that might offer such a hiding spot, but all of these were period pieces that were never owned by the Wrights. They had been donated to the Memorial over the years.

Biggs had become part of the operation based on postings that Smithson, through Grey, had noticed in obscure chatrooms and comments he'd posted on social media.

Smithson was looking for a project that was in the mold of his 3M Operation. That had been his only true failure and he wanted to revisit it, in a way, and show he had evolved.

He'd contacted Biggs, through encryption provided by Grey, of course, and they communicated for weeks before Smithson arranged a meeting. He flew to Dayton and took a rental car to the pigsty Biggs called an apartment. The walls of this dump were covered with thumbtacked articles from the net. There were some old newspaper clippings sprinkled in. Bulk food containers, Mountain Dew cans, and candy wrappers completed the picture.

And Biggs *knew* he was coming to visit.

They put the plan together. They would create a scenario that would compel Wright institutions and rightsholders to pony up money. Call it blackmail if you like.

To do this they would need some powerful material, as the Wright legacy was one of the best researched, most well documented, in the history of inventions.

Living in Dayton, Biggs had fairly easy access to primary source material on the brothers. Biggs had ticked them off on his chocolate stained fingers; the Wright Brothers Collection in the archives of Wright State University, Carillon Historical Park, the National Museum of the U.S. Air Force, the Aviation Heritage National Historic Park, and on and on and on.

Not all of the materials in these facilities could be penetrated electronically, so in this case Grey could not do everything that Biggs said *he* could.

Smithson was persuaded.

The deal was complicated. Biggs would find a hook in the material. He would then recommend a wish list of items needed to bolster the findings. Some might need to be fabricated. Smithson would bankroll this phase. He would also handle the "negotiations" with all relevant stakeholders.

Smithson even dove into some of the books written about the brothers. What they had accomplished was impressive, even to him. He supposed someone else would've eventually figured out the whole flight thing but the brothers, especially Wilbur, were very effective in their methodology and got there

13

first. Most men that were trying to fly at that time were derisively called "Cranks" by the general public. The Wrights were called that too, but not after their success at Kitty Hawk in 1903.

Biggs was paid $10,000 to start. Grey established the account. Once Biggs found the hook he began to send requests to Smithson for period materials. Biggs needed the same model typewriter that Orville Wright's secretary, Mabel Beck, had used. He needed vintage 7.5"x10.5" onionskin typewriter paper. He requested an antique set of instruments to alter the extruded letters on the strikers of the typewriter. Biggs explained that small idiosyncrasies in the shape of a letter acted like DNA and that the FBI could match a typed document to a specific typewriter. It was a common method of crime solving decades earlier and, though seldom employed today, could still sink the project. Biggs needed rare ink ribbons to craft the letter and, well, it just went on and on.

Early on Smithson decided it would be easier to just put funds in Biggs' account and let him source the items. Smithson was working with Grey on dozens of smaller projects that were providing immediate profits, so most of his attention was elsewhere. The total committed to Biggs rose to $35,000 over time, but it would be worth it. Wright brothers' patents had generated many, many millions of dollars over the years. There were plenty of entities that would pay to protect their interests. To start there was the Wright Brothers Foundation and the Curtiss-Wright Corporation. Virtually every aircraft-related company in the country, maybe the world, was a possible target.

Smithson christened the project *Operation Crank*.

He always used a code name for these more elaborate efforts. It seemed like a cool thing to do. The military named their operations. Why should they have all the fun?

A couple months into the project Biggs reported that he'd found a hook.

What Smithson found amusing was the fact that it would be another pair of rural Ohioans that would allow him to extort

14

the Wright interests. Edward and Milton Korn had grown up near Jackson Center, roughly 50 miles northeast of Wilbur and Orville. They, like the Wrights, were fascinated with flight.

Biggs had found evidence in the fourth floor archives of the Wright State library that the Korns had developed a rudimentary aileron for their airplane slightly before the Wrights achieved success in North Carolina.

This could be a problem for Wright heirs and rightsholders. What set the Wright brothers apart was that they had been first at powered, *controlled* flight. Others had soared in unpowered gliders. Some had put engines on their crafts and tried to get airborne, without success. The Wright brothers, without formal training, had put it all together.

Control was the key. Using a wind tunnel they built in their bicycle shop, the brothers tested wing shapes. They discovered by trial and error that formulas others used when it came to lift were incorrect. They proved their theories in North Carolina at Kill Devil Hills on December 17, 1903. The world would come to know the location as Kitty Hawk.

The key to their control was a concept they called "Wing Warping." In simplified terms it was a series of mechanisms that allowed the pilot to change the configuration of a wing. If done properly, he could control the path of the machine. Combined with rudders, wing warping allowed the user to direct the craft up, down, left, or right. Wing warping was the precursor to ailerons. Virtually every airplane flown since the Wright brothers used ailerons.

As far as anyone knew, no one else had any version of ailerons in 1903. Biggs had come across evidence that said otherwise. Smithson directed him to keep the evidence back in Dayton. It was sure to be challenged by anyone Smithson tried to extort. What he needed here in Nowhereville was the letter. The letter was the hammer.

It was forged to look like old Mabel Beck herself had composed it. Same paper, same ink, same brand of typewriter. The 'G' and the 'S' on the strikers had been modified to replicate those on original Wright letters found in the archives. In paragraph three, Orville "admits" the Korns beat them to the punch and agrees to pay Ed and Milt $5,000 for their silence. The fact that the letter was never mailed but was tucked away inside the Wright pump organ wouldn't matter. Lots of CEOs would pay a fee to keep the letter from seeing the light of day.

The discovery and exploitation of the letter would be engineered later. Smithson had a plan for that as well. He called it *Phase Three*.

They moved through the kitchen on their way to the stairway. Smithson glanced at the wood cabinet in the corner. It had a facing of decorative tin rectangles. During prep Smithson had pointed to a photo of this piece. Grey had captured it from a Michigan woman's cell phone. The woman had visited the Memorial three months earlier and posted several shots on her Facebook page. Smithson asked if it was the pump organ they were trying to locate.

"No, that's a pie safe," Biggs had said with a straight face.

Smithson waited for a punch line. When Biggs looked at him blankly Smithson blurted "Wait, these people had safes for fucking *pies!?!?*"

There was a carpet nailed to the wooden steps but they creaked just as loudly as the lower level floor. The men were perspiring freely now as there was no air conditioning in the house.

They covered the small rooms upstairs in less than a minute. They hadn't expected the organ to be upstairs but had to eliminate it as a possibility. Both men were on edge, eyes moving quickly.

"Damn," Smithson breathed. "It has to be in the other building."

Grey had discovered photos of the pump organ on numerous cell phones and social media accounts. The first mention was part of an extensive post on *rvhavinfun.com*.

Smithson remembered rolling his eyes when the name of that website was brought to his attention by Grey.

None of the pics were taken in such a way that one could see exactly where it resided in the Memorial complex. Two users, *BYE-Plane03* and *KittyHawwwkDammit* had also posted a picture of a framed item on the wall above the organ.

It read:

> The Wright family originally owned this 1865 parlor pump organ when they lived in Hartsville, Ind., their home after moving from here. Whether they had it while living here is not known. When the Wrights moved to Dayton, Ohio, they stored it in the rear of the church at Hartsville. The Birthplace was fortunate to get it in 1999. It is solid oak and all interior parts are original. It plays beautifully. Since Milton's diaries from this period are missing, we're not sure which Wright played the organ. We do know that Wilbur played the harmonica and sang bass with his friends.

Smithson didn't care which Wright played the organ. He didn't give a damn that the 1860s diaries of Milton Wright, Wilbur and Orville's father, were missing. And he sure as hell didn't care about Wilbur playing the harmonica.

He just needed to find the organ, stash the letter, and move on.

Smithson crept back downstairs and made his way to the rear of the house. He opened the wood door and eased the screen door outward. Confirming they were still alone he turned, motioned for Biggs to follow, and stepped down. He took several steps toward the museum building. It was back to the south, the way they had come in, and a few dozen feet beyond the jet they'd seen earlier.

Smithson congratulated himself for setting up the sequence they'd used. He decided to tackle the house first. It would be the furthest building from their hidden car. If the house was a dry hole, the museum would be on their way back to the car.

Smithson was sure this was good strategy. Or good tactics. Whatever.

He'd covered fifty feet with his head on a swivel, checking for cars, when he realized he was alone.

He turned and saw that Biggs had stopped ten feet behind him.

"Let's go, dammit!" Smithson was edgy. Sweat hung in his eyebrows and he wiped at them with a gloved hand.

Biggs was motionless. He appeared to be in a state of... panic?

"What the hell's wrong with you? We gotta *move!*" Smithson nearly shouted.

Biggs, in a modulated tone, said, "It's over...it's all a lie. Take me back to my car at the rest area."

Smithson froze.

"What the hell are you talking about?"

Biggs continued, "The Korn stuff, the fake letter, none of it will hold up. Any amateur will see through it." He looked at the ground. Both hands clasped the toolkit. He then raised his eyes to Smithson.

"I can't believe you fell for it."

Smithson reached under his hoodie and drew the stainless .357 Colt Python with the 4.25-inch barrel, walnut grip, and interchangeable front sight—it was a favorite weapon of Barry Burton, weapons expert of S.T.A.R.S. Alpha Team in the Resident Evil video game series—and shot Biggs in the forehead.

CHAPTER THREE

Paul made a right turn onto Wilbur Wright Road. A quarter mile ahead they saw a collection of houses. Paul slowed as they neared a sign. It proclaimed, "WELCOME TO MOORELAND, EST. 1882" and below that "HOME OF THE FORMER BOBCATS."

It was a small town, a village, really. Paul spent more than his fair share of time in small towns, having grown up in Wappingers Falls, New York. This place was a fraction of the size of his hometown. Paul guessed Mooreland was home to a few hundred people.

A block or so into town they came to Mooreland's one and only four way stop. As the SUV came to a halt the couple realized that the east-west cross street was no more than twelve feet wide.

Lauren giggled, "Do you think they wanted to keep up with all the other little towns in the area by adding these stop signs?"

Paul put on his half smile. "Hard to come up with another reason for them to put up a four way at an alley. I'm actually more baffled by the sign at the edge of town. What the hell does 'home of the former Bobcats' mean?"

"Maybe there was a school here once who had Bobcats as a mascot?" Lauren speculated.

Paul pulled through the intersection.

"Wouldn't it say 'former home of the Bobcats?'"

Lauren shrugged, "Hmmmmm."

They passed through the village a short distance later and continued south. Another historical marker urged them on. They continued for a couple miles. Wilbur Wright Road was a two lane, no different than thousands of other stretches in the Midwest. They'd passed only a few farmhouses before coming to a stop and being directed left by another sign. This road was narrower and covered with gravel, apparently the recent recipient of some type of resurfacing. They saw no buildings on this road, just cornfields on either side. After less than a mile they were again directed south onto a still-narrower road, "N.COUNTY RD 750 E."

"Well Paul, you really picked a hard-to-find place this time. I thought the Annie Oakley grave was off the beaten path. But this..." She let this hang in the air.

Paul laughed, "Hey, we'll get to see something very few people get to check out."

A quarter of a mile ahead on the right a small white farmhouse came into view. It sat just a few yards off the road. There was a handful of small buildings south and west of the house. This cluster was surrounded by tall cornfields. To the couple it seemed like the narrow county road was a bridge through a sea of corn and the Wilbur Wright site a small island.

A couple hundred feet before reaching the house Paul eased the SUV right and followed a short drive that then curled to the left. He found himself in the west parking lot a couple hundred feet behind the farmhouse.

Their SUV was the only vehicle in the lot.

Lauren tilted her head at Paul.

"Gee, I hope we don't have to fight the crowds to see everything."

Paul smiled, "I knew it would be closed. I just want to make a quick stop to get a feel for the place, see if it's worth visiting another time when it's open."

They got out of the Jeep. Lauren opened the rear door and rummaged through one of their bags, producing a black nylon camera bag. She knew Paul liked to take pictures at historic sites and that his older model iPhone did not take the best quality shots. They had invested in a relatively inexpensive DSLR camera, a Panasonic Lumix model, several years earlier when both were in the military. They'd taken it along on the rare occasions they'd vacationed together.

Lauren had put the 60X zoom feature to good use when photographing the Beaseley girls at a soccer tournament a few days earlier. They played on travel teams and both had games at Grand Park, the sprawling baseball and soccer complex in Westfield, a suburb of Indianapolis.

They began to walk toward the farmhouse, noticing a low white building on the right. A sign near the door revealed that this building was the Community Room and was available to rent. Another white building was adjacent to this. Block lettering identified it as the museum.

Paul was interested in the museum but knew it would be locked. He thought his best bet for picking up tidbits on Wilbur Wright was to check out the outdoor interpretive markers up ahead and to peek through the windows of the farmhouse.

In front of them to the east were two possible destinations. One was the farmhouse. Slightly right of that was a jet fighter, which was elevated on supports. Several medium sized trees were sprinkled about this area.

"Looks like there are some markers around the plane," Lauren observed, and angled in that direction. Paul followed.

A sign in front of the jet explained that it was an F-84 from the Korean War. It was placed at the birthplace site to show how aviation changed from the time of the Wright brothers to the jet age.

Paul stared up at the plane. A half smile again appeared on his face. He'd known dozens of pilots in the military. To them the F-84 would be considered an antique. It would've been retired decades before any of them had been born. It gave perspective to the fantastic advancements in aeronautics that had been made since the First Flight. In a way it had all begun here with the birth of Wilbur. He glanced at the farmhouse.

"I'm going to go check out the house, take your time here."

Lauren nodded as she raised the camera to take a shot of the jet.

Paul approached the birthplace. Okay, it wasn't the actual house, but he knew the builders had tried to duplicate the original structure and had situated it over the original

21

foundation. It was a small two-story frame with a porch in front facing the road. He walked in that direction.

Moving near the road, Paul removed his phone from the front pocket of his shorts. Its camera would not produce shots with the definition of their Panasonic but it would be nice to have a few pics on his phone to check out when the thought struck him. Phones were so convenient. No cords to connect to his laptop to download, as the camera required.

There was a small front porch. The roof angled down over it. Four spindly wooden columns were spaced across the front of the porch supporting the roof. There was a white door in the center, flanked by multi-paned windows on either side. Paul raised his phone and snapped a photo. He wondered what his boys from the service would think of him now, taking pictures of an empty house on a lonely road in Indiana.

Paul laughed out loud.

He glanced toward Lauren. She had moved to the other side of the jet and was reading an interpretive marker.

Paul smiled. When Lauren was pulled away from her technical journals and educational videos she could be just as locked in as he was on things that interested him.

Paul walked around the south side of the house

Lauren was very dedicated to her profession. She worked odd hours, often covering shifts for younger lab employees who asked her to trade, usually because of a son or daughter's activity. She was almost always amenable to this. It irritated Paul at times but he realized it was her way to help. Paul and Lauren did not have children. Her work was very important to her.

Still, it was fun to get away from time to time. Sure, they had to leave the Beaseleys in the middle of the week so she could get back to work tomorrow, but short trips like this with Paul were almost always fun.

Lauren moved a few feet to examine a tall concrete marker that displayed a photo of Wilbur Wright. The inventor looked dapper in a newsboy cap. She read the inscription.

A short life full of consequences. An unfailing intellect, imperturbable temper, great self-reliance and as great modesty, seeing the right clearly, pursuing it steadily, he lived and died.

It was written by Bishop Milton Wright, Wilbur's father, on the day his son died.

These stories often sucked her in. Lauren was sure that Paul knew this. This setting, a warm evening in a quiet corner of the country, made it easier to imagine a world with no internet or cell phones. Not one vehicle had driven past the site since they'd arrived.

Lauren raised the digital camera to take a shot of the marker and giggled at the irony.

After taking both horizontal and vertical images she looked about for another marker. She saw one several feet away near the road. She approached it and discovered it had the brass and iron look of many state historical markers. She didn't know what they were made of, but thought of them in this way. They were in every state along roadways. Few drivers seemed to take the time to pull over and read them.

This one seemed to be placed to tempt motorists. It was two-sided with the words "BIRTHPLACE OF WILBUR WRIGHT" at the top and featured an outline of the state of Indiana. Lauren approached to within a few feet. This spot offered a nice view of the entire site. She decided to take some shots. She glanced at the camera and remembered it had a video setting.

Maybe a panoramic video that showed the entire area?

Lauren checked the road in both directions to make sure no cars were coming and stepped to within two paces of its surface. She selected the video setting, pointed the camera at the marker, and began filming. Lauren slowly turned in the direction of the farmhouse, then the lonely road, and the corn across from her. She intended to come full circle back to the marker.

As she swept the cornfield a few yards away she heard Paul call her name. Lauren turned her head toward the farmhouse

23

while completing the circle. She stopped the video as she heard Paul call a second time. It seemed more urgent. She secured the Panasonic and headed in his direction.

Her turn of the head while filming prevented her from seeing a man peering from the corn.

The camera saw him.

CHAPTER FOUR

Smithson's T-shirt and hoodie were now saturated with sweat. He'd dragged the body a couple hundred feet. After pulling the trigger he'd watched Biggs drop, his arm and pistol still extended, now pointing at the house.

What the hell had Biggs done? This was so fucking... INCONVENIENT!

Smithson crouched instinctively and spun. He checked every direction. Nothing! He was incredulous that he could fire a pistol at a man in daylight and not draw attention from a single human being.

Gotta move!

Smithson returned the .357 to his custom ostrich shoulder holster. The gun shop owner had recommended a less expensive leather model but Smithson wanted something more exotic. His bulky hoodie had hidden it from Biggs.

Smithson had the mind of a gamer. He pushed down the surge of panic and let his brain work. His head was still flicking from right to left, sweeping from the south to the north, up and down the road. Still no traffic.

His eyes came to rest on the field directly east of the asphalt.

Gotta get this fatass into the cornfield. Gotta move!

Smithson had dropped the binder containing the letter when he'd drawn the Colt. He snatched it up and tucked it under his belt. He then grabbed Biggs by the ankles and dragged him backwards across the grass for ten feet. He dropped the legs, breathing heavily.

For Chrissake, how much does this guy weigh?

Smithson suddenly remembered Biggs' toolset. He loped back a few steps, grabbed the small bag, turned, and flung it across the road and several rows into the corn. Smithson moved back toward the road and bent at the knees, this time

25

facing toward the field. He lowered himself until he could again grasp Biggs' ankles. He took a few more steps. The sun was at his back and he saw his shadow creep onto the road. His crouched body position made the shadow appear ape-like.

Smithson couldn't help it. He snickered.

He dropped the legs again, turned, and frowned at Biggs. He wiped his forehead and took a deep breath, realizing for the first time that his heart was racing.

As he began to bend down again he noticed the greasy smear of blood and brain matter painted into the grass.

Smithson tried a new method. He now had the tips of Biggs' shoes, his old man white New Balance trainers, touching his cheeks. Smithson locked his own hands together near his chest and under Biggs' heals. This position redistributed the weight of Biggs' body and made it much easier to drag.

Smithson hunched forward and started across the road. He felt the body grating across the hard surface and, if it had been physically possible, would've turned to watch.

Smithson got the body across the road and down a small slope. He flopped on his stomach, gulping air. He looked again up the road to the north and thought he may have seen a vehicle in the distance. He turned to the left to check the opposite direction and found himself looking directly in the face of Biggs.

The gunshot wound was above the man's left eye. The long grey hair was tangled around the head and the right side of the face had scraped across the asphalt. The eyes were closed.

Smithson looked at Biggs. A part of him wishing the man would turn zombie and reanimate so he could shoot him again.

You can't believe I fell for it? You can't believe I fell for it?

Smithson refocused.

There was a thin trail of blood and flesh on the road. If he could get the body further from this spot and keep it hidden in the cornfield the blood trail might be mistaken for that of an injured animal, if it was noticed at all. He just needed to buy a little time.

Smithson began to drag Biggs south. The Audi was in that direction. He was behind the cover of the first row of corn. It hadn't rained in days and the soil was hard but dirt still clung to his boots and pant legs. He trudged on a few yards at a time, literally plowing the surface with Biggs' upper body.

The corn was seven or eight feet high. This surprised Smithson as it hadn't appeared that tall from across the road. The rough, sharp edges of the leaves raked at his face. He squinted to protect his eyes. The slight movement of his eyebrows released more beads of perspiration. Droplets trickled into his eyes. Despite the heat he was glad he'd worn his black tactical pants. He felt the leaves slide across his thighs. He hadn't noticed the strap of his binoculars until now. It rubbed at his neck as the damn Aussie set swung freely with his efforts. After a hundred feet he stopped. This was as good a spot as any to leave the body. Smithson wiped his face again with the sleeve of his hoodie and tried to slow his breathing.

Think!

Okay, take his wallet. The cops can't find out Biggs' identity until I've had time to go through his car at the rest stop... Get his keys!... And his phone, get the phone. I'm going to need to go through Biggs' shithole apartment to sanitize it before the cops find out who he is.

Smithson had pocketed the keys and phone and was patting down the body for any other item of importance when he heard a man shout.

"Lauren."

Smithson, without conscious thought, pushed his upper body out of the corn.

He stared into the lens of a camera not thirty feet away.

CHAPTER FIVE

Paul stopped at the first window on the side of the house. There were no shrubs or bushes so he was able to walk right up to it. His left leg ached a bit. He leaned toward the glass and cupped his hands around his eyes so he could look inside without glare. He unconsciously put most of his weight on his right leg. Paul could see a small room that contained an antique couch and a pair of small rocking chairs. There was an ancient wood-burning stove that had a pipe that rose vertically for a few feet before disappearing into the wall.

Paul saw a wooden rail with vertical slats that ran through the middle of the room, dividing it. The room was uncluttered on the far side of the rail. Paul decided that there was a path laid out for visitors to follow. He turned slightly to the right and could see the inside of the front door. Turning to the rear of the house he saw that a narrow internal doorway led to what must be the rear of the structure.

Paul left the first window and reached the second. He saw a small wooden bed inside with a washstand. There were small signs inside that must've offered information on the building and contents but Paul couldn't read them. The webpage for the site explained that the interior was set up to show the house as it had been in 1867. Wilbur was born that year on April 16. Two older brothers, Reuchlin and Lorin welcomed Wilbur to the world along with their father Milton and mother Susan. Orville came along a bit more than four years later on August 19, 1871 after the family had moved to Dayton. Sister Katharine came later.

Paul wondered if this was the room where Wilbur was born. He stared inside.

The inventor of flight—well, one of them—right here?

Paul backed away from the window and moved toward the rear of the building. He knew there was a back porch. He'd read somewhere members of the Wright family referred to it later in life as their "laundry room." The family's clothing was hung to dry there.

Paul edged around the back corner of the structure and took in the small porch. It was covered with a short roof, very similar to the front of the place. An outhouse stood several feet behind the porch

He smiled, imagining young Wilbur, who supposedly began to walk at ten and a half months, playing with his older brothers. They would've scampered in and out of the door...

Paul froze.

The inner door to the house was open. The outer screen door was closed but unlatched.

A charge ran through Paul. He shot a look toward Lauren and saw her two hundred feet away doing something to their camera. Paul quickly determined she was in no immediate danger. He decided to take a quick look inside the house. There were no other cars at the site but he reasoned that an authorized person could still be here performing some function and waiting for a ride.

There was another possibility.

Paul eased the screen door outward, wincing as the spring resisted with a muted screech. He was careful not to touch the doorknobs. He stepped softly through the opening and listened, trying to detect any minute sound that could bring him information.

Paul's heart rate rose, but only slightly. He slowed his breathing. He forced himself to not think of those building entries in Afghanistan and Iraq. He took a step into the building. The floor creaked. Another step. Another creak.

Well, if anyone's here they sure as hell know someone just came in the back door. Either I've scared the hell out of some volunteer or an intruder is in here waiting for me.

Paul decided to call out. If an authorized person was inside, there would be nervous a back and forth with a staffer followed by smiles. If it was someone else, well, Paul would deal with it. His leg no longer ached.

"Hello, anybody in the house?"

Nothing.

Paul repeated the call with the same result. Moving quickly he cleared the lower floor. He thought about checking the upstairs but his instincts, honed by those twelve deployments, told him it was unoccupied.

He needed to check on Lauren.

Paul exited the rear of the building, again careful to not touch the doorknobs. He took a few seconds to check for threats, then jogged toward his wife.

"Lauren!"

She didn't register his call. She was turning in a circle near a historical marker close to the county road. She held the camera several inches in front of her face.

Paul called out again as he passed the jet. This time Lauren turned her head to him. Her hands traveled on their path a few more inches before she lowered the camera and depressed a button. Her entire body now faced her husband.

Shit, Shit, SHIT!

Smithson ducked back into the first row of corn.

Who the hell was that woman? What had she seen?

"What?!" Lauren questioned.

"The door to the house was open."

Paul reported this as he reached Lauren. He was scanning the area.

Lauren was confused. "You mean someone is in there?"

Paul shook his head.

"No, the place seems to be empty. Either someone left in a hurry and didn't latch the door or something strange is going on here. Either way I think we'd better call the sheriff."

Lauren was now on edge. "Should we call 9-1-1?"

Paul shook his head as he pulled out his phone. "Let's see if we can figure out what county we're in and call the sheriff's office main number. It could be nothing."

But his head still slowly swung left and right.

Smithson lay motionless, barely breathing.

Now a man, too?!

He didn't dare raise his head. He was frightened, scared shitless. Incapacitated.

Smithson forced himself to function.

Get back in the game!

Smithson slowly moved his right hand toward his shoulder holster. He was lying on his stomach, again next to Biggs' body. He barely registered the presence of the corpse.

Get the gun. GET THE GUN!

Something was in the way. He slowly twisted his head and saw the binocular strap trailing down from his neck. The binos were wedged under his chest and blocked the path of his right hand. He shifted his weight and was able to get his hand to the walnut grip of the .357. He slowly eased it from the holster.

The couple was pleasantly surprised to find they could get online in this location and that they had a few bars on their phones, indicating they had service. Lauren quickly discovered they were in Henry County. She dialed the number and handed her phone to Paul.

"Yeah, we're out here at the Wilbur Wright Birthplace. It's closed. There are no other cars here but the door to the house is open. Anyone can walk into the building, take anything they want."

The dispatcher, a young man, asked a few questions then took Paul's name and number.

"We'll get someone out there sir. We have a deputy about fifteen minutes away."

Paul was looking at Lauren as he spoke.

"Do you need us to wait for him?"

The dispatcher considered for a few seconds before responding.

"No sir, you don't need to wait."

Paul persisted, "Are you sure? We're on our way to Ohio but we have no problem hanging around if you need us."

The dispatcher stated again, "No need, sir. We appreciate you reporting this. We have your contact information if we need to reach you."

"Okay." Paul ended the call and handed the phone back to Lauren.

With a slightly doubtful tone she asked, "They don't need us to wait?"

Paul shook his head, "Nope, he said a deputy would be here in a few minutes but we can take off. I'd really like to know what's going on here but..."

Paul glanced at his watch.

"I guess we can get back on the road."

Paul took one more look around the property before putting his arm around Lauren and leading her toward their vehicle.

Smithson heard the man speaking on the phone. He made out part of the man's side of the conversation and knew he was speaking to law enforcement. He had to make a decision quickly. The Colt was in his hand now. He was less than forty feet from the couple and imagined himself springing up from the field and quickly putting them down. There were five shots left in the revolver.

Had this been a video game the decision would be easy. Smithson was superb at first person shooter games. It would be two shots, two kills.

But this was real life. Smithson was sweaty and on edge. Despite the fact that he had shot Biggs through the forehead with his first shot, it had only been from ten feet. And Smithson had to admit that this was lucky. He had practiced sporadically with his weapons but it amounted to a small fraction of the time he dedicated to the shooter games.

Plus, two more bodies would really complicate the situation.

But the woman had caught him on camera. Biggs' body would be found eventually and the police, or sheriff, whoever the man had called, probably had their information. They would be contacted and the digital image could hang him.

Smithson had to get that camera, or at least the SD card inside. And he had to do it before pictures and videos it contained were posted on a damn social media site. He had to get at the couple. But he also had to get the hell out of here and clean up the whole Biggs trail.

What a clusterfuck!

Smithson risked a look through the cornstalks. He saw the couple walking toward the rear parking lot. The sun was getting lower in the west and they moved toward it easily. It looked to Smithson like the ending of a Hallmark movie.

Not that he watched Hallmark movies.

Smithson raised his Steiner binoculars and focused them on the only vehicle in the lot. It was a white Jeep Grand Cherokee.

Of course it was.

Smithson could clearly make out the front plate. He committed the number to memory, his lips moving.

Okay, I'll take care of that problem ASAP. Gotta get the hell out of here and get to the rest stop.

He took one more look at Biggs, focusing on the entry wound.

Helluva shot.

Smithson smiled and made for the Audi.

CHAPTER SIX

Ten minutes later Paul and Lauren watched a deputy sheriff's tan Dodge Charger Pursuit approach them from the east. They had found their way back to Mooreland and had traveled just two miles on State Route 36 when the tan Charger came into view. It passed by on their left, apparently in no hurry.

Lauren turned to watch it through the Grand Cherokee's rear window, then turned to Paul.

"Do you want to go back?"

Paul was watching the Charger grow smaller in the rear view window.

"No, you have the early shift tomorrow. I gave the dispatcher our number. If they need us, they'll get in touch."

He shifted his eyes back to the road.

"But..."

Lauren finished for him.

"But it would be nice to know what was going on back there."

They crossed the Ohio state line less than an hour later as the sun set. At Greenville they turned south on Ohio 127 for a short distance before taking a left and heading east on one of Paul's favorite two lanes, Hogpath Road.

Lauren generally had something amusing to say when she saw the road sign and today was no exception.

"Well, ole Hogpath is actually a nicer road than the one in front of the Wilbur Wright M'morial."

She said it with her head half turned and an exaggerated twang in her voice.

Paul grinned, "You know this is a better way to get back from Ronnie and Deena's than fighting that Indy traffic down to I-70."

The Beaseley's house was in Westfield, north of Indianapolis. There were basically two ways to make the trip to and from Troy. One was to take a circuitous route on major highways, Interstates 75 and 70 as well as the I-465 beltway around Indiana's capital. The other was to take smaller state routes and oddly named roads such as Hogpath.

Paul preferred the latter. Since he usually drove and Lauren was often listening to a medical recording he almost always chose this way. Besides, he got to pass through little burgs that drew his interest.

"Don't disparage Hogpath, girl."

Lauren, again tilting her head and smiling, responded. "What do you think Bill Burr would say about your road?"

The couple passed through Covington, the last small town waypoint before reaching their house outside of Troy. It was dark now with a nearly full moon overhead. With only a few minutes left in the drive their thoughts turned to the next day.

"So you have to be at the lab, what, at 7 a.m.?" Paul asked.

"No, 5:30. Paulette works third shift and she's usually there until seven but she has an appointment and needs to leave early."

Paul nodded. "Jumping right back into it I see. Well, you did have five days off so I shouldn't be surprised."

Lauren knew that Paul could get touchy about her covering for coworkers but didn't retreat.

"I don't mind helping out, especially if one of the moms in the lab needs to take one of their kids to an appointment."

Paul knew this was a showstopper when it came to any brewing argument. They had no kids of their own and Lauren went out of her way to be sort of a surrogate mom for friends and family. The photos she'd taken of Brinley and Shay in Westfield would be posted on her Facebook account as soon as she could get to it, no doubt accompanied by glowing comments about the girls.

Lauren shifted the conversation.

"So what do you have tomorrow?"

Paul considered, "Well, probably a workout in the basement in the morning. I have to take the Lariat in for new tires before nine. I think I'll toss my bike in the back and go for a ride after I drop the truck. I'll leave from the shop, do an hour or two, then come home. I can pick up the truck tomorrow before they close or wait until Friday."

He continued, "But first I'll get up when you do and make you a nice breakfast."

Lauren smiled then reminded him, "Aren't you going with Mike tomorrow to get firewood for his party?"

Mike McClary and his wife Marge were friends of the Hulls. They'd met a couple years earlier at a Dayton Dragons minor league baseball game. The McClarys were ten years older than the Hulls but they had many mutual interests. Lauren encouraged Paul to spend as much time with Mike as possible, hoping it would keep her husband occupied in a positive way.

"No, Mike has a meeting and bumped it to Friday, but that's fine because I'm hooking up with Woody tomorrow at the base."

"Gatewood? I didn't know that. That's great!"

Paul had been friends with Mike McClary for a few short years.

But he went way back with Gatewood "Woody" Dowdell.

The Hulls pulled into their driveway at 10:15 p.m. They lived in a three-bedroom single floor home. It sat on a one acre lot a couple miles north of Troy. The house was on Polecat Road, another name that could provide material for comedians.

After coming to a stop in the garage Paul collected his duffel and Lauren's suitcase. With his hands full he twisted the knob to the inner door and pushed it open with his shoulder. An orange blur flashed past his feet. Paul nearly lost his balance.

"Chappy!" He called. "Chappy's out!"

Lauren was gathering the camera case and her purse. She turned.

"Oh damn! Close the door!"

Paul stabbed at the switch on the wall. The overhead garage door began to descend. Paul tossed the luggage into the house and twisted back toward the interior of the garage. He felt a slight ache in his left leg.

Lauren had dropped the camera case and purse back on the passenger side seat and fell to her knees, calling out to the cat.

"Chappy!"

Paul moved behind the Jeep and watched as the door came down. He wanted to make sure Chappy didn't get out of the garage. The feline's usual modus operandi was to sprint into the garage, realize he was no longer housebound, then cower in a corner. He had done this several times in the past. Paul told himself it would be the end of a lot of aggravation if Chappy escaped. But he knew Lauren would be crushed.

The garage door reached the floor without Chappy reaching freedom and Paul turned back to the house, rubbing his left thigh.

Damn cat.

Lauren's voice carried into the house.

"I found him!"

She stepped into the kitchen cradling Chappy in her arms. He was an overweight orange tabby with, for a cat, a mean little face. He was difficult to hold with one arm. If you wrapped an arm around his mid-section the bulbous stomach of the cat tended to slide backward out of your grasp leaving just the head and front legs on the upper side. It always reminded Paul of trying to cradle a water balloon. Chappy's sour face would look up at you with disgust.

Chappy manifested a long list of other annoying traits.

His dashes through doorways seemed designed to trip any human up above. He generally made it a point to split the wickets if at all possible, bursting between the legs of the victim and, because of his physique, contacting both the right and left and startling the hell out of them.

He chewed through cords. His current total of nine—Paul noted that this made the cat an ace—featured six cellphone cords, two laptop chargers, and the cord of an iron. This while the iron was plugged in and teetering on the ironing board three feet above Chappy. There was no working theory on how he'd escaped electrocution.

Chappy also loved to chew shoestrings. Leaving a pair of shoes anywhere but inside a secure plastic bin in the walk-in closet was considered by Paul and Lauren to be as irresponsible as forgetting about a boiling pot on the stove. You were just asking for trouble.

The cat stretched his chubby body upward enough to pull down at the latch-style door handles in their house. This allowed him access to any room including Paul's office, the door of which was closed to keep Chappy from chewing said charger cords. Paul believed Lauren was at fault for these incidents by leaving his door open until he was in his office one day with it closed, heard the latch flick up and down several times, then watched with a combination of horror and amusement as the door opened and an ornery orange face poked inside.

Son of a bitch!

Paul had replaced all of the latches with standard round knobs. It had not yet registered with Chappy that he couldn't open these. He continued to paw at them with a single-mindedness that drove Paul crazy. It was usually done while he was reading or watching TV nearby.

Chappy also stretched upward to paw incessantly at vertical surfaces. He jumped on tables and countertops to paw at framed items, sometimes just leaving them out of balance but often knocking them off the wall completely. Paul had avoided putting any of his framed military awards and citations on the wall but Lauren was insistent. Chappy, apparently, was on Paul's side of the discussion as he went out of his way to make them tumble down, sometimes breaking the frames.

Chappy also pawed at the mirror above their bathroom vanity, leaving musky vertical streaks behind. Paul had googled this and learned that cats have interdigital glands in their feet that, when the legs and paws are extended, allow pheromones to be secreted. This is done to mark territory and helps them feel safe.

Paul felt it ironic that Chappy stared at his reflection the entire time he stretched and rubbed. It seemed the cat wanted to feel protected from the creature in the mirror.

Paul could relate.

Whatever, the streaks were disgusting. It seemed like the least distasteful thing Chappy brought to the household was his ability to fill a catbox, which was prodigious.

But Paul had chosen the cat's name when he was a cute kitten whose ability to disrupt was not yet evident. Lauren brought him home after visiting a co-worker who lived on a farm and whose barn cat had just produced a litter. In order to mollify Paul's doubts about pet ownership she encouraged him to pick the name.

Paul named the cute little guy after one of his heroes, Air Force Combat Controller John Chapman. The human Chappy was loyal, helpful, physically fit, and cheerful.

The orange tabby? Not so much.

Still, he was named Chappy, so Paul seemed stuck with him.

Lauren eased Chappy to the floor and returned to the garage to retrieve her things. Paul headed for the master bedroom with the duffel and suitcase. He dropped them on the bed and returned to see if Lauren needed help with anything from the Jeep.

She was back inside and set her things on the island in the center of the kitchen. Chappy jumped up on the island and inspected the items for exposed cords. In a pinch he would settle for straps or drawstrings if his favorite targets were unavailable. Lauren had to hang her purses from a hall tree to keep them safe.

"Down Chappy," Lauren commanded.

She again grabbed the tabby and lowered him to the floor.

Chappy immediately jumped back on the island and padded toward the purse. Lauren sighed.

She snatched up the purse and hung the strap on her shoulder. Looking at the camera bag she decided it would be a good idea to charge the Panasonic. She'd taken a couple hundred stills over the last few days and a good number of videos. She wouldn't have time to go through them for a day or two but didn't want a dead battery when she got to it.

The camera was charged by attaching one end of a short black cord to its side and plugging the other end into an outlet. The battery did not need to be removed and placed in a separate charging unit.

Lauren removed the camera from its bag and attached the cord. She reached to plug it into an outlet then remembered Chappy. She turned to the cat, whose green eyes were intent on the cord.

Lauren sighed again.

She walked to the dining room wall and opened one of the tall wooden cabinet doors. The builders had installed electrical outlets inside two of these cabinets. After buying the house, it took the Hulls six months to discover them. Lauren remembered thinking, *Why the hell would you need outlets inside dining room cabinets?*

Once Chappy moved in she found a use for them. It became an out of the way place to charge their devices. The cabinet doors did not have cat-attracting latches.

Lauren slid the camera onto a shelf that held cans of soup, vegetables, and Chappy's canned food. The charger cord was short so she had to slide the camera toward the rear of the shelf to make it connect. She plugged it in, and forgot about it. She left the empty bag on the kitchen table directly in front of the cabinets. It would act as a reminder for her to unplug the camera in the morning.

CHAPTER SEVEN

Smithson steered the Audi south on the county road, the low angle of the sun cutting through the passenger window. He forced himself to breathe slowly, trying to sort through the variables. He had to prioritize. Work the problem. He glanced over at the passenger seat where the leather folder with its now-worthless letter rested.

Thirty-five K!... Fucking Biggs!

The original plan was to return Biggs to his car then drive separately to Dayton. Biggs would go to his shithole apartment and Smithson would check into his Airbnb. Biggs' beater Toyota Camry was at the Indiana Welcome Center a short distance west of Richmond off I-70. They had looked at maps and decided on this location. Unfortunately there was no rest area nearby on the eastbound side of the highway. Smithson, coming from Indianapolis, had to drive past the Welcome Center, get off at Richmond, and double back to reach it. Biggs had come directly over from Dayton.

After planting the letter they would take small county roads and work their way southeast to Richmond then jump on I-70 West for a couple minutes before returning to the rest stop. After that they would re-enter the highway westbound, get off one exit later and drive east back past the Welcome Center on the way to Dayton.

Thinking about the plan now, Smithson realized that it was shit.

Gravel from the narrow road kicked up and dinged off his Audi. He winced.

What a convoluted fucking set up!

Biggs had made the suggestion, hadn't he? He was supposed to have local knowledge. Smithson shook his head, again wondering what he was thinking when he took on a partner. He was a lone wolf.

Smithson took comfort in the fact that he'd studied online maps the previous night in his hotel room in Indianapolis and saw an alternate route from the target site to the highway. He'd stayed at a place called The Alexander, a nice enough place, he supposed. For the local yokels it no doubt represented lodging nirvana. It had taken him three hard days of driving to reach this part of the country from his house in Nevada. He had no intention of roughing it and had stayed in four or five star hotels each night.

He'd noticed the Plan-B, Just-In-Case route by accident. It had drawn his attention because it had the shape of half a swastika. The upper left arm of the swastika began at the Wilbur Wright Birthplace. It ran straight down, or south, For five miles, turned left, east, at County Road 137 for five more, then south again at County Road 1 for the same distance before intersecting with I-70.

He congratulated himself now for his foresight. The straight sections of road allowed his mind to work. By the time he reached the first turn he had gamed it out. He really could be good at this operational stuff.

With the plan reformulated, his mind began to wander.

The Nazis. They were a bunch of crazy bastards, huh?

Smithson had spent very little time thinking about the social and historical aspects of the German Nazi party.

He'd killed a shitload of their soldiers in the 2017 version of Call of Duty on his Playstation 4 though.

Smithson had all of the major game systems back at his place in Nevada. After finding the place a half hour outside of Vegas, he had converted the living room to a gamer's dream. It had 75-inch flat screens on three walls. He'd situated a $2,000 chrome and black leather Vanquish barber chair in the center of the room. Its swivel feature allowed him to easily transition from one system to another.

He supposed it would look weird to any visitor coming in the front door. Thankfully he'd never had one.

He would like to add another screen to the fourth wall but that was the front of the house and featured a large picture window. He hadn't ruled out removing it and replacing it with a solid wall. No daylight would enter the house but Smithson considered this a plus for game play. He had closed the curtains in the Lair—he liked to think of the game room as the Lair—on the day he moved into the house and hadn't opened them since.

Smithson realized he was on the eastern leg of the drive now. He glanced at his speedometer and saw it was pegged at 88 miles per hour.

Dumbass! Slow down!

The last thing he needed was to be pulled over for speeding by some two-bit cop. His out of state tags would be remembered even if he had Grey wipe the records of the stop from the sheriff's computer system.

He remembered another time when this was necessary and allowed himself a smile.

Speed was both a blessing and a curse with this car. He'd first seen the Audi S8 in the original *Taken* movie. Liam Neeson's character Bryan Mills had stolen it from a bad guy by bashing his head into the side of the car. He then tore through the streets of Paris on his way to rescuing his dumbshit daughter.

Smithson identified with the badass Mills. He thought the Audi was super cool and filed away a thought that he would buy one at some point. That had become possible...more than possible...after Smithson's biggest hit ever, the Crypto Op.

He'd found the used 2009 Audi S8 v10 online. It had just 21,000 miles and was located in Whitehall, Pennsylvania. It was Phantom Black, a different color than Bryan Mills' ride but actually cooler. It had a 5.2 liter Lamborghini engine, could go zero to sixty in 4.9 seconds and had a top speed of 155 miles per hour.

Smithson paid the $29,500 asking price without batting an eye—he had just taken delivery of a fully loaded top-of-the-line Range Rover that cost $225,000—and had it shipped to Nevada.

The problem with a car this powerful was trying to keep it near legal highway speeds when traveling long distances. The mind-numbing journey from the Vegas area made him drift off mentally and he'd seen this same increase in speed happen. A ticket and fine were no big deal, but the gear in his trunk could not possibly be explained away.

Smithson resorted to using the cruise control for most of the trip. He crept across America with growing impatience, tempering his urge to swerve right into the slow lane and blow past some jackass in front of him on dozens of occasions.

Smithson was now heading south on County Road 1 and saw the ramp to I-70 a mile ahead. He jumped on eastbound and easily accelerated into the flow of traffic. Within minutes he could see the rest area ahead on the left across the westbound lanes. As he approached he squinted to make out Biggs' car, but the shadows were lengthening and the Camry was nondescript. It blended into the assemblage of vehicles like a pair of cargo shorts on the sidewalk of the Vegas Strip.

No worries. Smithson knew it was there and he had the keys.

Smithson approached another overpass. He was searching for a particular lighted sign. There was an exit ramp but he didn't see what he needed.

What he did see off to the right was an odd shaped building that appeared to have a thirty foot candle attached to one side. "Warm Glow Candle Co. Outlet Store" appeared on an arch near the entrance.

Smithson shook his head.

He'd committed a murder. Not his first. He had a complicated set of tasks to manage, and he was in danger due to the camera that woman possessed. His next priority was clear.

Find a McDonalds.

He needed to contact Grey.

Smithson took exit 151, Chester Boulevard. He came to a stop at the top of the ramp, saw the golden arches through the passenger window, and went right on red. He saw the lights of a Comfort Inn, a Red Roof Inn, and something called *Frickers*.

In his experience McDonalds locations tended to have fairly robust wifi. Smithson had a personal hotspot on his phone. He had actually modified it, boosting its capability. He didn't feel the need to employ it now. He could access Grey through the Mickey D's wifi. The level of encryption he maintained on his devices meant that he could jump on virtually any public wireless network in the country and be confident that no one short of Russia's state-directed Sandworm hackers would be able to track him.

Besides, he could use a Big Mac.

Smithson went through the Drive Thru and ordered a Mac, large fries, and large Diet Coke. The bottom half of the sun was below the horizon in the west. He pulled the Audi up to the pay window, reached for his back pocket, thought better of it, and lifted Biggs' worn leather wallet from the seat to his right. He opened it, removed a twenty, and smiled. He transferred the bill to his left hand.

The sliding window was closed so Smithson waited to pay. He ran a hand through his hair and discovered it felt matted. He glanced in the rear view and realized he looked like a homeless man. His longish red hair was tangled and moist. His face was streaked with mud. Smithson spit into his right palm and began to rub at the mud.

The sliding window opened.

"That'll be eight seventy ple... Oh!"

She was a twentyish girl with long dark hair. She stared at Smithson with an expression somewhere between disgust and pity.

Smithson saw the look and added a half sneer to his face.

You're no prize yourself, honey.

The exchange of money and food completed, Smithson put the Audi in an arc around the front lot of the McDonalds and parked on the opposite side.

He turned to the backseat and selected a case that was wedged between a collection of travel bags. He removed a tablet. It was a Panasonic G2 Toughbook, a compact unit with a keyboard. It had a small 10.1 inch screen and a super fast Intel processor. It could be dropped from six feet or utilized in a rainstorm. At 2.9 pounds it significantly outweighed larger devices. Smithson imagined that if computers were animated and became characters in a video game, the G2 could strut up to any macbook or Dell and tear it in half.

Smithson had read that top military units like the Navy's SEAL Teams used them in combat zones. He paid four thousand dollars for this one and had been itching to use it in a real operation. To "go downrange," as the military types said in podcasts and bestsellers.

Did he need a Toughbook on this Op?

Well, he was eating in his car at a McDonalds, not crouching on a freezing mountaintop in Afghanistan, so that was arguable.

But it looked cool as hell so he was going to use it.

He adjusted his seat back all the way, sat the G2 on top of his thighs, and opened it. While it spooled up he grabbed three fingers full of fries and thrust them into his mouth.

Fucking McDonalds...they have the best damn fries.

The screen came to life.

Now we're cookin'.

Smithson took a lumberjack-sized bite from the Big Mac and got started on the process of getting online, which was simple, and utilizing the encryption, which was not.

Like most of the tools he employed, the encryption was a blend of preexisting tech and wrinkles Smithson came up with on his own. His used Axcrypt as its foundational piece. This was excellent. But Smithson was always wary that the developers had a backdoor that would allow them, or law enforcement, to access his activities. He mutated the software with code he'd written himself and was now one hundred percent confident of its ability to withstand anything short of a high level military attack. And even that might not do it.

Smithson stuffed more fries into his mouth and watched as Grey appeared on screen and immediately asked how he could help.

Smithson typed:

FIRST PRIORITY: Immediately disable security cameras of Indiana I-70 rest area near exit 145. Location is on westbound lane. Designated as Indiana Welcome Center. Leave off until midnight, EST. Remove all history for last four hours.

SECOND PRIORITY: Access Ohio State License Bureau and report all relevant information on a white Jeep Grand Cherokee. He typed in the tag number.

THIRD PRIORITY: Access any doorbell video cameras in one block radius of Biggs' apartment. Disable them until midnight, EST.

Smithson signed off.

There was a quarter of his Big Mac remaining and he pushed it into his mouth. He stared out the windshield as he chewed, then took a long pull from his Diet Coke.

He reached for Biggs' phone and activated the screen. It asked for a password. Grey had given it to him weeks ago. Smithson scrolled through the phone for a few minutes and was relieved to see nothing in call history or in the photos that could incriminate him. He checked for any files that might be a problem and found nothing. He felt reasonably confident that anything problematic would be on Biggs' computer. Smithson believed this was in Biggs' apartment but would search his Camry for it just in case.

Smithson wiped the phone for a full minute using a sealed single-use sanitizing wipe he found in the Audi's consol. It was a leftover from COVID.

What else?

Smithson snapped his fingers. He went through the login process again to safely reach Grey. He added a fourth priority.

Erase geo history of Biggs' cellphone for entire day.

He would leave the phone in Biggs' Camry after searching it. If the cops tried to figure out Biggs' movements after finding his body they would assume that whatever happened, the phone never left the car.

Smithson sucked the last of the Diet Coke through his straw. He pried off the plastic lid and tipped several nuggets of ice into his mouth.

Fucking Biggs. That's it for me, no more partners. Just me and Grey.

Smithson chewed at the nuggets.
Fucking McDonalds has the best ice too.

He put the S8 in gear and headed for the rest stop.

CHAPTER EIGHT

Grey was not a person.

Grey was a collection of tech, code, and algorithms that were combined with a large dose of cunning from Smithson's brain.

The physical components of Grey were in a 25x40 foot building set just to the side of Smithson's house outside of Boulder City, Nevada. The town boasted a population of roughly fifteen thousand. It was twenty-six miles southeast of America's Playground, Las Vegas. It was near Lake Mead, the Hoover Dam, and the Colorado River. It was a quaint town that offered a number of recreational activities.

Smithson didn't care about any of that.

Grey was born in Smithson's mind. Ideas had coalesced there for over a decade before the thing that would become Grey began to take form.

Smithson had been a teenager that was average in every way but two.

One was looks, where he was somewhat less than average.

The second was in technological prowess, where he was decidedly above average.

He grew up in Boulder City and attended the local high school.

Go Eagles.

He never knew his father. He was raised by his mother who worked, as did many thousands in the Vegas area, in the hospitality field as a housekeeper in various casino hotels.

Smithson was heavily into video games from the age of seven. His mother's work kept her away from home much of the time. When she was home she was often too tired to do much more than heat dinner in the microwave.

Smithson was fine with that. He had his games.

Once he reached high school he began to tinker with writing code. His teachers took notice and one of them, Mr. Millian, took him under his wing.

Well, for about a year.

Near the end of Smithson's junior year Millian, who was also the girl's volleyball coach, discovered the lock on his desk was broken and a number of items were missing, including his 1992 Pepperdine University National Championship Men's Volleyball ring. Millian removed it daily when he went to practice. He still jumped in from time to time to demonstrate blocks or spikes.

Smithson was often left alone in Millian's computer lab after school. When the teacher confronted him, Smithson told him to go screw himself.

That was the end of the tutelage.

Despite this Smithson, during his senior year, entered the Imagine Cup, a national coding competition sponsored by Microsoft. He finished as runner up and gained scholarship money as well as quite a bit of notoriety.

Smithson thought he should've won. He had hacked into the judging site and viewed the other submissions. According to the rules one aspect of the competition was it must "take into consideration diversity, inclusion, and accessibility."

Smithson virtually ignored this requirement, throwing together some eyewash about helping handicapped kids. A submission from Delaware won the top prize.

It was complete bullshit.

Nonetheless, Smithson had opened some eyes and had his pick of colleges, to a point.

He chose Cal Berkeley and took his talents to the Bay area of Northern California. Pepperdine was his second choice.

After all, he already had the ring.

Smithson remembers being somewhat apprehensive about being accepted. He had a good chunk of the necessary money for tuition, at least to get started. He checked the boxes when it came to ability. But Berkeley's application process boasted they "take every aspect of your personal profile into consideration when calculating your admission chances."

If that was true Smithson might have a problem. By now he was stealing tests from teachers' files and selling them to fellow students. He'd also hacked into the computers of one male and two female teachers and copied photos of them in, uh, compromising positions. He set up an anonymous pay site and threatened to release the photos unless the subjects forked over money.

All three were reluctant until Smithson emailed them copies of their own pictures. They paid.

It was a learning experience for the budding hacker. People were willing to roll the dice when threatened and not pay. But when you showed them you were actually holding the winning hand, they caved.

Smithson enjoyed the control.

But Berkeley welcomed him with open arms. He breezed through two years. By now he had a nice little business extorting from a wide variety of online victims. He made his first foray into the Dark Web, buying lists of user names and passwords and cracking into them one at a time.

It was profitable, but tedious. He found that he had to concentrate his efforts on one or two targets a night. It generally took a week to gain a foothold with a victim. He could use an unguarded Apple ID password to link to his anonymous account and purchase $500 or $1,000 in Visa gift cards. Or he could crack into a user's unprotected Paypal account and send himself a similar sum.

By the end of his junior year Smithson was losing interest in school.

And then his mother died.

She was hit by a speeding car as she crossed the street in front of the New York-New York casino at the end of her shift.

Smithson left school.

After the funeral he stayed in his mom's small place for a couple weeks but couldn't stand it. He took part of his hard earned money and bought a ranch-style house three miles outside of Boulder City. He began to cobble together the first iterations of Grey in a back bedroom.

Smithson continued his hacking on the same level for a time. In two years his online accounts, now plural, boasted over $150,000. His needs were few. He ordered pizza and, occasionally, hookers when he felt the need. He read thrillers and military memoirs. The Global War On Terror was on by now and there was plenty of material. He collected guns. He had a good old boy from town use a bulldozer to create a berm behind his property and used it as a shooting backstop.

He also put together his gaming Lair.

And one day he received a random email.

It claimed that he was videotaped while on a porn site, doing his thing. The sender said he had accessed the camera on Smithson's device and recorded the action. He would send the video to everyone in Smithson's address book if he didn't immediately send $1,500 to a highlighted Bitcoin address.

Smithson laughed. He didn't give a shit who might see him do something naughty on video. He had no boss, no girlfriend, and no wife. He also knew there was no such video and this was a bluff.

But Smithson had two epiphanies at once.

One: *I can do this same scam. Only I can do it for real because I really can access the camera.*

Two: *Bitcoin?*

Smithson invested in more data and software from the Dark Web. He modified this with his own tweaks. He bought a dozen 10th gen Dell desktops and put them to work. They filled a back bedroom.

Money was coming in. He had more video material than some porn pay sites. And the subjects were completely unaware that they were being recorded. His suspicions were correct. Once they saw themselves in actual videos, they paid whatever Smithson asked.

Smithson almost always signed his emails with the word *Nightmare* in some form or fashion.

Your worst Nightmare

The Nightmare Man

I M Yo Nightmare

Like that.

He lost interest in watching the videos, often simply archiving them without viewing them. But he thought it was fantastic watching video of *victims watching the blackmail videos.*

Smithson would wait until the victim was online, get the naughty email ready, access the camera on the users device again, and send the video. He would sit back and watch the victim as he or she—usually he—watched himself on the screen.

It was priceless.

Smithson's bank accounts grew. He obtained and modified a number of hacker tools including Intruder, Aircrack-Ng, and Nmap. But he grew bored. On a whim he bought a piece of illegal keystroke logging software from the Dark Web. It allowed him to remotely and covertly record every keystroke made by the user of a targeted keyboard. He played around with it for a couple weeks but didn't see how it enhanced his already vibrant naughty video business.

He struck gold by accident.

Smithson's Dells alerted him that they had identified a possible video victim in Sierra Vista, Arizona. Research showed the man was a colonel in the Army and stationed in nearby Fort Huachuca a few miles north of the Mexican border.

Smithson researched the man's emails and saw that he had several weaknesses, mainly women and gambling. He also saw that the man had an extremely high security clearance, lord knows how he kept it, and had access to material that was classified above Top Secret.

Smithson blackmailed the colonel. Instead of money he asked for information. Classified information. He was fishing, really. A few thousand dollars from the colonel would be nice, but wouldn't change Smithson's life.

The resulting cache of information contained a bombshell.

It was generally believed that between 2005 and 2010 the United States Central Intelligence Agency was able to infect the centrifuges used to spin uranium gas to produce fuel for the Iranian nuclear program. They did so, it was believed, by placing infected USB flash drives in areas they could be found by plant personnel.

The Iranian facilities were believed to be completely secure from exterior cyber attacks. The only means of getting the malicious software, called Stuxnet, into the system was to embed it on flash drives outside the plant and hope a technician found one and used it in the facility in the course of their daily duties.

Stuxnet did infect the facility. The centrifuges spun out of control. The Israelis and Americans were blamed. Denials were made. The Iranian nuclear program was set back several years.

Despite official denials it was generally believed the CIA was responsible. The USB story was leaked.

But Smithson saw in the colonel's emails that the U.S. had actually penetrated the facilities remotely and planted a form of keystroke logging software.

Smithson had just such software, and he was a devious son of a bitch.

He leaned on the colonel for more details, eventually getting the whole story.

Smithson could now plant Dark Web keystroke software on any computer, tablet, or cellphone he liked.

The possibilities were endless.

Smithson had a contractor add a structure behind his driveway to house his computer operation. He upgraded the Dells. He had a system in place that combined regular internet aspects such as social media and the regular, *white*, internet with the Dark Net. It gave him access, and control, almost everywhere.

He called it Grey.

He delved into Bitcoin, or to be more accurate cryptocurrency, and quickly determined it was bullshit.

But that didn't mean there wasn't money to be made. Smithson learned through Grey that the co-founder of a crypto-currency exchange was siphoning millions from his investors.

Smithson set up his own crypto account then blackmailed the co-founder. He threatened to go public with the information unless ten million dollars were transferred to him. The co-founder paid.

Six months later the news broke by other means and the co-founder left the country.

Smithson had his ten mil. He didn't care.

This sounds relatively painless.

It almost wasn't.

The crypto billionaire, a 32-year old, employed a security firm. One of their employees came very close to catching Smithson before the payment. He'd tracked him all the way to the house outside Boulder City.

The man rang Smithson's doorbell.

Smithson, in his barber chair playing Fortnite on his Xbox on screen three, ignored it. Minutes later he got up to take a piss and glanced out the curtain. He saw a dark Chevy Tahoe in his drive. There was no person in sight.

Smithson grabbed a tablet and accessed Grey. He ran the plates. Within seconds he saw that the Tahoe was owned by a security company employed by Mr. Crypto.

Goddammit!

Smithson retrieved his Colt Python from a bedroom closet and crept to his kitchen window. He saw a man on his tiptoes shading his eyes and trying to peer into the single window in Grey's building.

Smithson withdrew from the window, took a deep breath, and made a decision.

Well, It's been a good run.

He returned to the kitchen and saw the man disappear around the rear corner of the outbuilding.

Time to rock and roll.

Smithson slid open the rear glass door and strode purposely to Grey's building. He reached the corner, took a deep breath, and stepped forward.

The man was walking back in his direction. He was wiry, in his fifties. He looked intelligent. He wore hiking boots, jeans, and a golf shirt with a navy sport coat.

Smithson shot him twice in the chest.

The vehicle and body disappeared into the desert, as many had before at the hands of organized crime.

Grey took care of the man's device history.

The crypto co-founder paid.

Smithson learned a valuable lesson. He needed to take more precautions. Analysis of a laptop in the dead investigator's vehicle revealed that the security firm had a recording of his voice. He had made two phone calls to the crypto guru.

The first was five minutes after Grey alerted Smithson that the man had opened the initial blackmail email. Grey had discovered Mr. Crypto's unpublished cellphone number. Smithson called. Crypto ignored the first two calls but Smithson was unrelenting. Crypto finally answered on the third attempt with a wary tone in his voice.

"Hello?"

Smithson jumped right into the man's head.

"Pretty fucking slick how I figured this out, huh?"

He spent nearly a minute explaining exactly how he would release the sensitive information to the media, and repeated the demand for ten million that was in the email. He could almost taste the astonishment and terror coming through his wireless headset. He'd made the call from the Lair and was slowly spinning on the barber chair, a grin on his face as he hung up.

The act of manipulation energized Smithson.

When it appeared Mr. Crypto was dragging his feet, Smithson made a second call. In threatening tones he warned that he had now decided to contact Crypto's customer base directly and provide evidence that their accounts were being pilfered. He would start with one of the executive level members of a leading Mexican drug cartel.

"That would suck, huh Crypto-Boy?"

Once he gained access to the security company's files he discovered that this second call was recorded. Crypto had acted quickly after the initial contact and was obviously doing all he could to neutralize the threat. Smithson had Grey eliminate all digitally stored copies of the recording but he had no way of knowing if there were copies stored on devices that were not connected to computer systems.

He determined that he would limit himself to one call to any future target. One call should be safe. Sure, most cellphones could record phone calls, but who was going to nimbly navigate "Settings>Calls>Incoming Calls" then toggle "Incoming Calls Record" while being threatened out of the blue with financial ruin?

Smithson was also tracked, in part, because of his propensity to use the handle *Nightmare* in the course of his online operations.

He determined that he would use forged identities in all significant operations going forward.

For example, in the Wright brothers op.

Smithson wasn't his real name.

CHAPTER NINE

The man who was calling himself Smithson cruised into the Welcome Center parking area. The last rays of the sun were fading. Vapor lights came awake on the tops of poles spaced about the lot. There were a handful of parked vehicles, all but one of them within a short walking distance of the entrance.

Smithson eased the Audi past the grouped cars and trucks. There was a man in a Dodge pickup scrolling through his phone, a woman at the wheel of a red KIA SUV talking on hers. Everyone else was apparently inside. The Audi, its motor purring, drew even with the front doors. Smithson saw a young man staring at a wall map inside.

The building looked new. It was constructed of sand colored brick and exuded a look that Smithson would call "efficient penitentiary." He noted that every rest stop building he'd passed since entering the Hoosier state from Illinois had a similar look.

Smithson guided the Audi to the left and angled toward the outlier vehicle, a tired looking six-year-old maroon Toyota Camry. It filled the last space in the lot and faced in the direction of the interstate. He pulled in to the left of the Camry facing the same direction.

Smithson was again wearing the gloves he'd used at the Memorial site. He eased open his door and was silhouetted by the dome light as he stepped out of the car.

Liam Neeson probably would've disabled that light first.

Smithson smiled and stepped around to the dead man's vehicle. He surreptitiously scanned the lot and noticed two cameras. There were probably more. He had supreme confidence in Grey, though, and knew he wouldn't be recorded.

Smithson removed Biggs' keys from the pocket of his hoodie. The fob and keys hung from a metal ring, which in

61

turn was connected to a piece of oblong green plastic. He depressed the button to remotely unlock the door and—

Nothing.

Slightly panicked, he tried a second time. Again nothing. Had he grabbed the wrong set of keys from Biggs' pockets? Smithson tried to think.

No, these are right. I saw him put these in his pocket right here earlier today. Had it only been a few hours ago?

Smithson selected the largest key and inserted it into the driver's door lock. It slid in easily and he turned it to the right. The lock on the door popped up.

Smithson thought idly that it had been a helluva long time since he'd had to turn a key to open a car door. He retracted the key and pulled it toward his hoodie pocket when light caught the green plastic. He stared at it and realized it actually depicted the head of an alien. The words *THEY EXIST* were printed across its wide forehead.

For Christ's sake, how the hell did I let myself get hooked up with this asshole?

Smithson quickly searched the car and found little of importance. It was clean.

Well, it was filthy. It was a rolling version of the man's apartment. Candy bar wrappers, a balled up Burger King bag, a couple errant dental floss picks...

Wait, Burger King?! Wrong fries, dude.

A half full container of Pedialyte sat in the cup holder.

Weird.

He opened the console and dropped in Biggs' phone, closed it, thought better of it. He reopened the console, moved the phone aside, and scooped up a dollar or so in change.

You owe me $34,999.

Smithson locked the door and moved to the trunk. He noticed for the first time several bird droppings on the hood and roof. He glanced up instinctively before remembering there was no garage at Biggs' apartment and he parked in the open. The trunk held nothing of consequence.

Good. This will be a dead end for the cops.

Smithson locked up, returned to the Audi, and headed for the highway.

He still had to check Biggs' place before crashing at his Airbnb.

Smithson crossed the Ohio state border thirty minutes later. His navigation system said he had forty-one minutes until he reached Biggs' place. He'd had the nav components retrofitted into the car. The Liam Neeson 2009 S8 hadn't been blessed with a modern system. Smithson had shelled out another three grand to have it done right. He'd had to travel six miles west from the Welcome Center before getting off the highway and doubling back eastbound. He realized again how haphazard the plan had been.

Forty-one minutes to think.

That damn camera.

He thought back to earlier in the evening and tried to remember everything possible about the couple with the camera.

Nice looking woman. Pretty good shape, too, for her age. Gotta be...40...45?

Too old for Smithson.

The guy was about the same age...a little grey in his hair. A few inches taller than her but not that physically impressive.

He considered. Smithson had to admit that even though the man wasn't above average in height or broad across the chest and shoulders, he did appear to be in pretty good shape.

Well, better shape than Smithson.

But who wasn't?

He sniffed out a smile, then frowned.

Fucking Biggs...that's who. He was in waaay worse shape than me. And he played me.

Smithson would focus on Biggs when he got a bit closer to Dayton. For now his attention went back to the couple. The man told the cops they were on their way home and that they lived in Ohio. They were on a small road so there was a fair chance that they didn't have far to go once reaching the state line. Of course they could also jump on I-70 at multiple points and end up across the state.

He was relying on Grey. Getting the plate number had been key. Grey should have the pertinent information for him next time he checked in. Smithson would stay in the Airbnb tonight then drive to wherever the couple lived in the morning.

Then... what?

He would have to get into their place, preferably when no one was home. Have Grey probe for security devices. Get the camera. Get the hell out. It had to be done quickly. As soon as Biggs' body turned up the country bumpkin cops in Indiana would try to reach the couple. So he couldn't wait days for an empty house or apartment. If one or both of the couple were there and he was running out of time...well.

You gotta do what you gotta do.

And Smithson had no doubt he could do it. He certainly had the gear. He mentally took inventory of the contents of the Audi's trunk.

- A Colt M4A1 carbine capable of fully automatic fire, obtained via the Dark Web. It was the favored weapon of the United States Special Operations Command. It was stowed in a custom Pelican hard case. The weapon had traveled the world, originating in the U.S., being transported to Afghanistan sometime in the last decade with hundreds of thousands of other weapons, being left behind when America bugged out, then sold to an Uzbek arms dealer and finally being purchased by a Dark Web marketeer in Vancouver who smuggled it back into the states.

- A SOPMOD Special Operations Modification kit that came in a hard case chock full of futuristic components to add on to the rifle, including a suppressor. Again, Afghanistan, arms dealer, back to the good old US of A.

64

- A burglar kit that included a rake pick set for defeating locks. Smithson had barely practiced with it. He'd expected to learn from Biggs this week but that hadn't happened. Biggs had really disappointed.

- A Velocity Systems Plate Carrier bulletproof vest with Hesko armor plates. He bought this online from Offbase Supply & Tactical Gear. The plates were priced "too low to publish...buy two or more and save BIG."

- A Winkler Stealth Axe LT custom made combat axe in a fast draw carrier. It was made in Master Bladesmith Daniel Winkler's Boone, North Carolina factory. Winkler tomahawks were rumored to be carried in combat by some Tier One military personnel.

- A PVS-14 Night Vision Monocular attached to a lightweight black ballistic helmet. Smithson bought this from the bulldozer operator who had formed the shooting berm on his property. The bulldozer guy had purchased it from a gun show.

- Plenty of ammo for the M4 and the Colt Python revolver.

Smithson felt fortunate that the S8 had a good-sized trunk. It held well over one hundred thousand dollars worth of goodies. When he left Boulder City he would have pegged the odds of having to use any of the gear on this trip at maybe one in fifty. He had already used the revolver and it was looking like the chances were down to one in two on the remaining items.

So, get the camera...no matter what.

Bolt for Nevada.

But first, Biggs' place.

He looked at the nav and realized he was barely ten miles from his exit. The lights of Dayton brightened the eastern sky.

The Stillwater River flows lazily into the Dayton region from the northwest. The name is a reflection of its relatively slow current. By the time it reaches the northern suburbs of the city it angles due south. It intersects with the Great Miami River before coursing through the downtown area.

Early road builders constructed Riverside Drive a few short yards to the west of Stillwater. It acts as the right arm of a narrow V-shaped collection of neighborhoods. The left arm, to the west, is Main Street. Though Riverside ends a couple miles north where it intersects with an east-west road, Main continues northwest for miles. It becomes State Route 48 and connects with I-70.

Biggs lived in an apartment in the Redcrest neighborhood, located more or less in the center of the V. Most houses dated from the 1930s, the predominant style being Cape Cod. There were also a number of two-story brick homes. Biggs' apartment took up the entire first floor of one such building on Knecht Drive. It was one of dozens of east-west streets that connected Main with Riverside.

Smithson took the Route 48 exit off of I-70 and followed it past the usual collection of restaurants and gas stations, eventually reaching Knecht. He made the left, passing a Bail Bonds business, and eased the black Audi down the moderately lit street.

There was a light on upstairs. Smithson had to assume the tenant was in for the night. He knew that a single mom lived in the apartment with her young son.

A one-car garage sat at the end of a narrow, black asphalt drive. It was situated on the east side of the house. The garage was not connected to the larger structure. A set of wooden steps angled down from the upper floor and ended near the garage. The landlord had decided that the tenant inconvenienced with the climb would be compensated with use of the garage, hence the bird droppings on Biggs' Camry.

Smithson drove past. He reached the last house before Riverside and pulled in the drive. He reversed back onto Knecht, pointed the S8 back toward Biggs' place, and pulled to the curb two houses from the apartment. He selected one of the travel bags on the rear seat and moved it to his lap. He unzipped it and removed a black device that was roughly the size of a TV remote and slipped it into the front pocket of his hoodie.

Smithson pulled on his gloves then opened the console and removed a flimsy facemask. It was the style that became ubiquitous during COVID, white on one side, light blue on the other. He looked at it.

Never did figure out which color was supposed to face outward.

He fit it onto his face, looping the elastic over his ears. Smithson was not sure that the masks helped prevent transmission of the virus one iota, but he was sure of one thing: they made it a hell of a lot easier to commit a crime and not be identified.

Even now, a few years after prime COVID hysteria, a burglar or hold-up man could enter a building wearing his disguise and barely draw a second look. He could commit a crime in front of multiple witnesses and have a reasonable chance of remaining unidentified.

Smithson saw no potential witnesses on Knecht. He had Biggs' keys so would not need to fumble with the lock pick set. Anyone who happened to see him enter wouldn't notice anything out of the ordinary.

Smithson opened the door—*that damned dome light again*—and pulled himself out of the Audi. He lowered his head slightly and walked toward the apartment at what he hoped was an unremarkable pace. The moon was bright, not quite full. The keys were in his right hand and tucked inside the hoodie pocket. His left hand gripped the black device. His eyes jumped furtively from side to side. He tried to keep his head still. He softly whistled a cheerful tune that had been stuck in his head, reasoning it was something a guiltless person would do. He reached the front walk, made a right turn, and arrived at the door. He'd examined the keys earlier and determined there was only one that could possibly fit the front lock. It slid in cleanly. He pushed the door open and quickly stepped inside.

Smithson had also ruled out using the night vision device. The helmet wouldn't fit in his hoodie and would be too obvious dangling from his hand. And he sure as hell wouldn't be inconspicuous if it was fitted to his head. He'd decided to get in quick, close all the curtains, and risk turning on the lights. It would be much easier to search using interior lights than fumbling about with the unfamiliar device that made everything appear green.

Should've practiced more with the damn things.

The front picture window was to his left. Through the dim light he could tell that the curtains were partially open. He moved in that direction. With his second step he tripped over a coffee table and fell forward. He reached out and, fortunately, contacted a couch that sat in front of the window.

"Goddammit!"

Smithson said it out loud, too loud.

He stood and listened, straining to hear anything unusual from upstairs. After thirty seconds he exhaled. He reached for the curtains and drew them shut. He then felt his way across the wall, searching for a light switch. He came to a bookshelf and let his gloved hands traverse it until again feeling the wall, then finally contacted a switch. He flipped it on.

The light revealed a room with threadbare furnishings. Tall bookshelves crowded two walls. A waist high shelf, also stuffed with books, was situated against a third wall. A mid-sized flat screen television sat on top.

Smithson remembered the books. It was the thing that most impressed him when he'd flown out earlier in the summer to meet Biggs. That and, well, not much else come to think of it.

Biggs had been employed by a small Dayton company that specialized in producing high quality hard cover editions of Civil War books, some of which had been out of print for decades. It was based out of a Civil War era—of course—home in an older section of Dayton. The business owner employed a handful of staff members. Biggs was his right-hand man.

The shop itself had limited hours, 10a.m.-4p.m. weekdays. A sign on the door read, "Doberman has access to entire building. Please allow us time to put the animal away."

Thousands of volumes were housed on the sagging floor-to-ceiling shelves that lined the walls. Extra shelving stood in the interior, creating aisles. Biggs had an office in the rear of the building with a desk surrounded by stacks of boxes. A sealed fireplace on the rear wall was the only space not covered by books in some fashion.

The shop did no printing of its own. It contracted with various houses across the country. Standards were high. Biggs acted as liaison between the owner, the printing facilities, and the rights owners of the books. His expertise in methods, typeset, and paper and bindings were a key factor in producing the finished product.

Biggs told Smithson that he loved his job. Then came the internet and online books. The shop held on for a few years until, in 2013, the owner passed away unexpectedly. The doors were closed permanently leaving a great many book lovers to mourn not only the passing of the owner, but the books themselves.

None of them more than Biggs.

Biggs worked part time for a while in one of the glorified coffee shops that passed as a modern bookstore, but his heart wasn't in it. For the past three years Biggs spent most of his lonely waking hours at a library or online. That is where Grey had come across a number of his posts.

Smithson removed the small black device from his hoodie. It was a Scout Hidden Camera Finder, purchased from SpyGuy.com.

Grey would take care of any security camera footage that could be problematic. In his sweep, Grey would find any hidden camera that was linked to the internet. There was another type of camera, one that records directly to an SD card. Those devices could not be detected by Grey.

But the lens on this type of camera would almost certainly have an infrared filter. This filter would reflect light. Cameras could be hidden in electrical outlets, smoke detectors, nightlights, or any one of dozens of other obscure spots. The Scout was designed to reveal these lenses.

Smithson checked the batteries in the unit. He got his bearings in the room to make sure he wouldn't trip again before switching it on. He then flipped off the overhead light. He raised the device to his right eye and peered through its small aperture. He then slowly turned 360 degrees. Lenses would appear as red dots.

There were none.

This was not unexpected. It was difficult to believe Biggs had a security system set up in his rathole apartment but Smithson wanted to be sure.

He quickly searched the room for anything related to Operation Crank. He found nothing obvious. The books would be a problem. If Biggs had hidden something in one or more of these, Smithson would play hell trying to find it. He checked the books on the shelf directly in front of him and saw titles such as *LEE'S SHARPSHOOTERS, THE ATTACK AND DEFENSE OF LITTLE ROUND TOP, and SOUTHERN HISTORICAL SOCIETY PAPERS, Volumes 1-52*. There was simply not enough time. He'd hoped that the dead man had everything he was searching for in one place and that it was accessible.

This living room area was fairly tidy. There was an empty pizza box and a couple copies of *Gettysburg Magazine* strewn on the coffee table, but everything else appeared to be in its place.

Smithson moved to the bedroom.

He flipped on the lights. The room was a mess. The bed was unmade. Whiteboards and old style cork bulletin boards covered a significant percentage of the walls. Notes and printed articles filled these spaces, just as Smithson recalled from his previous visit. But it seemed there was even more material than he remembered.

A desk took up a corner of the room. A wooden swivel chair sat in front. The desk was covered with papers. Some were stacked neatly while others appeared to have been haphazardly strewn on top. An older macbook laptop computer was situated in the center of the desk. Several books and printed material of various sizes, all related to the Wright brothers, surrounded the floor in a semi-circle around the chair. A wastebasket overflowed on the far side of the desk.

Smithson sighed.

For Christ's sake Biggs, really?

He flipped off the lights and ran the Scout camera finder around the room, then switched them back on. No reflections.

Time to go to work.

Forty minutes later Smithson returned to the Audi. He lugged two large pillowcases filled with material. The laptop was inside one. A dozen manila folders stuffed with eight and a half by eleven papers went in that sack. The other held a number of clipped articles that had been tacked to the corkboards as well as the contents of two desk side drawers.

The other side drawers had held Civil War and alien conspiracy material. The center drawer was filled with bills, including several from medical providers. Many with older dates were marked "Overdue," but several of the more recent ones were stamped "PAID."

Smithson had stared at these for a few seconds. He had a good idea what had happened to his thirty-five thousand.

He had erased the word "Smithson" from one whiteboard and scribbled over it. He'd searched through the seven books on the floor to see if anything important fell out. A brochure labeled "WRIGHT STATE UNIVERSITY LIBRARIES SPECIAL COLLECTIONS & ARCHIVES" flapped to the ground. He tossed it into the pillowcase.

Smithson had to move a standing TV tray to get to the wastebasket. The tray held a paper plate with pizza crusts and an empty can of Warped Wing Flyer Red beer. Smithson held the can in his hand and scrutinized it.

It hit him.

The Wright brothers' concept of wing warping may have been their biggest breakthrough in their road to flight. A craft brewer in Dayton had seized on this and named their product after it.

Smithson sniffed and allowed a half smile to come to his lips. He sat the can down and reached for the wastebasket. He turned to the bed and dumped the contents on top. There were two more empty Warped Wings as well as three Pedialyte containers.

Smithson mused, *I don't know what the hell was wrong with you....but I guess we don't have to worry anymore, do we?*

He smiled.

Smithson searched through the discarded items, finding two or three scraps that went in the case. Near the bottom he came across a manila folder.

Across its top Biggs had scrawled the words "PHASE THREE."

It was empty.

Fucking Biggs!

CHAPTER TEN

THURSDAY

Paul heard Lauren's alarm at 4:20. She hit snooze and rolled over. Paul sat up and swung his feet onto the floor. He tried to remember to test his leg before starting his day but often forgot. Today he remembered. He stretched it out then stood, leaning slightly from side to side. The leg ached but he was certainly used to that by now.

He slipped on a pair of Ugg moccasin-style slippers and made for the kitchen. He gathered eggs, bacon, shredded cheese, and butter from the refrigerator and selected two skillets from a cupboard. Next, he turned on two of the six burners on the Thor stainless steel stove.

Paul smiled whenever he did this, remembering asking the salesman why it was advertised as a seven-burner unit. The man explained that there was a grouping of four burners on the right side, a stainless cover in the center of the unit, then two more burners on the left. The cover hid a built in griddle.

"The griddle surface is your seventh burner, sir."

Paul had countered, "Shouldn't it be advertised as a six burner, one griddle stove?"

The man smiled nervously, unsure of how to respond.

Lauren punched Paul in the shoulder.

First things first. Paul hadn't filled the coffee maker the night before. He got that going. It was a commercial Bunn unit. All those years on the go had made Paul particular about his brew. The Bunn was easy to operate and would crank out a potful in no time flat.

He cracked six eggs and walked the bowl to the corner of the dining room. They kept three small ceramic bowls there for Chappy. One held dry cat food, the second one, now empty, was used for canned food, and the third held water. Paul spooned three of the yolks into the empty bowl and walked back to the stove.

Spoiled cat.

He fished a handheld whisk from a drawer and mixed the remaining yolks with the egg whites. The skillets had heated sufficiently for Paul to add strips of bacon to one. He added a splash of olive oil to the second and spread it across the surface with a wooden spoon.

Back to the refrigerator, it was also a stainless unit from Thor. It was a twenty-two cubic foot version with French doors. It was certainly larger than two people needed, but it served Paul well during the cooking phase of his initial retirement years. The Hulls has splurged when setting up the kitchen. Lauren had some definite ideas of how it should be outfitted. Paul's recent interest in cooking made him an equal party in the selection of appliances and components. It wasn't that money was no object, but all those years of combat pay combined with Lauren's income made a dream kitchen possible.

On top of this, Paul received a significant disability payment each month. This was not totally based on his leg injury. It was a little understood fact that a very high percentage of combat veterans returning from the GWOT qualified for disability at levels somewhere below one hundred percent. For the shooters, the personnel out at the tip of the spear, almost all of them had one or more qualifying conditions, hearing loss and back and joint issues being the most common. Tack on combat wounds and training injuries and the compensation levels could rise. Paul was assessed as having a sixty percent level of disability upon separation from the Air Force.

He selected a half-gallon container of milk—Lauren preferred organic—and added a small amount to the eggs. He whisked for twenty seconds then poured the contents into the second skillet. The bacon began to crackle, the fragrance mingling with the aroma of coffee.

Paul opened the sliding glass door to the patio and stepped out. He closed it quickly so Chappy didn't escape. The cat hadn't yet made an appearance this morning but the presence of the egg yolks should change that. The patio was constructed of pavers and ran nearly the entire width of the back of the house. It was partially surrounded by a matching block wall. This wall held over a dozen pots of various sizes. They constituted the Hull's garden. They were bursting with vegetables and flowers. Paul selected two small sweet Italian peppers from one and a mid-sized tomato from another.

He stepped back inside, again on the lookout for Chappy. He cleaned and chopped the veggies, intermittently working the eggs. Finally, he added the peppers and tomatoes as well as sprinkles of cheese before reducing the heat.

Paul moved to a cupboard and selected two mugs. His had simple block lettering, "THE 24." Lauren's sported the logo of the Albuquerque International Balloon Festival. He filled his from the Bunn before reaching down to pull out the door to an under-counter icemaker and scooped Lauren's full. She'd recently become a fan of iced coffee.

Paul sipped his coffee and pushed the eggs with the wooden spoon to prevent them from burning. He used a fork to turn the bacon. He heard the noise of the hair dryer coming from the master bathroom. He realized he'd forgotten the toast. He opened a drawer built into the island and took out a loaf of wheat bread. He removed four pieces and crossed to the toaster. It was a four-slice model with dual controls. Lauren liked hers very lightly toasted. Paul preferred his, well, *normal*.

He depressed the levers then decided strawberry jam sounded good. As he reached for the refrigerator door, Paul felt the eyes of a predator. He looked up.

Chappy was in his sniper hide. It was an old rectangular Longaberger basket. The Hulls kept it on top of the refrigerator, ostensibly to hold rolls of trash bags and other miscellaneous items. Chappy decided early on that this was an excellent perch. No matter how many times he was pulled from the basket and placed on the floor, he invariably returned. After a few weeks Paul and Lauren gave up. Chappy would jump on the counter, pad to the side of the Thor, and jump up. His chubby body fit comfortably now that the trash bags and widgets had been removed.

Paul crossed his arms and peered at the cat.

"Good morning Chappy, all clear this morning?"

Chappy sunk lower, green eyes barely visible above the edge of the basket.

"You're pretty well concealed today."

Lauren walked in, her hair fragrant and slightly damp.

"Mmmmm, breakfast smells fantastic. Talking to Chappy?" she asked.

Paul smiled as he found the jam.

Lauren doctored her coffee as her side of the toaster released. They both filled plates and sat next to each other at the island.

"Make sure to tell Gatewood I said hi," Lauren said as she glanced at a wall clock.

Paul sprinkled Old Bay on his eggs and smiled, "Will do. Bet he asks about you inside of a minute when we hook up. I think he has a thing for you."

"Oh he does," she agreed. "It's a big brother-little sister thing. Nobody better mess with Gatewood's adopted little sis, even you." She tilted her head to him.

Paul chuckled, "I wouldn't dream of it. I can't think of anyone that would want to mess with Chief Master Sergeant Gatewood Dowdell."

Paul considered. It should be obvious based on the differences in skin pigmentation alone that Lauren and Gatewood were probably not blood relatives. But he also knew she had a point. The person who considered doing harm to her with Woody in the world was going to have an extremely bad day, even after the man's own severe wound.

"Oh geez, I completely forgot about the clothes," Lauren announced with a bit of a startled look on her face.

"Clothes?" Paul lowered his mug.

76

"I promised Elaine I'd bring her some clothes from the closet. Her daughter goes back to college next week and the stuff from the eighties and nineties is back in again," she explained.

Lauren stood but Paul stopped her.

"No, no, you finish your breakfast. I'll get them. Where are they?"

Lauren replied, "In the plastic totes on the floor of the walk-in closet in our bedroom."

"There's like four of them in there, I trip over them a couple times a week. Which one do you need?" Paul asked.

Lauren, deadpan, said "All of them. Does that break your heart?" She smirked.

"Not in the least."

Paul stood, gave Lauren a sarcastic salute, and headed for the bedroom.

The totes were just large enough to be in the way regardless of where they were stashed. They currently resided on the floor of the closet along the left side. This was under Paul's hanging shirts. He really did run a toe into or trip over them every week or two so it was well worth his effort to carry them out for his wife.

He moved to the tote deepest in the closet and bent to slide it out. His attention was seized by something he saw in the corner. It was behind the tote and tucked under several long sleeved dress shirts on hangers.

It was his little Ruger 10/22 rifle. He'd owned it since high school. His grandpa Hull gave it to him for Christmas one year, apparently without the approval of Paul's mom. Paul grinned, remembering the withering look she cast at her father-in-law and the shameless smile he gave her in return.

Paul and his buddy John Foster had plinked around in the woods with it for two summers and sporadically during the corresponding school years. John went off to college, Paul eventually headed to the Air Force, and the Ruger had spent the past twenty-five years in various closets and storage units on or near military installations across the United States.

Paul recalled his younger sister Patrice, two years his junior, watching him shoot at soda cans near a creek behind their Wappingers Falls home. They were soda cans in New York. Here in Ohio they would have been called pop cans.

Patrice seemed curious so Paul asked if she'd like to try her hand. To his surprise she said yes. She fired five times and didn't come close to hitting a can but she came back to the creek the next time she heard the crack of the rifle, and most every time after that. By the end of that summer Patrice was a more than respectable shot.

Years later, after Patrice and her husband Kevin were married, she told Paul she wanted him to teach her future sons or daughters to shoot with that same rifle. Paul had just completed the demanding twenty-plus month series of training evolutions necessary to begin a career as a Combat Controller. It was known as "The Pipeline." He was home for a week before joining his first operational squadron. It was 2003 and the conflicts in Iraq and Afghanistan were hot. Paul was eager to do his part. He laughed and told Patrice that of course he would teach her kids to shoot.

After the deployments, and the things he had seen, he was much more circumspect. Patrice was his sister. She and Kevin now had Leo, fourteen, and eleven-year-old Frankie. If Patrice revisited the conversation, Paul would keep his promise.

She was his sister. He would do anything for his nephews.

But Paul was not unlike some other former special operations personnel. They vowed to lay down their weapons forever once they were out of the service.

"Paul?"

"Coming!" he turned from the rifle and grabbed the first tote.

"I need to leave in five," Lauren reached for the coffee pot.

"No worries, I'll get them all out of the closet and make a couple stacks on the table. Get your coffee and go open the Jeep's hatchback. I should be able to carry two at a time out the door to the garage if you hold it open for me."

Paul stacked the totes on the table.

He questioned, "What the heck is in these things, anyway?"

78

Lauren laughed, "Well, tube tops, high-waisted jeans...I think they're called 'mom-jeans' now... spandex..."

"You're telling me all that stuff is popular again?" Paul feigned incredulity.

Lauren winked, kissed him lightly on the lips, and said "That's what I'm told, and I'm sure not wearing any of it again."

She was out the door. The stacks of totes had blocked her view of the camera bag.

CHAPTER ELEVEN

Paul rinsed the dishes and stacked them in the dishwasher. He refilled his mug and strode out of the kitchen toward the converted office. The house had been listed as a three-bedroom structure but the previous owner had set up one of them as an office. It had all of the necessary connections to utilize modern devices. As a bonus, a rear window offered a view of a line of woods a quarter mile distant that reminded him of his boyhood home in New York. Paul had seen no reason to revert the room to its original purpose and Lauren agreed. It continued to function as an office.

Chappy was obsessed with the room. To him it seemed to bristle with cords that needed chewed and wall mounted photos to paw. If allowed to enter, he tended to rub his body against any occupant of the office chair. If he received no attention in the form of head scratches or petting Chappy would plant himself on the laptop keyboard or writing pad, whatever seemed to be absorbing his human's scrutiny. He would roll his rotund body to one side and stare up expectantly. Paul and Lauren kept the door closed when it was unoccupied and only allowed the cat inside when they could keep an eye on him.

On this day Paul wanted a few minutes to concentrate while online without "assistance" from Chappy. The feline must have assumed he would be welcomed in to the office on this morning and followed Paul. When the door closed before he could enter Chappy began to paw urgently at the doorknob.

Paul opened his laptop and went online. He searched for and found the Henry County Indiana Sheriff's Office site. He navigated to the Sheriff's Log area and saw no mention of activity at the Wilbur Wright Birthplace. Sipping coffee, he also checked the Sheriff's Office Facebook site without result. Paul continued, checking the Henry County Courier Journal and Indianapolis Star newspaper sites as well as the local news sections of Indiana television outlets' websites.

Whatever led to the odd circumstances at the birthplace Memorial the previous day had not generated any media attention.

Paul realized Chappy was no longer working away at the door. He closed the laptop and walked back toward the kitchen.

Maybe one more cup before my workout.

He entered the kitchen and saw gooey egg yolk footprints leading from Chappy's bowl. They went first to the base of the island then appeared on top of it. They trailed the cat, who stood there looking at Paul with a scrunched up face.

Paul groaned and reached for the paper towel holder.

This cat.

After cleaning up both the kitchen and Chappy, Paul changed into workout gear and headed for the basement. He closed the door to keep the cat from joining him. Chappy had a habit of inserting himself into Paul's workout in a variety of inconvenient ways.

Paul had remodeled half the basement. He'd added a wall across the center creating two separate spaces. The far space became his workout room. There were windowed double doors in the center of the new wall. The long-term plan was to finish the other half of the basement at some point. The couple would have the ability to keep the workout area semi-private when the doors were closed. For now they remained open most of the time.

The room was roughly 20x24 feet. It had a synthetic wood floor. A number of machines stood on rubber mats, which protected the floor. There was a Circuit Fitness stationary bike. Paul wouldn't need that today as he intended to ride outside after his workout, hopefully before the heat of the August day took hold. There was an Obsidian Surge water rowing machine and a Champ free weight rack with pull up bar and pyramidal storage for extra plates. There was also a Hyperwear Advanced Weighted Battle jump rope and a Pilates table.

The back wall opposite the doors was covered with dark brown pegboard. Paul had added it to allow storage of stretch bands, weightlifting accessories, and workout towels. Added shelving held a variety of foam rollers. A large whiteboard was situated amongst the assemblage, displaying notes on various workouts.

A third wall was covered with floor-to-ceiling mirrors. The final wall held a wall-mounted fifty-five inch flat screen television mounted over waist high cabinets. These were topped by butcher block and housed a small built-in refrigerator. Speakers in the corners allowed audio from the TV, a cellphone, or a laptop or tablet. Paul could execute any number of exercises in this small space. He varied his workouts to avoid boredom and work different muscle groups.

Today Paul would be doing a full-body Tabata workout, aimed to yield the most benefits in a short amount of time. He would complete eight sets of ten different exercises. For each exercise he would do twenty seconds of strenuous activity followed by ten seconds of rest, then repeat it seven more times before moving on to the next one. This meant he spent four minutes on each of the following; jump rope, pull ups, bench press, rear foot elevated split squats (RFESS), Russian twists, Romanian dead lifts, overhead tricep extensions, planks, Arnold press, and Zottman curls.

It was an exhausting routine. Paul had only in the last six months been able to complete the RFESS's on his left side with anything approaching the same level of strength as his right. His left leg was still improving from the parachute accident.

When he'd finished, Paul was covered in perspiration. He toweled off and grabbed a Gatorade from the refrigerator. It was not yet 8 a.m. He had until nine to get his truck to the shop. He planned to get in a bike ride of an hour or two before meeting Gatewood for lunch.

Paul went upstairs and passed a scowling Chappy on his way to the bedroom. He changed into padded shorts and a high visibility green shirt made of wicking material. He filled a water bottle on the way back through the kitchen then entered the garage and opened the overhead door. Walking around his

Ford Escape, he made his way to a small rack on the far wall. It held his bike, which cost Paul $1,500. In the world of serious bikers this was not at all extravagant.

Paul wheeled the bike out the door. His helmet was balanced on the seat. The driveway flared out to the side of the two-car garage, allowing a third vehicle to be parked without blocking access. Paul's pickup truck was parked there. It was a 1989 Ford XLT Lariat. It was black with a thin red pinstripe running its length and had a reupholstered red interior. It had been well used but well maintained by its previous owner, Paul's friend Mike McClary.

Two years earlier Mike and his wife Marge purchased a camper and needed a larger truck to pull it. It was a 24 foot Dutchman Aspen Trail unit they christened *The Bourbon Trail'r*. They bought a Dodge Ram 1500 and the Lariat became expendable. Mike offered it to the Hulls at Blue Book price and they quickly agreed to the deal. A number of Paul's military buddies drove pickups and he saw firsthand how useful they could be. Lauren's dad had owned several over the years and she'd learned to drive in one of them.

The truck had over a hundred thousand miles on its odometer and was ready for its third set of tires. Paul tried to do as much business as possible with a small family owned truck and auto repair shop. It was located two miles south of the Hull's house, on the north edge of Troy.

Paul slid the water bottle into the bike's holder. He lowered the Lariat's tailgate and swung the bike up and into the bed. He was at the auto repair shop, J.D.'s, three turns and five minutes later. He grabbed the pair of Oakley sunglasses that hung from his rear view and headed for the office.

J.D. himself was at the desk in the small office. Or, as Paul liked to call him "J.D. Actual." J.D. was a grizzled man in his mid-sixties. Paul learned that the mechanic had done six years in the Army after high school as an enlisted man. He had seen no combat, spending the bulk of his time completing repetitive tasks for low pay. But it had suited him. He learned a trade—he had been an Army Wheeled Vehicle Mechanic—met a few lifelong friends, and had done his small part for the country.

J.D. had used a vanity license plate that read "MOS 91B" on a series of vehicles he owned ever since. This was the military occupational specialty designation for his job.

Paul's moniker for J.D. stemmed from the first conversation the men had. Upon learning that Paul had been in the Air Force, the man asked "Enlisted or officer?"

Paul had smiled and replied, "Got out as an E-7."

J.D. smiled back.

"We're going to get along just fine."

J.D. confided he had no love for officers. In his opinion the great majority of them "let a little bit'a power go to their head."

It was customary in the military to add the word "actual" on radio traffic when referring to the commander of a unit. The officer in charge of Hotel Company, for example, would be "Hotel Actual" on the radio. This let anyone listening know they were communicating directly with the commander. Paul added the word to J.D.'s title as a friendly dig, implying the mechanic was carrying himself like an officer.

J.D. always grinned. He was definitely in charge at the shop.

"We'll get the new rubber on that Lariat of yours, Sergeant," he grinned. "Lola will be in before noon and I'll have her call you when it's ready."

Paul grinned back and tossed him the keys.

"I left it unlocked. Thanks Actual," and winked.

Paul returned to the Lariat, removed a garage door opener from the visor above the driver's side, and slid its clip over the top of his shorts. He walked to the rear of the truck and lowered the tailgate then lifted his bike, setting it on the ground and letting it lean against the fender. He remembered the first time he saw a high-end bike and discovered it had no kickstand. He had not realized this. He was now accustomed to it.

He attached his cellphone to the holder on the handlebar and double-checked to make sure the water bottle was secure. It was just past 9 a.m. but the temperature was already nearing eighty and the humidity level nearly seventy percent. After the workout earlier he would definitely need to hydrate during the ride. Paul eschewed clip-in style biking shoes, preferring standard flat bottoms. It allowed him to easily detach himself from the pedals if necessary. He had seen bikers injured after losing their balance. They had failed to right themselves because the clip-ins cost them a split second of recovery time.

Paul donned the helmet and adjusted his glasses. He opened his exercise app, MapMyRun, and selected the Road Cycling feature. He turned to see J.D. through the window, back at his desk.

Paul smiled and saluted.

J.D. laughed and returned the salute.

Paul started the app and eased into the bike lane on the street. After a few blocks he reached the Great Miami River Bike Trail. He decided to ride south and within a minute was accelerating down the paved surface as he passed Miami Shores Golf Course. The path would be mostly clear of walkers and joggers on a Thursday morning, allowing Paul to maintain a brisk pace.

Several geese stood next to a tee box, unmindful of the nearby foursome of morning senior golfers. One of the men raised a hand and smiled at Paul as he cruised past. Paul returned both the wave and the smile.

He glance up at the blue sky with the sun rising to his left then picked up his pace.

It was a nice day to fly.

CHAPTER TWELVE

Smithson woke up at the exact time that Paul was finishing his Russian twists.

It was ridiculously early.

Smithson was wiped when he reached the Airbnb the night before. He knew his main priority, his "Prime Directive" if he'd been a Trekkie, was to find the couple with the camera. He had selected a four-bedroom, two story home with a full basement. It was chosen based on the fact that the ad for the place claimed a wifi speed of above 50 Mbps and that the basement featured a seventy-five inch television with a surround sound system.

Smithson had chosen the house weeks earlier and intended to spend large blocks of the next few days with his games while waiting for Phase Three of Crank to be implemented. That was gone now.

Smithson frowned, again remembering how he had been played by Biggs.

The home was located on Homeview Drive, midway between Biggs' apartment and I-70. Smithson had pulled into the drive and retrieved the key from a lockbox near the side door. He took only a small travel bag and the Toughbook into the house. He expected to leave the place for good early Thursday morning to travel to wherever the "Camera Couple" lived.

Nearly three hours had passed between the time Grey had been given the license plate number and when Smithson entered the rental. Smithson expected a significant amount of information to be waiting for him. There was a better than average chance that the couple lived hours away and he would have to get back on the road shortly to travel to their location.

Smithson sat in the first chair he came to and opened the laptop. He completed the protocol required to safely access Grey. The screen brightened and he watched a small icon float across. For Operation Crank, he had chosen a small Wright Flyer. He smiled as it crossed the screen.

Smithson saw that Grey, as usual, had arranged the data in sections. Smithson selected the first section and read.

> *Grand Cherokee registered to Lauren Rose Hull, 45*
> *Address: 880 Polecat Rd. Troy, Ohio, 45373*
> *Occupation: Medical Technologist, Kettering Health,*
> *600 West Main, Troy*
> *No previous marriage*
> *No children*
> *Spouse: Paul Robert Hull, 50*
> *Address: Same*
> *Occupation: Retired, United States Air Force*
> *No previous marriage*
> *No children*

Smithson immediately opened a secure browser and searched for Troy. He was elated to see it was barely a half-hour from his current location. He could bunk down in the Airbnb for the night and wouldn't need further travel. He would use the current rental for as long as necessary before heading back to Nevada. It shouldn't take more than a day or two to tie up loose ends.

Smithson continued through the data.

The husband had both a Facebook and Twitter account. The wife had both of these, as well as Instagram.

There was a three-year-old Ford Escape, grey, registered to the husband.

An older 1989 pickup truck was also registered to the husband.

Smithson yawned. A load seemed to disappear from his shoulders now that he knew he could rest. He gave Grey a set of instructions:

Immediately disable all posting functions for both subjects on all social media accounts. Allow other features to continue normally.

Assess level of electronic security in couple's house.

Search for any extortion leverage, i.e. affairs, improper activity, criminal history.

Access wife's work schedule for remainder of week.

Access husband's military records.

Collect customary information on extended family and circle of friends.

Assemble log of cellphone calls and geo data for the past 12 months on both subjects.

Access Ford and Jeep vehicle communication/ entertainment/navigation systems.

Collect information from all law enforcement agencies in Indiana referring to discovery of a body near Wilbur Wright Birthplace.

Smithson set the alarm on his phone with a smile and went to bed.

Now, Thursday morning, it was time to go to work.

But first, donuts.

He hadn't eaten since the stop at McDonalds the night before. He'd seen the sign for a nearby Mom and Pop donut shop just off I-70 on his way to Biggs' apartment. It was closed at that time. Smithson assumed it would be open in the morning. But it was an unfamiliar shop and he had a craving for Dunkin'. He pulled up the web on his phone and saw there was a Dunkin' Donut shop fifteen minutes away. He threw on Wednesday's hoodie and was out the door.

Fifteen minutes later on the dot he parked the Audi outside of the shop on Woodman Drive. There was one customer in front of him, a middle-aged woman. As he waited, Smithson looked at the selection of remaining donuts. It was 8:05 and the displays were barely half full.

How early do these people wake up in this town?

Smithson noticed four peanut donuts on the right side on the bottom rack.

Damn straight!

These were his favorite. The customer ahead of him had ordered a dozen mixed donuts and was directing the counter attendant around the display as if he were a remote controlled drone.

"...and one chocolate filled...and an apple fritter, umm, two glazed..."

For Christ's sake lady, let's go!

The woman turned to her right and seemed to lock on the peanut donuts.

No! Don't you dare take my donuts!

She turned back to the center of the display and completed her order.

"Two cinnamon and a French Cruller."

Smithson mentally pumped his fist. He paused a beat then pumped his actual fist. Moving forward he smiled brightly.

"Four peanut and an extra large coffee to go."

The attendant, an overly cheerful woman in her forties, gathered the order and sat it on the counter.

"That'll be $6.89, sir. Would you like to round up for Rico?"

Smithson was handing her a ten. He hesitated and stared at her dumbly.

She pointed to a laminated paper taped to the counter. Smithson leaned forward and saw a photo of a young man in a hospital bed. His lower face was covered by a plastic mask, which was attached to a tube.

He read:

> University of Dayton basketball player Rico Hawken collapsed on August 6 in his hometown of Baltimore, Maryland. All Dayton area Dunkin' locations are supporting the family with ROUND UP FOR RICO. By rounding up your order total to the next dollar you can assist his recovery. Dunkin' will match the total amount donated. GO FLYERS!!!

90

Smithson thought back to his time at Cal Berkeley. The basketball and football players were catered to on campus. Their education was free. They had their own meal facilities. Those that bothered with schoolwork had tutors. They were celebrities on campus. They were invited to all the best parties and had all the hot women. Now, since the advent of Name, Image, Likeness, or NIL rights, they were actually *paid* to grace the school with their presence.

He looked back at the smiling attendant.

"No."

Her smile disappeared. She handed him back three ones, a dime and a penny.

Smithson walked to the Audi, thinking *Screw Rico.*

CHAPTER THIRTEEN

A quarter of an hour later the black S8 pulled back into the driveway of the rental on Homeview. Two donuts and nearly all of the coffee remained. Smithson gathered the pillowcases from the back seat that held items from Bigg's apartment. He carried them inside with the Dunkin' bag and cup and sat it all on the dining room table. He went to the bedroom and fished out the Scout Finder.

He was too tired to do a sweep of the house when he arrived the night before so he set to it now. He was methodical, taking a full twenty minutes. Users of rental sites such as Airbnb, Vrbo, and HomeToGo were encouraged to set up a Virtual Private Network, or VPN, for internet security when staying at a property. Because of Grey, Smithson didn't need to take this step. But he counted himself among the fifty eight percent of guests that worried about hidden cameras and was also in the eleven percent that had found them.

He was impressed by the video setup in the basement. It had the appearance of a mini amphitheater with semi-circular seating arranged around the large screen. Smithson cleared the basement, took a longing look at the setup, and climbed back up the stairs. It looked like he wouldn't have time to give it a whirl.

He thought he had a positive reflection in the smoke detector above the bed in the master bedroom. But closer inspection revealed it was a style with a glass component in its interior. For a second it appeared he had a repeat of the situation in Vancouver. He'd gone there to pick up his M4 from the arms dealer. He'd found a camera in the smoke detector of his rental the night before taking possession of the weapon. It would have captured video of him opening the rifle case on his bed had it not been discovered.

Smithson was livid.

Fucking criminals! This is illegal!

He immediately accessed Grey and tracked the owner of the rental. He was the sales manager of a Mercedes dealership on the outskirts of Vancouver. Smithson directed Grey to insert two years of history on the man's work computer. It featured hundreds of views of child porn sites and, as a kicker, photos of the wife of the owner wearing a bikini while vacationing in Hawaii.

A simple anonymous call completed the payback.

Smithson settled into a chair at the kitchen table. He again accessed Grey and saw that most of the information he requested barely an hour earlier was already assembled in sections.

There was no evidence of extramarital activity for either the husband or the wife. Also, no criminal history. No evidence of drug use.

Hmmm, OK, blackmail is out.

The husband, Paul, had family. Both parents were still living and had retired to Florida. A sister lived in Ohio. She was married with two young sons. Cellphone call and text history showed that he was very close to her and her family.

Interesting.

The wife's mother and two brothers lived in New Mexico. Her father was deceased. Her work schedule showed 5:30 a.m. start times each day until the coming weekend. Her shift ended at 2:30 p.m.

5:30?!? No wonder the donuts were picked over.

Grey had accessed both the information systems of the husband's Ford Escape, which used the SYNC system, and the wife's Jeep, which used Uconnect. Separate folders were available with vehicle histories for the past year. They were sizeable. Smithson saved them to review later if it became necessary.

The husband's military records were attached. Smithson had programmed Grey to flag peculiarities when assembling these reports. If he had added this feature prior to the 3M operation he could've avoided a significant amount of inconvenience. A note in red flashed at him.

Paul Hull retired from Air Force with honorable discharge 38 months ago. Receives disability check monthly. Level of disability 60%. Portions of Paul Hull military records classified. Unavailable through standard probing methods. Employ Stuxnet Level attack?

The question mark blinked at Smithson. He considered.

Stuxnet level penetration should be able to defeat any firewall. But...if any organization would be able to defend against it, wouldn't it be the military? It would be nice to have all of Hull's information but...

Smithson decided he didn't want to risk revealing himself. He remembered being on the defensive during the 3M affair and he was damn near caught during the crypto thing. Besides, all he had to do was grab the camera and disappear.

He moved on.

No indication of body discovery near WW birthplace.

Okay, he had some time.

He pulled up Google Earth and found the Hull house. It was outside of Troy, a small city of just over twenty-five thousand, a bit larger than Boulder City. Despite its closeness to the town the location appeared to be very rural in nature. It was located on a winding road northeast of Troy. There were farms sprinkled every mile or so on both sides but the stretch that included the couple's house was wooded.

He moved deeper through Grey's report and found the answer to his query on electronic security at the house.

No indication of security system/burglar alarm/doorbell camera.

Smithson sat back. He crossed his arms, turned his face to the ceiling, and closed his eyes. After a few seconds he went back to the Toughbook. He instructed Grey to show the current location of the wife's Jeep, the husband's Escape, and both cell phones.

Smithson opened another window on the laptop and accessed a map application. He knew that Grey could sync his location requests here. He found Troy and manipulated the map so the town and the surrounding area filled the screen. He sipped his coffee and reached for a third donut.

Something about this taste combination. Little chunks of peanuts...some sweet glaze on there making the peanuts stick. Why the hell don't they have these every day? Seems like half the times I stop—

Two red dots appeared on the screen.

Smithson took a large bite from the donut and leaned in. He had programmed Grey in such a way that cellphones would show up as red on the map. Most of the location requests he made were for phones. Everyone had their phone with them at all times, either in their hand, their pocket, or within arm's reach.

One red dot was located at Kettering Hospital.

Right where you're supposed to be.

The second was northeast of town. Smithson zoomed in and saw it was at the residence on Polecat Road.

Probably sleeping in while his wife's at work...Lazy bastard.

Biggs pushed the remainder of the third peanut donut into his mouth and reached for the fourth.

Two blue dots now blinked onto the screen. These would be the vehicles. One was nearly touching the red dot at the hospital. The other overlapped the one at the house.

OK, the Jeep is with the wife, probably in the hospital parking lot. The Escape is at home with the husband.

His mind worked the problem.

Smithson pushed back from the table. He stood and took a sip of the coffee. He scowled.

Room temperature coffee, ugh.

He walked to the sink and dumped the remainder of the cup. Absent-mindedly he walked back toward the table, picking up the remainder of the last donut as he passed, and made for the master bedroom. His mind continued to appraise the situation, determining a course of action.

96

Smithson shoved the final half-donut into his mouth. He entered the bedroom and grabbed a travel bag before continuing into the connected bathroom. He sat the bag on the vanity then leaned forward, head down. He rested his hands on its edge and chewed slowly.

She's at work. Her Jeep's there. Outside chance the camera is in the Jeep...probably not...

He's home. The Escape is there. They could've tossed the camera in there when they got home last night...probably not. Probably in the house.

Outside chance he isn't home. He could be driving the old pickup. Grey can't track it, no linked nav system on something that old...but doubtful. He would take his phone. Nobody goes anywhere without their phone.

Smithson raised his head and looked at the reflection. He stopped chewing.

The stringy hair was pushed straight back on his head. He hadn't showered for two days and it had developed a bit of an oily sheen. The rumpled black hoodie covered an upper body that, he knew, was just as rumpled.

Smithson remembered the incident in the Fiesta Rancho, a hotel casino in Las Vegas now permanently closed due to COVID. He was celebrating his big score against Crypto Boy and had hired two hookers. High-end girls who worked through the most reputable escort service in the region, if escort services could be reputable.

He was in his hotel room bathroom. The girls were in the bedroom...preparing. He could hear them talking and noticed they had switched from English to Spanish. Weird. He heard bits and pieces of their conversation and caught the words "verde," "linterna," and "el villano." They were giggling.

Afterwards, when the girls had left, he went online and realized they were comparing him to the bad guy in the movie *Green Lantern*. He vaguely remembered the 2011 film. It was based on a character from DC Comics. He searched for images of the villain, Hector Hammond.

The stills from the beginning of the movie showed a man that resembled Smithson. Well, he was actually a bit more attractive. But the character is exposed to something called "yellow energy" and he mutates, his brain growing to enormous size. He was borderline disgusting midway through the movie and even worse by the end.

Smithson was pissed.

He instructed Grey to penetrate the employee records of the escort service.

Who the hell did these women think they were?

He found that both women had mid six-figure incomes with glowing credit reports. Well, he could change that.

He set up online gambling accounts for both and diverted large amounts of cash from their mutual funds, placing risky bets that inevitably lost. When he was finished with them, the women had little savings and shitty credit.

But he still looked the same.

Well, what the hell am I supposed to do about that? I sure as hell won't start jogging...running around in public wearing yoga pants? Half the people out there have no business wearing that stuff. There are even some GUYS wearing it. Fatasses, and they don't even know it.

Smithson had considered anabolic steroids at one time. He thought they might be the magic bullet that could give him a physique that belied the fact he spent most of his days in the barber chair in his Lair. But a bit of research revealed that steroids didn't just make muscles appear on their own. They required the user to work out. In fact they allowed the user to do so incessantly. Anabolic steroid use allowed fatigued muscles to recover quickly, permitting the user to reduce the time between workouts.

That was the last thing he wanted.

Maybe HGH. That might do it. Will have to check into that.

Smithson decided to reconnoiter the Hull house. He was a half hour away. The husband was home so he would have to be discreet. He removed his sweatshirt, and unconsciously pulled his eyes from the mirror when his bare upper body appeared.

He sniffed his underarms.

Whew! Where's my deodorant?

Smithson rummaged through his travel bag and produced a stick of Old Spice High Endurance. He'd found this brand the most effective. After applying it he selected a clean T-shirt and hoodie. The shirt was beige with a large orange and black numeral "2" on the front. This was a logo for the *OVERWATCH 2* video game. The hoodie was navy blue with no logo. He added clean underwear and shorts.

Maybe shower later.

Smithson didn't plan to wear his shoulder holster but wanted to be prepared. That was the reason for the T-shirt. The damned ostrich skin contraption would be a pain in the ass if he wore in over bare skin. If he decided to put it on later he would be ready. Still, he now wore two layers, including his trademark dark hoodie, and it would suck being outside in Ohio's heat and humidity.

He walked back to the bedroom and slipped on his socks and a broken-in pair of black Salomon Tactical boots. He had read that special operations personnel wore them.

Smithson returned to the table and collected the Toughbook and phone. He took one last look, decided he was ready, and headed out the door.

Let's do this.

CHAPTER FOURTEEN

Paul propelled the bike away from Troy, his speed on the mostly level bike path hovering between sixteen and twenty-two miles per hour. He could monitor this on the odometer that was attached to his handlebar. It was mounted next to the phone holder and linked to a sensor on his front wheel. Coupled with the MapMyRun app it gave him two ways to view his speed. The app, though, provided significantly more data. Average speed, elevation gain, calories burned, and distance covered were a few of these.

Paul cared to some degree about the distance. He generally rode by feel, cutting rides short if conditions warranted or if he'd had hard rides several days in a row. Wind was the biggest factor. If winds were stiff he often rode into it at the beginning of his ride, breezing home with it at his back. Occasionally he reversed the order, making the ride more of a challenge. He understood that his most demanding physical tests, and there had been an untold number, lay in his past.

Most of the cyclists he knew used the Strava app. It seemed to have been developed with biking in mind. It had a "Share and Connect" feature that allowed interaction with others. This had no appeal to Paul. He had no desire to broadcast his exercise results to the world, or even to a small group of friends.

Paul installed MapMyRun on his phone long ago, several years before his parachute accident. He was a runner then and the app worked well. After he bought the bike he discovered the app allowed the user to select "Road Cycling." It did everything he needed it to do so he stuck with it.

As expected the path had very little traffic. Two women approached from the south and waved to him without taking a break in their conversation. Both carried water bottles. It was warm, edging toward sultry, but Paul barely sensed the heat.

The path was shaded for most of its length and the prevailing southwesterly wind helped to cool him as it angled in obliquely from his right. A mile out of Troy he moved to his left to pass an older man on an electric bike.

The first time he saw one he was amused.

Doesn't it defeat the purpose? Do you really get any benefit from one of those?

But he came around to a different opinion when talking to one of Mike McClary's friends at one of the many parties Mike and Marge hosted. Scott, a pleasant man with a semi-permanent smile, related that his mother rode an electric bike to "get back out in the world."

Paul had sipped his bourbon—there was always bourbon available at a McClary party—and nodded. He got it. He had spent months going from hospital bed to wheelchair, wheelchair to crutches and, finally, from crutches to a cane before getting back out in the world. Anything that helped people enjoy the outdoors was fine by Paul. He simply raised his glass to Scott and took another sip of his Buffalo Trace.

Paul flashed past the man, well to his left, and said "Lookin' good."

He didn't see the man's reaction. He hoped he didn't sound like too much of a jackass.

Biking had been almost a new lease on life. The significant damage done to his left leg limited Paul's ability to exercise. Separating from the Air Force was nearly as traumatic, but in a different way. The difference between the day-to-day routine of being a CCT—Paul knew it was anything but routine—and full-stop retirement were impossible to express, even to Lauren.

Paul had been a member of a select group of warriors. In fact, the select of the select. He had not only made it through the daunting nearly two year journey known as The Pipeline to receive the red beret of a Combat Controller, he had gone on to become a member of the most elite unit in Air Force Special Operations.

This was the 24th Special Tactics Squadron. It was known to its members as "The 24," or "The Two Four."

His path to the unit was certainly not preordained. Paul remembered sitting next to the Fosters' swimming pool in Wappingers Falls the week before their graduation from high school. John's mom had just brought them tomato and mayonnaise sandwiches and tall glasses of iced tea. If it was a warm day in early June and one of the Foster kids had friends over there would be tomato and mayonnaise sandwiches.

John was lamenting the fact that he had not received a baseball scholarship offer from a Division 1 college. He was a left-handed pitcher, a good one. He had received offers from smaller schools as well as a few junior colleges.

"It's bullshit," John fumed. "Complete bullshit!"

He was talking to everyone, and no one in particular at the same time.

"Horton has offers from all the big schools and I don't have a single one!"

John's mom was pulling open the sliding door to the house. She turned back to the boys.

"Johnny."

She said it in an even tone and it got her son's attention. She nodded at Paul, who was staring into the pool, his mind obviously elsewhere. John took the cue and focused on his friend.

"Uh, sorry dude," he began. "I didn't mean to be an ass."

He knew Paul had no set plans after graduating.

"Any new possibilities?"

Paul had been on the baseball team with John. His best sport was wrestling. He'd been all conference in that sport for the John Jay Patriots in his junior and senior seasons. He had no offers to continue his wrestling career at the collegiate level and his parents were not in a position to contribute much financially.

Paul continued to stare.

"I don't know. Maybe get a loan? Maybe go to Dutchess Community College."

He paused then looked to John.

"Patrice thinks I should join the military, do something with computers."

Then, somehow dejected and hopeful at the same time, "What do you think?"

John considered.

"Well, you are pretty good with computers. I don't know much about the military but I think the Air Force has a lot to offer when it comes to techie jobs."

Paul looked up, his face brighter.

"That's what Patrice says, too!"

It did not happen right away. Paul spent a few years working for a landscaping company in Wappingers Falls after high school. The work was physically demanding—which didn't bother him—but it had no real future. Paul was in career limbo, not quite a lost soul, but not fulfilled. It was Patrice's continued encouragement that finally led to his enlisting at the age of 24.

John went off to Louisburg Junior College in North Carolina. They remain close friends to this day.

The bike path entered Tipp City, a town of ten thousand that was founded in 1840 along the Miami and Erie Canal. It was a very bike friendly community. Paul had actually purchased his bike from a shop in the town. He slowed as he reached Main Street where it intersected with the path. A car decelerated and Paul motioned it to continue. The driver raised a hand and eased past. Paul looked to his right and saw the permanent bike maintenance and air station the town had installed for cyclists. He reached an index finger under his Oakleys and wiped the sweat from his eyes before continuing across the street.

Paul enlisted for four years and attended Basic Training at Lackland Air Force Base in San Antonio, Texas. He found himself shuttled into Material Management after finding that the computer-related specialties he requested had no openings. He was assigned to Whiteman Air Force Base in Missouri. He found the work less than fulfilling and was leaning toward leaving the Air Force as he neared the end of his enlistment period.

Then came the terrorist attacks of September 11, 2001.

Paul was furious. The World Trade Towers had not been visible from Wappingers Falls, but nearly so. They were the backdrop to his many trips to the City. Trips to watch his Mets or, less often, the Yankees.

It was personal to Paul. The United States Air Force was going to war, but Paul had gone to Knob Noster.

Whiteman Air Force Base is home to the 509th Bomb Wing. It is assigned to the Air Force Global Strike Command, Eighth Air Force. It is a descendant of the 509th Composite Bomb Group, the unit that had been commanded by Colonel Paul Tibbets and dropped the atomic bombs on Hiroshima and Nagasaki at the close of World War Two. Whiteman is a sprawling base that in 2002 boasted a contingent of twenty B-2 Spirit Stealth Bombers, the two-billion-dollar-a-copy futuristic heavy bombers that were the cutting edge of U.S. military power. Whiteman is located next to the western Missouri town of Knob Noster, a town of fewer than three thousand people.

Paul was an Airman E-3 tapping a keyboard in a cubicle.

Whiteman was making headlines.

The Spirits were flying forty hour round trip missions to and from Afghanistan, a staggering accomplishment.

After three months of war, Paul had yet to see a pilot or air crewmen. He was frustrated and, to be honest, a bit homesick. Patrice wrote to him every week. This made it better, and worse.

He made a few friends and went out on the town but...Knob Noster?

The next significant event in Paul's career path happened on March 4, 2002.

Takur Ghar was an obscure mountaintop in southeastern Afghanistan. It is located on the eastern border of the Shah-i-Kot Valley. In the early morning hours United States Special Operations units were inserted in various parts of the valley to act in a reconnaissance and observation capacity for the largest endeavor to date for the coalition, Operation Anaconda.

105

At the summit of Takur Ghar one helicopter, a CH-47 flown by the most elite helo unit in the world, the "Night Stalkers" of TF-160, was hit by rocket-propelled grenade and machine gun fire on its approach. A member of the Navy's SEAL Team Six, Neil Roberts, fell from the open rear ramp. The helicopter dropped down the side of the mountain. Miraculously, it was brought under control by its pilot.

But Roberts was on the mountaintop facing dozens of Al Qaeda fighters. The ensuing several hours included Roberts' fellow SEALs returning to retrieve him under withering fire, another helicopter carrying a Quick Reaction Force of Army Rangers being shot down, and the loss of seven American servicemen including Roberts and, to Paul's consternation, two members of the United States Air Force.

Paul was horrified. He was, again, furious. And, he was almost ashamed to say, curious. What the hell were two Air Force guys doing in the middle of something like this?

He discovered that one, Jason Cunningham, was a Pararescueman, or PJ. The Pararescue motto is "That Others May Live." They specialize in battlefield trauma care, personnel recovery from crash sites, and combat search and rescue, or CSAR. PJ history went back several decades. The war in Vietnam produced countless stories of heroism by these men, who adopted a uniform patch with the grinning Cheshire Cat from *Alice In Wonderland* surrounded by the phrase "We're All Mad, You Know."

So it made sense that Jason Cunningham was part of the mission. But who was John Chapman, the other Airman?

John Chapman was an Air Force Combat Controller, a CCT.

Combat Controllers were, arguably, the most dangerous men in the history of warfare. Technically their job description was twofold. One aspect was to run airfields, typically airfields seized in contested hostile areas. They are trained to expertly assume the role of air traffic controller when put in place at an airport, a lonely desert site, or a storm-ravaged island.

The second, and more significant aspect of CCT, is their ability to integrate with Special Operations units and direct devastating air strikes.

The CCT motto is "First There" and hails from World War Two when the first iterations of CCT, Army Pathfinders, jumped in ahead of airborne assaults. Their abilities were honed in Vietnam, Grenada, Panama, and the Gulf Wars. By September 11, 2001 CCT was a force multiplier with no peer.

Paul read everything he could get his hands on about Roberts Ridge. He bought the March 18, 2002 issue of Newsweek that's cover featured pictures of the deceased Americans, including Roberts and Chapman, under the banner "THEY WERE SOLDIERS."

Stories of heroism on the mountain trickled out. Paul was consumed by it. He found it difficult to do his job. In his cubicle nearly four years after he joined the Air Force, it hit him that a Basic Training classmate had attended a briefing on Combat Control while at Lackland.

Paul researched it and noted the procedure for applying to the program. Two months later, after passing the initial physical fitness tests, he accepted an assignment to the Air Force Special Warfare Training Squadron at Kirtland Air Force Base on the southeast edge of Albuquerque, New Mexico. Paul's time at Kirtland was a springboard to his career in Special Operations. It was also where he met his future wife, a native of the "Land of Enchantment."

Paul was in The Pipeline. He was 28, one of the oldest men in his class.

What followed were months and months of some of the most demanding physical and mental training the Air Force had to offer.

CCT hopefuls were combined with aspiring Pararescuemen. Paul's class featured forty-nine hopeful CCTs and seventy-one Airmen attempting to become PJ's. In the initial stages of the Pipeline they go through the same training as the CCT candidates.

This includes the OL-H phase in the Lackland pool and featured the dreaded "Crossovers." Fifty percent of the class starts on one side, the remainder the other. Candidates must swim underwater without coming up for air, half taking the "high" path, half the "low." This is done multiple times and breaking the surface means immediate dismissal.

There is a significant amount of water training in Air Force Special Operations. It bewilders some, but the oxygen deprivation is used to stress the candidate and reveal his capabilities.

There was Army Special Forces Combat Diver School in Key West, Florida and Air Force Water Survival School in Homestead, Florida. These were followed by Airborne School at the Army's Fort Benning in Georgia. Next came Air Force Airman Survival School at Fairchild Air Force Base in the state of Washington. Several other schools followed.

The ultimate course, from Paul's point of view at least, was Air Traffic Control School at Keesler Air Force Base in Biloxi, Mississippi.

If you couldn't demonstrate expertise in handling aircraft, you couldn't be CCT.

Air Force Special Operations Training stresses quality over quantity. Of the one hundred twenty original hopefuls, just five PJ and two CCT candidates graduated.

It was at Keesler that Paul first met Gatewood Dowdell.

Paul had been churning along on the path. He broke from his thoughts. He realized there was an Airbus 350 passing overhead. It was gliding downward, meaning he was near Vandalia Ohio, the home of Dayton International Airport.

Oh shit.

He checked his odometer.

"14.5 Mi."

He had to get back, get cleaned up, and meet Woody for lunch.

CHAPTER FIFTEEN

Smithson took the first Troy exit, Market Street, and angled northeast. The map showed that this street would bring him to a traffic circle in the middle of town. From there he would continue north for a couple miles before taking a right on the Hull's road.

The drive from his Airbnb had taken twenty-five minutes. He'd departed Homeview and jumped on I-70 East. A few miles later he arrived at a large interchange and transitioned to I-75 North. The concrete retaining walls of the interchange featured bas-relief images of a Wright Flyer every forty feet.

It reminded Smithson of the purpose of this trip. Operation Crank. He'd thought the word was humorous. But it did accurately depict how most people thought of wannabe flyers before the Wrights' success. Man had always dreamed of flying. Many died trying. Flight was a mystery.

Damned if Wilbur and Orville didn't figure it out.

On the drive up I-75 to Troy, Smithson thought back to what brought him here.

Once he had Grey working, really cooking, he had a steady stream of income. The blackmail videos were almost always successful. People paid. And there were an ongoing and seemingly limitless number of targets. Once Grey had penetrated the porn site databases it was game over.

The financial security was nice, but Smithson quickly became bored. Wasn't there more of a challenge out there? Something.......*fun?*

He was jotting down a short grocery list on a Post-It Note one day when he wondered absentmindedly how the damn little yellow things worked. He researched it and found that in 1968 a scientist in a 3M lab working on adhesives discovered a peculiar formulation. The substance was strong enough to hold paper together but what made it unique was when it was removed it would stick again. It could do this repeatedly without harming the paper.

The scientist was Spencer Silver. He searched for applications for the adhesive for several years without success. Then in 1974 a fellow 3M Scientist named Art Fry used it to prevent bookmarks from falling out of his hymnal while singing in his church choir.

Fry began to work on practical applications and eventually the Post-It Note was born. Fifty billion are produced each year by 3M in various shapes and colors.

OK, it wasn't the airplane, but Smithson now thought of Silver as the Wilbur and Fry as the Orville of sticky notes. Silver made the discovery. Fry worked to implement it.

But just as the Wrights had to battle competing claims and lawsuits after their breakthrough, so did 3M. In 2016 a man named Alan Amron filed suit, claiming he invented the sticky note in 1973 and called it Press-on Memo. He said he showed it to 3M stationary executives at an invention trade show in New York in 1974.

There was an extensive litigation history between Amron and 3M. Smithson grew bored reading the competing claims. But the amount asked for in the lawsuit, four hundred million dollars, certainly caught his eye.

This might be fun.

Smithson had Grey penetrate the Minneapolis-based company's computer system, looking for evidence that Amron had a case. Nothing concrete was discovered.

Still, Smithson was intrigued. He emailed the company through secure means provided by Grey and threatened to release information that could damage their defense. He asked for a mere ten thousand dollars.

He was stunned at the response. 3M came at him hard. Their cyber security people were good, very good. If not for Grey they probably would've identified him. They spent at least a quarter of a million dollars in the attempt, much more than the extortion demand.

Smithson had stirred up a hornet's nest. He'd seen how they reacted to protect their intellectual property. It was an interesting divergence from his usual video revenue stream. He filed it away and decided he would tackle something like Post-It Notes again in the future when he had more material to leverage against the target. It would be an opportunity to exert a different kind of control over his victims.

Operation Crank was supposed to be his triumphant return to the genre.

That fucking Biggs.

Smithson saw a Kroger supermarket ahead on the left. He pulled off Market Street and into the parking lot. As the Audi idled he opened the Toughbook and accessed Grey. Before continuing to the Hull's house he wanted to again verify the whereabouts of the couple.

He pulled up the map and watched as the red and blue lights appeared.

Hel-lo, what's this?

The blue dots were in the same locations as before. So was the red dot at the hospital. But the second red dot was south of Troy. It was moving. Not particularly fast, but steadily away from Troy.

Hull is moving? How? His Escape is at the house.

Then he had it.

It's the pickup truck. Gotta be.

Smithson sat, pondering.

I should check this out. Head in the direction of Hull. If he's going to be gone for any length of time I can get into the house now. Grab the camera.

Smithson sat the laptop on the passenger seat with the screen angled toward him. He followed streets east, then north, arriving on Dye Mill Road. The road continued south into the distance. Smithson pulled into a small parking area and watched the red dot. It was still moving but now appeared to be coming back north.

What the hell?

111

Smithson looked up and turned his head from side to side. It was a cartoonish action that had no real possibility of explaining the movement of the red dot.

But it did.

Smithson was parked in front of a wooded sign. It was covered by a map that was labeled "Miami Valley Bike Trail."

Hull is on a bike! He must be, what, ten miles away?

This development changed everything. Smithson could enter the house *right now*.

Okay think. Game it. Cruise the house. Get in, grab the camera, get the hell out. No, go by the hospital first, it's on the way to the house. Find the wife's Jeep just in case. If the camera isn't in the house it's still in the Jeep. I'll have to hit the Jeep on the way back through town. How long would it take Hull to ride all the way back to his house?

Smithson had no idea, but he knew his time was limited. A sheen of perspiration had formed on his forehead. He turned up the air conditioner.

He instructed Grey to disable the Kettering Health security cameras that view the parking lots. He then searched Grey's reports and found the wife's four-digit code that could be punched into the driver's side door to unlock it.

Two Four Two Four. Easy enough to remember.

Smithson backed the S8 onto Dye Mill and drove toward the hospital. He used the two dots at that location to guide him. He reached the traffic circle and slowly wheeled around it, exiting on West Main. Kettering Health was five blocks ahead on the right.

Smithson approached and saw that it was a new three-story structure. An elevated area in the center hinted at the existence of a fourth level. There were parking lots on both the east and west sides. A Tim Horton's restaurant and a Valvoline Instant Oil Change were across the street.

He reached a cross street at the west side of the property, North Elm, and turned right. He saw just a few vehicles in this lot. The ambulance entrance was on this side of the building and access to parking spaces appeared to be limited. He saw no white Jeep Grand Cherokee.

Smithson continued to Water Street and made another right. He could see the rear of the building. There was no vehicle parking on this side. A sidewalk ran the length of the building just a few feet from the structure. The building seemed to grow directly out of a rectangular-shaped city block and filled the space completely. He continued east and saw that the lot there was larger than he thought when he viewed it from the front.

Smithson decided to cruise the lot. Grey would've had time to shut down the exterior cameras by now. Fifty feet inside he saw the Jeep. It was parked on his left, on the outer edge of the lot. It faced east, its rear pointed toward the hospital.

Smithson braked, letting the Audi idle.

Okay, got the Jeep.

He was edgy, aware that his window of opportunity was limited. He shot a look at the Toughbook and saw that the second red dot was nearing a town to the south, Tipp City. Hull was definitely on his way back but was still several miles away.

A horn honked behind him.

Smithson flicked his eyes to his rear view and saw a woman in a Honda SUV. She was an officious-looking shrew, wearing a pair of ridiculously large sunglasses.

He instantly raised a middle finger and, with heat in his voice, shouted "Screw You!"

But he had to get moving. He rolled the Audi forward, navigating to the far side of the lot then back to the Water Street entrance. He saw the woman select a handicapped spot on his left. She turned toward him and he scowled. Smithson again flipped a middle finger.

As he headed out of the lot, Smithson berated himself.

Pretty stupid. Pretty fucking stupid. Should've just moved on, not bring attention to myself.

But the horn was that high-pitched bleating type. The kind that some sound engineer designed to piss you off. And the driver...

She was probably parking illegally in that handicapped spot.

Smithson didn't anticipate needing to get into the Grand Cherokee, but the gamer in him forced him to plan. He would prefer not to park in the lot near the Jeep. There would be no video of him but witnesses might remember a man moving from one vehicle to another carrying a camera bag. He eased down Water Street looking for options. A block and a half ahead to the east he saw it, the Troy Public Library.

Perfect. A back-up plan if I have to come back and hit the wife's vehicle. Park at the library, walk to the hospital lot. Get to the Jeep. In and out.

He headed for the house.

What the hell is a Polecat?

Smithson found the Hulls' road six minutes later and glanced at the sign as he made the turn. He saw that the blue dot of the husband's Escape was perhaps a half-mile ahead. Smithson checked the addresses of the few houses he encountered and soon came to 880. Mature trees lined both sides of the road. The house was on the right. A gravel lane led back from the road a hundred feet or so where it connected to a concrete driveway. This led to a two-car garage that was attached to the left side of the house. The driveway expanded on the left creating a space for an extra vehicle. It was empty.

The house itself looked nice enough, Smithson supposed. It was actually not that different from his place outside Boulder City. No outbuilding that could house something like Grey, though.

Smithson smiled.

Grey is a gamechanger, the difference between winning and losing.

He continued on Polecat, now traveling northeast at barely forty miles an hour. He glanced again at the laptop and saw that Hull's red dot was now on the northern edge of Tipp City.

Gotta go NOW!

Smithson ducked into a farm lane, checked traffic, and reversed. He steered back to the target house. An SUV approached from the other direction—everyone in Ohio seemed to drive an SUV—and Smithson slowed to allow it to pass. The driver flashed by without so much as glancing at him. Smithson saw the vehicle grow smaller in his mirror and slowed further as he arrived at the target.

Smithson pulled into the lane. As he approached the concrete driveway he had a thought.

Angle the car horizontally so no one on the road can see my plates, just the side of the car.

The Audi had stolen Nevada plates. Smithson had Grey enter the Nevada DMV database and tie them to his assumed name, Glenn Smithson, and a fictitious address. In his trunk he had a second set of stolen plates, tied to another alias. Nevertheless, he didn't want anyone seeing the set on the car.

He manipulated the S8, stopping when the rear of the car was near the left edge of the flared driveway. Any curious passersby would see only the passenger side of the Audi. Perspiring now despite the air conditioning, he looked again at the Toughbook.

Not quite halfway between Tipp and Troy. Still... running out of time.

He popped his trunk and exited the car. He let it run. Inside the trunk he shifted the rifle case and SOPMOD kit so he could reach the lock pick set. He pulled two disposable gloves from a box and snapped them on. As he did so, he glanced at the Colt revolver and shoulder holster.

No time. Shouldn't need a weapon.....still...

Smithson reached past the Colt and selected the Winkler Combat Axe. He removed it from its fast draw sheath. He had no time to properly connect the carrier to his belt. The axe, or tomahawk, was a scary piece of weaponry. From the bottom of the dark walnut handle to the top of its steel head it was nine inches. The head measured four and three-quarter inches. It had a black oxide, no-glare finish.

And it was uber badass.

Smithson gathered the lock pick set and axe and closed the trunk. He checked the lane then moved quickly to the front door. He was ten feet from the door when he had a thought.

What if they have a dog? Hell, they could have two or three of the damn things. Aww shit. Well, can't stop now. Will have to have the tomahawk ready.

Smithson reached the door and opened the pick set. And this is where the operation hit a wall.

He fumbled with the picks for what seemed ten minutes. It was actually less than two. But after one hundred seconds Smithson was red-faced and fuming.

Fucking Biggs! He was supposed to be good at this and I would've learned how to use them better. That son-of-a-bitch! This is HIS fault!

Smithson stood, checked the lane again, and closed his eyes. Five seconds later he opened them and leaned toward the door. He tried the knob. It *was* locked but he still felt sheepish for not trying it earlier. The center of the door had an arch-shaped design that was formed by multiple windowpanes. Smithson peered in, seeing no evidence of a dog.

He glanced at the axe lying at his feet. The evil front blade was curved and razor sharp. But the rear tapered to a chiseled spike.

He smiled.

Smithson lifted the Winkler, blinking at perspiration. He wiped his eye with his right sleeve, realizing a split second later that he'd narrowly missed slicing his forehead open with the blade.

"For Christ's sake," he rasped out loud.

One more glance at the lane, no cars. Then with his left forearm in front of his face to deflect any shards of glass, Smithson swung the axe in a short, chopping arc. It struck the pane nearest to the doorknob and shattered it. He used the blade to chip the jagged pieces of glass from the frame. He was careful reaching through the opening. The hoodie protected his right forearm. He groped for the knob, found it, and undid the lock.

He was in.

CHAPTER SIXTEEN

Smithson closed the door and turned. He sat the lock pick set down near the door. He had a tight grip on the Winkler. It was a standard bland American TV room. No barber chair.

A flat screen was attached to one wall above a console table. A round coffee table occupied the center of the room surrounded by a semicircle consisting of an upholstered couch with leather recliners on both flanks. The couch and chairs were configured to face the television. A large framed photo of colorful aerial balloons with mountains in the background dominated another wall.

Smithson checked the chairs and couch and saw no sign of a camera. The coffee table held nothing but two television remote controls. He scanned the remainder of the room and noticed a drawer near the top of the console table. He quickly stepped to it and yanked it open, saw a collection of miscellaneous items topped by a channel guide for the local cable provider, and left it open.

No need to be tidy. They'll see the broken window.

He had two options as he moved deeper into the house. A hallway to the right no doubt led to bedrooms. Straight ahead was the dining room and kitchen area.

Smithson went right. The first door on the right led to a small bathroom. Smithson cleared it in thirty seconds. He opened a door on one wall and pushed items around, spilling a container of Q-tip cotton swabs to the floor.

Move!

He reentered the hall and moved down its length, saving the room across the hall for his return trip.

Or, what would the military call it, egress?

The room ahead on the right was the master bedroom. The door was open. The large bed was unmade. Smithson searched nightstand tables on both sides of the bed finding no camera and actually pulling one shelf completely out of its track. The contents spilled out. He scattered the items to confirm it didn't hold his objective, and moved on. He entered a large walk-in closet and slid clothes and their hangers from side to side looking behind and through them.

He could feel nervousness and edginess transition to desperation. Above, shelves ran the length of the closet on both sides. He pulled down stacks of sweatshirts and T-shirts. He couldn't reach the stacks in the corner and had to use the Winkler to sweep them down. They tumbled to his feet and caused him to stumble on his way out.

Out of the closet, now pawing through the dressers, first his, then hers.

No time to check out her stuff, too bad.

He hurried into the master bathroom. There was a black hair dryer sitting on the vanity. He saw it and instantly identified it as the camera, and just as quickly recognized it was not. He swung the Winkler and sheared it nearly in two.

Smithson detected movement. He immediately turned his head it that direction, tensing for action, and saw a nightmarish figure in the mirror gripping a primitive weapon.

He flinched. Then grinned.

Nightmare, yeah!

Back to the hall, a quick step into the room on that side. Guest bedroom. No joy.

He moved toward the kitchen. There was one more room in the hall, the bypassed room across from the small bathroom. This door was closed. Smithson pushed it open. Something brushed against his right leg and he jumped.

What the hell?!?

He saw movement below and instinctively raised the Winkler.

It was an animal. It bolted under a desk in the rear of the room.

They DO have a dog? Didn't hear it bark.

Smithson cautiously leaned down and saw...

A CAT? It's a big fat cat!

He stood and allowed a quick laugh, then got back to work. The desk was situated just to the right of a window that looked out at the back of the property. Smithson saw that the view consisted of bland farm fields with uninspiring trees in the distance. A stand next to the desk held a printer and a clear display case with a red cap or beret inside. A laptop sat in the center of the desk, an iPad to one side. Stacks of papers and printed literature covered almost every square inch of the desk's surface. Charger cords led down to a wall plug. Smithson's eyes followed the cords and he noticed the cat had tucked behind a stack of books. He was staring at Smithson with a baleful look.

Smithson eyed a book with a white dust cover on top of the stack. It was *The Wright Brothers* by David McCullough.

Hell, I've read that.

Smithson hastily scanned the stack and saw at least two others he'd read.

Hunh.

He went through the room quickly finding no camera but pausing when he noticed some framed items on the wall. There was an 8x10 black and white photo of a Wright Flyer passing near the Statue of Liberty. Smithson had seen it in more than one book.

Hunh, he mused again.

There were also four certificates arranged in a square. They were military awards. They all displayed the words "Bronze Star with Combat V."

So our boy DID do some things in the military. How the hell did an Air Force guy...

He let it go. He had to keep moving. On the way out of the room he noticed another group of frames. They included a certificate for the Purple Heart. This frame was paired with an 8x10 picture of Hull in a hospital bed. His left leg was elevated in a cast. A black man with a shaved head stood next to him. The man was leaning to his left and holding up a prosthetic leg. Both men were smiling at the camera.

What the hell?

Smithson hurried into the kitchen. The island had collected day-to day junk. He checked it all closely. No go. The counters held a large coffee maker, a toaster, and a number of unremarkable items that by their very existence angered Smithson. None of them was a camera.

He saw a number of kitchen cabinets and drawers in the island. He opened them as quickly as he could. He found keys, change, utensils, Post-It Notes—of course—and Tupperware. Desperate now, his eyes wandered through the kitchen.

Nice ice make—nuggets?

He let his eyes slide into the kitchen.

There was a camera bag on the table.

THERE WAS A CAMERA BAG ON THE TABLE!!!

He rushed to it and knew as soon as he grabbed it that it was too light to hold the camera.

FUCK!!! Fuck, Fuck, Fuck!

Smithson saw tall cabinet doors behind the table. He flipped them all open and saw canned food, bags of corn chips, boxes of crackers, cat food... it was useless. This was the pantry.

He turned to see a door to the basement. He held out a measure of hope for a short time but found that the lower level held nothing but a laundry area in a corner, an open room, and a workout freak's paradise through a door in the back.

Back upstairs he opened the door to the garage. The Escape was on one side. The other side was empty. He flipped on the overhead light, stepped out, and turned in a circle, surveying shelves full of...junk.

Why the hell even check here? The damn thing must be in the wife's car.

Still, he took a minute to quickly rifle through the Escape, finding no camera.

Smithson went back into the house and rushed to the front door. After checking for movement he collected the lock pick set and went out the door.

He was gone.

CHAPTER SEVENTEEN

Paul allowed thoughts to float through his head. It was the best part of the ride. His brain was always doing its own thing during a ride. Sure, he could direct it to work on a specific task or to recall a particular memory, but it always seemed to be running a completely separate data stream in the background. Like a crawl across the bottom of a TV screen. The brain often became bored with Paul's set of instructions and pushed a more interesting subject to the forefront.

He was pedaling out of Tipp City, having crossed back over Main Street and passing the bicycle maintenance and air station, and trying to concentrate on his leg. Paul made it a point to monitor the leg during a ride. His physical therapist had told him to be cognizant of any pain.

"The leg will tell you if you need to slow down."

Paul respected his PT. One of the reasons he and Lauren had settled in the area was to have access to health care at Wright-Patterson AFB and the nearby Dayton VA Medical Center. But he had been a high school wrestler and an Air Force CCT. His mentality had always screamed *push through*.

He tried to focus on the leg, the left leg, when his mind assigned him a related but more interesting channel to watch.

Yes, Paul had broken his left leg in the accident. It resulted from crosswinds and a lack of visibility. His night vision device had malfunctioned on the night training drop, and the inability to properly judge his altitude when the wind shifted resulted in an off balanced landing that was more than awkward. It was calamitous. Ultimately it was career ending.

Paul's mind would rather think about another broken left leg—Orville Wright's. It had happened during a crash at Fort Myer, an Army installation adjacent to Arlington National Cemetery.

It was September 17, 1908. The Wright brothers had spent nearly five years after the first powered, controlled flight in Kitty Hawk developing and improving their invention. Much of the testing was now done in Ohio. Kitty Hawk was chosen by Wilbur because of the prevailing winds. The dunes allowed elevated areas to facilitate launching of their gliders and eventually the powered Flyer. By 1904 they were testing and flying in an area known as Huffman Prarie on the northeast outskirts of Dayton. The brothers had developed a catapult launching system that negated the need to travel to Kitty Hawk.

An odd sort of standoff had taken shape. The Wrights had offered their invention for a significant but, they believed, *fair* fee to the United States government on multiple occasions. They were asked to demonstrate the capabilities of the Flyer before funds would be committed. The Wrights balked at this. They did not want to reveal their secrets to competitors.

This situation persisted for nearly five years. It allowed competitors to develop their own flying machines. None had yet approached the capabilities of the Wright Flyer, but they were advancing. The Wrights believed many of these advancements were due to infringements on their patents.

The Wrights had originally applied for a patent on March 23, 1903. They would not accomplish powered flight for nine months but they felt they had established control of the three axes of flight—pitch, roll, and yaw—with their successful experiments at Kitty Hawk in 1902.

The brothers wrote the patent application themselves and it was rejected. This patent application was at some point misplaced by the National Archives. It was rediscovered on March 23, 2016 in a storage facility in a limestone cave in Lenexa, Kansas.

In early 1904, a few months after achieving their first flights, they hired Harry Toulmin, a patent attorney from Ohio. He helped write and submit an application that was finally accepted on May 22, 1906.

One of the most persistent violators of the Wright patents from the brothers' point of view was Glenn Curtiss. Considered by many to be the finest builder of internal combustion engines in the world, the Hammondsport, New York native became known for mounting motors on two-wheeled frames. He rode one of his "motor-cycles" to a then unheard-of speed of sixty-four miles per hour in Ormond Beach, Florida in 1903. Builders of dirigibles were attracted to Curtiss engines because of their relatively light weight and power. Curtiss became enamored with flight while manufacturing custom engines for the balloon makers in his small shop.

He was soon mounting engines on his own flying machines with varied success. He became acquainted with the Wrights and even offered to build engines for them on more than one occasion. The brothers declined, preferring to use their own. An employee of their bicycle shop, Charlie Taylor, had impressed the brothers with his ability to produce designs that met their needs.

The Wrights were famously protective of their methods and advancements. Some, like Curtiss, thought they were protective to a fault. Curtiss did not believe that it should be possible to patent certain concepts of flight. They were not products, like an engine. They were ideas and were, or should be, available to anyone inventive enough to figure a better way.

He began to experiment with ailerons. The Wrights, particularly Wilbur, were incensed. They demanded Curtiss pay rights fees to them, taking the position that the use of any controlled surface on a flying machine was an infringement on their patent. This claim has been argued and scrutinized by scholars ever since. Curtiss claimed he wasn't building his machines for profit. The Wrights scoffed at this.

Curtiss became associated with the Aerial Experiment Association, which was formed in 1907 at the summer home of Alexander Graham Bell, the inventor of the telephone. Bell was fascinated with flight. He had experimented with giant kites constructed with tetrahedral-shaped cells and was interested in the development and expansion of powered flight. The club had members from many fields. The Wrights saw the AEA as a serious competitor.

Another member of the AEA was Thomas Selfridge, a United States Army Lieutenant. Selfridge was interested in possible military applications of powered aircraft.

By 1908 the Wrights had made the decision to aggressively pursue the sale of their invention to governments. Wilbur sailed to France and was dazzling audiences with demonstrations of the Flyer. Until this time, many people had doubted the Wrights' claims of distance and speed. On August 8, 1908 near the Le Mans racetrack, Wilbur flew for two minutes, making two figure eights. One of the two hundred onlookers, French pilot Leon Delagrange, muttered "Nous sommes battus"—"We are beaten."

Wilbur had demonstrated control.

By the end of 1908 Wilbur was drawing crowds of over one hundred thousand and on one flight logged a mind-numbing distance seventy-seven miles, staying in the air for two hours and twenty minutes.

Meanwhile Orville was set to make a similar exhibition in the United States. The Army had set up distance and speed requirements that the Flyer needed to meet in order to facilitate a sale. They also required it to be able to carry two people. They designated an officer to make the flight. To Orville's dismay they chose Thomas Selfridge. The Wrights did not trust him due to his association with the AEA.

On September 17 Orville, accompanied by Selfridge, circled Fort Myer four times. On the fifth circuit, at the height of one hundred and fifty feet, one of the Flyer's two propellers, the right, broke. The Flyer dove. Orville fought for control. Selfridge uttered his final words—"Oh! Oh!"

Selfridge suffered a fractured skull and died hours later. He has the dubious distinction of becoming the first fatality of powered flight. Orville broke several ribs, injured his hip, and sustained a broken left femur.

Paul winced, remembering the moment he hit the ground at Fort Bragg. He did a mental assessment of his own leg. So far, so good.

What thoughts must've gone through Orville's head? He didn't trust Selfridge, but he must've felt some guilt over the man's death.

Paul checked his odometer. He was coming up on twenty-three miles.

Five to go, give or take.

Paul edged to the right side of the path. A walker ahead was approaching him. He was getting closer to Troy and should begin to encounter more people from here on out. On weekends and holidays Paul avoided the path and rode on country roads. There was just too much traffic on the bikepath on these days and the starts and stops made for a disjointed ride. Plus, he was afraid that someone would step in front of him without warning. A surprisingly high percentage of people on the path had their attention diverted. They were talking or scrolling on their phones. They were texting. Many were streaming audio to their earbuds.

Paul was most apprehensive about hitting a child. He couldn't stomach seeing harm to a child. An image popped into his head of that time in Afghanistan....

He made his mind change the channel. He didn't want to think of that.

What else can I think of? The difference between bike workouts and running? Experts say one mile running is equal to three miles on a bike. Seems wrong. Running is much harder. I'd say it would be equal to five.

That avenue of thought trickled to a halt very quickly. His mind was blank for a quarter mile then it went to work, examining the remainder of his day.

Get home, shower, lunch with Woody...

That did it. His mind was on another track. Gatewood.

Gatewood Dowdell hailed from Birmingham, Alabama. He attended Hoover High School where he lettered in football and track. His senior year he returned a kickoff ninety-six yards for a touchdown in the Alabama Class 7A state football championship at Bryant-Denny Stadium on the campus of the

University of Alabama. That spring he won the two hundred meter state championship and finished second in the one hundred.

Gatewood joined the Air Force in 1994 after graduation. He entered the Pipeline in late 1995 and by 1997 was the youngest CCT in the Air Force. Woody was intelligent and affable. In the squadrons he was everyone's friend and biggest supporter.

When CCT went to war after September 11, Gatewood deployed to Afghanistan. He proved himself in battle, making a name for himself not just among CCT, but with their "customers," the American and coalition partner special operations units to which they were attached.

By 2003 Dowdell was tapped to be an instructor at the Pipeline's Air Traffic Control School at Keesler Air Force Base in Biloxi. The Air Force needed controllers.

They still do, Paul thought. *There are six hundred CCT active right now and only 3,700 in the history of the Air Force.*

It was at Biloxi that the two men met. Paul's class had been whittled down to fourteen men. This school may have been the most important one of the entire two-year Pipeline. The skills taught here needed to be mastered, or everything that came before was meaningless.

Paul remembers a smiling black E-5 with a deep, booming voice greeting the class. His head was shaved. He had his right hand in the air.

"Show of hands. Who is gonna make it through this school and become CCT?"

The entire class smiled and raised their hands.

Not all made it, actually. But Gatewood had set a positive tone. This stuck with Paul, who came to learn that Gatewood loved to start a group session or even a conversation with those same three words—*Show of hands.*

It became somewhat of a trademark. That and his shaved head, refreshing enthusiasm, love of Crimson Tide football, and absolute competence in all aspects of CCT. Paul learned a lot from Gatewood. He employed these skills on the battlefield and knew he owed much of his professional success to the man.

Combat Controllers do not spend significant stretches of time together as a unit when deployed. They are imbedded with their customers, often the only member of the unit from the Air Force.

Paul remembers his first deployment. He was assigned to the 21st Special Tactics Squadron. He was to be integrated with an Army Special Forces A-Team, Green Berets. Gatewood had stayed in touch with him after Paul joined the squadrons as a full-fledged Controller. As he was stepping on the plane at Pope Field in North Carolina, bound for the war, Paul heard a man call his name. He turned as Gatewood, recently returned from a deployment of his own, neared the ramp.

Woody delivered some last minute advice.

"Don't suck, and don't get killed."

Both men laughed. Paul went off to war.

He didn't get killed... and he didn't suck.

There were many more deployments ahead for both men. Both narrowly avoided death or injury several times. This ended in May, 2016 near Fallujah, Iraq, when an IED detonated under Dowdell's Humvee.

Gatewood lost his right leg, and eventually his slot in CCT.

A Navy Corpman with a Marine Company got to him first, applying a tourniquet and saving his life. He was flown by a UH-60 Blackhawk to the 28th Combat Support Hospital, which had just arrived from the States. He spent two days there before being flown to Rhein Main Air Force Base in Germany, and finally to Walter Reed National Military Medical Center in Bethesda, Maryland.

Gatewood was fitted with a series of prosthetic legs. It took him nearly two years but he worked his way back to active duty. Just not as a CCT. The demands of the job made it impractical.

But Gatewood, optimistic as ever, had befriended a member of the security detachment at Bethesda. The man related that

Dowdell's combat skills would be an asset to any base in the United States military. Gatewood put this advice to good use, holding assignments in base security at a series of installations since his wounding. He was now an E-9 Chief Master Sergeant and the senior enlisted member of the 88th Security Forces Squadron at Wright-Patterson Air Force Base.

He and his wife Roberta had two sons and a daughter and lived in Huber Heights, a few minutes from the base.

Gatewood had connections everywhere. He had networked with personnel on multiple bases over the years and stayed in touch with his CCT brethren. In addition, he seemed to know important people outside of the military. He was associated with golf tournaments for veterans' organizations, fundraisers for children of deceased servicemen, and sporting events honoring service members.

Gatewood continued to network. Rumor had it that two different major sports franchises had asked him to take over their security operations but he had declined. He loved the Air Force and planned to complete a full thirty years before getting out.

Paul thought back to his own leg injury. Gatewood used his clout to fly from his duty station at the time, Eglin AFB in Florida, to Womack Army Medical Center at Ft. Bragg.

He walked to Paul's bedside, removed his prosthetic leg, and held it up.

"Show of hands, who is gonna get fixed up and walk outta this place?"

Paul raised a hand, laughing through the pain.

A nurse snapped a picture.

Paul smiled. A woman walking a dog looked at him quizzically as he passed. He was on Dye Mill Road, nearing the golf course. He'd be hanging with Woody soon.

The smile stayed on his face.

CHAPTER EIGHTEEN

Smithson hopped in the running Audi. He tossed the axe into the back seat. He looked at the lock pick set for two seconds then hurled it into the back. The kit popped open and several picks spilled across the seat.

"PIECE OF SHIT!"

He screamed it twice and was about to scream a third time when his eyes fell on the fuel gauge. The tank was nearly empty.

"WHAT???"

He was horrified.

HOW CAN THAT BE?

He made the calculations in an instant. He had stopped for gas an hour or so west of Indianapolis before checking into his hotel. *Or was it two hours?* Then came the drive to the Wright birthplace and back and forth from Richmond to the rest stop. Add the drive to the Airbnb, the trip to Dunkin'...

Well hell... IDIOT!

He hurriedly rolled down the lane. Thankfully there was no traffic in either direction. He wheeled to the left and accelerated.

Gotta get to that Jeep...then gas....DAMMIT!

Smithson drove back to Troy, making a conscious effort to stay near the speed limit. He made it to the library and pulled into the lot at the rear, quickly switching off the ignition. He gave the gauge a hateful look before pulling up the hood of his sweatshirt. He still wore the gloves. His eyes searched the area. He saw a bit of pedestrian traffic but no one was looking his way.

He took a deep breath and stepped out of the car. He was staring directly at a security camera mounted near the rear entrance to the library.

OH SHIT!

Smithson turned quickly and walked a few steps to the sidewalk. He turned again and strode in the direction of the hospital.

Gotta get Grey to wipe that camera...

The sidewalk took him past a sprawling two-story brick building to his left that sat next to the library. He glanced at lettering above the entrance and saw "Hobart Center For County Government."

Damn, they probably have cameras too.

He tugged his hood down toward his eyes. After what seemed a ridiculously long distance he found himself at a short cross street. It had been barely one hundred yards. The Kettering Health parking lot was just across the street.

He checked traffic—*Don't get hit by a car, on top of everything else*—and crossed the street.

The Grand Cherokee hadn't moved from its position earlier in the day.

That was less than an hour ago. Okay, get it together... Grey has taken care of the cameras up here. He glanced up at the hospital. *Gotta go.*

Smithson walked directly to the Jeep as if he owned it. He concentrated.

Two Four Two Four.

He punched in the numbers on the outside of the door. It remained locked. He pulled the glove off his right hand and tried again. The lock popped open and he used his sleeve to wipe away any fingerprints. He jumped in and closed the door, struggling to pull the glove back on. He found himself wedged between the car seat and the steering wheel. The wife was smaller than Smithson and had her seat adjusted accordingly. Smithson struggled to turn his upper torso, scanning the inside of the vehicle. He reached over to the glove box and popped it open. He saw vehicle manuals and little else.

He opened the console and found the usual crap. No camera.

The back seat was clear.

DAMN!

He could not see into the rear cargo area from his point of view.

Last chance.

Smithson found the master lock button on the driver's side armrest and pushed. He heard pops all around. He checked quickly for witnesses, seeing none, but realizing that his situational awareness had gone to shit and he could've easily missed something. He opened the door and as nonchalantly as possible moved to the hatchback door and pulled it open.

He saw four plastic bins. No time to be cute. He pulled the lids off of each of them and dumped the contents. He threw each lid and emptied bin into the back seat. Women's clothing piled high in the cargo area.

No camera.

FUCK! He struggled to not scream it out loud.

Smithson slammed the hatch shut and walked briskly toward the library.

At that moment Lauren was sitting in the hospital cafeteria. The day had not been particularly smooth so far. There had been a medium-sized stack of lab tests on her desk when she'd arrived. This was not unexpected. The reports collected on her desk daily and by now she could predict the height of the stack based on the number of days she'd been gone. There were also three notes from fellow lab personnel requesting changes in their work schedules. Lauren made the monthly schedule for the entire department. There was a specific policy to follow for trading shifts but she found it was just as efficient to keep the process informal. It allowed her to interact quickly with multiple employees before adjusting the computerized form.

While she sorted through these requests another of the Med Techs, Josie, appeared in the doorway with unwelcome news.

"The analyzer is down again. The phlebots are bringing down the morning draws and they're stacking up in the fridge."

Phlebotomists drew blood samples from patients in their rooms on the second and third floors early each morning and brought them to the lab. Doctors ordered specific tests run for

131

each patient, depending on their affliction. There was a finite period of time that blood could be stored before it no longer yielded accurate results.

Lauren sighed and asked Josie to call the manufacturer of the machine.

"Transfer the call to me when you get someone."

Lauren knew the call could result in being put on hold for some time. She worked through more paperwork while waiting to be connected.

It was past 11 a.m. before she came up for air and announced she was going to the cafeteria for a quick lunch. Paul's breakfast had sustained her for hours. She smiled.

All that cooking he did last year, trying new recipes, and he always comes back to something tried and true...bacon and eggs.

She picked at her salad then set down the fork.

Maybe try this again.

She reached for her phone and located the Find My iPhone app. She and Paul used this to keep tabs on each other. Paul generally accessed it to check on Lauren's location if she hadn't returned home from work when expected. Invariably she was still at the hospital, shopping, or visiting a friend. Lauren used it for a different reason. She looked in on him during his bike rides. As long as the icon on her screen was moving, Paul was safe.

She wished there had been a way to ensure his safety when he was with CCT.

She'd checked the app twice earlier today during a short break and was frustrated to see that the screen was frozen. The app was typically very reliable. She tried to open it again now and encountered the same problem.

Don't get too excited. He probably took the bike path today. Probably rode south toward Tipp or north to Piqua.

She had come to rely on the feature and found herself growing frustrated with the lack of electronic information.

My God, I feel like part of Gen Y!

She worried about Paul.

Not like she worried when he was a Combat Controller. That had been like a long tightrope walk at a frightening height. Lauren dreaded a surprise visit from solemn Air Force officers with a chaplain in tow. When she was finally informed of Paul's parachute accident she actually felt a degree of relief.

He'll live through this. He won't deploy for months, years, maybe ever.

Lauren thought back to the first time she saw him.

She was working at the VA hospital at Kirtland Air Force Base as a member of the 377th Medical Group. She was learning the trade that had served her well for nearly three decades.

But she was not happy.

She was still in Albuquerque.

She had nothing against the city. In fact, she loved it. She enjoyed the balloon festival every October and loved to jog, relishing in the scenic backdrops. She had dozens of friends and knew the city inside and out. That was the problem.

Lauren grew up in Albuquerque.

Her dad, Joe, spoke often of his time in the Army and the places he'd visited. He'd been a tank crewman in the 1960s. It had been peacetime duty. It was only four years, but she had the impression more than once that her dad secretly considered it the time of his life.

If I had a latte for every time he told that Munich beer stein story...

During her senior year of high school she spoke to recruiters for the Army, Navy, and Air Force. She wanted to see the world. She decided on a career as a medical technologist. Her research showed it was a field constantly in need of applicants. She believed the Navy gave her the best chance of travel, but the creepiness of the recruiter was off putting. It came down to the Army or the Air Force. Her dad, if he was disappointed, hid it well when she chose the Air Force.

She wanted to blaze her own trail. She was happy.

He had a daughter in the military. He was happy.

But she didn't get to see the world, at least not yet. Her first two duty stations after basic training were both in her home state, the second being just seven miles from her house. She was unhappy and more than a little disillusioned, wondering if she'd made a mistake that would waste some of the best years of *her* life.

Then she bumped into Paul.

Literally bumped into him.

She was jogging on the Embudo Trailhead near the Sandia Mountain foothills, just east of the city. Technically, at the instant they met, she was hiking, or maybe walking. She was making her way down a steep trail, concentrating on keeping her balance, when she saw an athletic man charging toward her from below. His head was down, his legs churning and arms pumping.

Lauren stepped to one side as he neared. She was in a bit of a cut with the terrain rising on both sides so there was little room to maneuver. Just before he reached her she stepped to her right and shouted, "HEY!"

He was startled and tried to stop but his front foot slid across loose rock and he tumbled into her.

And the rest, sports fans, is history.

Lauren smiled.

Paul was mortified. He'd scraped his knees pretty badly but was more concerned with her bleeding elbows. He insisted on helping her down to her car. She learned he was in the Air Force and had just arrived in Albuquerque from Whiteman AFB in Missouri to "do a training thing here." He had arrived three days early and was trying to get acclimated to the altitude.

He offered to take her to lunch and she accepted. He didn't know the area so she mentioned a couple places with outside seating, "Where our dripping blood won't stain the floor."

He laughed. So did she.

She told him her first duty station had been at Hallomon Air Force Base, roughly 200 miles south of Albuquerque. She'd spent three years with the 49th Medical Group. Hallomon was located between White Sands National Park and the city of Alamogordo. Kirtland AFB was her second duty station and she'd been there less than a year. He was impressed by her knowledge of the area for having been in Albuquerque such as short time.

She gave a sad smile, "I've been in New Mexico pretty much my whole life, other than the eight weeks at Lackland."

They spent two hours at the café. Lauren revealed that she wanted to see the world but was "stuck" in Albuquerque.

Paul, deadpan, said, "Yeah, not everyone gets to spend time in Knob Noster."

They laughed again.

Lauren talked about her family, her dad, her mom Lisa, and brothers Josh and Jack. She told her dad's Munich beer stein story. She remembers thinking *Why the hell am I telling the beer stein story?*

He said her dad seemed like a great guy, and it sounded like he meant it.

They dated. They fell in love.

They saw lots of the world, some of it together, most of it apart.

They were together now and would be for the rest of their lives. Her worry for Paul now had nothing to do with combat. He needed a purpose again. His leg was mostly recovered. He was still young and in otherwise fantastic health. He needed something beyond history books and bike rides.

She had talked to Gatewood about it. The man had connections everywhere.

He had nodded and said "It'll happen Lauren...in due time."

Gatewood said things that could sound so profound. She kidded him from time to time that he was full of shit, but hoped he was right in this case.

"Well it's not just our stuff."

Lauren looked up to see Josie sliding into the chair across from her. She was peeling the lid off of a peach yogurt cup.

"What?" Lauren was confused.

"It's not just our stuff in the lab. I just talked to Jerry from maintenance and he says they're having trouble with the security cameras."

Lauren looked at Josie. Then eyed her phone.

135

"Gadgets," she said under her breath.

CHAPTER NINETEEN

Paul pedaled the final few hundred yards on Polecat Road. He was in the right lane and unconsciously checked his helmet-mounted mirror every few seconds to monitor traffic coming from behind. A box truck from a delivery company appeared in the mirror and Paul picked up the pace. He decided to beat the truck to his lane, not to finish strong, but to remove himself from the path of the truck.

Why take a chance right at the end of the ride.

Paul reached twenty-eight miles per hour before braking hard and veering into his lane. He stopped a few feet inside and dismounted. The truck pushed past creating a breeze that rustled the trees on either side of the lane. Paul pulled up the MapMyRun app and stopped the distance feature. He'd logged nearly twenty-nine miles. He removed his helmet and glasses and dabbed at the perspiration around his eyes with his upper sleeves.

Paul turned and walked his bike toward the house as gravel crunched under his feet. There was a bit of a ritual to this. Paul had a good friend, an attorney that lived outside of Sidney two towns to the north. Paul and Lauren needed to update their wills and the man, Rich, had been recommended to them. Rich was ex-Navy and a bike rider. He lived in a semi-rural area in a house that also had a gravel lane. Rich wore clip-in shoes on his rides. He kept a pair of beat up docksider shoes in his garage and slipped them on before walking the bike down the lane. At the bottom of the lane he changed to the clip-ins. He reversed this process after the ride. While he was logging miles, the docksiders sat a few feet from the road waiting for him to return. Rich had been told several times over the years, "Hey, somebody left an old pair of shoes in front of your place."

Paul smiled. For him the ritual was more about cataloging. He reviewed the ride. He filed away any adjustments that needed done to the bike. He also assessed his leg.

Not bad today, especially after the early workout.

He reached the concrete section and pulled the garage remote from top of his shorts. After engaging it he waited for the door to reach a sufficient height and ducked under while it continued upward. He stored the bike in its rack and hung his helmet on the shelf above before grabbing a towel from the stack kept there for this purpose. Paul walked to the door to the house with his phone, sunglasses, and door opener in one hand. He worked the towel over his face and neck with the other.

Alright, I have to remember to watch for Chappy.

Paul entered the house.

Something was off.

He could see that three of the kitchen cabinets were open. He quickly scanned the room, seeing no immediate threats. Paul stepped back into the garage. He laid his phone, glasses, and garage door opener on top of a red rolling toolbox, tossing the towel aside. He slid out a drawer and selected a claw hammer. He reentered the house.

Paul moved from room to room, advancing cautiously. The disarray of the first floor increased as he moved to the rear of the house. Drawers were open on dressers. The floor of the walk-in closet in the master bedroom was covered with items from the shelving above. The place had been ransacked. He gripped the hammer and made his way back toward the kitchen. He passed the open office door with his senses heightened and heard a strained wailing.

MYOWWWWWW

Paul turned and whispered, "Chappy!"

He closed the door, sealing the cat in the office, and moved on. He noticed broken glass at the foot of the front door and saw that a pane was missing. Five minutes later he had cleared the house and was sure whoever broke in was gone.

What the hell?

Paul returned to the garage and retrieved his phone. He called 9-1-1 and reported the break-in. He was told that a Miami County deputy would respond. The Hull's place was outside of the Troy city limits and was in county jurisdiction.

He needed to call Lauren. Hospital employees were not supposed to utilize their cell phones unless on break. He decided to call the number for the lab. Josie answered and said she would get Lauren.

"Heyyy Paul, I was trying to track you on my phone. Good ride?"

"Listen, somebody broke into the house, I—"

"WHAT?" Lauren cut him off, drawing the attention of the entire lab.

Paul tried to concisely give her all the information he had.

"It happened while I was on my ride. They broke a window on the front door to get in. I can't tell if anything is missing, it looks like they were in a hurry and looking for valuables."

"What about Cha—"

"I have Chappy, he's fine." He answered before she completed the question.

Lauren paused, then, looking at the clock asked, "Should I come home?"

Paul responded, "I don't think so, not yet. Let's wait for the deputy to get here and see what he thinks. You just got back to work this morning. I'll call you after I talk to the deputy."

The responding deputy was Tyler Wilks, a fit young man whose uniform shirt fit tightly over his protective vest. He was all business. He pulled his black Sheriff's Department SUV up to the garage and got out, a clipboard in his left hand. His right hand rested on his holster. Paul waited for him in the garage. After introducing himself Wilks began taking down Paul's information.

Minutes later a second SUV turned into the drive. Detective Amos Bunker got out and moved to the pair. Bunker was a fortyish man with short, prematurely grey hair. He was an inch shorter than Paul. He wore a sport coat and tie, rather than a uniform.

139

"Mr. Hull?" He extended his hand.

"Yes sir... Paul."

They shook.

"I'd like to do walk-through if you don't mind. You can come with us. Let us know if you see anything missing."

They made a circuit of the house. Paul put Chappy in the basement and closed the door when they finished there. When they entered the office Bunker's eyes were drawn to a power strip under the desk. Several cords were plugged into it. One, an iPhone cord, was in two parts. The block was plugged into the strip. Small gouges appeared on the white casing of the wire about eight inches from the block. The cord was severed at that point. Small metal strands poked out. The larger section of the cord lay beside it with similar markings on one end.

Bunker knelt to examine it.

"Uhh, that was probably done by our cat."

Bunker looked at Paul with a raised eyebrow.

Paul thought, *Chappy's tenth cord...this makes him a double ace.*

They continued through the house. Paul saw nothing missing. In the bedroom he pointed to a softball-sized ceramic container on a dresser.

"We keep some cash in there, I haven't checked it yet."

He pulled the cork stopper from the top and tilted it toward the detective and deputy. There was several hundred dollars inside.

"Looks like it's all here."

Bunker nodded thoughtfully.

They entered the master bathroom.

Wilks whistled and said "Whoah!"

All three of them stared at the ruined hair dryer. Paul had missed it in his haste to clear the house.

"Looks like someone was frustrated," Bunker stated. He turned to Paul.

"It looks like they were looking for something specific. You wouldn't have any idea what that would be would you Mr. Hull?"

Paul looked at him and smiled.

"What are you thinking, drugs?"

Bunker, not embarrassed in the least, smiled back.

"Well, ordinarily in a situation like this, I would allow for that possibility. The house torn apart, a stash of cash left behind... but I saw those Bronze Star certificates on the office wall and I don't figure you for a dealer."

Bunker continued.

"And the Sheriff's Department has most of our vehicle maintenance done at J.D.'s. I happened to be at his shop one day when you rode past on a bike. You were new in town and I like to stay informed. I asked J.D. what he knew about you and he said you were 'Good Troop.' I took that to mean that you were a military guy that he would vouch for."

Paul laughed.

Good old J.D. Actual.

Paul said he had no idea what a burglar could've been looking for.

Wilks cleared his throat and ventured, "Maybe a case of mistaken identity? If it was a druggie, he might've had the wrong address. Happens from time to time."

Bunker nodded and began to say something about dusting for fingerprints when Paul's phone vibrated. He checked the screen.

Sticks, you getting close? On the base yet?

It was from Gatewood.

"Damn, excuse me guys, I need to make a call."

Paul walked to the kitchen, selected Gatewood from his contacts, and placed the call.

"Sticks! Are we meeting at the Pit?" Gatewood's optimistic tone accompanied his words.

Paul allowed a small smile. Only his Joint Special Operations Command, or JSOC, buddies called him "Sticks."

"Sorry Woody, we have a little problem here. Someone broke into the house and the sheriffs are here."

Gatewood's voice changed, dropping an octave.

"Everybody alright? How is Lauren?"

Paul assured him they were fine.

"Lauren's at work. Listen, I need to take a rain check on lunch. Maybe catch up tomorrow? I'm meeting Mike tomorrow to load some wood but I should be able to swing by around noon."

Gatewood responded with one word.

"Check."

It was special operations speak for "acknowledged."

Paul ended the call and returned to the men in the bedroom.

Smithson was sweating and pumping gas in Tipp City at a BP station just off I-75. It was a nine-minute drive from the Troy Library to this exit and he had a death grip on the wheel the entire way. His eyes bounced from the road to the fuel gauge and back again.

What a helluva thing it would be if I ran out of gas. What a helluva thing.

He wanted to get away from Troy before stopping. Things were closing in on him. He hadn't anticipated all of the cameras. Yes, he'd disabled the hospital recordings but there were at least two more buildings that could've had cameras that now had him on video.

Not a big deal if no one is looking for me, but the wife will see I was in her car. She's probably already heard from her husband and knows I hit their house. The cops might start canvassing for video. DAMN!

He had to get Grey on it pronto. He watched the fuel counter on the pump tick higher. Even here, getting gas, he was beginning to get paranoid. He glanced inside the Audi and saw the facemask on the passenger seat. He'd tossed it there the previous night after going through Biggs' apartment.

Probably should've put the damn thing back on before getting out to pump this gas.

He was using one of the Glenn Smithson credit cards. It just wasn't convenient to use cash for everything. He'd brought plenty and used it at restaurants, but when he planned Operation Crank he figured he'd be fine using the cards for some things. He hadn't anticipated complications of this magnitude.

To be safe he may have to switch soon to his second fake ID and set of credit cards. He pulled his hoodie lower and turned another five degrees away from the camera mounted above the convenience store area of the station. In so doing he turned directly toward a young mom pumping gas into a green Subaru Forester. A toddler sat in a car seat in the back with a pacifier in her mouth. Smithson frowned at the kid and checked out the woman.

Not bad...now THAT chick belongs in yoga pants.

He smiled to himself at the irony of the second name on his fake documents. It was Oliver Haugh.

Smithson grinned.

Wilbur would be rolling over in his grave.

The gas flow stopped. Smithson gave the Audi one more squirt and hung the nozzle on the side of the pump. He noticed a McDonalds in the next lot.

The hamburger chain's 2003 slogan swam into his head and he let it come to his lips, "Ba Ba Ba Baa Ba, I'm Lovin' It."

The woman at the next pump locked the doors of her Subaru.

Smithson headed for Mickey D's.

The Pandemic had strained staffing levels in every sector of the economy. Nowhere was it more apparent than the restaurant business. Wait times were doubled, even tripled. Staff was overworked. Management struggled. It led in some cases to the easing of standards in many businesses. Many establishments with drug testing policies waived them to get more applicants.

143

In other businesses the easing of standards occurred in different ways. Such was the case at the Tipp City McDonalds. Their once strict no cellphone policy for workers on duty was not rescinded, but the managers allowed quite a bit of leeway as long as the lines kept moving. This was well received by the hourly employees, if not those actually in the lines.

Dart Johns and Rebecca Goody were two such employees. Dart was a nineteen year old sophomore at Sinclair Community College in Dayton. He lived at home in Tipp. He took all the hours his manager, Mr. Baker, would give him. He had flesh tunnels in both ears lined with black plastic rings that were a half-inch in diameter. He planned to expand them over time to a full inch.

People just don't realize how much time and patience this takes.

Rebecca was a seventy-year old widow who lived near the airport in Vandalia. She had her hair styled to look like Meg Ryan in *Sleepless In Seattle* and it still worked for her, at least she hoped it did. When the manpower shortage hit, she decided to go back to work for the first time in twelve years.

The pair were a godsend to Baker so he looked the other way when they were texting. Oddly, they were usually texting each other. Rebecca worked the pay window while Dart took care of dispensing the orders at the second window. Rebecca had a nice seat at her station. She was pleasant and enjoyed talking to the customers. Dart was constantly on the go and had to be doing something at all times.

This worked well as there was a need for both Rebecca's customer service and Dart's near-attention-deficit-disorder-level of cleaning and organizing.

The pair struck up a friendship. The type that only happens with people stationed adjacent to each other in a work environment. They would ordinarily have nothing in common but learned over time that they both had somewhat abnormal interests in celebrities. This interest, though, was from wildly different genres and time periods. Rebecca liked old movies, some sports, popular TV from the seventies and eighties, like that. Dart preferred current actors and actresses as well as social media personalities, rappers, and hip-hop artists.

They were working the windows one day when a customer passed through.

Rebecca commented, "He kind of looked like Jimmy Stewart."

"Who is Jimmy Stewart?"

Rebecca was incredulous and a long discussion ensued about celebrities of different eras. A week or so later Dart finished with a customer and, seeing Rebecca was conversing with the next driver in line, sent a text to her phone.

That last guy looked like Tupac.

This developed into a back and forth. They found it the most fun when they texted each other with their separate opinions about the same customer. They could compare notes and then google the name they didn't recognize.

You're right, your Rebecca Romijn customer DID look like young Barbara Eden.

There were many examples:

George Clooney/Cary Grant

Kendall Kardashian/Young Elizabeth Taylor

Melissa McCarthy/Rosanne Barr

Denzell Washington/Sidney Poitier

Fat Joe/David Ortiz

Joe Rogan/Telly Savalas.

This one had confused Rebecca as she remembered Rogan in the 1990s television sitcom *NewsRadio* when he had hair. Dart added a modifier—*Podcast* Joe Rogan.

Kid Rock/Scruffy Larry Bird

They retired this last pair of identifiers after a week of the game when they realized a full ten percent of their customers looked like Kid Rock and Scruffy Larry Bird.

They actually texted each other the same name on a few occasions. Donald Trump Jr., Derek Jeter, and Rick Harrison from *Pawn Stars,* displaying some commonality.

After the sweating, agitated man in the black Audi came through the Drive Thru, Rebecca and Dart texted each other.

Rebecca: *Philip Seymour Hoffman in the phone scene from Punch-Drunk Love*

Dart: *Jim Gaffigan if he had longer, stringier hair*

CHAPTER TWENTY

Lauren checked her watch on the way out of the east entrance of Kettering Medical. The lab's location on the east side of the first floor made the parking lot on that side convenient. It was 3:10. Just forty minutes after her shift was supposed to end. Paul urged her to limit her overtime.

He'll be happy I'm not staying later.

She had to admit that if not for the break-in she would probably still be at her desk. There was just so much to do in the lab, a constant stream of samples to process. She had been so busy she hadn't had time to slip out to the parking lot and move the totes from the Grand Cherokee to Elaine's car.

But she wanted to get home to gauge the level of damage. Paul had said there was not much broken. Things were mostly out of place.

It's the invasion of privacy, though. A stranger had been in their house!

Lauren dug through her purse and came out with her keys. She squinted in the afternoon sun, the heat of the day closing around her. A line of parked vehicles was between her and the Grand Cherokee. As she cleared the last car in line she came to an abrupt stop.

There was a pair of purple spandex leggings on the ground. They were near the left rear tire. Lauren was confused. She stared at them for two beats, her mind racing through different possibilities.

Could those be mine? How could they fall out of the car?

Then she knew.

Someone got into my Jeep!

She turned, frantically searching for any threat. Seeing none she edged cautiously toward the Jeep, looking for any sign of an occupant. There was no movement so she angled in a bit closer. She remembered to grip her keys so one protruded from between her forefinger and middle finger at the knuckle. She was prepared to defend herself.

When she got to within ten feet she could see the totes and lids piled haphazardly in the back seat. That confirmed it.

Lauren turned and walked briskly back toward the hospital. She palmed her phone and dialed Paul.

He answered on the second ring.

"Hey, still at work?"

Lauren approached the automatic door. It detected her and slid open.

"I think someone broke into my Jeep!" She made an attempt to sound calm but knew it came out sounding strained.

"WHAT?!?"

Paul was working on the front door. He had cut a piece of plywood to fit over the broken pane and was working to fit it into the opening. The county fingerprint tech had left a few minutes earlier after dusting some areas that had obviously been contacted by the burglar. He dropped the wood and stood.

"Are you alright? Have you called the police?"

As he talked Paul closed and locked the front door and hurried to the kitchen. He grabbed his keys and rushed through the door to the garage on his way to the Escape.

"Hold on," she said.

Lauren walked to the information desk and asked the attendant to call security. She returned to Paul, having no doubt he was already on his way.

"I'm at the east entrance."

Tommy Walters from hospital security met Lauren at the desk and after hearing a brief version of events escorted her back to the Grand Cherokee.

"Yep, sure looks like somebody tossed things around in there. Any way you could've forgotten to lock it?"

Lauren's glare was all the answer he needed.

Walters was forty-six years old and twice divorced. He had seen that look before. Many times.

"Okay, pretty doubtful, huh? Well even if it *had* been unlocked, no one should've been inside the vehicle. I think we need to call the police."

The Troy police officer arrived at virtually the same time Paul pulled into the lot. The entire group approached the Jeep. Lauren tried the hatch door and it lifted upward.

"Not locked now," she observed.

They saw piles of clothes in the rear compartment. All four of the empty totes were tossed into the back seat. Two of the lids were there as well with the other two spread across the front console.

"Looks like someone was in a hurry," offered Walters.

Paul, composed but with some steel in his voice, said "I think you better call Detective Bunker with the Miami County Sheriff's Department."

Smithson took another pull of the Diet Coke. The Big Mac and fries were gone. Even the squirters that made it out of the french fry holder and into the bottom of the bag. He had finished them before getting off I-70 on the return to the rental. Smithson read somewhere that the official name for the red holder for Mickey D's fries was "French Fry Scoop." He couldn't decide if that was stupid or not.

He pulled into the drive of the Airbnb five minutes later. He got out of the Audi and surreptitiously checked the neighborhood. It had the look of an area that was home to a number of school-aged children. On a Thursday early afternoon the sidewalks were clear. He popped the trunk and returned to the driver's seat, reaching into the back for the lock kit and the Winkler. The second he turned he remembered the picks had scattered over the seat and floor.

"Dammit," he hissed.

He spent a full minute collecting the picks and stuffed them back into the kit, bending at least one of them in the process.

Junk, fucking junk!

He pushed the kit into the pocket of his hoodie. Stepping back out of the S8 he held the handle of the Winkler in his right palm, the shaft and blade pointing upward on the inside of his forearm. He tucked his arm into his body, effectively hiding the axe from wandering eyes. Smithson stepped back to the trunk and flipped the Winkler inside, then pulled at the lock kit. It was hung up in the pocket.

"GODDAMMIT!"

He cringed.

Dumbass! That was too loud!

He worked the kit free and, with contempt, tossed it into the trunk. He grabbed the trunk above his head and was about to pull it down when his eyes fell on the second set of license plates. They were from Nebraska and, like the first set, stolen. It was not difficult to find someone in Vegas looking to make some extra cash for gambling or drugs. Most were willing to do far more than remove a couple screws from a tourist's car.

Two heavy rubber bands held an envelope against the plates. He paused, then grabbed the envelope and pulled it away from the plates. He walked around to the passenger side and picked up the Toughbook before locking up and heading to the house.

Smithson went directly to the dining room table and opened the laptop. He began the necessary steps to establish the encrypted connection. He had to get Grey on the cameras near the hospital. He finished the last step and waited impatiently for the confirmation. The screen brightened and the Wright Flyer began its journey from right to left.

Smithson instructed Grey to find any cameras within a two-block radius of Kettering Medical. This meant a search of multiple security systems and could take some time, even for Grey. Smithson figured it would be a minimum of several minutes and possibly an hour. Rather than close down the connection and checking in later he elected to leave the screen up. A notification would appear and he could act upon the results immediately. It was critical to wipe any video evidence before the cops had the chance to seize the recordings.

Smithson minimized the screen and navigated to a set of documents he labeled "Action Plans." While he waited for Grey to complete the assigned task he would formulate a new game plan. He paged through past operations. Some prompted a smile. None more than the highly lucrative "CRYPTO-BOY." Others like the 3M "GO POST-AL" summoned a frown.

Smithson found the "CRANK" file. He scrolled to the end of Phase Three... *Fucking Biggs...* and began to add notes on a page he titled "Supplemental."

STATUS*****
Husband & wife alerted to my presence.
Location of camera/SD card unknown but best guess, still in house.
Biggs body not yet discovered.
Grey has cached files on vehicle geo histories.
File also cached on family/friend cell and social media interactions.

To Do List
Wipe cameras vicinity of Kettering Hospital (Grey engaged)
Terminate Hulls?

He stared at the last line.
Hmmmm
He slowly shook his head. No, he couldn't kill the Hulls, at least not yet. He had basically ransacked the house and the woman's Jeep. The cops were involved. It was apparent that someone wanted something that the Hulls possessed. As soon as Biggs' body turned up in Indiana the shit would really hit the fan. The Henry County yokels will have the report that the couple made last night.
Holy Hell! Was it just last night?
It had been less than twenty-four hours since he and Biggs had hit the Wright site. Smithson shook his head again. A niggling thought was germinating in the back of his mind.
You didn't plan this very well.

You gave Biggs too much leeway and it came back to bite you.

You missed on the camera at the house and may have been recorded passing the buildings by the hospital.

You're playing catch-up. You had no solid back-up plans.

"Aw Fuck!"

Didn't he improvise this morning? He had planned to just cruise the house and settle on a plan later. When Grey alerted him to the husband riding a bike, he adapted and put together a course of action.

Pretty damned bold one, too.

No, he would be fine. He just had to be more careful. He had to come up with a plan to leverage the couple into giving up the camera and its video evidence. He had to do it in such a way that the Henry County cops didn't get the evidence from them. Smithson would be an instant murder suspect and with the current state of facial recognition software he would be in deep shit.

At worst he would be tracked and apprehended. At best he would be in hiding the rest of his life.

WWLD?

What Would Liam Do?

In the movie, Neesom's character was on the phone with his daughter's kidnapper. He told the man that he was coming for him.

Maybe the direct approach is best with this couple.

Smithson looked at the screen. The "To Do" list was woefully small.

He typed: *Status of pickup truck?*

He leaned back. Grey was still working on the security task. His eyes fell on the envelope he'd brought from the trunk of the Audi. He slid it over and opened it. A Nebraska driver's license and Visa debit card were inside. Smithson stared at the name on the card and grinned.

The name was Oliver Crook Haugh.

Smithson wanted two fake IDs for Crank. He had nearly been caught by the 3M probes. He hadn't shielded his identity properly. Going forward from there he obtained fakes from the Dark Web and went pretty much unchallenged until the Crypto-Boy Op. It had been a fantastic success financially, but he'd had to kill the investigator to preserve his identity.

Smithson learned from this. He purchased two full sets of identification for Crank. He spent some time selecting his new names.

The voice in the back of his head told him he spent significantly more time on this than he did on the planning phase with Biggs.

STFU!

The first name was Glenn Smithson. In was a combination of Glenn Curtiss and the Smithsonian Institution.

Curtiss was a rival flyer that had a long history with the Wrights. He was perhaps the most talented builder of engines in the world. He gravitated to aviation and built flying machines that rivaled the Wrights'. The problem, from the Wrights' point of view, was Curtiss was building upon their advancements and resisting paying them rights fees. They had acquired patents through the courts.

Curtiss, rather than using wing warping for lateral control, employed ailerons. He flew in many exhibitions. The Wrights were to receive payment for this. Curtiss argued that aviation was advancing, whether the Wrights liked it or not, and he was part of this evolution.

The men may not ever have been close, but they had been friendly at one time. Their relationship grew more strained. But there was an incident that involved the Smithsonian Institution that caused a complete break. There was animosity, certainly from the Wright family toward Curtiss.

It went back to one of the early competitors of the Wrights, Samuel Langley. At the same time Wilbur and Orville were using their wits and limited funds to develop their theories, Langley had been the recipient of fifty thousand dollars from the United States War Department to do the same thing. This was a fantastic sum of money at the time.

Langley was the third secretary of the Smithsonian. He developed a flying machine he called "The Aerodrome" using the money from the government. The Aerodrome was mounted on a barge on the Potomac River. It made highly publicized attempts at the first powered flight on October 7 and December 8 of 1903.

Both were spectacular failures. Langley's design had no effective means of control. The Aerodrome ended up in the river both times and Langley's chosen pilot, Charles Manley, was nearly killed.

Nine days after the second attempt the Wrights successfully logged the first controlled, powered flight at Kitty Hawk. They had photographic evidence to prove it.

Langley died in 1906. The Smithsonian became caretakers not only of Langley's reputation, but the Aerodrome itself. As advances in aviation transpired, the Smithsonian partnered with Curtiss. In 1914 they engaged him to extensively modify Langley's creation. Curtiss lowered the craft's center of gravity, strengthened its structure, modified the engine, and changed the wing aspect ratio. He even added propellers that were based on the Wrights' design.

With the changes, Curtiss was able to get the Aerodrome airborne for a few seconds. Curtiss participated in this to bypass the Wright patent on aircraft. The Smithsonian did it to vindicate Langley. The museum promptly put the craft on display as the first heavier-than-air craft "capable of flight."

Orville Wright was furious. His older brother had died of typhoid fever two years earlier at the age of forty-five. This affront to Wilbur's legacy sparked a feud that lasted decades. Orville refused to allow the Wright Flyer to be displayed at the Smithsonian. Most observers backed the Wrights. Visitors to the museum wondered why the Wright Flyer, possibly the most important invention in history, was not showcased, while Langley's fifty thousand dollar boondoggle was.

The brothers had stored the original flyer in a shed behind their bicycle shop at 1127 West Third Street after returning from their 1903 success in Kitty Hawk. It remained there for nearly ten years until a devastating flood covered a large portion of western Ohio, including Dayton, on March 25, 1913. Water and mud damaged the Flyer. It was later restored.

The dispute with the Smithsonian continued. In 1928 Orville loaned the Flyer to the Science Museum in London. A new generation of Americans wondered why this piece of history was not prominently displayed in their country.

By 1942 a new secretary, Charles Abbot, was in place at the Smithsonian. He directed his staff to publish a list of the Curtiss modifications to the Aerodrome, there were thirty-five of them in total. The Smithsonian then rescinded the claims it had made about Langley's brainchild.

Orville warmed to the idea of bringing his Flyer back to America. But World War Two was now raging and the United Kingdom was being ravaged by German bombs in what came to be known as The Blitz, or the Battle of Britain. Orville watched from an ocean away as the invention he developed with his brother was employed to indiscriminately kill thousands.

The British moved the Flyer to an underground facility built in a quarry near Corsham, roughly one hundred miles west of London. It safely rested there until the end of the war. It finally returned to the United States in November of 1948 aboard the RMS Mauretania.

Orville, who died of a heart attack on January 30 of the same year, was not there to witness it. On November 23 Orville's estate signed an agreement that allowed the Smithsonian to purchase the Flyer for one dollar. The agreement contained strict provisions for exhibition. Orville's heirs no doubt shared his trust issues of the Smithsonian.

The Flyer was finally put on display at the Smithsonian on December 17, 1948, forty-five years to the day after its First Flight at Kitty Hawk.

The inspiration for Smithson's name came from both Glenn Curtiss and the Smithsonian. He took his first name from the Wrights' nemesis. The name of the museum was too recognizable. People would certainly remember any interaction with a man who had the same last name as the institution. Smithson found that removing the last three letters left him with a name that was much less memorable.

But *HE* knew. His smile widened. Curtiss and the Smithsonian were two entities that presented slights and threats to the Wrights. Smithson was to be a third.

But Biggs screwed it up.

His smile fell.

Smithson looked again at his second driver's license.

Oliver Haugh.

This name was derived from a completely different part of Wright history, though it was no less difficult for them, particularly for Wilbur.

The original Oliver Haugh was a bully. He lived in Dayton just two blocks from the Wrights. In the winters the neighborhood kids often engaged in an outdoor form of ice hockey known as "shinney." During the winter of 1885-86 Wilbur took part in this.

At the time, Wilbur was an excellent student at the local public school. Family lore has it that he intended to enroll at Yale after graduation. Then came the game of shinney with Haugh. The bully struck Wilbur in the face with his stick. This caused significant damage to his teeth and necessitated the use of painful dentures the rest of his life. Wilbur went into a three-year depression. He didn't graduate and did not attend Yale. It was only his curiosity for flight that brought him out of his despondency.

Smithson remembered a drawing that Grey found on display at the Wilbur Wright Birthplace Museum. It showed Wilbur on the ice, knocked on his ass by another boy brandishing a curved stick. The drawing was signed by Dennis McMahan and was titled "Wilbur, Hurt In A Game Of Shinney, Gives Up Plans For Yale."

Smithson's smile reappeared.

The mean little bastard in that drawing kind of looks like me.

Then, *Oliver really got into your head, didn't he Wilbur?*

Smithson believed almost no one would recognize Haugh's name, even with his subsequent history, so he appropriated it as his second identity in Crank.

That subsequent history was notable. Haugh was a bully, but a smart bully. He became a doctor. He was obsessed with Robert Louis Stevenson's *Dr Jekyll and Mr Hyde* in which the main character develops a potion to separate the good and evil aspects of his personality. He experimented on himself seeking to prove that two beings could exist in one body. Haugh had at least nine wives in his life, some simultaneously. Four died while married to him. It is believed Haugh was responsible, using hyoscine injections to their spines. Many of his patients also met unexplained deaths.

Haugh learned his parents had cut him out of their will. On November 5, 1905 his father, mother, and brother died in a fire. Haugh was tried for the crime. He claimed he was addicted to cocaine-infused toothache medication, pleading not guilty by reason of insanity. He was found guilty and executed by electric chair on April 19, 1907 at the age of thirty-six. He was believed to have killed sixteen people.

Haugh was one of the first serial killers.

Smithson continued to stare at the name on the license.

Am I a serial killer too?

He examined the question. He had now shot two men. Technically two qualified as a series, a small one, but a series. But Smithson thought of serial killers as psychopaths, creatures who stalked their victims and had a compulsion to kill. Smithson's shootings were not that at all. They were acts of self-preservation.

Well, at least the investigator shooting had been. To a large extent Biggs had just pissed him off.

No, the two shootings didn't put him in psychopath territory.

Smithson pondered.

Now if you consider that thing with the girl in Belize a third murder, maybe I would qualify as a serial killer.

But he didn't. She wasn't even an American.

CHAPTER TWENTY-ONE

Once Amos Bunker arrived at the hospital the group convened in a small conference room on the first floor. In addition to him it consisted of the responding Troy policeman, Jeff Graves, a Troy detective named Todd Borland, Tommy Walters, and the Hulls.

A second Troy police cruiser was posted next to the Grand Cherokee to discourage anyone from tampering with the scene. The officer sat inside the running cruiser with the air conditioning on high.

Inside the conference room the air conditioning was also running, but observers may not have noticed. There was an atmosphere of low-level tension. After some initial jurisdictional wrangling it was agreed that Bunker would be the lead investigator with Borland in a supporting role. That sorted out, Bunker got their attention.

"In a large city these incidents might not cause a ripple. Nothing seems to be missing from the house or the vehicle. But in this area we," he tipped his head to Borland and the Troy policeman Graves, then continued, "jump on something like this."

Borland and Graves nodded.

"Our Sheriff's Department tech has dusted for prints at the house. We wouldn't ordinarily check for fingerprints on a simple vehicle break-in, but I believe the Troy Police will send someone to check the Jeep. Mrs. Hull, you opened the hatchback so we don't expect to find anything there, but we'll still check."

Lauren blushed.

"No, no, don't misunderstand me. You did nothing wrong. In fact I've talked to our fingerprint folks and their initial opinion is the person or persons involved wore gloves. If it's the same perpetrator, and logic suggests it would be, and he wore gloves at the house, he almost certainly would've worn them here."

Bunker looked around the room.

"The next thing on our checklist is to view the security video from the overhead cameras that look down at the lot. This is a new facility and we expect to see high resolution images of the incident to ident—"

Tommy Walters cleared his throat loudly, interrupting Bunker.

"Uhh, actually, our cameras went down a few minutes before this would've happened." He smiled nervously and added, "First time that's ever happened."

Bunker pulled his eyes from Walters and found Hull. Paul's eyes were already locked on him with a look of.......something other than fear.

Hull held his gaze for another second then turned to his wife, putting his arm around her.

Bunker remembered the Bronze Star certificates and thought, *This cat is capable.*

When a notification blinked onto the screen of the Toughbook it drew Smithson's attention. He saw that Grey had identified four cameras that had the potential to record his walk from the library to the hospital and back. Two were indeed on the library and the Government Center. The other two were from businesses down the street. He had Grey corrupt the storage files of all four. He did not have the time to focus on specific windows of time.

This done, he relaxed somewhat. He wandered down to the basement.

Maybe some games? It always helps me think.

Some of Smithson's boldest plans emerged from a corner of his brain while the conscious portion was engaged in first person shooter games. The basement was equipped with the current versions of both the Xbox and PlayStation gaming systems. Multiple controllers were arrayed on a low table in front of the angled seating. Smithson chose the Xbox.

What shall we play?

160

As the system came alive he reviewed the Xbox games he'd been investing his time in recently. There were five; *APEX LEGENDS, CALL of DUTY: MODERN WARFARE II, FORTNITE, OVERWATCH 2, and PUBG BATTLEGROUNDS.* He chose *OVERWATCH 2*—he was still wearing the T-shirt— and logged in with the username *RandumGener8*. His proclivity to use a variation of the word "Nightmare" was a thing of the past.

Smithson entered "Player vs. Player," or "PvP" mode, and entered the queue. He found that his mind often went on autopilot during game play. Time passed, he entered another world. It calmed him. Occasionally he experienced significant inspiration.

While he waited, he went to the shooting range. In less than two minutes he was admitted to the game.

Not a bad wait.

Smithson's "Main" in *OVERWATCH 2* was Reaper. There were thirty-five characters to choose from. Reaper was a Damage Hero. These characters had the largest capacity to do damage to enemy players and tended to move quickly around the map. Smithson loved these traits. On the other hand Damage Heroes were more vulnerable to attacks from the other team and had lower Hit points, which indicate how much damage they can sustain. This was the tradeoff the player had to consider.

Smithson had racked up points by completing daily, weekly, and seasonal challenges. He refused to buy tiers. He had too much integrity. He was a Diamond Level player, a ridiculously high rank. Diamond was the seventh of eight levels. Only "Top 500" was higher.

Reaper was an American mercenary and terrorist. He wore a black trenchcoat with a white skull mask. He could teleport using *Shadow Step*. He could also employ *Wraith Form*, which granted him a brief period of invulnerability and increased speed. He could heal himself by consuming the souls of fallen enemies.

Smithson navigated through the scenario. He liked to get to the top of buildings before carrying out an attack, believing opposing players did not expect him to be there. Smithson realized that he and Reaper shared many of the same qualities and abilities. Grey served as Smithson's special ability. Grey granted him the defensive capabilities of stealth and concealment that his adversaries couldn't match. Grey also gave him proficiency for technological attack that was unparalleled.

Reaper's ultimate ability was *Death Blossom,* a fusillade with twin Hellfire Shotguns that dealt massive damage. Reaper was vulnerable when executing *Death Blossom,* so it worked best when employing the element of surprise, taking out enemies before they got a chance to react.

Smithson smiled.

He paused the game, reached for his phone, and brought up the DoorDash app. Ideas were beginning to coalesce.

He ordered pizza.

Smithson resumed the game and played for ten minutes before signing off and going upstairs to wait for the pizza. He moved to the kitchen and noticed the pillowcases from Biggs' apartment. He sat and began to remove items. When he'd finished he had three stacks, each a foot high, give or take. This was the hard copy material. He set the laptop aside. He would take it back to Boulder City where he and Grey could do a thorough examination of its contents.

Smithson pulled a file towards him and opened it. The first item on top was the brochure from Wright State Libraries that he'd noticed the night before. He opened it. The Special Collection and Archives section of the library was located on the fourth floor. According to the details mentioned, it housed a wide selection of significant material, including a collection from Dayton poet Paul Laurence Dunbar. The library itself was named after Dunbar. But the first line on the listing of available resources was "The largest Wright brothers collection in the world." There was little doubt that this compilation was the star of the show.

Below the brochure were a yellow legal pad and a stack of copies. Biggs had made notes on the legal pad and numbered each. Every number corresponded to a notation on one of the copies. It appeared to Smithson that Biggs had taken pictures of items he found in the research material with his cell phone. Fingers of Biggs' left hand could be seen in some of the photos. He apparently sent these to his laptop and then ran copies later. Smithson could have Grey confirm this if it became necessary.

After months of on and off prep on the Wrights, even Smithson was fascinated by some of the things in this file. There were copies of both Wilbur and Orville's wills. The actual guestbook from Orville's funeral at the First Baptist Church in Dayton was in the collection. The service was held before he was interred next to Wilbur in Woodland Cemetery. Biggs had photographed several pages of signatures. There were a number of typed pages listing who sent flowers. Smithson saw the Edison Institute of Dearborn, Michigan, as well as numerous political, military, and world figures on the list. Far and away the most prevalent category of donors was the American aviation industry. It seemed they all realized the debt owed to Orville and his brother.

Someone had gone to the trouble of keeping the small sympathy cards that were attached to floral arrangements. They were slipped into plastic holders. Biggs had taken shots of several of these. Smithson flipped through the copies and selected one at random. On the front in green ink was "Engineers Club of Dayton," written in cursive. Biggs had also taken a shot of the rear. In pencil in a different hand was "Basket, pink gladiola, white stock, Lavender iris."

My god, these people were packrats!

There were copies of telegrams, old newspaper clippings, and pictures of all four pages of the agreement to turn the original Wright Flyer over to the Smithsonian. Smithson saw that a page was attached to the back of this document from The Library of Congress, who must've been included in all correspondence on this matter between the Wright Estate and the Smithsonian. Typed at the bottom of this page was "Sending the attached back to you is a real honor, believe me." It was signed by a Richard Eells and dated 17 May, 1949.

All this was interesting, but nothing here really would've helped with Operation Crank.

Smithson continued through the stack and came to a photo of a man seated on a plane. It appeared to be a slightly more modern craft than the original Wright Flyer. Scrawled across the bottom in cursive were the words "Edward A. Korn and Benoist Type XII Aeroplane, Sidney, Ohio, Fairgrounds, Nov. 9, 1912."

"Son-of-a-BITCH!"

Smithson continued through the stack and found many more copies of Korn photos. Almost all were dated after 1910. The brothers were flying a full ten years after the Wrights' Kitty Hawk breakthrough. They were not even close to beating the brothers. One of the notes said the Korns *trained* on a Wright Flyer that was manufactured years after Kitty Hawk. The Benoist planes were not produced for sale until after 1908.

Smithson's face grew crimson. The enormity of his screw up, believing the scenario put forth by Biggs, hit him.

Hell, the Korns actually donated all of their aviation related items to the Wright collection. They weren't even competitors.

Smithson took a moment to compose himself before moving to the next stack.

It appeared that Biggs had invested some time and effort in his search for a plausible wedge to use against the Wright brothers' interests. There was a large file labeled "Dayton Metropolitan Library" filled with papers. These consisted of notes written in Biggs' hand on yet another legal pad as well as photocopies of nearly one hundred yellowed pages. These appeared to be copies made from a manuscript produced on an old typewriter. Smithson examined several sheets and discovered they were from an unpublished composition by Ivonette Wright Miller.

Ivonette was a niece of Wilbur and Orville. She was the daughter of their older brother Lorin. The manuscript was filled with Ivonette's memories of her famous uncles. The copies read like the transcript of a court case, with printed questions, followed by Ivonette's answers. Ensuing sections included answers from other members of the Wright family.

Smithson realized that he was reading a memoir titled "Uncle Wil & Uncle Orv" that while published, was not widely circulated. He looked at Biggs' corresponding notes and saw several interesting facts.

Neil Armstrong took a piece of cloth from the wing of the original Wright Flyer to the moon. Smithson had read this in other places. But the manuscript revealed the cloth was in Armstrong's boot.

How has that not been in print before?

Smithson saw that Biggs had noted "Cassette Side 3" next to this. He stared at this dumbly.

Next was a photocopy from "Cassette Side 4" stating that only one known printed copy of the catalog from the Wright bicycle shop currently existed.

Notes from "Cassette Side 12" mention an organ in the Wright house. That word was circled in red ink. Next to it were the words "Maybe This?"

Fucking Biggs. He was reaching for something to hook me with.

The papers labeled "Cassette Side 14" discussed an Agnes Osborn, who the family members agreed was Orville's girlfriend. Everything Smithson had read indicated that neither Wilbur nor Orville had a romantic relationship with a woman.

Smithson flipped ahead through the stack of notes. He saw there were several more "Cassette Sides" listed. At the bottom of the file was a printed set of instructions under the heading "The Dayton Room-Local History+Geneology." The first line under that read "items were not to be removed from this room." It struck him that Biggs must've sat in a room in the Dayton library for hours listening to old cassettes and making notes and copies of the manuscript pages.

There were what, sixteen sides of cassette tapes? Twenty? How long is a side, a half-hour? An hour? It must've taken him days to do that, maybe weeks.

Smithson went online and checked out Ivonette Wright Miller. The first entry was from *Find a Grave*. She had quite an interesting life. She lived to be ninety-nine. She had christened an aircraft carrier named after her uncles. She and her husband Harold preserved thousands of items that were donated to the Smithsonian, the Library of Congress, and the National Museum of the United States Air Force, among others. On August 29, 1911 at age 15 she went up in a Wright Flyer with Orville. At the time of her death she had been the last living person to fly with one of the Wright Brothers. Ivonette died in 1996 and was buried in Woodland Cemetery in Dayton.

Smithson hesitated.

Woodland?

The doorbell rang. His pizza had arrived.

CHAPTER TWENTY-TWO

When the fingerprint tech had finished with the Grand Cherokee, Lauren and Paul drove home separately. On the way Paul took a call from J.D.'s auto shop.

"Paul? This is Lola from over to J.D.'s."

Paul smiled at her Tennessee accent.

"Oh hi Lola, what's up?"

Lola continued, "We gotcher tires on the Lariat. Ya'll can come pick it up whenever it suits ya." She pronounced tires "tars."

Paul liked Lola. She was a spitfire of a woman from Tellico Plains in the Volunteer State. It was not far from the Tennessee-Georgia-North Carolina tri-state axis so she came by her accent honestly. She met J.D. during his Army years. They'd been together ever since and had raised four sons.

"It'll probably be after you close. I'm kind of on the run right now. Can you lock the keys in the glove box? I'll have Lauren drop me off with the other set later. Okay if I settle up in the next day or two?"

Lola snickered, "My J.D. might never ask you to pay if it weren't fer me. That man likes you." Then, "You weren't an officer were you?"

Paul laughed, "No Lola, tell J.D. thanks. 'Preciate the call."

He disconnected, realizing it had taken him less than thirty seconds to be lulled into Lola-speak.

He could've stopped on the way home and paid for the work. J.D.'s was just a few blocks away and not out of his way. But Paul knew Lauren was anxious to see the house. He didn't want her to wind up there by herself. Not on a day that had already had twin break-ins.

They arrived home. Paul pulled into the garage first, then Lauren. Paul insisted on going into the house before she did. He glanced at the toolbox, thought about grabbing the hammer, shook his head slightly, and pushed through the door.

Lauren entered and looked around apprehensively. After setting down her purse she made a tour of the house. Paul trailed behind. Lauren found Chappy lying on the couch of the front room and bent to scratch behind his ears.

"Are you okay Chappy? Were you scared?" She bent to look him in the face.

Chappy stared back impassively.

Paul pointed out the broken pane on the door. The plywood patch lay underneath where Paul had let it fall.

"That's how they got in. It's actually not as disturbing as how they got in your Jeep."

He almost added the follow-up *you're sure you didn't leave it unlocked?* Paul did not want to be on the receiving end of the look Tommy Walters had experienced earlier in the day.

"Could they have guessed my door code?" She asked this almost to herself, and turned to Paul. "I guess I should change it, right?"

Paul nodded. "I guess it makes sense. Err on the side of caution."

They continued through the house. Lauren froze when she saw the wrecked hair dryer.

"Well, that's disturbing."

Paul agreed, "Yeah, it's the biggest red flag in this whole thing. Makes you wonder if whoever did that is unhinged."

The faux marble vanity top was gouged under the remnants of the dryer.

Lauren commented, "We'll have to turn that in to our insurance. I wanted to remodel in here anyway." She made a vain attempt at a smile then let it die.

Paul said he would call their homeowner's insurance agent in the morning since Lauren would be back at work.

"Well, if I'm going to work tomorrow we'll need a new hair dryer. Maybe we can run out to Meijer after dinner?"

Meijer was a supercenter chain operating in several midwestern states. It was one of the all-things-to-all-people twenty-first century general stores on steroids. It featured thousands of square feet of grocery space and an equal area of clothing, electronics, sporting goods, and just about anything else a shopper needed. There was a Meijer on the west side of Troy near I-75.

"Sounds good. My truck is ready. You can drop me at J.D.'s on the way."

They decided to make loaded baked potatoes for dinner. Paul heated the oven while Lauren busied herself tidying up the walk-in closet. Paul had done a bit of a triage on the strewn clothing. Lauren was now doing surgery.

Paul popped in the potatoes and went to work creating a large salad. He used a number of vegetables from the patio planters.

The oven reached the proper temperature and beeped to notify them. Paul was slicing a cucumber and asked Lauren to bring him the potatoes from the pantry. She turned to approach that part of the kitchen and the camera bag caught her eye.

"Oh, I forgot to unplug the camera. I meant to do that this morning."

She reached for the pantry door and pulled it open. Paul turned to see her busying herself with moving food out of the way so she could get to the camera.

He froze, thinking *The camera? What possible reason would someone have to break in for the camera? Everyone has one on their phone now.*

But he made a mental note.

Lauren took a call during dinner. It was Marge McClary, calling to coordinate some things for her and Mike's party Saturday. Each couple brought a side dish to these parties and attendees helped themselves. There was no entrée, so Marge called or texted in advance to try to limit duplication. Paul listened to Lauren's side of the conversation for a few minutes. When his wife brought up the break-ins, Paul could hear Marge's voice rise and made out the words "Oh my god, are you alright?!?"

Within a minute Paul received a text on his phone from Mike. He had obviously been within earshot of Marge.

WTF?

Paul answered, typing details of the incidents. Their text conversation went on for a few minutes. At the end, Mike asked if Paul wanted to skip helping load wood the following day.

I can get someone else, no problem

Paul responded, *No worries, I'm in. Will see you then.*

The phone and text conversations ended within a minute of each other and the Hulls returned to their salads and potatoes.

After dinner they took the Jeep to J.D.'s. Paul jumped out with the extra set of keys and turned to Lauren.

"Don't be too long out there. Pick out a dryer and come home. If you don't like it tomorrow we'll get a different one. Just...don't take too long."

Lauren saw the concern in his eyes and tried to brush it away.

"I'll be fine Paul, it's just a quick trip to the store."

It was 8:10 p.m. and the sun was just setting. The moon, now full, was rising on the opposite horizon. Though the temperature still hovered near eighty degrees, a slight dip in the humidity level gave relief from the heat of the day.

Paul watched her pull away, then pulled up the Find My iPhone app so he could follow her progress.

The pizza was from a place called "Marion's Piazza." They had nine locations in the Dayton area and according to the information online had been voted as having the city's best pizza several times. Smithson had actually ordered two larges with pepperoni, mushroom, and banana peppers. He wasn't sure exactly how long he'd be at the house and figured anything he didn't eat tonight would be versatile enough to fill in, hot or cold, as a breakfast, lunch, or dinner. While on the DoorDash app he saw Marion's sold beer. He checked the selection and saw they offered Warped Wing Flyer Red.

Oh I gotta try that stuff.

The delivery was made by a gangly young man that was probably exactly what he looked like, a college freshman trying to earn beer money. Smithson opened the door and the kid, overburdened by the pizzas and twin six-packs, screeched "DoorDash, sir."

As Smithson reached for the boxes he saw the kid look past him, apparently searching for other occupants that would help devour the pies.

Smithson grabbed the pizzas and snapped at him.

"It's just me, alright? Yeah, that's right....one fuckin' guy is gonna eat both pizzas!"

The kid put his right hand up. His left still balanced the six-packs.

"I'm sorry sir, I didn't—"

"What the fuck kind of customer service are they teaching you jackasses?"

Smithson snatched the beer and slammed the door.

He returned to the dining room and dropped the pizza boxes on the table.

Seems like every damn time I have food delivered they send somebody with a real attitude. It's bullshit.

Smithson had long ago set a policy of giving the minimum fifteen percent tip when using online food delivery services. Unfortunately it was customary to select the tip before the delivery was made. He had actually looked into the process of how to lower a tip after the fact and found it was possible but not really worth the effort.

If I have to go to that much trouble I might as well turn Grey loose on them.

He smiled, considering.

The pizza and beer were both more than acceptable. Smithson devoured all but two pieces of the first large pie before sliding it into the refrigerator to join its twin. He took it easy on the Warped Wings, limiting himself to four cans. He admired the design. It was a red can with a white band displaying the word "Flyer" prominently. Below that in a blue oval was a design that drew Smithson's attention. It was a representation of wings being warped. He thought this visual did as good a job as anything explaining the concept. Lord knew it was difficult to read a description and come away with a full understanding.

While eating and drinking Smithson shifted his attention from the Biggs hard copies to files Grey had assembled on the Toughbook. He was particularly interested in two areas.

The first was a wedge. He always looked for a wedge. The wife was the obvious answer. He had already proven that he was a danger to her by getting into her Jeep. Smithson could use threats against Lauren to control her husband. But he suspected Paul might just cling to her like a bodyguard once he became completely aware of the situation they were in. If the Hulls had children, *that* would be the answer. But they didn't so he had to find something else. Or rather Grey did.

It appeared that the couple had close friends in Dayton, a Mike and Marge McClary.

Hmmmm, but who really gives a shit about their friends?

He continued through the report. The wife's mother was living in New Mexico. One brother was still at the same address, one living on his own.

New Mexico is two states away from Boulder City. If it became necessary to make a physical threat on them I could do it, but Biggs' body could turn up at any time. The logistics just don't work.

The husband's parents were in Florida.

Same logistics.

Then he got to the sister.

Patrice Chamberlain was forty-four years old. She lived in Columbus, Ohio with her husband, Kevin, and two sons, Leo and Frankie.

Now we're getting somewhere.

Smithson went to the geo data on the Escape and the Grand Cherokee and saw that both vehicles made semi-regular trips to Columbus. The sister's address was associated with the trips most of the time. Occasionally the destinations were elsewhere in Columbus. Smithson found the Columbus Zoo and The Ohio State University on the list as well as something called

COSI. He checked online and saw that this was the Center of Science and Industry.

Looks like Uncle Paul and Aunt Lauren like to broaden the horizons of their precious nephews.

Smithson next pulled up records of calls and texts to Patrice and found that combined there were over one hundred in the last six months alone.

Bingo, I can threaten the sister and her kids.

Smithson took a final pull on his second beer and opened a third.

Now that he had found the wedge, he turned his attention to the second key area. How would he actually use the wedge? How could he use it to get physical possession of the camera and SD card before it found its way into the hands of law enforcement?

He had the genesis of an idea when reviewing the Biggs material. The husband, Paul, seemed to be a Wright brothers buff. He had a stack of books on the subject in his office. Searching his memory he believed that some of the material on top of the desk was also related to the brothers

What are the chances that I get to screw with ANOTHER guy that is interested in the Wrights? Until I started Operation Crank I don't remember a time in my life that I gave two shits about them. Now, Biggs, then this guy Hull.

Then the sharper part of his mind cut through the thin alcohol haze.

Dumbass, of course he had Wright brothers stuff at his house. Who the hell else would show up in the middle of nowhere to look at the site where Wilbur was born?

Smithson continued through the data. Halfway through his fourth and final beer of the evening he gave Grey another task.

Locate all references to the Wright brothers in Paul Hull's online history. Correlate and plot on area map all corresponding physical coincidences with vehicles or cell phone.

He watched the blinking cursor. There was no additional information on the missing pickup truck. But Smithson knew it wasn't at the house. The husband, the wife, and their two primary vehicles were all accounted for when Smithson broke into the house and he knew the truck wasn't there. It must've been on loan to someone, he knew pickup owners did that often. Whatever, it was a small data point in a larger picture that was becoming clearer.

Smithson hit send.

CHAPTER TWENTY-THREE

FRIDAY

It was 8:15 a.m. Friday morning and Granger Gorsuch was whistling a happy tune. This would seem odd for most people if they'd experienced his last hour firsthand. Granger had picked up the stinking carcasses of two groundhogs, a raccoon, and an overripe skunk by himself. In addition, his partner had helped him wrestle the remains of a large female deer onto the liftgate.

But Granger was a happy sort. He was twenty-two years old and had a job with the state. He was set for life. He and his partner, Anthony Joseph Voit, worked for the Indiana Department of Transportation, or INDOC. They were based out of the Greenfield District, which was one of six in the state. Greenfield was located ten miles east of Indianapolis on I-70.

Granger sat in the passenger seat of the white Ford F-550 flatbed crew cab. The truck featured side gates to compliment the rear liftgate and sported the blue and yellow INDOC seal on both front doors.

Voit always drove. Both men knew that INDOC policy was that the two-man crews were to rotate but Granger didn't mind sitting on the passenger side. It allowed him to be slightly more attentive scanning the roads for victims and the sky for carrion. He believed it was a difference-maker in the long-running informal contest he participated in with a friend, Whitey Stanley, on the other roadkill crew in the district. Both he and Whitey bought five-dollar scratch off lottery tickets and put them in an envelope every Monday. At the end of the week whoever had accumulated the most points—there was a points system—earned the tickets.

Voit loved to drive. He told people it was in his blood. He was named after four-time Indy 500 champion A.J. Foyt, a tough talking Texan. Foyt started in thirty-five consecutive Indy 500s, beginning the streak in 1957. He was a love-him-or-hate-him sort. Voit's dad loved him.

His son loved his name, *A.J. Voit.*

Being named by their fathers was one of the few things Granger and A.J. had in common. Granger was a twin. On the day he and his brother were conceived, a Saturday, their father got a haircut and attended a meeting at Fairview Grange #2177 in Goshen, Indiana. Barber and Granger arrived nine months later. Granger often wondered how the name thing would have shaken out if his dad had eaten at Wendy's instead of going to the barber.

They were traveling westbound on Indiana State Route 38. They'd picked up the groundhogs and the skunk at three different points on I-70. The raccoon was collected on Indiana State Route 1. INDOC was responsible for roadkill pickup on state and federal highways. As on most days they began their morning by rolling east on I-70. They almost always had a list of dead animal locations, known as the "Hit List," in hand before leaving the garage. Their supervisor posted it with a magnetic clip on the breakroom refrigerator. This had been a point of contention for a number of the INDOC road crew workers as they didn't like to start their days, and in some cases their breakfasts, staring at a list of dead animals.

Granger thought it was funny.

The pair had clocked in minutes before their 7 a.m. start time. After filling their travel mugs with coffee and doctoring them appropriately they pulled the list from the refrigerator and were out the door. It was a light day. The three smaller animals were all located at points on I-70 between the garage and State Route 1, thirty-five miles to the east. No calls had come in about roadkill east of Route 1. There were no deer strikes reported on this day on I-70—a bit of a rarity.

In addition to making the pick-ups on the morning list, they were to look for targets of opportunity. These were typically fresh kills. Crews often reached these animals before rigor set in. There were no additional pick-ups to be made this morning on the stretch to Route 1 so the pair appeared to have a light day ahead of them.

The next animal on their list was the doe. She was to their north, just outside of Hagerstown on State Route 38. After the pair slid the doe onto the liftgate Granger used the hydraulic controls to first raise the animal to the level of the bed, then to angle the gate until the deer tumbled deeper into it. A.J. stood to the side, unwrapping a Swisher Sweet Blunt cigar. The deer secure, both men returned to the truck.

"What's next on the list?"

A.J.'s question had to work its way past the cigar that was now in his mouth. He sucked on the Swishers, never lighting up. There was a strict no smoking policy in the state vehicles. A.J. had to constantly remind himself to not touch the cigar with his gloved hand after handling a carcass.

Granger looked concerned.

"Nothing until we get up to 36. Whitey has me right now."

A.J. did not take part in the contest. A light day on a Friday meant an early return to the garage where they could take their time delivering their cargo to the incinerator before pressure washing the bed and putting the truck away until Monday. Then they would wait for the time clock to reach 4 p.m. and head home.

They were running parallel to State Route 36. To reach it they had to take county roads. Though not responsible for removals on these tracks they would occasionally do the county crews a solid and clear a larger animal. They never stopped on county roads for something small.

They turned north on North County Road 750E and were five miles from linking up with 36 when the ever vigilant Granger, eyes squinting, said, "I think we might have something."

A.J. looked in the distance but saw nothing that got his attention.

"What? Where?"

"Up there, not quite a half mile. By that little group of buildings. See the buzzards?"

A.J. adjusted his gaze.

"Granger, I'm telling you. If a Sasquatch ever got hit by a train in the middle of the night and knocked into a field ten miles from nowhere, you'd make history and find the damn thing."

Granger snorted.

"Whitey and I actually have a Sasquatch on our points list... worth a hunnert."

They drew closer and saw there were several buzzards circling to the right of the buildings. It looked like they were centered above a cornfield across the road. No roadkill was visible.

"Pull up there A.J. I'll get out and check the ditch."

Voit removed his Swisher and said "Not our monkey, not our circus, Granger."

"Aww, c'mon A.J. We'll get back to the garage early either way. Plus if we call the boys over at Henry County and tell them, they'll owe us one."

A.J. caved.

"What the hell."

The F-550 eased to the side of the road. A.J. engaged the flashers as Granger hopped out and surveyed the ditch.

"I don't see it. Mighta' gotten knocked into the corn. Think I'll take a look."

A.J. shook his head and stepped out of the truck himself. His attention was drawn to a bronze marker across from the cornfield. He checked for traffic then walked toward the marker, his eyes on the words, *BIRTHPLACE OF WILBUR WRIGHT*.

A.J.'s attention was sidetracked a moment later as Granger's voice rose from inside the cornfield.

"Uh, A.J.? Better c'mere."

CHAPTER TWENTY-FOUR

Paul and Lauren were up early again on Friday morning. Lauren showered while Paul made for the kitchen. He decided to make something light today. After starting the coffee he sliced a pineapple and toasted cinnamon raisin bagels. He made sure that the setting on Lauren's side of the toaster was suitably light.

Chappy padded into the kitchen and hopped up onto the island. Paul looked at the cat with exasperation. Chappy was told to get down every time he did this. It never helped. They kept a yellow squirt gun in a basket on the island and used it to deter the cat. It was usually effective in hastening Chappy's retreat but the cat's memory was short, or non-existent, and he would be back up minutes later.

Paul looked for the basket but it was gone, no doubt moved by Lauren during yesterdays clean up. He put both elbows on the island and rested his chin in his hands. Chappy had tucked his front paws underneath his body giving him the appearance of a nesting hen.

A thought occurred to Paul. He and Lauren watched a Netflix documentary about cats a few weeks earlier. One segment focused on ways to form a better link with your pet. They key component of the segment was the "slow blink." Studies showed that cats with close ties to their owners often showed this by looking them in the eyes and blinking at them very slowly, sometimes more than once. These same studies postulated that owners that returned the blink were communicating in a positive fashion.

What the heck, nothing else seems to work.

Paul looked directly at Chappy and slowly closed his eyes before opening them at the same speed. The cat looked at him as if he were deranged. Paul imagined a thought bubble above

Chappy's head, filled with the words "Maybe I need a new owner."

"Good morning boys, having a heart to heart?"

Lauren smiled as she breezed into the kitchen and reached for a coffee mug.

Paul smiled back sheepishly.

"I was trying that slow blink thing on Chappy. Guess what?"

"He just stared back at you?"

"Like I was a lunatic."

Lauren was giggling at this twenty minutes later as she drove to work. For all Paul had experienced in the military, she still liked to think of him as kind-hearted. He would've made such a great father. She watched him interact with their friends' kids and Patrice's sons in Columbus. He lit up when he was around them.

He reminded her of her dad.

When Lauren was born, the story went, both parents agreed the new baby brightened their lives. So much so that they considered a name that reflected this.

"What about a flower? Her mom had asked.

"Well," her dad began, "the state flower of New Mexico is the blossom of the Desert Yucca Plant. I don't think 'Lauren Yucca Silva' has much of a ring to it."

Her mom laughed and said "How about the national flower?"

Lauren Rose Silva it was.

Joe Silva was a patriotic guy and couldn't resist the symbolism, especially since it was attached to his only daughter. Years later, when Lauren and Paul were dating, she overheard her dad telling the story to her future husband. The men were in the Silva garage. Joe had asked Paul to help lift some old furniture into the bed of his pickup truck. The job complete, Joe retrieved two bottles of Dos Equis from the garage refrigerator. It was a beat up old Frigidaire that was covered with decals, many of which displayed some form of the United States flag.

180

Lauren was inside the house and had intended to grab a soft drink from that same refrigerator. As she turned the knob she heard the men talking and hesitated. Could Paul be asking for her dad's blessing and permission to marry her? She put her ear to the door in time to hear her dad finish the "Lauren Rose" story. Then she heard two bottles clink and Paul's voice.

"That's a damn good story, Joe."

At the time Lauren rolled her eyes. She was primed to eavesdrop on one of the most memorable events of her life. Instead she got an old soldier and a future Combat Controller toasting the connection between her middle name and the national flower.

The proposal eventually came. Her dad was there to give her away. Lauren would never forget how proud he was that day, just as she had always been proud of him. She remembered the time in February 2008 when one of the Navy SEALs that Paul had worked with was killed in a training accident. His funeral was at Arlington National Cemetery. Joe had met the SEAL at a military event a couple years earlier when he was visiting Lauren and Paul. Joe and the SEAL had hit it off, discussing their love of 1957 Chevys. The SEAL owned one and Joe had always wanted to. Joe asked Paul if it would be appropriate for him to attend the funeral. When told it would be fine, he traveled across the country, quietly paid his respects, and excused himself from the ceremonies, returning to New Mexico. More than one of the frogman's teammates commented on Joe's attendance, saying it was "damn classy."

At their wedding Joe's Father-of-the-Bride speech concluded with "Paul, take care of my girl." Paul had simply nodded. And he *was* taking care of her.

Lauren lost her dad in 2022. It still hurt. It always would. But she still had Paul, even after all the times she could have lost him. She realized her eyes were now full and wiped at a tear as she came to Piqua-Troy Road at the end of Polecat. Her left turn signal was on and she waited on traffic coming from her right.

Paul was an anachronism. He was a terrific partner that quickly earned the friendship and respect of others. He was also a warrior so efficient that many of the country's most elite combatants praised his abilities. She had heard them with her own ears. Many times. At a party a few years earlier she found herself in a corner of the room with Gatewood. After more than a few adult beverages he nodded at Paul, who was across the room, and sung his praises.

But she, of course, had never seen this side of her husband. That was reserved for his deployments. The Paul she experienced firsthand kidded her for doing the Jeep Wave to other Jeep drivers. He made omelets in the morning, geeked out on history, and fought comical losing battles with Chappy.

The last vehicle in line had its left signal on. As Lauren waited for it to turn onto Polecat she realized it was also a Jeep Grand Cherokee. She smiled and raised the first two fingers of her right hand. The other driver returned the wave, and the smile.

Lauren thought this was a sign that it would be a good day. The smile stayed with her until she reached the Kettering Health parking lot. She glimpsed to her left and saw the space that her Jeep occupied yesterday during the break-in. Her smile disappeared and the words Gatewood has spoken at the party came to her.

"Woe to the sonofabitch that messes with your husband, Lauren Rose."

After Lauren left for work Paul cleaned up the kitchen then changed into his workout clothes. He had a completely different routine in mind today. He went downstairs to the exercise area. He looked at the whiteboard with his hands on his hips. The components of two supersets were written there. He reviewed them as he stretched, then got started.

Paul completed the first superset in twenty-five minutes. It consisted of multiple sets of bench presses, renegade rows, band pull-aparts, and hammer curls. After a break of a few minutes for water and to towel off, he jumped right into superset two.

A half hour later a thoroughly worn out Paul climbed back up the steps. He had finished off multiple sets of barbell deadlifts, banded good mornings, mountain climbers, and crunchy frogs and was feeling every one of his 50 years. He carried a fresh towel and his water bottle into his office, making sure to close the door before Chappy came in. He thought he'd get in another bike ride this morning on the path before the weekend joggers and cyclists took it over.

First, though, he would check again for any news on the Wilbur Wright site in Indiana. The break-ins of the previous day had pushed the incident to the back burner.

Paul opened his laptop. He decided to check the weather before getting on with his search. He saw that the current pattern of temperatures in the high-eighties with mid to high humidity would continue until at least Sunday when a front was due to bring rain and possible thunderstorms.

Maybe a little shorter ride today, then go long tomorrow before the weather changes? Might not get a ride in Sunday.

Paul then navigated to the Dayton Dragons homepage. The Dragons were a minor league affiliate of the Cincinnati Reds. They began play in Dayton in 2000 in what is now known as Day Air Ballpark. The team received fantastic support from the fans in Dayton and the surrounding communities. He searched to see how the team fared yesterday but found no score.

Oh yeah, Thursdays are travel days in the Midwest League. The Dragons just started a road trip and are out of town until next Friday.

That done, he found the Henry County, Indiana Sheriff's homepage and searched for the log.

And there it was.

7:44 p.m. Wednesday. Deputies responded to a report of unlocked doors at the Wilbur Wright Birthplace Museum, 1525 N. County Rd. 750E. Deputies found no evidence of foul play. Staff was contacted to secure site.

"That's it?"

Paul allowed himself a short laugh.

183

*I guess someone really DID just leave the doors unlocked.
Well, hope they didn't get chewed out too bad.*

Paul closed the laptop and slowly spun his office chair. He looked out the window at the woods in the distance. The sun was well above the horizon in the east and he could sense the heat beginning to build outside.

The incident in Indiana hadn't been particularly frightening. Just...odd. But the break-ins the following day, the destroyed hair dryer, the failure of the security cameras at the hospital...could this all be coincidence?

Paul had begun to think it was all related. But the innocuous entry in the Henry County Sheriff's Log eased his concern.

He heard Chappy pawing at the door. He spun his chair in the direction of the door and his eyes fell on the photo of the Wright Flyer circling the Statue of Liberty. It was one of Paul's favorite images. It was taken in 1909 during the New York Hudson-Fulton Celebration, an event honoring the one hundredth anniversary of Robert Fulton's first commercial paddle steamer and the three hundredth anniversary of Henry Hudson's discovery of the Hudson River. The photo had been crooked yesterday when the fingerprint tech checked the room.

"Better check that for prints," the tech said as he stared at musky streaks on the glass.

Paul told him not to bother.

"No, I think there was definitely some unusual contact here," insisted the tech as he leaned closer.

Paul smiled remembering his reply and the tech's mystified expression.

"Have you ever heard of interdigital glands?"

Paul made a note to remember to call the insurance company after his ride. He opened the door slowly, careful not to injure Chappy. After reclosing the door he headed to the bedroom to change into his biking gear. Chappy resumed pawing at the door.

Now changed, Paul refilled his water bottle in the kitchen then dropped the insurance reminder note on the island. As he reached for the door to the garage his eyes fell briefly on the camera bag. He hesitated for the briefest of seconds then walked out to begin his ride.

CHAPTER TWENTY-FIVE

Smithson woke up at 7:35. His head ached slightly from the beer the night before. He used the bathroom before making his way to the kitchen. He opened the refrigerator and removed the pizza box that held the two surviving slices. Sitting the box on the dining room table, he opened the Toughbook and began the protocol to link to Grey. While the laptop was doing its thing Smithson reached for one of the slices.

Mmmmm, banana peppers on cold breakfast pizza...very underrated.

The Wright Flyer appeared on the screen as the connection was made and began to glide. Smithson preferred to work with a "hot corners" type of screen set-up when he was coordinating data for an operation. It allowed him to quickly switch from one window to another. He first checked for warnings from Henry County. There was no new information, meaning Biggs was still in his uninterrupted deep sleep in the cornfield.

What was that saying? *Sleep the sleep of the just.* What the hell did that mean exactly? Smithson googled it.

"Noun. A deep and worry-free sleep."

Smithson smiled and took another bite of pizza.

He selected another screen, the one containing information on Hull's sister. Grey had assembled an impressive amount of data on her and her family. Smithson knew this was culled primarily from open source material such as employer and school district websites as well as the typical social media goldmines of Facebook, Instagram, et cetera.

The family lived in a house on the west side of Columbus in the suburb of Hilliard. Their address was on Hayden Run Road.

Well, doesn't that sound fucking exclusive?

Patrice worked from home. It looked like she actually did so even before the pandemic. The practice was so widespread now that it didn't raise an eyebrow. Smithson had come to believe that the American work force was morphing into a bunch of lazy bastards wearing pajamas, at home on their computers.

He reached down to his underwear, scratched himself, and continued.

Patrice Chamberlain worked for the National Veterans Memorial and Museum. Her title was "Event Sales Coordinator."

The building opened in 2018. It had a modernistic look that, Smithson mused, must've been a bitch to build. The information he found showed that it encompassed fifty-three thousand square feet and cost over seventy-five million dollars. It housed thousands of artifacts and its mission was to tell the story of the American veteran.

The facility also featured expansive sections that could be used for temporary exhibits, speaking engagements, or even outside group functions. This is where Patrice came in. She coordinated events involving Columbus-area firms that made use of the space for a unique experience. Smithson saw that a local investment firm had recently held a catered customer appreciation dinner in the building that, if social media postings could be trusted, seemed to have been quite well received.

Patrice networked with companies all across the region. It looked like she had an office in the building a few doors down from the retired Army General who was the President and CEO. She spent time in the building when doing walk-throughs with clients when they were in house to review the set-up options. But most of her work was done from home. She was evidently able to shoehorn many of her phone and video calls around the schedule requirements of her two boys.

Kevin Chamberlain, her husband, worked as a structural engineer. He was a well-respected member of his firm's staff. The company was located in downtown Columbus. He had a company parking pass that was linked to a digital log. It showed he spent long days at the office followed by two or three days away. Smithson added a task to Grey's list.

Check airline records from Columbus airport for Kevin Chamberlain's travel schedule.

Smithson had a hunch that Patrice's husband may have been traveling to building sites during these absences from the office. It would be a welcome development if he were out of town now. Patrice would be unprotected. Smithson's mind considered how he could use this to influence Hull. He let this incubate as he swallowed a piece of crust and reached for the second slice.

The boys were in the Hilliard school district, which had just begun the new school year this week. The system consisted of fourteen K-5 elementary schools that fed into two buildings that housed sixth-graders exclusively. The students then funneled into one of three middle schools. Finally, they would attend Darby, Davidson, or Bradley High School. The method for determining who goes where was not clear to Smithson, but he didn't concern himself with this. Right now the older boy, Leo, was an eighth-grader at Heritage Middle School and Frankie a sixth-grader at Hilliard Station.

Smithson instructed Grey to access bus timetables and extracurricular activity schedules for both boys. He gazed at the screen, wondering if he had forgotten anything. Deciding not, he opened the file that included Paul Hull's geo data in relation to known Wright brother sites.

As it loaded, Smithson sucked at a small piece of pepperoni that had wedged between two of his upper teeth. They were #9, his central incisor and #10, his lateral incisor. Smithson memorized much of the dental tooth chart after the *Demon's Souls* 2020 game for PS5 was introduced. It allowed players to customize teeth when using the create-a-character feature. Smithson was able to slap some absolutely gnarly sets on his personas.

Kudos to Bluepoint Games.

The pepperoni remained stuck so he used a fingernail to loosen it, not considering it was the same finger he'd just used to scratch himself. The data loaded, it displayed on the screen, and Smithson leaned in.

Grey had configured the information in such a way that Smithson could instantly process it. The screen showed an overview of the entire Dayton region. It stretched from Troy, north of the city, to Springboro, a suburb several miles south. Wright brothers related sites were indicated by blue stars. They were sprinkled across the map with a number of them concentrated in the west-central section of the city.

If the geo data showed that Paul's phone had been to a site, a red "P" flashed beside it. Similarly, a green "E" or a black "J" indicated the Escape or the Jeep had been there. Smithson did not have Grey track the wife's phone. He wanted to know where the husband had been, with either vehicle. If Lauren had been to a site without him it was inconsequential.

Smithson would be dealing with Paul alone.

If the data he was viewing gave him what he hoped, the interaction would be decisive.

And final.

Smithson examined the screen. The overhead map perspective combined with the flashing icons reminded Smithson of an in-game map from a first person shooter game.

His eyes narrowed slightly and his fingers hovered over the keyboard of the Toughbook. He began his review.

The site closest to Troy, northeast of Dayton proper, was the Huffman Prarie Flying Field Interpretive Center. It was located adjacent to Wright-Patterson Air Force Base in Fairborn. The elevation lines showed that it was a raised area of ground. Smithson checked Grey's attached notes and saw that the site was managed by the National Park Service. The elevation, Smithson saw, was due to the fact that the center was built on what was designated as "Wright Hill." A seventeen-foot pink granite obelisk known as the "Wright Brothers Memorial" had been dedicated there on Orville's sixty-ninth birthday, August 19, 1940. He was in attendance.

Both Paul's phone and his Escape had been to this site twice in the last year.

Wilbur and Orville had used a nearby piece of property known as Huffman Prarie to perfect their Flyer after the first flight in December 1903. Their work here in 1904 and 1905 resulted in what came to be known the first "practical" flight. Huffman Prarie was now an eighty-four acre site, designated as a National Historic Landmark in 1990. It was located roughly two miles northeast of the Interpretive Center and was surrounded by Wright–Patterson Air Force Base.

Paul's phone and his Escape had been to this site once.

Smithson shifted his attention to the sites closer to downtown Dayton. The Engineer's Club of Dayton was located at 110 East Monument Avenue. The building sat just yards from the Great Miami River as it meandered through the downtown area. It was a grandiose building, founded in 1914 by Dayton icons Charles Kettering and Colonel Edward Deeds. Orville Wright spoke at the opening on February 2, 1918 and later served as the club's fourth president. One of Dayton's nine "Bowler Benches" stands outside of the building. These were bronze benches cast by sculptor David Black in 1996. Each of the nine features two bowler hats in the style often worn by the brothers.

Hull's phone had been to the club three times, his Escape twice. His wife's Jeep had been there once. Apparently the couple has gone together once in her vehicle.

Nearby, at 111 West Monument, was the First Baptist Church. The large gothic structure was the site of Orville's funeral on February 2, 1948, a grand affair that brought Dayton to a standstill.

There was no evidence to indicate Hull had visited the site. In theory this made it a candidate for the final phase of Smithson's plan. But Smithson did not believe it was a suitable setting for what he had in mind. This was not because it was a religious structure. No, it was because it was located in the downtown area and presented many difficulties to his egress.

The site furthest to the west was the Wright Company Factory at 99 Cowart Avenue. It was the first factory built in America for the purpose of manufacturing airplanes. Located roughly two miles west of downtown Dayton, it was a multi-building complex that had been closed to the public since 2008. Building 1 was completed in 1910. The complex grew and changed hands several times. At the time of its closing the facility manufactured auto parts for Delphi. The site was currently in planning by the National Park Service and managed by the City of Dayton. Overhead views showed the buildings were surrounded by open concrete, apparently former parking lots. It appeared to be protected by fencing that separated it from residential neighborhoods on three sides.

Neither Hull's phone nor his vehicles had been to the site, making it a candidate for the final phase.

Just over a mile east of the complex, nearer the center of town, were two sites that sat within a couple blocks of each other.

The Wright Cycle Shop was located at 22 Williams Street. It was a two-story brick building that housed the brothers' business from 1895 to 1897. The Wrights used profits from their bicycle business to help fund their aeronautical studies. The Wright Cycle Company successively occupied six different locations over the years with this being the only existing building on its original foundation and in its original location. The building that housed the last location of the cycle business, at 1127 West Third Street, was moved to Greenfield Village in Dearborn, Michigan by Henry Ford in 1937, with Orville's blessing.

The Wright family house where the brothers lived with their father Milton and sister Katharine was located two short blocks to the south at 7 Hawthorn Street. This was one of the most famous private residence addresses in United States history. The house itself was also moved to Greenfield Village. A recreated facade of the porch stands on the property on its original location.

Hull's phone and Escape had been to both the cycle shop and 7 Hawthorn on two occasions.

To the east, on the other side of I-75, the north-south artery that acted as a dividing line for the city, was Woodland Cemetery. Smithson popped the last of the second piece of cold pizza into his mouth. He had run across this site in the Biggs research on Ivonette Wright Miller. It featured two hundred acres of rolling hills set in an urban area. Stewart Street, which bordered Woodland on the south, separated it from the University of Dayton campus. A number of famous figures from American history were interred in the cemetery. None, however, were more famous than Wilbur and Orville Wright.

The phone and vehicle data showed that Hull had not been there. This was a second possibility for the end game.

A mile or so southwest of Woodland sat Carillon Park, a sixty-five acre open-air history museum. It housed a phenomenal collection of significant historical artifacts. Most had local connections. The shining star of the park was the Wright Brothers National Museum. It housed the only airplane designated a National Historic Landmark, the 1905 Wright Flyer III. Orville was involved with preserving the plane for Carillon, his last major project before dying in 1948. He had a hand in selecting the site of Wright Hall, the building that housed the Flyer, but did not live to witness the park's opening in 1950.

Paul's phone had been there twice. The Escape and Jeep once each.

A mile southeast of Carillon Park, and less than two miles south of Woodland Cemetery, stood Hawthorn Hill, which some called "Orville Wright's success mansion." Both Wilbur and Orville planned the mansion, but the older brother succumbed to typhoid fever before it was completed in 1914. It sat on a rise in the fashionable suburb of Oakwood. Its white pillars and twin porches reminded some of the White House.

Paul's phone had been there, as had Lauren's Jeep. Apparently the couple visited together. Smithson saw that the visit was on a Saturday. He checked the Hawthorn Hill website and saw that tours were offered on a limited schedule and had to be accessed via a shuttle from Carillon Park. The Hull's visit to Hawthorn Hill corresponded with one of their visits to Carillon.

Lastly, twelve miles south of downtown Dayton on North Springfield Pike in Miamisburg, was Wright B Flyer, Inc. This was a free museum that offered flights on a Wright B Flyer lookalike. It housed historical exhibits on the brothers and their path to powered flight. To Smithson, it appeared to be a hangar-like building near a small airfield.

Paul's phone and Escape had been there once.

So, there was the intel. Grey had assembled it. It was up to Smithson to sift through it and finalize his plan. Two sites stood out, the Wright Company Factory complex and Woodland Cemetery. He needed to recon both sites. He checked the time and saw that it was nearly 8:30.

Smithson headed for the bedroom. He needed to put on a clean hoodie.

CHAPTER TWENTY-SIX

Paul removed his bike from the rack and walked it out of the garage. He leaned it against the Lariat and slid the water bottle into the holder connected to the bottom tube. He attached his phone to its central position on the handlebars. Before mounting he reached back with his left hand as he raised his foot. He found the front of his shoe and gently pulled it upward. Though technically this was a quad stretch, Paul found it useful to gauge the level of strain on his injured femur. The earlier exercise session had been strenuous.

Hmmm, not bad. I think it might be time to stop worrying about this leg.

Paul walked the bike up the lane. He checked for traffic on Polecat, started the MapMyRun app, and was off. He rode west on Polecat with the sun at his back before taking a right at Piqua-Troy Road. Less than a mile later he turned west again on Eldean Road. He climbed a slight rise and was rewarded with a view of Eldean Bridge ahead on his left.

At 231 feet, the bridge was the longest Long Truss style structure remaining in the country. It was built in 1860 and for decades served as the main means of transiting the Great Miami River for residents of farms and small towns in the vicinity. The bridge was no longer on Eldean Road. The modern version of the road now ran slightly to the north over a newer bridge. The bypassed bridge was kept intact nearby and could be accessed by runners and walkers.

Paul looked at the red wooden siding of the old bridge as he crossed the river and smiled. A few yards ahead, a bike path intersected with the road. This was the Great Miami River Recreational Trail. Paul turned north on the trail and picked up his pace. Again, there was little traffic. Within a few hundred yards the path was swallowed by wooded terrain that would follow the river north for four miles before reaching Piqua.

Paul loved this stretch. It provided shade that he always appreciated when returning home from a hard ride. Today, though, he planned to keep the distance and intensity on the lighter side. The relative coolness of this section of the path always seemed to put his mind on automatic pilot. This morning was no exception.

Paul thought of some of the men he'd served with. After completing the Pipeline he was assigned to the 21st Special Tactics Squadron. This was a fantastic unit with an impressive history. In fact John Chapman had been in the 21st before going through selection for the 24th STS.

The Two Four, though, was operating at an entirely different level. It was a component of JSOC, the Joint Special Operations Command. This command oversees the Special Mission Units of the United States. These were the U.S. military's Tier One units. The ones Hollywood made movies about.

The two most well know were the Army's 1st Special Forces Operational Detachment-Delta, commonly known as Delta Force, and the Navy's Naval Special Warfare Development Group, known as DevGru, or SEAL Team 6. These were the military's premier counter-terrorism units. The 24th STS attached personnel to Delta and DevGru as enablers to provide air traffic control and fire support. This created a lethal symbiosis in the Global War On Terror.

The American public had the impression that the Tier One units were extremely capable.

They had no idea.

It would be difficult to determine the effectiveness of these units in terms of enemies killed or captured, but suffice it to say the percentage that the Tier Ones were responsible for far exceeded their size. Published reports say that by 2006 Delta was running three hundred missions a month and by 2009 fifty percent of their operators had been awarded the Purple Heart.

SEAL Team 6 was running a similarly high volume of missions. Operators, most of whom had several deployments under their belts, were honing their craft with real world missions, sometimes more than once a night. And it *was* typically at night. The men took on the hours of vampires, sleeping during the day and hunting at night. Occasionally there was a highly publicized hostage rescue missions or the elimination of a High Value Target, or HVT. These missions made headlines for a day or two before fading as the public anticipated the next news cycle.

Then came Operation Neptune Spear, the killing of al Qaeda mastermind Osama bin Laden, on May 1, 2011. It was accomplished by Red Squadron of SEAL Team 6. The attention of the world was on America's Tier One units. This mission, carried out with specially modified stealth helicopters, came to be held up in the media as the ultimate achievement of United States Special Operations.

But not by Paul.

He had worked with several of the Red Squadron assaulters in the past. He certainly wasn't on the helos with them that night, but had no doubt they performed with incredible skill.

The press focused on certain types of missions. Hostage rescues were a good example. On December 8, 2012, SEAL Team 6 was tasked with the rescue of an American citizen, Dr. Dilip Joseph, in Afghanistan. Petty Officer 1st Class Nicolas Cheque was shot and killed when entering the compound where the hostage was held. His teammate, Ed Byers, rushed through the door and engaged several terrorists. He killed two, immobilized a third until another member of the team eliminated him, and threw his own body over Joseph to protect him. Byers—also the units' medic—then tried to resuscitate Checque.

On October 22, 2015, Delta Master Sergeant Joshua Wheeler was part of a combined operation in Iraq. Thirty American special operators and a number of Kurdish counter terrorist soldiers assaulted an ISIS prison that held approximately seventy hostages. Information indicated the hostages were in imminent danger of being executed and that their graves had already been prepared. When a group of assaulters breached the compound and were pinned down by gunfire, Wheeler climbed a wall to get to them and was killed by enemy fire. Delta trooper Thomas Payne braved severe enemy fire to cut the locks from the cell doors.

Byers and Payne were deservedly awarded the Medal of Honor for their actions. The deeds of all four men gave the public a glimpse at the level of skill and dedication manifested by those on the JSOC rosters.

But for Paul, the capabilities of Delta and SEAL Team 6 were best displayed in their day-to-day performance when deployed in a war zone. They were absolutely unmatched when it came to taking down enemy networks. They fought a foe that hid in the shadows, used multiple layers of deception, and utilized decentralized control, to confound the efforts of coalition forces. Delta and ST-6 acted on intelligence. They took down targets, generating more intel and more targets. Their mission cycles became shorter. Often multiple targets were hit in the same night. Opposition forces were knocked off balance and eventually crumbled.

This happened over and over again in both Iraq and Afghanistan. Paul had been attached to both units while downrange and saw it firsthand. The impressive thing was the short amount of time they required to prep for a mission. They took intelligence from an interrogation or electronic device at Target One, then used it to hit Targets Two and Three on the same night. This generated more intel, and more targets.

The operators, or "shooters," worked to the point of strain, and sometimes beyond. But they pressured the networks into collapse. The enemy simply could not match the combat skills of these units. The few hundred operators of SEAL Team 6, for instance, are said to fire more live rounds in training in a year than the entire United States Marine Corps.

Paul was particularly impressed by the mission-planning and briefings these units exhibited. It was carried out by both officers and senior enlisted men. But junior enlisted personnel were encouraged to contribute as well. Several times Paul became aware of new information coming to his "customer" unit, watched the men assemble and devise a plan, and saw them put it in place immediately.

The bin Laden mission had been damn impressive, but months of planning were involved at every level, including the very top, to prepare the SEALs for Neptune Spear.

Like missions were carried out innumerable times without the fanfare. The boys from Red Squadron had pulled off similar missions many, many times.

Once one of America's Tier One units set up shop in a bad guy's neighborhood, that bad guy, no matter how much help he had and how well he was concealed, was going down.

Paul crossed a bridge that provided wonderful vistas of the Great Miami River on two sides. The river was now on his left. He felt the sun on his right side and realized he had come out of the canopy of trees. The path continued to follow the river northward. Ahead the asphalt path ended and was replaced by a wide concrete surface. A small complex of structures rose on the right. The first, the Piqua Waste Water Treatment Plant, raised no eyebrows amongst bikers or joggers.

The second, though, caused many to do a double take. It was the decommissioned Piqua Nuclear Generating Station. In the 1960s the Atomic Energy Commission authorized the construction of seven nuclear power facilities under the U.S. Government's small reactor construction program. The Piqua facility operated from 1963 to 1966, producing forty percent of the city's electricity. Technical problems caused the plant to cease operations in 1966. A scram, or emergency shutdown, actually occurred on May 6, 1965.

Paul slowed to a stop and got off his bike. There was a historical marker near the river that told the story of the plant. He had read it before so ignored it to look at what remained of the facility. A fifty-eight foot high dome dominated his view. Paul knew it contained the reactor, which was entombed in tons of concrete.

Didn't work out the way they hoped.

He began to walk the bike toward a rusty steel bridge that crossed the Great Miami directly across from the nuclear facility. Paul didn't know the original purpose of the span but it had been modified to accommodate bicyclists, walkers, and runners. There was a steel channel that ran the length of the bridge. Bike tires slipped into the channel easily. This made it easy to walk them to the other side where the path resumed.

Paul took one more look at the nuclear sarcophagus. He had no idea it existed when he and Lauren settled in the area. He learned about it one day when dropping off his Escape at J.D.'s for service. He was pulling his bike out of the cargo compartment when J.D. ambled over.

"You gonna ride home? I can drive you."

Paul explained that he rode the bike for exercise and he planned to take the path up through Piqua before returning home.

"Don't come home a-glowin'."

Paul didn't know what J.D. was talking about until he saw the marker for the first time.

He resumed his ride, once again on the west side of the river. The path skirted Piqua's downtown, which was to Paul's left. It was a city of slightly more than twenty thousand and hadn't changed much since the heyday of the nuclear plant. The bike path dipped lower into the river basin. There were no trees in this area. Other than the river, the primary feature of this stretch seemed to be geese and their droppings. Paul did his best to avoid the majority of the droppings but made a mental note to clean his tires before his next ride.

The bike path hugged the river as it bent to the west. In another mile the path would diverge and travel through Piqua's west side. It was at that point that Paul would leave the path. He intended to transition to two-lane roads. He decided to ride a few miles south on these roads until he came to the Lockington Dam. The trip there and back to the house would give him nineteen miles or so.

Paul steered off the path onto State Route 66. He was on it for just a half mile before taking a right to continue northbound on Hardin Road. It took him past the Johnston Farm and Indian Agency on the right. This site occupied ground that was mentioned in the works of author Allan W. Eckert. His most famous book was *THE FRONTIERSMEN.*"

Paul smiled remembering that one of the Delta troopers read that book on a deployment. Paul thought it had been in 2009 or 2010. The trooper was known in the unit as 'Johnny Combat." It was sometimes shortened to J.C. He was an E-7 at the time. He'd spent four years in the 75th Ranger Regiment before screening for Delta. A high percentage of Delta operators came from the 75th.

Johnny was well read and scored very high on intelligence tests. These traits did not separate him from his fellow Tier One operators. The general public would be surprised to discover the level of intelligence possessed by these men, particularly the enlisted cadre that did not have college degrees. What did separate Johnny was that he was constantly trying to help his fellow soldiers. As a rule sergeants make excellent den mothers. But Johnny took it to another level.

Paul remembered his favorite story about Johnny. It took place several years earlier when J.C. was in the Ranger Regiment. He had been at Fort McCoy in Wisconsin at the Army's Cold-Weather Operations Course. The students had very little opportunity to fraternize with the locals. At a bar in nearby Sparta one of J.C.'s men was hitting on a barmaid with no success. When they returned to McCoy, J.C. went on eBay and purchased a gold-plated, size 13, American Bowling Congress 300-game ring for $39.99. Bowlers that roll a 300-game are eligible to buy these from ABC. Many end up on eBay after their owners pass on or simply lose interest.

The ring arrived four days later. J.C. presented it to his subordinate, and the man spent the next Saturday night with the barmaid.

Paul, J.C., and eleven other Delta troopers were in eastern Afghanistan preparing for a mission when he first heard the story.

"Wait, you're saying the ring made the difference?" a trooper asked.

Johnny Combat responded.

"Those local girls have Rangers comin' in hittin' on them every week. But a guy starts flashing around a 300-game ring......"

"Bullshit," said another operator as he adjusted his NVG's. "My wife would laugh at that."

J.C. had smiled and nodded sagely.

"Your wife is from Texas. 300-game rings only work in Wisconsin, Minnesota, and parts of Iowa."

Fifteen minutes later Paul rounded a bend and saw the Lockington Dam. He rode closer and pulled off the road into a turnaround. He brought up MapMyRun and stopped the counter. He had been periodically taking sips of water but he took the opportunity now for a longer pull.

Paul stared at the dam. It was gigantic. It was 6,400 feet long, seventy-eight feet tall, and 415 feet wide at its base. It was one of five Miami Conservancy District dams that were constructed after the devastating 1913 flood.

Not only had the original Wright Flyer been threatened by the flood, so had the hundreds of glass negatives the brothers had accumulated. The Wrights had purchased a Korona Series V camera made by the Gundlach Optical Company in 1898 for eighty-five dollars. This was a substantial sum for the time. Many of the negatives were damaged by the floodwaters. The most important one, however, survived.

This was the shot taken at 10:35 on the morning of December 17, 1903, four miles south of Kitty Hawk. Orville had set up the camera on a tripod and pointed it to a spot where he thought the Flyer might be in the air. Soon three members of the U.S. Lifesaving Service Station approached to help out, a not uncommon offer. Wilbur handed John T. Daniels the bulb that would activate the shutter and asked him to squeeze it if the Flyer got airborne.

It did, and he did.

Daniels is often referred to as the "photographer" responsible for taking one of the most consequential photos in history. In truth he had never taken a photograph before this moment. Most accounts say he had never before even seen a camera.

Paul had seen the camera. It was on display at Carillon Park in the Wright Brothers National Museum.

He saddled up, restarted the app, and headed for home, smiling again at Johnny Combat's 300-game ring story. The Delta and ST-6 guys were known in the teams by their nicknames. Paul looked inward and remembered some of the names and faces. Harp, Bull, ChaCha, Doogie, Special Ed, Kanker, and B-Man from Delta. Dutch, Magua, Turbo, Dusty, Val, Tofe, and Burnsie from ST-6.

They were all hard men. Some did not survive the War on Terror.

Paul was proud to have served with them. He had gone from being referred to simply as "Air Force" when he was first assigned to their teams to getting his own Operator name.

He was "Sticks."

Gatewood hung the name on him the first day Paul fell under his tutelage at Keesler AFB. Paul walked into the barracks with a green duffel bag on his shoulder, his last name printed on it in large letters. The upper half of the L's were straight up and down. The lower, horizontal part angled downward. Paul had signed his name like this since he was a kid.

"Those L's look like hockey sticks!" Gatewood boomed. "And your name is H-U-L-L, like the hockey player? I'm calling you Sticks."

Sticks stuck.

After just one deployment Paul found that he seemed to be developing a reputation as a Controller that rucked his gear, coordinated the air assets, and put bombs on targets. This reputation grew over the years. The accident had ended his career but he hoped those warriors remembered him as an effective teammate.

He sure as hell would never forget them.

CHAPTER TWENTY-SEVEN

Smithson steered the Audi into the flow of traffic on eastbound U.S. Route 35. He had driven south three miles on Main Street before jumping on I-75 south for a short distance. His GPS directed him onto 35 and he was looking for his next turn, Abbey Avenue.

Online photos of the Wright Company Factory showed a facility that looked largely intact. It was difficult for Smithson to tell from the photos how accessible the site was, or how secluded. For his needs he preferred it to be both.

U.S. 35 was one of those odd highways that had intersecting city streets and stoplights. Smithson's GPS told him the turn on Abbey was less than two miles from I-75. As he continued east he noticed that the buildings on both sides of the highway appeared to be private residences. There were few businesses and none of the fast food joints that typically lined a well-traveled roadway.

A half-mile from the Abbey Avenue intersection the homes on his right thinned out. Smithson saw the factory complex come into view a moment later. It sat several hundred feet north of U.S. 35 near the center of an expansive lot covered by concrete. The building, or buildings, seemed to be a series of single story concrete-block affairs with high, rounded roofs that gave Smithson the impression of several quonset huts pushed together. The exterior walls were painted a faded white and he saw splashes of graffiti.

Smithson put on his right turn signal as he came to the light at Abbey Avenue. There was one car in front of him that was apparently continuing on U.S. 35 so he had to wait for the light to change before moving on. He surveyed the area. It was not quite apocalyptic, but headed in that direction. He thought the factory and its surrounding area would fit nicely into the landscape seen in the *Fallout: New Vegas* video game. To his right, and weirdly out of place, was a Dayton Metro Library building. It had a modern design and looked like it been plopped down in this neglected area by some giant, rich, suburban mom who was trying to spread the wealth.

The light changed and Smithson wheeled north. Once he cleared the library on his right the factory came into clearer view. There was several hundred feet of concrete surface on the east, south, and west sides of the building complex. Weeds sprouted up from cracks. The old plant entrance access road was on the north side. The Audi's GPS was guiding him there.

Smithson came to an intersection and again turned right. He saw businesses, or their remnants, on all four corners. Two of the buildings housed competing off-brand wireless phone stores. They could have been diners in their past lives when hundreds of factory workers toiled yards away. Heading east now he slowed at the entrance to the factory. The entire facility was surrounded by a chainlink fence, topped with three strands of barbed wire. A small security gatehouse stood inside the rusted front gate looking forlorn. Smithson turned into the drive and pulled up to the gate. From here, perhaps two hundred feet from the factory, he could see that the white paint was not just faded but had completely flaked off in some areas.

If the National Park Service is going to turn this place into a museum it will take a SHITLOAD of money.

Smithson sat with the Audi's engine running. This spot didn't feel particularly safe and he swiveled his head, checking the area for threats. No one was in sight so he directed his attention back to the factory.

This would be a great fucking place to defend against a zombie attack. Put a few automatic weapons up on that roof...a clear field of fire all around the building...great fucking place to kill zombies.

The site did have some positives. Smithson thought it would be easy to eliminate Hull and take the camera if he could lure the man into the building. The place was the perfect location for a post-industrial slasher movie. It was close to a highway, which would allow him to quickly put distance between himself and the crime scene. And, he noted, there did not appear to be any security cameras.

But the site posed several dilemmas. There were several houses ringing the fenced-in property. Gunfire, even suppressed gunfire, might be noticed. After taking down Hull he would have to somehow return to his vehicle outside the fence. This meant crossing a wide expanse of open area with no cover.

Just getting into the complex presented a problem. Smithson had hoped to find a gate with a lock meant to deter trespassers. He no longer had fantasies about picking locks—*fucking Biggs*—but he could sure as hell find a Home Depot and buy a set of bolt cutters. The front of this place, however, featured a forty-foot wide gate suspended on rusted out rollers. There was no way of getting through at this spot.

That meant getting over the barbed wire fence at another point. Smithson thought he might need a ladder to do it. He could not see a spot where a ladder would go unnoticed. Add to this the fact that two unfamiliar vehicles, his and Hulls, would almost certainly draw the attention of area residents.

Smithson filed this away for future examination. He needed to act quickly but not necessarily immediately. He still had time to let the plan distill. He punched in the address for his next destination, Woodland Cemetery, and saw that it was just eleven minutes away. He retraced his route back to U.S. 35 passing a business he hadn't noticed on the way in. It was the Delphos Market & Carryout, a worn brick and wood structure that had absorbed several coats of brownish-gold paint over the years. A weathered sign out front included the words "Deli & Grill." It looked like a rural gas station in a movie from the 1960s.

That place probably has the best barbeque in the state.

He considered for a second.

Or the worst.

Smithson took Route 35 east past I-75 and exited at Warren Street. He followed this south through increasingly gentrified blocks for a mile or so until Warren bent slightly to the right and became Brown Street. Seven blocks later he came to Woodland Avenue and turned left.

Smithson saw open wrought iron gates just ahead. They were flanked on either side by two-story stone structures. He pulled through the gate and found a spot in the small parking lot.

Smithson got out and looked back toward the gate. He saw that the structure on the north side was the Tiffany Chapel and the one on the south the Administrative Office. He headed to the office. At the door he paused to run a hand through his hair then straightened his hoodie.

Gotta look respectable.

Upon pushing through the door Smithson was greeted by a bespectacled older woman sitting behind a wooden desk.

"Hello, how may I help you?"

A smile appeared on Smithson's face. He had expected a bespectacled older woman behind a wooden desk.

"Good morning, young lady." His smile could not have been more insincere. "I'd like some help finding the Wright brothers' graves. I understand they're buried here?"

Smithson had decided on the drive over to use the direct approach. It would be unproductive to drive randomly around the two hundred acre property. There was a map on the Woodland website that was laid out with the numbers of each section and included several points of interest including the location of the Wright family lot. But Smithson believed it could be tedious to drive through the cemetery while comparing the real world with the map on his phone. Plus it had been his experience that most cemeteries lacked proper physical markers that would correspond to map locations.

Besides, he theorized that a fair percentage of visitors who came to the office were, like him, searching for the Wright brothers' resting place. A courteous man in a hoodie—he gave himself the benefit of the doubt—asking for the same directions would not raise suspicion.

In addition, if Smithson chose this location for the final phase of what he'd come to think of as the modified Operation Crank, he would get Grey involved. He was probably recorded coming through the gate. It was possible he was being filmed right now. Grey would wipe these files. On the day of the big finish he would make sure the security cameras would be shut down.

The woman, her nametag read "Marna," smiled hesitantly.

"That's correct. They're in section 101. It's in the northeast portion of the grounds."

Smithson could not remember the last time he heard the word "portion" used when it wasn't followed by the word "control" and associated with a weight loss program.

"I'm sorry, I'm not very good at reading maps." He gestured at a stack of cemetery diagrams on the corner of her desk.

Marna stood and selected a copy of the map from the stack.

"Here, let me show you."

She walked past Smithson and out the door. He followed.

Marna pointed toward the interior of the cemetery and began to give directions, tracing each step on the map with an index finger.

"You came in on Woodland Avenue. It continues into the property for a few hundred feet until it meets Central Access Road." She pointed to the spot.

"You take a right, then a quick left on Boy and Dog Road."

"On what?" Smithson thought he heard her incorrectly.

"Boy and Dog Road. It's named after the grave marker of a five-year-old boy named Johnny Morehouse who fell into the Miami and Erie Canal in the 1860s. His dog tried to save him but Johnny drowned. The dog came to the gravesite for weeks after the funeral. The marker shows a sleeping little boy with a dog protecting him. It's very touching. People leave toys and dog bones at the site all the time."

Smithson made an attempt at stifling a yawn that wasn't completely successful.

Marna continued to indicate the route on the map with her finger before concluding.

"The Wright family graves are near the top of a hill between Wright Brothers Road and Dunbar Road. Look for three flagpoles in a line. They mark the site. You can't miss it."

Smithson would've bet every cent of the money he'd extorted from Crypto Boy that Marna would end her directions with those four words.

He thanked her and returned to the Audi. As he reached for the door he noticed a bench at the base of a hill. It was one of the "Bowler Benches." Smithson didn't know that one of these was in the cemetery. He walked over to take a closer look.

The bench was roughly four feet wide and looked like it was heavier than hell. It had a brown-green hue. Smithson had read that they were cast in bronze. There were two bowler hats on the right side of the bench. They looked as if they could be lifted off of the bench but when Smithson pushed on one he confirmed that they were permanently connected.

Why do they call it a bowler? Isn't it really just a derby?

Smithson saw that there were words on the front edge. He bent to read them.

> *DEDICATED TO THE IMMORTAL SPIRIT OF DAYTONIANS ORVILLE AND WILBUR WRIGHT.*

Smithson stood and said quietly, "You have a little bird shit on your hat there, Wilbur."

He smiled and lifted his eyes. A large boulder with an attached plaque sat several feet behind the bench. He couldn't read it from the distance but saw a nearby sign.

> *GRAVESITE OF AUTHOR & HUMORIST ERMA BOMBECK.*

Smithson stood and walked to the Audi.

Never fucking heard of her.

Smithson guided the S8 over the narrow roads. The grounds of the cemetery consisted of a number of tree-covered hills. Most were low and rolling, but a few rose steeper and higher. One of these presented itself to him as Boy and Dog Road and bent to the north.

He made no effort to look for the marker that Marna had referred to.

What the hell was that kid doing playing by the canal?

The irresponsibility of little Johnny reminded Smithson of Bryan Mills' daughter in *Taken*.

Running around Europe, following U2, no supervision... she had it coming.

The roadway merged with another on its left to form Wright Brothers Road. Smithson slowed and scanned for flagpoles. He caught sight of them ahead to the right and steered the Audi in their direction. When he'd reached a point below the flags he put the car in park and stepped out. He was about one hundred feet from the flagpoles and couldn't quite tell how the site was configured due to the intervening grave markers.

The heat and humidity of the August morning closed in on him. Smithson raised his gaze beyond the Wright site and saw another road. It was closer to the flagpoles than he was now.

Must be Dunbar Road. The hell with walking up from here, I'll drive up top and walk down.

And that's what he did.

He left the car near the crest of the hill. The Wright site was several yards below, to the west. On the other side of the Audi a line of large markers were dispersed amongst small and mid-sized mausoleums. Past this the east face of the hill fell off at a steep angle. A pond was visible several hundred yards in the distance with the barrier fence of the cemetery a short distance beyond.

Smithson turned back to the flagpoles and began to pick his way through the markers. To him they all seemed ancient.

People back then had a thing for cherubs.

The poles were in a line running north to south. The tallest, in the center, was every bit of fifteen feet high. The flanking poles were a foot or two shorter. Smithson stepped onto a paved walkway in front of the center pole, which flew the flag of the United States. At the foot of the pole was a bronze marker. It read:

An impressive monument sat on the other side of the poles. It was rectangular in shape and reached the height of Smithson's chest. It appeared to be made of concrete. There was no lettering on this side of the monument. A ledge ran around its top and the bottom tapered outward until contacting the ground.

Smithson saw that the pavers lined the entire site so he worked his way around the right corner of the monument until he could view the other side. There was a single word, "WRIGHT," on its face.

A small plexiglass case connected to thin black metal legs stood near Smithson's waist. It was of the sort that some realtors used to post information sheets in front of properties for sale. Or at least they did before Zillow. Smithson saw that it held pamphlets labeled *Remembering The Wright Family and the Brothers of Aviation.* He removed one and continued down the side of the gravesite.

He saw that the pavers ringed an area that was perhaps 15x30 feet with the long sides running east to west. Green groundcover filled the interior of the paved area with grave markers peeking up above. There were two short lines of markers. Smithson came to those in the center of the rectangle. He saw markers for Susan Wright, the inventors' mother, and Milton Wright, their father. The markers—they appeared to be granite—rose just a few inches above the ground and were rounded on top. Their shape reminded Smithson of the roof of the Wright factory he'd visited earlier. Between Susan and Milton's markers was a tombstone that stood over a foot high. Its face was worn. Smithson could make out just one word, "WRIGHT."

I wonder if the Bishop and his wife lost a baby at birth?

Smithson consulted the pamphlet but found no mention of this stone. He moved on.

At the bottom of the enclosure formed by the pavers was a line of three additional markers. They were identical to Susan and Milton's in size and shape. They read:

WILBUR WRIGHT 1867-1912, KATHARINE WRIGHT HASKELL 1874-1929, ORVILLE WRIGHT 1871-1948.

A black coffee mug with a U.S. Space Force logo sat atop Wilbur's marker, as did several white seashells. Orville's marker held a small metal Wright Flyer. Someone had adhered a single word, "FIRST," onto the top wing. It looked like it had been made with an old-fashioned label maker. More seashells surrounded the Flyer.

What's the deal with the seashells? Maybe people bring them from Kitty Hawk?

Several pennies had been placed on all three markers.

Wow, the Wright brothers...right down there...Okay then.

Smithson lifted his eyes and surveyed the area. He hadn't come here to pay tribute. He had come to recon. He was on a hillside surrounded by markers, some the size of a small car. Mature trees were scattered throughout the grounds. Many were within what Smithson considered easy rifle range of the Wright site.

Maybe lure him in here and wait for him up in a tree? A couple quick shots—double tap—then vamoose.

He looked back up the slope. His eyes were drawn to a mausoleum behind and just to the left of the Audi.

The high ground! That might do it. Doesn't look like the shot would be too tough from there. Gotta step it off.

Smithson took a step in that direction then had a thought. He removed his wallet and pulled out both fake I.D.'s. He held them toward Wilbur's marker.

Whaddya think Wilbur-boy? Glenn Smithson and Oliver Haugh. They were all pains in the ass for you weren't they?

He grinned widely and sidestepped to the right.

Gotta let you get a look too, Orv.

Smithson realized that if the original Operation Crank was carried out to its final phase, he would have, in effect, hacked the Wright brothers from across time.

Well, now you boys get to help me take care of Hull.

The entire scenario had a bizarre tang that struck Smithson as funny. He laughed out loud then quickly caught himself and checked to see if he had attracted attention. He saw only a man walking a dog on a cemetery road a good one hundred yards away.

"Okay, time to move."

Smithson returned to the flagpoles then began to pace toward the mausoleum on the crest. He angled slightly left as he climbed the slope, weaving now and then between markers. He reached the road, then the structure.

Sixty-five paces. I can make that shot!

The mausoleum was constructed of large slabs of stone. Smithson estimated it was fourteen feet across and twenty deep. A locked metal gate stood in front of a sealed door on its front. Above the door was an arch with the word "ARCHER" pushed out from the surface.

Smithson went to the left front corner and leaned in for support as if assuming a shooting position. He had a clear view of the flagpoles and most of the Wright site.

Yes!

This would be perfect. He could wait for Hull behind the mausoleum, get him in the open, then....*Pop, Pop.*

This decided, he now needed to plan his entry to the shooting position. A fence ran the entire circumference of the grounds. Smithson looked at a section in the distance and saw that barbed wire topped it as well.

Grey will take care of the cameras. Gotta get over that damned fence.

He remembered his ladder idea from the factory but realized he hadn't thought it through.

So even if I find a spot in one of the neighborhoods that butt up to this fence and get a ladder there unnoticed, how do I get back over the fence after doing the deed? Gotta think about this.

Smithson was beginning to perspire. He got back in the Audi and cranked up the air conditioner. He slowly made his way back toward the front gate. His mind worked on the problem.

Could I park outside the cemetery and come through the open gate, then just wait until they close? Well, yeah, but how do I get out, and how does Hull get in?

He passed the man walking the dog, thinking the closing time angle might be worked if he gamed it. When he reached the office he pulled over. Letting the Audi idle he again entered the office.

Marna looked up and smiled.

"Find it?"

Smithson's insincere smile returned.

"Yes ma'am, but I have a question. What time does the cemetery close?"

Marna, ever helpful, answered, "Both the gate and this office open at eight. The office closes at five. The gate stays open until seven then it gets chained and locked."

Smithson could've kissed her.

The bolt cutter idea! Come after dark. Park on the street. Cut the chain and come through. Close the gate but leave it so Hull can get in. Hoof it up to the mausoleum. Take care of business!

"Marna, you're wonderful!"

The woman blushed as Smithson went back out the door. He nearly skipped to the Audi. He opened the door, unable to suppress a grin. As he put the S8 in gear he heard his phone chirp from the passenger seat. He reached for it and saw there was a notification from Grey.

Biggs' body had been found.

Smithson's grin disappeared.

215

CHAPTER TWENTY-EIGHT

"Are you shitting me?"

Smithson said it out loud. He took a moment to try to regain his composure, but seconds later repeated the question in an even louder voice.

"ARE YOU SHITTING ME!?!"

He cocked his right arm and drove his elbow violently into the vertical section of the passenger seat before regaining control. Instantly self-conscious, he quickly checked his surroundings. He didn't see anyone outside but there was no way to tell if Marna could've been watching him through the office window. Thinking quickly, he punched up the S8's audio system and jacked up the volume. His personalized gaming soundtrack was dialed in and *Not Ready To Die* by Sevenfold came up. It was created specifically for the video game *Call of Duty: Black Ops*. As the speed metal riffs pounded the interior of the Audi, Smithson, making sure to not look toward the office, lowered his window with his left hand while simultaneously repeating his elbow attack on the passenger seat.

Satisfied that he had convinced any onlookers that he was just enjoying the music, Smithson drove off.

Marna stood a few feet back from her window. She *had* been watching.

What a wacko.

Smithson began to work his way back to the rental.

Why the hell does everything happen to ME?

He chewed unconsciously on a thumbnail, navigating through traffic.

Gotta get on top of this fast. They'll try to reach Hull soon. Gotta move!

Smithson had only had a day or so to begin to put together a plan for retrieving the camera. He had hoped to put off the next phase for at least another day. He wanted to check out one of the other Wright brother sites, Huffman Prarie Flying Field. He hadn't considered it as a setting for the end game due to its proximity to the Air Force base. But its distance from the other sites meant that it could be useful if he sent Hull scrambling about Dayton before finally arriving at the cemetery.

That was the plan crystallizing in Smithson's head. He wanted to keep Hull off balance. Bounce him around town for a while, keep him guessing before the final act. Plus, it would show Hull who was in charge. Smithson needed to hit Hull with an overwhelming amount of information from the get go to convince the man he had no choice but to accede to his demands. To do this he would need specific information on the sister and her family. Grey was working on that.

Once Hull was properly motivated it would just be a matter of coordinating the final events.

As the Audi cruised through Dayton, Smithson began to feel more in control of the situation. Grey would furnish him with the raw data he needed. Usually Grey served him in an almost passive mode, sifting through indicators on the customer bases of porn sites, detecting tendencies, then collecting data on specific users that was reported to him. From there it was easy. Grey set them up. He knocked them down.

But the computer entity could also be used in another way. This method was a directed effort at a specific target. In effect, no one could withstand this. The ability to plant keystroke software on virtually any private device meant that Smithson had access to waves of data, in fact, too much data. They were tidal waves. Thankfully Smithson had become adept at giving Grey the proper amount of instruction to achieve the desired result.

He could direct Grey to "find the best restaurants in Dayton, Ohio," for example and would receive an answer immediately. The list would be customized to fit his tastes, featuring pizza places, burger joints, and donut shops. This was nothing new. Anyone who had ever shopped on Amazon.com and had the algorithms immediately suggest related products would recognize this. But Grey took it to a much higher level, especially when doing one of these targeted, blunt force, attacks. Grey knew from past operations the type of data Smithson selected.

It was a form of artificial intelligence, or A.I., but there was more. Smithson had taken a class at Berkeley on Ethical Hacking. It was the process, now widespread in business and the government sector, of detecting vulnerabilities in an organization's systems that an attacker could exploit. The professor spent an inordinate amount of time stressing the responsibilities that ethical hacking companies had to their clients. Smithson disregarded this, of course, and concentrated on the worms, viruses, ransomware, and malware that were highlighted in the course.

Along the way he had an idea. What if you could hack the Ethical Hacking industry? These companies partnered with the end users that had the big money. They then spent time fooling around in client's systems. If Smithson hitchhiked in with them, he could have some fun later. He knocked around for a couple years trying to piggyback with a few of these companies without success, nearly being caught a couple of times. He'd backburnered the idea. But now, with a fully functional Grey, it might be time to turn his attentions back to this.

Smithson was now traveling north on Main Street and realized the next side street was Knecht Drive, the site of Biggs' apartment. He had a quick thought.

I should drive by... make sure the cops haven't identified the body already.

He angled the Audi to the right lane and was immediately greeted by a honking horn. Smithson swerved back and looked to his right in time to see an older man in a midnight silver Tesla Y zip past. There was a black and yellow "MENSA" sticker on the rear bumper. The man was wearing a bucket hat and holding up a middle finger.

Smithson screamed at him.

"Go screw yourself, old man!"

He was furious. He would like nothing better than to cut off the Tesla in traffic, pull the M4 out of the trunk, and walk 5.56 rounds right into the bucket hat.

But he couldn't. Knecht was right there. So he checked his mirrors and made the turn, all the while thinking, *fucking quiet electric cars.*

Smithson passed the apartment and was gratified to see it was not swarming with law enforcement vehicles. He continued to Riverside and made a left.

Maybe he should turn his attentions to older people. A number of the phishing emails, purporting to be from reputable companies but actually just attempts to get people to reveal personal information for malicious use, came from Russia. Since that country's invasion of Ukraine, patriotic Russian hackers had concentrated their efforts on their neighboring country rather than retirees in the West. This created a bit of a void. One that Grey could fill. But Smithson was uninspired by the prospect of swindling grandmas out of their nest eggs. This had never been solely about money, certainly not since the hit on Crypto-Boy. It had been about power. About having the ability to screw with people, disrupt their lives.

Crank was not turning out the way it was originally planned. But this thing with Hull promised to be most satisfying. Smithson first needed to make sure the camera stayed out of the hands of the police. He would have to contact Hull with credible threats, and quickly. But after that he could mess with the man, control him, and ultimately kill him.

Smithson had to admit that last component was becoming more attractive to him. Killing Biggs had been impulsive and had unquestionably created significant complications, but *damn* it was satisfying. Theoretically he could let Hull live and probably escape capture if he simply took the camera and let the man go on with his life, but what fun would that be?

He thought again about serial killers and re-examined his first incident. It was a few years after leaving Berkeley. He had nearly two hundred grand in his accounts and decided to treat himself. He had read online about Adults Only resorts in Belize, a country on the Caribbean coast of Central America. Some catered to couples, but many encouraged single visitors.

Smithson had never been particularly successful with the ladies—other than the professionals—so he thought *why not?*

On his second night there he hit it off with a hot little Latina number in one of the resort's tiki bars. She made it clear that she was willing and soon the two were on the way to his room. Once inside she made her mistake.

"Now Señor, we discuss payment."

Smithson was incredulous. He could have *paid* for it back in Nevada.

"You're a prostitute?!?"

Her look of condescension was the final straw. It screamed *why else would I be in this room with a man such as you?*

Smithson strangled her.

It happened almost without conscious thought. When it was over he was in a state of near panic. The rest of the night was a blur. He went online and booked a flight out of the country for the next day. A seat wasn't available until nearly noon. He left the body on the floor of his room and covered it with a bedspread. The next morning he woke early and scouted the halls for over an hour before finding an unattended laundry cart. He wheeled it to his room and lifted the body into it, covering it with bedding.

He'd been able to access the hotel security cameras to disable them after the murder, so his trip to the room with the cart wasn't recorded. He had also wiped his name from the hotel records. But Grey was not yet fully developed so he didn't have the capability to reach back into the recorded history that the cameras stored.

He ditched the cart in a maintenance room before leaving for the airport. Thankfully he'd had the sense to use a fake I.D. He'd chosen the name "Felix Millian" after the high school teacher that unfairly accused him of stealing his damn volleyball ring. He made it home safely and had never been questioned.

But there were images of him in that hotel that he'd not been able to destroy, or even locate. This was worrisome, and the reason he was so intent on getting the camera from the Hulls.

CHAPTER TWENTY-NINE

Paul returned from his ride covered in sweat. He had not been quite as successful on the return leg at avoiding the geese droppings near the river. He found the collapsible bike stand that he used for repairs and set it up in the garage in the space usually occupied by Lauren's Jeep. He spent twenty minutes cleaning the entire bike before applying a thin coat of bike oil to the chain. That finished, he placed the bike back on its rack and put away the stand.

When Paul entered the house Chappy made an attempt to get out. But Paul was ready for him and blocked the opening with his leg until the door swung shut. Chappy looked up at him. The cat seemed to slowly lower his eyelids partway, then stopped. Chappy seemed to be glaring at him.

Paul thought *I didn't see anything like that in the Netflix documentary.*

It was not quite ten o'clock when he got in the shower. After toweling off and getting dressed he walked back to the kitchen and saw the note reminding him to call the insurance company. He spent a few minutes on his cell with their agent when another call came in. Paul glanced at his phone, saw "No Caller ID" and ignored it. A minute later an identical call showed on his screen. Paul looked at the phone and frowned.

Persistent jackass. He can leave a voicemail if he'd like.

He'd answered a final question from the agent when his phone vibrated, indicating an incoming text. Paul's eyes focused on the screen.

And the world changed.

If you don't get off the line with your insurance agent and take my next call, Paulie, you're not going to like what happens to Lauren. Or to Patrice and the boys.

Paul was rocked.

He realized the agent was waiting for him to talk.

"Uh, sorry, that's all I have. Something's come up, I have to go."

He disconnected without waiting for a reply and stared at his screen. The words of the text message seemed to be disintegrating right before his eyes. His screen seemed to flash —no, sparkle—and portions of every word disappeared with each spike of light.

What the hell?

His phone rang again as he watched the screen. Again it read "No Caller ID."

Paul answered immediately, his voice a bit strained.

"Who is this?"

Caller: "Pretty neat trick with that text on your phone, huh Paul? I call that 'shimmer.' It burns texts off a phone's screen so you can't take a screenshot. No evidence left that you ever received it. Comes in real handy in my business. I came up with that myself. Could probably make millions selling it to people who threaten their exes, but I'm going to keep it for myself right now."

Paul was angry, confused, and alarmed. He took a breath and tried to push that all aside. He repeated himself, already assuming the tone he'd used when directing strike aircraft during high stress situations overseas.

"Who is this?"

Caller: "Let's not worry about that right now. Let me get right to it. You have something I need and you're going to give it to me. If you don't, I will destroy everything you love."

Paul fought an urge to scream into the phone with threats of his own. He knew he needed to focus on every detail of the call. There was a legal pad on the kitchen table. He'd use it to make notes on the insurance claim. He moved to the table. As he sat, his eyes slid toward the camera bag. He knew the answer to his question before it was asked.

"What are you talking about?"

Caller: "Your camera. Not your cellphone camera. Your fucking DSLR."

Paul: "You broke into our house."

It was a statement, not a question.

Caller: "And your wife's Jeep. And I don't have time to fuck around anymore trying to get it. Let me let you in on a little secret, Paulie, you have a picture of me on that camera. Well, a video. You're going to give it to me."

Paul's eyes narrowed.

"Why the hell—"

Caller: "Before you get an idea to hang up and go straight to the police, let me give you a little demonstration. Go get your laptop."

Paul had the thought of calling Detective Bunker already in mind. The caller had obviously anticipated this.

"My laptop?"

Caller: "Go get your fucking laptop and open it." His voice had raised in pitch.

Paul walked to his office and opened the laptop. A picture of Lauren appeared on the desktop. She was at the balloon festival in Albuquerque. Her hands were to either side, palms up. They were situated in such a way that it looked like she was holding up two balloons in the background. Paul loved that photo.

"It's open."

Caller: "Watch this."

Lauren's image disappeared. It was replaced by a black screen.

Caller: "That, Paulie, is the screen of death. You will not be using that computer again. I've done the same thing to your wife's tablet. I've also disabled some features of your cell phones."

Paul fought an urge to lash out.

Caller: "Speaking of phones, watch your screen."

Paul's phone vibrated in his hand as a text came in. It was a photo of his eleven-year-old nephew, Frankie. The boy was staring intently at the camera. Patrice was in the background, apparently talking to the boy.

"What—"

Caller: "Your sister must be one of those mean moms that won't let her kid get a cellphone until they reach a certain age. That picture was taken a few minutes ago. Frankie is using your sister's phone to play video games since he doesn't have one of his own. I remotely accessed the phone and took the pic myself."

Paul wondered how this could be possible.

The caller continued.

"Keep watching your phone."

The screen cleared before filling with a copy of the incident report filed by Detective Bunker of the Miami County Sheriff's Department on the break-in at Paul's house.

Despite being knocked mentally off balance, Paul had little doubt that the report was genuine. As he watched, the report sparkled and, as before, disappeared from the screen.

Caller: "I've accessed all the family phones. Did you know your nephew Leo has a girlfriend? No? Well why would you? His mom doesn't even know. Her name is Cecelia and they've been texting regularly for the last couple weeks. Nothing hot and heavy yet but I'll be there to see it if it goes in that direction."

Before Paul could think of something to say, the caller continued.

"I'm going to rattle off a set of facts to you that will confirm how serious this situation is, Paulie. I know your brother-in-law Kevin is in Wichita for three days. I know exactly how, where, and when, both your nephews get to school. I know what soccer fields they practice on and their schedules. Really, Paul. Soccer? I know Patrice's work schedule for the next week. I've accessed the National Veterans Museum's computerized appointment book for staff—very well organized by the way—so I know exactly where she'll be. *Exactly*. I have your wife's schedule, which, by the way, seems a bit worthless, don't you think? All those extra hours and shifts on her time card."

Paul began to make notes on the legal pad, jotting each of the caller's claims as quickly as he could.

Caller: "I have accessed the geo history of all of your relevant devices. I know where your phones are currently and where they've been for the last year. I accessed your Escape SYNC system and your wife's Jeep Uconnect and I know where they've been and where they are now."

Paul scribbled.

Caller: "Here's the deal. If you give me the camera and the SD card you've used the last few days, I go away."

Paul thought of the Wilbur Wright Birthplace and the open doors.

Caller: "You see, I shot a man the other day in Indiana and you and your wife came along a few minutes later. I was hiding the body and I know your wife took a video that I will appear in. The cops found the body this morning. I know you called the sheriff about doors being open at that damn museum. I actually listened to your call from thirty feet away."

Paul blinked, "The cornfield?"

Caller: "You're catching on, Paulie-boy. Now before you get any idea that you hold the high cards because you have the video, listen to this. I have an M4. Suppressed. You're familiar with those, right? I've killed people. Not with the M4...yet. But I have. Got a sweet .357 Colt Python like Barry Burton uses. Different barrel length, though."

Paul jotted down *Barry Burton*. He added a question mark. He had no idea who that was.

Caller: "So I've popped a couple people with the Colt. Even had to do one chick with my bare hands. But I'm looking forward to using the M4. If I don't get that camera and SD card, I'll pop one of your people. At least one. You might be able to keep your wife home, but Hilliard's not far away. You can't be in two places at once, Paulie."

Paul felt like he had parachuted into the middle of a gunfight and he had not yet acquired situational awareness. *Where are the bad guys? Where are my guys? Gotta get some help in here.*

Caller: "So, I know we share a mutual interest in the Wright brothers. Of course we do! That's why you were at that museum, right? I'd tell you why I was there but it isn't relevant. Anyway, I know which Wright brother sites you've visited and which ones you haven't. Tomorrow I'm going to text your phone and tell you where to go. Bring the camera and the card. Drive the Escape. A little bit of a pedestrian vehicle, don't you think? You should see my rides."

Paul wrote, *Nuts?*

Caller: "Make sure you have plenty of gas. I'm going to run you around a little while, see some sights. I think you'll enjoy it. Every location will have something to do with those two inventors. Cranks. Did you know that's what people called men who were trying to invent an airplane? Ahh, you probably knew that. You've already been to most of these sites so it'll be like old home week."

Paul scribbled, *gas, W.B. sites.*

Caller: "But you'll be delivering the goods to me at a place you haven't visited. I'm a bit surprised, actually. Seems like a place you would really be interested in. Anyway, it will be a secluded spot where nobody can bother us. I'll direct you in to a specific point. It will be dark. You'll see some flagpoles that will help, more on that later. You'll leave the camera bag on the ground. I'll be watching with NVG's. Did I mention I have NVG's? I'll have the M4, so no funny business. You get back in the Escape and.......escape."

Paul heard the caller giggle as he jotted, *flagpoles, NVG's, M4.*

Caller: "So, the thing is, I've penetrated the systems of all the relevant law enforcement organizations: the Henry County Sheriff's Department in Indiana, your Troy Police, and the Miami County Sheriff's Department. I can do the same with the Dayton PD or anyone else if you decide to get creative and invite someone to our party. As I'm running you around the area I'll be monitoring all of these, and others, and I'll know if you've brought someone in. If you do, I pop your people, understand?"

Paul was silent.

"*UNDERSTAND?!?*"

"I understand," Paul gripped the phone, fighting to control his urge to lash out.

Caller: "I'll text you tomorrow. Be ready late afternoon, early evening. Leave your wife at home. You can do that can't you? Do you wear the pants in the family? It will all be done by text. You see, and I waited until the end of our call to tell you, I don't want my voice recorded... didn't want you to scramble for a recorder. Shimmer will burn all the texts. You won't have any proof I ever existed. I'll have the video so I'll be happy. I'll be gone. You go back to your bike rides. Everybody's happy, get it?"

"Yes."

Paul could think of nothing else to say.

Caller: "OK, the Henry County yokels will probably be trying to get in touch with you because you called in that report. Maybe not, who knows how efficient they are. But probably. I've blocked all calls to your phone from the 765 area code so they won't get through on a landline, but everybody has cell phones now and they might try to reach you from a phone with a different area code. Avoid talking to them. When the time comes that they finally get in touch with you, don't say anything about the camera. Just give them the same info you did on the original call. Remember, if you give them information on me, I'll know it. I'm in their computers."

Paul again was silent.

Caller: "OK, that's it Paulie, tell me you got it."

Paul, through gritted teeth, managed "I got it."

The caller disconnected.

CHAPTER THIRTY

Paul held the phone in his hand. He had the sensation that he'd been drinking water from a fire hose and it suddenly shut off. So much information to try to process then....click. He sat the cell down on the table and studied the legal pad.

Is there an easy way out of this?

After less than five minutes he concluded there was not. He reviewed the pluses and minuses of following the directions of the man.

If I follow his directions there is no reason for him not to take me out. Why leave me alive after the exchange? He has to know I'd go straight to the cops in an effort to catch him. If he's not caught he remains a threat to my family...and I won't have that.

Paul considered.

I'd be willing to take the bullet to keep Lauren, Patrice, and the kids safe, but it wouldn't guarantee a thing. This...... guy....what do I call him? He didn't give a name. This Crank will still be out there and could still go after my family. So, if I can't go to the cops, and doing it his way isn't an option....what?

He glanced at the clock. It was 10:45. The original plan for the day was to meet Gatewood for lunch at noon at WPAFB then link up with Mike McClary outside of Tipp City to help him load firewood. Obviously things had changed. He looked again at the pad then flipped to a new page.

Did he have another option? He couldn't go to law enforcement.

There was the law. And there was justice.

Do I have enough information to take this guy out before he hurts more people?

Paul spent the next twenty minutes consolidating the information. Much of what went onto the pad was factual, if he could take Crank at his word. But much of what Paul added was based on deductive reasoning.

He probably plans on shooting me.

I could be wrong, but I got the feeling he doesn't know what I did in the military? How can that be if he can hack into any computer system? Maybe he can't get into military systems.

He was all over the Escape and the Jeep, but he didn't mention the Lariat.

Paul pondered this.

It's too old! It doesn't have a manufacturer communication and navigation system that he can piggyback onto and get my data.

"Now we're getting somewhere."

Using the facts that he knew, and the assumptions he made, Paul began to construct a plan. It was very structured. At JSOC, he and his teammates utilized warning orders and operational orders. Each had five components: Situation, Mission, Execution, Administration and Logistics, and Command and Signal.

Paul had spent several deployments watching these planning guides assembled. Then, they were put together in order to go after an armed, crafty enemy that was extremely dangerous. They were constructed many times with incomplete or spotty intelligence. It was a very, very, difficult thing to do properly.

But Paul had been there with the best the world had ever seen at doing this sort of thing. Men like Dutch, Harp, Special Ed, and Val. Paul had participated in constructing a number of the orders and had been on the ensuing missions. He'd done this sort of thing.

Many times.

At the end of the twenty minutes he did an assessment.

Was it feasible?

Yes.

Paul stood up from the table.

I guess my original plan for the day is still in place, first Woody, then Mike.

He turned to go to the bedroom and saw that Chappy was up on the island watching him. The cat had to know he was in a forbidden area. Paul had been too intent on his task to notice Chappy's presence. He walked towards the cat but instead of putting him on the floor or reaching for the squirt gun, Paul had a few words for him.

"Time to go to work, Chappy. First there."

It was the motto of the Air Force Combat Controllers.

Chappy looked at him and blinked, very slowly.

Paul hurried to the bedroom. A lot had to happen in a short time. He went into the walk-in closet and found a small duffel bag. He selected a white button-down linen shirt, a pair of light brown dress shorts, and his favorite pair of flip flops and stuffed them in the bag. He found his travel kit that held toiletries and tossed it in as well.

He went to the dresser and pulled the cork stopper from the ceramic container that held their cash. He removed it all.

No doubt Crank would see any credit card purchases.

Back to the kitchen, he picked up his cell phone, began to search for something, thought better of it, and set it down. Instead, he went to a kitchen drawer that held stamps and envelopes. He opened it and removed an address book. Quickly flipping through pages he found two phone numbers and jotted them down. In the age of cell phones it seemed no one memorized another person's number. They simply searched for a name on their phone and selected that. Paul was pretty sure he knew these two numbers, but he couldn't take a chance.

And he didn't want Crank to know he'd searched for them right after their conversation.

He opened the wall cabinet and grabbed a handful of Clif Bars, picked up the camera bag, and snatched the keys to the pickup. He turned to see if he'd forgotten anything, saw the legal pad, and tucked it under an arm. He left his phone on the island. After one last scratch on the head for Chappy, Paul was out the door.

Paul pulled the Lariat onto Polecat Road, heading toward Troy. When he reached the traffic circle in the middle of town he took a right and headed west. He hit a red light near Kettering Health came to a stop. He stared at the hospital.

How the hell am I going to explain this to Lauren?

The light changed and Paul continued on Main Street. He passed over I-75 and made his way to the Meijer parking lot. Once inside the store he made his way to the back and angled toward the electronics section. He searched the aisles until he found the prepaid phones. There were several models. They were kept inside a locked case. He looked for help, knowing he was short on time. He saw a young man wearing the blue polo of a Meijer employee. He was doing something inside a case that held video games.

"Excuse me, can you answer some questions about these phones?"

The man turned. He walked toward Paul. He had long blonde hair that fell over his eyes. He pushed it to one side as he approached.

"Sure, what do you need to know?"

Paul asked questions about the texting options and data plans of the various models. The other man answered every question. He pushed his hair out of his eyes three more times. Each time the hair returned.

Paul nodded.

"Okay, I'm ready to buy. Do you open the case for me?"

"Yes sir," he answered. "Which one would you like?"

Paul pointed to a Tracfone.

"I'll have four of those."

The attendant had been looking at the phones. He swiveled quickly toward Paul. His hair swung back into his eyes.

"Four burners? Dude!"

Paul eyed the man, realizing he must've thought Paul had several mistresses.

"It's not what you think."

The man put his hands up.

"Sorry mister, I didn't mean anything by that."

Now he had a look of fear in his eyes.

Paul shook his head and smiled.

"And I'm not a drug dealer."

Paul walked out of the store with the four phones and more than enough data for his requirements. He'd spent just over three hundred dollars. He got inside the cab of the Lariat and immediately opened one of the phone packages. He scanned the accompanying instruction sheet for one minute, and he went to work.

Paul was not a hacker. He was certainly not a computer genius on par with the likes of the man he thought of as Crank. But as a CCT, he had been adept at utilizing some of the most sophisticated equipment in the United States military. He had carried the AN/PEQ-1 SOFLAM, or Special Operations Forces Laser Acquisition Marker, for example, every time he went on a mission.

It was a pain in the ass to hump. It weighed over eleven pounds, blew through batteries requiring him to carry a number of extras, and had a tripod that never seemed to fit on his gear. But it allowed him to mark targets and generate coordinates for close air support and artillery. It saved the operators of his customer units more than once. It was rugged, but all equipment in the field eventually had issues. Paul could repair and recalibrate it. In the dark. Under fire.

He could handle setting up a burner phone.

Once he finished, he selected one of the phone numbers he'd taken from the address book—Gatewood's—and sent a text.

Hey Woody, this is Sticks. New phone. Running a half hour late. Meet me at the Visitor Center at 1230 hours?

He started the Lariat and headed for the highway. As he waited at a red light an answering text came to his phone. A distinct "ding" caught his attention.

Gotta remember to set these phones to vibrate.

Paul checked the screen.

Why the V-Center? Not the Pit?

The "Pit" was the Pitsenbarger Dining Facility. It had a cafeteria-style format and served military personnel over a quarter-million meals a year. There were many other dining options on or near the base, but the Pit was the usual choice for Gatewood and Paul. It had several things going for it. First, the food was top notch as well as plentiful and affordable, always big draws for military personnel. Second, it was located in Kittyhawk Center, Building 1214, not far from Gatewood's office with the 88th Field Security Squadron. And finally, it was named after Staff Sergeant William H. Pitsenbarger, a member of Air Force Special Operations, a PJ, who was killed in Vietnam in 1966.

Bill Pitsenbarger grew up in Piqua, Ohio. On April 11, 1966 he was inserted to an ambush site to treat and evacuate wounded Americans. He loaded wounded one at a time onto litter baskets dangling from a cable. The cable lifted the men to a hovering helicopter. It was a tedious process, more so when under fire. One helicopter was hit by small arms and had to pull out. Pitsenbarger had the opportunity to jump in the basket but waved off the helo, electing to stay with the survivors. For the next hour and a half he treated wounded, delivered ammunition to the men, and picked up a rifle, helping defend the position. He was killed by a sniper. His body was found with a rifle in one hand, a medical aid kit in the other. Although he didn't survive the battle, sixty Americans did.

There was no better example of an Air Force PJ.

Pitsenbarger was originally honored with the Air Force Cross. Nearly thirty-five years later, in December 2000, it was upgraded to the Medal of Honor. That ceremony was held at the National Museum of the United States Air Force, which was also located at WPAFB.

Paul and Lauren had visited his grave outside of Covington, Ohio on the way back from one of their trips to see Ronnie and Deena Beaseley in Indiana.

Paul sent a simple two word answer as the light changed.

Long story.

CHAPTER THIRTY-ONE

As the Lariat merged onto I-75 South Paul tore open a Clif Bar with his teeth. There would be no time to sit with Gatewood for a leisurely lunch. But he did want to talk to the man in person. What he was about to ask had to be done face-to-face. If Woody declined being a part of this, or Mike for that matter, Paul would go ahead with his planned course of action.

It would just be more difficult.

One reason he moved their meeting place to the Visitor Center was they could talk outside in the parking lot with no one within earshot. This would be difficult in the Pit during lunchtime.

The other reason had to do with logistics. In 2022 Wright-Patt was one of many Air Force bases that implemented a new biometric identification system to streamline the visitor pass process and decrease foot traffic. Developed by the Air Force Security Forces Center, the system prompted visitors to register through a pre-enrollment website. Their information, which includes the name of the sponsor on base that they're visiting, and a copy of the applicant's driver's license, is processed. The applicant reports to the base, in the case of WPAFB it is Building 286, and a biometrics profile is created. The applicant is fingerprinted and photographed and a background check is done.

Once this process is completed the visitor is sent a unique QR code that can be scanned upon entry, streamlining the process for subsequent visits.

Paul's QR code was on his cell phone at home. He could not bring it with him to the base without the Crank caller knowing. And he did not want the man to know he was meeting with Gatewood, or with Mike.

Paul took I-70 East to State Route 444. He passed the massive Huffman Dam, a clone of the structure he'd viewed on his bike ride earlier in the day at Lockington. Both were constructed following the 1913 flood. In the next five minutes he saw signs for both the Huffman Prarie Interpretive Center and the Flying Field itself. He pondered both, wondering if they would be part of the run-around that Crank had planned for the following day.

Paul arrived at the Area B Visitor Center at 12:15 and pulled into a small parking area after explaining to the two Airmen at the security checkpoint that he did not have his QR code and that Gatewood was coming to meet him.

Both security men beamed. One saying, "Chief Master Sergeant Dowdell. He's the man!"

Paul smiled in return.

"You got that right, Airman."

In the lot Paul opened the other three Tracfones and entered a single number into their contact lists. It was the number of the phone he'd used to text Gatewood. He set all the phones to vibrate. He had just finished when a white Dodge Durango with the word "POLICE" emblazoned on either side pulled into the space to his left. A smiling Gatewood Dowdell sat at the wheel.

He wore the mottled green and brown OCP, or Operational Camouflage Pattern, utility uniform, with the navy blue beret of the Air Force Security Forces. He rolled down his passenger side window to speak to Paul.

"Let me guess, Sticks, you don't have the QR on your new phone?"

Paul had rolled down the driver's side window of the Lariat. The midday sun beat down on the asphalt parking lot and seeped into both vehicles.

"Something like that."

Paul said it without a trace of humor.

Gatewood kept his smile, but his eyes narrowed a bit.

"You're not going to give me crap about the color of my beret?"

The navy blue beret, though desirable, did not have the cache of the red version worn by Air Force Special Forces. When Gatewood transitioned to Security from CCT after his injury, he became one of the few to ever qualify to wear both versions. He wasn't wearing the blue one every time he met Paul, but when he did, the younger man never missed an opportunity to yank his chain.

Until today.

Paul's face remained serious.

"We have to talk, Woody."

Gatewood noted the urgency in Paul's tone. His smile disappeared. He pointed first to the Lariat, then to his Durango.

"Your place or mine?"

Paul climbed into the Durango carrying two of the Tracfones, the legal pad, and the camera bag. His jaw was set, not a hint of a smile.

"What is it, Sticks? Is Lauren alright?"

The trousers of Gatewood's left leg were bloused into his boot. On his right side they were tailored to blouse to the top of his prosthetic device. This one was constructed of black carbon. He had several others. His body was angled slightly toward the passenger side. Paul knew that this wasn't solely in order to talk to him. Gatewood found it easier to drive using his left foot to operate the brake and accelerator so he angled his lower body accordingly.

"She's alright right now, but..."

Gatewood's face darkened.

"What the hell is going on, Sticks?"

Paul took a deep breath.

"Woody, Lauren and I have a big problem."

Gatewood had two words.

"Tell me."

Paul used the legal pad to give as complete an account of the situation as possible. He began with their return drive from the Beaseleys two days earlier. He gave specifics of the stop at the Wilbur Wright Birthplace as well as the two break-ins. He then recounted the phone call with Crank in great detail. When he got to the threats the caller made against

239

Patrice and the boys he paused. Paul's face was set in a mask of grim resolve.

Gatewood's face mirrored the look.

When Paul finished the briefing Gatewood asked two questions.

"What do you have in mind, and what do you need from me?"

Paul looked at his friend.

"Woody, you have too much to lose if this thing spins out. I'm going to do what I'm going to do. I don't expect you to drop everything you're doing to get a piece of this thing. I knew you would light me up if I went forward with this without telling you."

Gatewood and the love of his life, Roberta, had three kids. It was a family the man could only have dreamed of growing up in Birmingham. Roberta, or "Bert" as she was known throughout Air Force Special Operations and, now, the Security Forces, was a smart, capable woman who was a perfect match for her husband.

Their oldest, Vida, attended West Point and now flew the V-280 Valor. This was the new Army tilt-rotor aircraft similar to the V-22 Osprey flown by other branches of the service. Vida—the word meant "life" in Latin—was an impressive combination of her mother's looks and her father's personality. She finished third in her graduating class at the Point and had a long-term goal of becoming that institution's second female astronaut. Twenty-one West Point graduates had gone on to the astronaut program. To date Anne McClain, class of 2002, was the only woman.

Paul had very little doubt that Vida would be the second.

The Dowdells' second child was named William, but was know to all as Billy. He was in his final year at the Air Force Academy and was also near the top of his class. He had his eye set on jets when he graduated rather than his dad's choice of Special Operations. His parents were just fine with this. They were looking forward to the following year when Billy was expected to attend AFIT, the Air Force Institute of Technology, right here at WPAFB. It was the Air Force graduate school of engineering and management.

Paul knew that Roberta had threatened to put so much weight on Billy with his favorite home-cooked meals that he would no longer fit into a cockpit.

The couple's youngest, Henry, was a junior at Wayne High School in nearby Huber Heights, where the Dowdells resided. He had pursued Gatewood's first love, football, and excelled as a wide receiver. He was ranked nationally as a four-star—out of five—talent and already had dozens of scholarship offers. Henry had whittled his choices to a half-dozen schools and all three Service academies were on that list.

Paul knew that the head of recruiting for the Alabama Crimson Tide had recently contacted Henry. Gatewood wore a wide grin for three days after that call.

"I know exactly what I have to lose. I also have no intention of losing any of it. I would think you'd know by now that I have a pretty good idea of how to get things done. Let me know what you need and I'll figure out how to do it right. I *do* have a few connections."

He emphasized the word "do."

Paul looked his friend in the eyes and smiled.

"Well, I have no intention of giving this guy the camera."

He paused.

"I can't take it to the cops. I don't think there is any doubt that he has penetrated their computer systems. So...I thought I'd give it to you. Maybe you have a way to get some information on this guy through military channels that won't set off any tripwires he has set up."

Gatewood looked at the camera bag.

"Have you looked at the video yet?"

Paul, a bit sheepishly, admitted he had not.

"My hair's been on fire trying to put together a plan since I took his call."

Gatewood pointed to the camera.

"Let's have a look."

Paul removed the camera from its bag and turned it on. He selected the playback feature. The default setting of the unit was to show the last photo or video taken. Generally, when Paul was searching for a shot on the camera he had to scroll back through a number of exposures before he found what he was looking for. In this case, he realized, the video in question may well be the last item in its history. To be sure he covered all possibilities he skipped back several shots until he reached the final photo Lauren had taken of Brinley and Shay Beaseley playing soccer.

"Okay, everything after this was taken at the Wilbur Wright site."

He began to slowly scroll through the images. The camera had a 2x3 inch screen on the back that showed each shot, allowing both men to view them at the same time. Lauren had taken ten exposures at the site. They included a couple views of the farmhouse. Paul used the playback zoom feature to bring the rear door closer on one photo.

"Look, you can tell the interior door was open!"

Gatewood nodded, concentrating on the image.

Paul continued to scroll.

Lauren had taken pictures of a couple interpretive markers. One was labeled "Success At Last" and included photos and text from the brothers' time at Kitty Hawk. Another was entitled "Home Sweet Home." It included facts and pictures about the farmhouse. She had framed the shot of the marker by including the house itself in the background.

Paul smiled.

The next photo showed an old jet on concrete supports.

"Looks like an F-84," Gatewood intoned.

Paul looked at his mentor, showing surprise.

"Hey, my guys are responsible for security over at the Air Force Museum too. I'm not just a pretty face, Sticks."

Paul smiled and continued.

Next was a tall concrete obelisk with an image of Wilbur near the top with a quote from his father Milton carved below. This was followed by a still picture of the historical marker nearer the road that included an outline of the State of Indiana at the top, above the words "Birthplace Of Wilbur Wright."

Paul zoomed on this image. There was a cornfield in the background. He knew this had to be where Crank was located. At the instant Lauren had taken this shot, the killer was just a few feet from her. Paul had been checking out the back door on the farmhouse. Paul completed the search of the photo's background without noticing anything out of place.

He advanced the camera to the last exposure. It was a video. It started from the exact position as the previous shot, framing the historical marker. It then slowly panned to the right. The gift shop came into view, followed by the obelisk, the jet, and then the farmhouse. Paul stopped the video at this point and zoomed in to see himself at the back door, turning toward the camera. He continued. Once the farmhouse disappeared off the left side of the viewscreen there were no more structures, just a couple Hawthorn trees, the county road, and the cornfield. As the camera swept toward its original position, Paul's voice could be heard faintly, calling Lauren's name. A split second later, an image could be seen emerging from the corn.

"STOP," Gatewood commanded.

Paul stopped and toggled the vertical and horizontal playback controls to fit the image into the center of the screen. He felt like a Predator drone operator lining up a missile shot....and wished he was.

"So this is the son-of-a-bitch that is threatening our Lauren, not to mention your sister and her family?"

Gatewood said it matter-of-factly, but Paul detected some menace. He continued.

"Ugly piece of work, isn't he?" Before Paul could comment Gatewood reached for the camera. "I'm in, Sticks. I'll see if we can do anything with this without warning our boy here," he nodded at the screen.

Paul handed over the camera and the bag. Gatewood accepted them then removed the SD card and handed the camera and bag back to Paul.

"You might need this. How do I get in touch with you if this asshole is in your phone?"

Paul handed him one of the Tracfones.

"I took care of comms. The number of my new phone is programmed into this one."

Gatewood smiled.

"I knew I did the right thing when I gave you passing grades down at Keesler at Air Traffic Control School."

A smile passed over Paul's face before it took on a serious tone.

"Thanks Woody, I'll never forget this."

"Get the hell out of my Durango, you have a lot to do."

Paul was out.

CHAPTER THIRTY-TWO

By the time Smithson neared the rental on Homeview Drive his anxiety had subsided substantially. He had known there was a good chance that Biggs would be discovered in the cornfield. Anticipating this, he had given Grey a variety of tasks designed to stay ahead of the police.

His next step would be to contact Hull directly and make sure the man did not cooperate with law enforcement. It had to be made abundantly clear to the man that to do so would result in the loss of some of his loved ones. Originally Smithson theorized that he just needed to project a believable threat to Hull, not that he actually needed to be ready to carry it out. But now, the more he thought about it, an actual attack really appealed to him, especially if it involved the M4. It was such a cool weapon and it was such a pain in the ass obtaining it. Shouldn't he get some real-world use out of it?

It was just after 10 a.m. when he returned to the Airbnb. It had been a productive morning but there was much more to do. Inside the rental he immediately established the encrypted link with Grey. He saw that a 911 call was routed to the Henry County Sheriff's Department at 8:38 a.m. An INDOC road crew had come across the body.

Smithson glanced at the clock.

An hour and a half ago. Not enough time for them to connect the dots to the Hulls. Gotta seal off contact with them.

He instructed Grey to access both of the Hulls' cellphones and block all incoming calls from Henry County's area code. He didn't remember what area code it was, but Grey would figure it out. This bought some time, but it was a stopgap measure. The authorities would find a way to reach one of the Hulls, probably Paul since he'd left his number when he called from the Memorial site Wednesday.

Have to get to Hull, lay down the law.

He shifted to the file Grey had assembled with results of his last set of assignments and began to sift through.

He found several interesting nuggets.

Lauren's work schedule was in the data. It had been updated since Grey last accessed it.

Seems like the damn thing changes pretty often.

Smithson saw limited benefit from this. He assumed that, if pressed, Hull would circle the wagons around his wife and make sure she was protected. But he couldn't be in two places at once, so the information on his sister's family would be key.

Hull's brother-in-law, Kevin Chamberlain, had taken a United flight out of John Glenn International Airport in Columbus, switched planes at O'Hare outside of Chicago, and landed at Wichita's Dwight D. Eisenhower International. He would be gone through the end of the weekend.

Smithson smiled.

Wichita has an INTERNATIONAL airport?

He dug into the sister, Patrice's, information. Grey had penetrated her work appointment book at the Veterans Museum in Columbus. She had a total of five meetings scheduled outside of the office the following week. Three were lunch appointments with clients. He plotted the locations and times and added them to his supplemental "To-Do List."

He went into the family's cell phone information. They owned three, one for each of the parents and one for the older boy, Leo. All of the relevant tracker/stalker information that Smithson had requested was present. Grey had added a nice little Easter Egg for him. It seemed the younger boy, Frankie, used his mother's iPhone to play games. Before school that morning he was on it. Grey noticed and, knowing it was the sort of thing Smithson utilized, accessed the camera and snapped a picture of the boy. He was staring into the screen with the transfixed gaze that Smithson knew well.

Attaboy Grey, good work.

Curious, Smithson dug through the data to see what game the boy was playing. He found that it was *Hero Wars,* a game about building up a team of heroes and watching them make their way through dungeons.

Not a first person shooter. C'mon kid, you should be killing things by now.

Smithson spent just two minutes scrolling through Leo's texts and saw over twenty to and from a girl named Cecelia. Very tame, but useful.

Awww, puppy love.

Smithson burst out laughing.

I crack myself up sometimes.

He paused, wondering.

Am I losing it?

It seemed that he was becoming more impulsive. Certainly his immediate reaction to shoot Biggs was not well thought out. Even Smithson could not argue that he had considered all the ramifications in the short moments between Biggs' final words and the pull of the .357's trigger.

One genre of books that Smithson enjoyed was thrillers. They contained their fair share of psychopaths. A common theme in the stories was that psychopathic behavior accelerated over time, to the point that the individual no longer had control of his actions.

Similarly, serial killers were portrayed as creatures that, in the early stages of their development, have mastery over their dark impulses and can bide their time when choosing victims. Later, they are often shown to be subordinate to their desires. They begin to act without sufficient preparation. It leads to shorter cycles between murders and more loose ends, often leading to their capture.

That's how it was portrayed in the fictional accounts. It happened in almost every one of the books in the *Prey* series by John Sandford, one of Smithson's favorite authors.

He wasn't completely sure that this is how things played out in the real world, but it seemed convincing. Smithson decided he needed to make an honest self-assessment.

Were the mistakes in the Operation Crank plan an indication that he was not devoting enough attention to detail? Being hoodwinked by Biggs with the Korn brothers angle, something that he or Grey could've easily checked? The illogical escape route from the Wilbur Wright Birthplace to the rest stop where Biggs had left his car? The fact that he burglarized the Hull house with a gas tank that was nearly empty?

Smithson studied each point. He trusted Biggs. It was the mark of a good partner. Could he be criticized for that? Perhaps, but it wouldn't be fair. The escape route? Who in their right mind would've believed an escape route would ever be used. It should've been an uneventful return to the rest stop by both he and Biggs. And the gas thing, well, there was a lot going on. It was a simple oversight.

Was he losing it?

Naaaahhhhhh.

He looked at the assembled information and decided he had enough material to make contact with Hull. He had to be sure. The phone call had to be done properly. It had to get Hull's attention and convince him to do things Smithson's way. This was not an easy thing to accomplish with a man like Hull in a single phone call. Smithson could not take a chance of being recorded in subsequent calls, so this would be his one and only discussion with the man.

Even though each passing minute gave the authorities time to find a way to reach the Hulls, Smithson hesitated before making the call.

Was there more leverage he could apply?

He gave himself a few more minutes to think. Using the time to access the security system at Woodland Cemetery. He discovered that there were several cameras on the exterior fence that ringed the property. There were a few more that recorded parts of the interior, including the Tiffany Chapel and the Administrative Office.

Smithson saw that the video security company used at Woodland was the same as one of the systems he had accessed in Troy after breaking into Lauren Hull's Jeep at the hospital. It was an easy thing for him to breach their database a second time. He wiped the video records from earlier that morning, eliminating all record of his visit.

While he was in the system he decided he might as well prepare for the following day. He instructed all cameras at Woodland to shut down at 7:05 p.m., five minutes after the gates were locked for the night. This assured that anything that happened at the fence or inside the grounds would not be captured on video.

He smiled.

Back to Hull.

It seemed logical to continue with his *WWLD* theme. What would Liam do? Neeson's character went right after his adversary. No screwing around. He needed to slap Hull in the face and get his attention during this phone call. Make him realize he had no choice but to fall in line.

He needed....a demonstration.

How could he exhibit the capabilities he had. He would hit Hull with all the proprietary information Grey had ripped from the devices, including the shot of the younger boy playing *Hero Wars*.

He had to let the man know that the camera held information from the site in Indiana. Hull was going to eventually find out there was a murder, so why not play it up. Show him he wasn't fooling around. Let Hull know how serious the situation was by emphasizing his willingness to kill. It would help amplify his threats against Hull's family.

And, hey, while he's at it, why not let Grey fry Hull's laptop while they were talking on the phone?

CHAPTER THIRTY-THREE

The call went well.

Smithson considered himself an excellent judge of people and the read he got on Hull from their conversation was that the man went from taken aback, to outraged, to accepting, to almost...pliable.

It was like listening to the seven stages of grief compressed into a ten-minute telephone conversation.

Smithson reviewed his performance. He had hit all the high points. He'd gotten on top of Hull. Wasting his laptop was a nice touch. And he could feel the man's outrage when he'd texted the picture of his young nephew.

It was apparent that Hull came away from the call aware that he could not involve law enforcement in the matter. The Incident Report from the Sheriff's Department proved that Smithson could access police computer systems.

Smithson felt he'd given Hull the proper impression of his willingness to use lethal means to get what he wanted. He flat out told the man how he'd taken out Biggs. This should convey his prowess with the Colt Python. He'd also made sure to emphasize that he had an M4.

Had he also mentioned he'd killed a woman with his bare hands?

He searched his memory of the call, which had occurred just minutes earlier, and found that he wasn't sure.

No matter, his mention of the M4 planted the seed that he could reach out and destroy Hull or any of his loved ones. The raw intelligence provided by Grey combined with Smithson's willingness to carry out the threats made for a devastating combination. He felt confident he had gotten this point across to Hull.

Still, he could not trust Hull. That was why he planned to manipulate him tomorrow, to keep him moving before bringing him in close for the final act. Smithson had the ability to monitor Hull and he would take full advantage.

Smithson had chosen the spot for the end game. He still had some work to do on the preliminaries. What did they call it in boxing? The undercard. The events that occurred before THE event. Smithson planned to take care of most of this preparatory work tomorrow.

Right now he needed food. He hadn't eaten since the two slices of cold pizza hours earlier. He considered all his options and decided, once again, on McDonalds. He had no shame about this choice. Why the hell should he? He liked their fries. He liked their ice. The Big Mac was a consistent performer. If it were an FPS video game, it would be *DOOM*. It's been around forever and it's still getting it done.

He pulled up McDonalds locations on his phone and saw the closest one was just to the north on Main Street, near I-70. Smithson remembered passing it Wednesday night on his way to the rental. While he was checking locations he remembered he needed to pick up a pair of bolt cutters for the lock and chain that would be on the cemetery gate. He looked for home improvement stores and found the closest was a Lowe's, located a few minutes to the west in an area known as Trotwood.

Might as well kill two birds with one Hellfire Shotgun.

He decided to pick up the bolt cutters first then swing through the McDonalds Drive Thru and take the food back to the rental. Before leaving he paused.

Shower first?

He couldn't remember when he'd last cleaned up. Wearing the hoodie in the heat and humidity of an Ohio summer must've left him in a condition that would be improved upon by a shower. Smithson sniffed his underarms and shrugged. He couldn't tell. Deciding it could wait until after his errands he walked back to the master bathroom and dug out the Old Spice High Endurance.

Smithson took Homeview Drive east to Main, drove north a few blocks, and jumped on Shiloh Springs Road. Lowe's was just two miles west. He pulled into a parking lot that held fewer than two-dozen vehicles.

Lowe's was one of those stores that had entry doors at the left front of the building and exit doors to the right. They were separated by over a hundred feet and always presented Smithson with a quandary.

Where to park?

Does he park nearer the entrance to make for a shorter walk in, or the exit to make his return trip easier? What were the chances that he was going to buy something? If the chances were good, it made sense to park closer to the exit so he didn't have to carry the item far to reach his car. If he didn't find the item and left without making a purchase, he had needlessly walked extra steps to get in.

It's bullshit. I'm not a fucking triathlete.

The entire concept made him angry. It wasn't just Lowe's. All the home improvement companies and a great many of the computer supply businesses Smithson visited were set up this way. It was like a new generation of architects who had learned their trade designing corn mazes were put in charge of creating retail spaces across the country. Why not one main doorway that served as both an entrance and an exit? It had worked in America for two centuries.

Smithson selected a space somewhat in the center of the lot. It was slightly closer to the exit. When he got out of the Audi he realized the temperature was again climbing. But it was the humidity that set this place apart from his home state of Nevada. He could feel the dampness build under his hoodie. The temperatures were often much higher at home, but this humidity... Smithson realized it also put you in a bad mood. He walked toward the sliding doors. Before they opened, admitting him into the air-conditioned interior, he viewed his reflection.

Boy....I look really pissed.

He stopped several feet from the door so he could get a longer look.

He burst out laughing.

He must've leaned in far enough to activate the sensor. The doors slid open. Smithson found that he was confused.

Hadn't he been in a good mood after the phone call to Hull? Yes! It had gone well. Why was he so angry now?

He decided he needed a reset.

Get your head out of your ass. Get the bolt cutters.

He looked for the tool section and saw it was to his right, past the registers. He made his way there and read the signage above the different sections. The section that seemed the most relevant was under a sign reading "Pliers & Wire Cutters." Smithson walked the length of the aisle without finding what he was looking for.

He strode through the other tool aisles, finding no bolt cutters. An older man in the red vest of a Lowe's employee was restocking items in the power tool section. He glanced at Smithson at least twice.

Smithson hated to be asked if he needed help. It was a know-it-all employee's way of conveying that the customer didn't know what the hell he was doing. It was an insult. He circled back to the "Pliers & Wire Cutters" section a second time. Still no bolt cutters. What the hell did he expect? He'd already checked here.

Where are the fucking bolt cutters?!?

"Can I help you, sir?"

It was the old guy in the vest that wouldn't help Smithson before, now trying to embarrass him.

"Where the hell are the bolt cutters?" he demanded.

The man pointed to the bottom shelf.

"Uh, right there, sir."

They were indeed on the bottom shelf. Smithson had missed them. He bent to get a better look and saw there were two sizes. Both were made by Kobalt and had bright blue grips. He selected a pair of the larger size, twenty-four inch. They looked like they would cut through a solid inch of steel. He looked at the price tag and saw they were just $29.98.

Helluva deal!

He was in a fine mood now, whistling a tune. He cut the busybody shelf-stocker a break and waved to him on his way to the register. When he arrived there, however, this changed.

It was a self-checkout station. The regular registers were not open, apparently due to the low volume of store purchases at that time of day. Smithson had no trouble scanning the bolt cutters but the machine would not accept his bills when he tried to pay cash. He had a tri-fold wallet that left his bills bent in two places. They would not process no matter how he tried to slide them.

Sonuvabitch!

Smithson saw three different points where the monitor to the self-checkout register was connected to its base unit. He reached for the bolt cutters......

"Here sir, let me give you a hand."

It was a grey-haired woman wearing that damn red vest. She took Smithson's two twenties and smoothed them several times before inserting them into the bill slot. The sale was processed.

"Thank you for shopping at Lowe's."

Smithson accepted his change and walked to the door without saying a word. He exited into the sun and squinted, the humidity instantly upon him. Disoriented, he looked for the Audi. He located it and walked in that direction. As he reached the driver's door he froze. His eyes had passed over the entire lot.

There, one row over and set back several yards from any other vehicle, was a midnight silver Tesla Y with a Mensa sticker on its rear bumper. Smithson couldn't believe it.

Fucking Bucket-Hat!

He made his way to the trunk of the Audi and opened it. After dropping the bolt cutters inside he rooted around for thirty seconds before locating the Winkler combat axe. He found that if he palmed the blade and tucked it into his forearm, it fit snugly into the front pocket of his hoodie. He walked to the Tesla with a smile on his face.

Witnesses later reported that the perpetrator apparently used a weapon of some kind to scratch deep gouges in the paint of the Tesla. After scouring all sides of the vehicle, the man, described as "homeless" by one witness and "a wild-man" by another, swung his weapon several times at the rear bumper.

He then walked to a black Audi, apparently in no hurry, and drove off. Onlookers reported he was whistling the entire time. When pressed, one witness, a retired music teacher from Vandalia High School, swore the tune was *Whistle While You Work* from Disney's "Snow White and the Seven Dwarfs."

CHAPTER THIRTY-FOUR

Paul took Route 4 west toward Dayton. His original plan for the afternoon was to meet Mike McClary outside of Tipp City. The logical route there would be to link up with I-75 and head north. But a mile before the interchange Paul guided the Lariat off Route 4 and onto Valley Street. He followed Valley southwest for a mile until it ended at Keowee Street. After taking a left, he headed south into the downtown area, crossing the small Tony Stein Memorial Bridge as he passed over the Mad River.

Paul knew that most Daytonians had no idea who Tony Stein was. He was sure that very few of them were aware the bronze marker on the structure even existed. Stein, a Dayton native, was a corporal in the United States Marine Corps in World War II.

A toolmaker before joining the Marine Corps, Stein, with the help of a marine armorer, customized a .30 caliber Browning machine gun from a wrecked Douglas SBD Dauntless dive bomber. He attached it to a M1 Garand rifle butt, added a bipod, and finished with a one-hundred-round box-magazine. He used his ingenuity to create a very effective weapon out of spare parts. He named it the "Stinger," and carried it into combat.

On February 19, 1945, Stein was the first man of his unit to hit Green Beach at Iwo Jima, a name that would become synonymous with sacrifice and vicious combat. It was Stein's fourth Pacific campaign. He was a member of the famed "Lions of Iwo Jima," the Twenty-Eighth Marines, the regiment that would later raise the flag on Mount Suribachi, resulting in one of the most famous photographs in history.

Stein used his Stinger to great effect that day, eliminating Japanese pillboxes and personnel. The high volume of fire of the weapon resulted in his running out of ammunition quickly.

As the marines moved inland, Stein made no fewer than eight trips back to the beachhead for fresh ammo. Each trip back he carried a wounded marine on his back. To expedite his trips across the black sand, he removed his boots. Later, on March 1, Stein was killed while leading a patrol against a machine gun emplacement that had his company pinned down.

Tony Stein was posthumously awarded the Medal of Honor for his actions on February 19. The bridge in Dayton was dedicated to him in 1998. It featured a concrete abutment with a plaque affixed to its face.

As he passed, Paul noted the ten flagpoles that flanked the marker. It reminded him of the reference Crank made to flagpoles in their phone conversation. Paul was sure he knew where they were.

The next aspect of Paul's plan was important, and would be the lead-in to a difficult component, perhaps *the* most difficult component. Certainly the act he was planning later that day would generate a fair amount of guilt. But it couldn't be helped. Paul intended to inject an element of misdirection into the affair. He didn't initiate the situation with Crank, but he intended to end it. And he saw no reason that he had to sacrifice his freedom in order to resolve things.

He turned right on Monument Avenue, driving slowly, and four blocks later passed Day Air Ballpark on his left. He knew the Dragons were out of town so the activity around the stadium was significantly less than on the day of a home game. Monument Avenue ran beyond the left field barrier of the ballpark. Two massive green dragon heads topped the seven-story scoreboard. The dragon heads produced smoke and their eyes glowed red after a homerun by the home team. Paul had seen it many times during the dozens of games he'd attended.

Paul continued a few blocks beyond the ballpark before turning left at Jefferson Street, and then left again at 1st Street. He was now moving east, back toward the ballpark, again very slowly. He tried to take in every relevant aspect of the area. What once had been a sagging area of Dayton had been revitalized by the ballpark. The team was extremely well supported. Vacant warehouses were turned into bars and restaurants. There was a significant amount of construction equipment in the area.

Paul passed Day Air, took a right, and repeated his reconnoiter on 2nd street, moving back to the west. He was now a full block south of the ballpark. He came across a possible location for what he had planned. To be sure, he repeated his drives across 1st, Monument, and 2nd one more time. He feared doing it more than that would attract undue attention. The spot he'd found on 2nd wasn't perfect, but it would have to do.

Paul came to a red light and picked up the Tracfone that he'd come to think of as *his*. He selected the second number that he'd written down earlier, Mike McClary's, and sent a short text.

New phone, running late. On my way to Tipp. See you in 20.

As Paul merged onto I-75 North he thought back to the day he and Lauren met Mike and his wife Marge. Lauren had won two Dragons tickets in a drawing at Kettering Health for a Saturday night game. They were pleasantly surprised to see that the tickets were in the 200 section. This was behind home plate in the second deck. The seats were just a few rows up and offered an excellent view of the action. Paul had always been a baseball fan, going back to his childhood in Wappingers Falls cheering for the Mets. Lauren had not grown up as a baseball fan but enjoyed the few games they'd been able to attend during their military careers.

The Dragons, like most minor league franchises, prided themselves in the fan experience. For the most part they did not have recognizable names on their rosters like big league teams. They made up for this by packing contests, music, and scoreboard videos into down times of the game.

The franchise stumbled upon a fan favorite, Roof Man, a few years after the opening of the ballpark. Roof Man was a team employee—the actual person varied from year to year—that dressed in a form-fitting white superhero costume complete with green cape. He ran on top of the roof of the second deck between innings. He threw spongy, soft baseballs to fans while shouting "Look out below!" He had his own theme music and, eventually, his own baseball card.

Paul and Lauren were standing between innings of the game and turned to watch Roof Man overhead. Paul was working on his second twenty-ounce beer and enjoying the evening. As he turned to watch Roof Man's antics he saw the T-shirt of the man behind him. It was grey and had blue lettering outlined in orange, spelling out "THE FRANCHISE." Below this was a white circle, inside of which the numeral "41" appeared.

Paul took one look at it and, out of character, blurted out "Tom Terrific." He later thought the beer had much to do with his overture. The man, Mike, responded with "Yes! Tom Seaver," and held out a fist to be bumped.

Tom Seaver was a member of Major League Baseball's Hall of Fame. In 1969 he led the "Amazin' Mets" to an improbable World Series victory over the stacked Baltimore Orioles. He went on to play for other teams, but he would always be a Mets hero. A statue of Seaver was unveiled outside of their new Citi Field ballpark in 2022 in Queens, New York.

Paul and Mike immediately began an extended conversation on baseball. It lasted through the remainder of the game and two more beers each. They were both transplanted Mets fans in Cincinnati Reds territory. The conversation continued that night at a local watering hole and, if Paul was honest with himself, had barely diminished in the intervening years. The two men meshed so well that they didn't notice until later that night that their wives were just as good a match, having exchanged life stories and phone numbers while their husbands droned on about arcane baseball subjects like pitch framing and infield shifts.

Paul was impressed to learn that Mike had pitched professionally, reaching the Triple-A level for the Cleveland Indians. He had emphasized that he played for the Indians organization, not the new iteration of the team's name, the Guardians. Mike admitted that he once gave up what was believed to be the longest home run in the history of professional baseball, a five hundred and eighty-two foot blast in Denver's old Mile High Stadium.

The two men were amazed to discover that they'd each taken full advantage of a promotion run by the DairyLea Milk Company in New York in which coupons were printed on the side of their cartons. If you saved enough coupons, you could attend a free Mets game. The games were on specific dates, usually weeknights, and usually in the upper deck. No matter. Both Paul and Mike remembered the games and the promotion fondly.

Mike and Marge lived in South Park, a twenty-four block, one hundred fifty acre neighborhood located just south of downtown Dayton and just north of the University of Dayton campus and Woodland Cemetery.

They hailed from Yonkers, New York. It was roughly midway between Paul's hometown of Wappingers Falls and New York City. They attended Manhattan College. Mike was drafted as a pitcher after beginning his college career as a catcher, a not unheard of metamorphosis. The McClarys were a few years older than the Hulls but they shared common interests in many areas, including, but not limited to, current events, travel, and, of course, baseball.

Neither of the McClarys had a military background but they had a deep respect for service. Mike's late father had been a New York City policeman. Mike told the story that years before he was born, his father was on duty outside of the Polo Grounds when the New York Giants' Bobby Thompson hit "The Shot Heard Round The World," the home run off of the Brooklynn Dodger's Ralph Branca that clinched the 1951 National League pennant. Mike and Marge were suitably impressed by both Paul's and Lauren's military history.

Mike had an engineering degree and was putting it to use in New York State a few years after his baseball career ended. One of his clients just happened to be a distillery. A discussion with the company president led to a long-term friendship. Mike was a bourbon aficionado and impressed the man with his knowledge. The distillery was in the process of expanding their business and the president needed knowledgeable employees. Mike didn't accept the job offer, but thought long and hard about it. He and Marge had two young children, Brendan and Kaitlyn, and the time wasn't right for a career change.

Years later, after Mike had added sales experience to his repertoire, another opportunity came along. This time it involved a consortium of small distilleries that were looking to hire someone to represent them in dealing with the various state liquor agencies in the northeast. In some states, liquor agencies determine what spirits can be sold in authorized liquor stores. In others there are more arcane methods. The consortium wanted a representative to navigate the various state systems and help get their products on the shelf.

Mike was extremely successful at this. As the bourbon industry exploded in the early 2000s he and Marge, an electrical engineer by trade, started their own business, Jasper Spirits Consulting, and moved to Dayton. From this location they not only remained relatively close to their original customer base in the northeast, but benefitted greatly from their proximity to the hotbed of bourbon, Kentucky.

The word "Jasper" was a nod to the McClarys' alma mater. The nickname of the Manhattan College sports teams was the "Jaspers." It was a running joke between the two men that the abbreviation for McClary's consulting business was nearly identical to Paul's former employer, the Joint Special Operations Command.

Now firmly entrenched in Dayton, the couple ran the business from their small two-story house on Oak Street. Mike remodeled the interior and Marge decorated it in what she jokingly referred to as "Cheerful Irish." The small back yard had been completely replaced by a paved courtyard that featured a large firepit in its center.

The McClarys entertained often and took full advantage of their firepit area. They had parties every few months, many with offbeat themes, and had a wide circle of friends. Most of the parties featured several couples, sometimes referred to as "the usual suspects." Paul and Lauren were happy to count themselves among these couples.

The couple's business had branched out to other spirits, hence the inclusion of that word in the company name. Marge, in addition to being responsible for the day-to-day operation of the office, was making inroads in the wine industry. Mike dealt with all liquors but bourbon was his first love. Parties at the McClarys' always featured the latest samples from their clients.

The McClarys had a party scheduled for the following evening. No rain was in the forecast so the back yard area would be put to good use. Mike needed to stock up on firewood and planned to load his pickup truck at a farm outside of Tipp City. Paul had met him there in the past and agreed to help again today. On Sunday, the day after the party, Mike and Marge planned to pull their camper, known as "The Bourbon Trail'r," to Tennessee. They would leave the camper at a KOA while visiting their son Brendan, an intern for the Nashville Sounds minor league baseball team. Their daughter Kaitlyn was now a teacher and certified athletic trainer in a Dayton-area school system.

As Paul neared the Tipp City exit he realized he might not get home before Lauren. She needed to be brought up to speed on the situation. He had hoped to do this in person.

He decided he had to at least give her a synopsis of what had happened. He couldn't take a chance that she might go somewhere other than home when she got off work. He reached for his Tracfone and called the number of the lab from memory. When Josie picked up Paul asked for Lauren. He was put on hold for a short time before his wife came on.

"Hi Paul, what's up?"

Paul sighed.

"You might want to set down."

He explained as concisely as possible, ending with instructions.

"When you get home, stay there. Remember, he tracks the phones. Both of ours will be in the same place and this Crank guy will think we're together. I don't think he'll try anything as long as he thinks you're with me."

Five minutes later he came to a stop at the end of the ramp at Tipp City. As his turn signal blinked, Paul reviewed one difficult conversation, the one he just had with Lauren, and became apprehensive over another he was about to have.

CHAPTER THIRTY-FIVE

Gatewood watched from his Durango as Paul guided his pickup truck back through the security gate and onto State Route 444. As the Lariat merged with traffic and disappeared to the west, he looked at the camera in his hand. The story he'd just been told infuriated him. As a Combat Controller, Gatewood prided himself on professionalism. Being able to focus on the task at hand was not just a desired quality for that job, it was a necessity. This skill also served him well in his current position in the Security Forces.

Gatewood would proceed in a calculated manner. He knew it was the most efficient way to get results. But this was personal. He thought about the threats this Crank character had made to his friend.

Make no mistake, asshole. I'm coming for you.

He made the short drive to the 88th Security Forces Squadron building on Z Road and parked the Durango. He picked up the SD card from the cup holder and tucked it and the Tracfone into his breast pocket before swinging his legs out the door. He nimbly hopped out and made for his office. On the way down the hall he stuck his head inside a room with several cubicles and computers. Eight enlisted personnel shared the room. Several were at lunch but the one Gatewood was looking for was at his cubicle.

"Airman Alabaster?"

A thin man looked up from his computer screen. He was in his twenties, had short black hair, and wore dark-framed government-issued prescription glasses. His eyebrows went up when he saw Gatewood.

"Chief Master Sergeant Dowdell?"

Gatewood pointed toward his office at the end of the hall.

"A minute?"

Alabaster nodded and shut down his computer, a personal security measure that he insisted on whenever leaving his workstation. That completed, he followed Gatewood down the hall.

"Close the door and have a seat, Airman."

Alabaster complied.

Gatewood sat behind his desk, his fingers steepled.

"Lets dispense with military decorum for a few minutes, that alright with you?"

Alabaster's countenance did not change. He remained attentive, but nodded.

"Sure, Chief Master Sergeant."

Gatewood smiled.

"I believe you remember my friend, retired Master Sergeant Hull?"

Senior Airman Charles Sterling Alabaster produced a wide grin. He had met Paul twice, both on occasions that the retired CCT had visited Gatewood in their building. Alabaster had a history of struggling to fit in. In high school in Maine he was a bit of a loner, not necessarily of his own choice. He didn't play sports, had no steady girlfriend, and fought a scorched earth battle with acne. Consequently, he buried himself in computer-related activities. This served him well when he joined the Air Force.

Alabaster became an enlisted Cyber Systems Operations Specialist. He had a skillset that was in high demand. It didn't seem to matter when he came to WPAFB. His government issued glasses, called "BCGs," or Birth Control Glasses, by some based on their ability to repel the opposite sex, combined with his fastidious manner, meant that he continued to be a bit of an outcast.

His name didn't help. Synonyms for "alabaster" include *extremely pale, lacking color,* and *anemic.* His family's British heritage was the basis for the last name. Alabaster was derived from the word *arbalester,* which was a term for a man who built or used crossbows in the 12th century. Charles tried to explain this to those that made fun of his name, calling him

"Airman Pale" or simply "Blanco," Spanish for white. It did no good.

And that was just his last name. He went to great efforts to conceal his middle name, knowing from experience it would make things worse.

Sterling? What were my parents thinking?

When Gatewood came to the 88th, he was preceded by his reputation. Rumors flew about the new Chief Master Sergeant that was about to move in, a former "Snake-Eater," or member of the Joint Special Operations Command. At Gatewood's introductory meet and greet with all the enlisted personnel of the unit he asked a question that got everyone's attention.

"Show of hands, who here is working at their absolute highest potential?"

The question was designed to show that every person in the room could up his or her game. Gatewood expected everyone to stare nervously, more or less admitting that they could perform at a higher level for him than they had for the outgoing Chief Master Sergeant.

One hand had gone up. Alabaster's.

In a movie, Alabaster would be singled out as a know-it-all that thought he was the smartest person in the room. He would be run out of the unit by the new boss. In fact a number of sets of eyes turned to Alabaster that day with barely concealed derision.

Not Gatewood's. He looked at the E-4 with raised eyebrows.

"Hello...what have we here? Okay Senior Airman, come see me after this meeting."

A few in the room smiled, believing Alabaster was about to get chewed out.

Alabaster went to Gatewood's office that day and left an hour later having laid out the reasons for his confidence. Over the next couple weeks Gatewood came to understand that Alabaster was right. His work product was fantastic. In part this may have been due to Alabaster's lack of interests outside of work. No matter, he became the person most trusted by Gatewood to get things done.

When Alabaster met Paul Hull for the first time, he was pleasantly surprised. Instead of coming across as a don't-screw-with-me type, Paul was friendly and cheerful. He spent several minutes talking to Alabaster. One topic was fantasy football. Alabaster was taking his lunch at his workstation and reviewing printouts of his team. Paul was curious.

"You know, I never got into that. How exactly does the point system work?"

Alabaster enthusiastically explained. Months later Paul visited again and made a point of checking in with the Airman to ask about his team.

"Hey, I forgot to ask. What is the name of your team?"

Alabaster had answered, a bit sheepishly.

"The Ala-Blasters."

Both men laughed.

"Sure, I remember Master Sergeant Hull...great guy."

Gatewood nodded.

"Great guy, great family, fantastic Combat Controller."

He paused then looked Alabaster in the eye.

"What I'm about to tell you is a close hold, understand Charles?"

Gatewood's use of his first name as well as his change in tone got Alabaster's attention. He nodded.

"There has been a threat to Master Sergeant Hull's family by," he searched for words, "some nut-job."

Alabaster's eyebrows went up.

Gatewood gestured to the SD card.

"There is a video of the guy on this card. I want to find him. I believe you know I have a number of uh...*connections* that I can access?"

Alabaster nodded again.

"What I need is a high-resolution still photo of this guy taken from the video at the end of the SD card, one that I can get in the hands of the right people. People that can help track him. This is completely off the reservation. It will not go through official channels, I can't tell you why. If you're not comfortable doing this there will be no repercussions. I completely understand."

The men looked at each other for three seconds before Alabaster reached for the card.

"Give me ten minutes, Chief Master Sergeant."

After Alabaster left, Gatewood put his personal cellphone and the Tracfone on his desk. He spent several minutes going through his contacts and jotted down over a dozen names. It was quite a list.

It included a current Master Chief Petty Officer at SEAL Team 6, a Master Sergeant at Delta, and senior enlisted CCTs that were based at Hurlburt Field in Florida, Pope Air Force Base in North Carolina, and Kirtland AFB in New Mexico. Also on the list was an E-9 at Space Operations Command, a former Marine Corps Captain that ran a security company in Texas, and a private security consultant from Oregon that Gatewood had played golf with at a Wounded Warriors outing.

Lastly there was an E-8 that was stationed at Air Force Security Forces Center at Joint Base San Antonio-Lackland in Texas.

Gatewood pulled up contact numbers on his phone and dialed on the Tracfone. Several of the calls went to voicemail, as the person on the other end did not recognize the number of the burner. A few picked up, usually with challenge in their voice. All received the same greeting from Gatewood.

"Don't hang up. This is your boy, Woody. I need a favor."

Gatewood worked the phones. His calls went out. Calls were returned by those who let Gatewood's first call go to voicemail. He juggled conversations, asking for and receiving secure and personal email addresses. Two hours in, he had created and activated a loose intelligence network that was highly motivated to assist him.

As promised, Alabaster had produced an extremely high quality still inside of ten minutes. He sent it to Gatewood's Tracfone. The former CCT stared at the image and shook his head. He spoke in a low tone.

"You are one unfortunate son-of-a-bitch."

The image went out to Gatewood's net. It would take most of a day, but it would produce results.

CHAPTER THIRTY-SIX

Paul approached the familiar farm two miles west of Tipp City. A sign near the property announced "Firewood, U-Load." Almost as an afterthought, a second sign read "Split." Paul saw the McClarys' new grey Dodge Ram backed up to a large woodpile near the barn. Mike was tossing pieces of firewood into the bed of the truck.

Mike was a solid man. He stood six feet, four inches and weighed in the vicinity of two hundred and thirty pounds. He'd done some running after his baseball career but a knee injury relegated him to walking for a good portion of his exercise. At this, he generally set a fast pace, and not just when exercising. His wife Marge, a petite woman, joked that she'd spent the last few decades hurrying to catch up to him.

Paul parked the Lariat next to the Dodge Ram. At the sight of him Mike, who was wearing cargo shorts, a plain grey T-shirt, leather gloves, and a well-worn low profile blue Mets cap over his short brown hair, grinned.

"There's the Lariat! If I didn't need something bigger to pull the Bourbon Trail'r I'd be loading her right now. How's she..."

Mike's voice trailed off. He had a piece of firewood in his hands. Like Gatewood earlier, he had seen something in Paul's face.

"Looks like those break-ins are still bothering you. Hope you and Lauren can still make it tomorrow night. You look like you could use a bourbon or two."

Paul stared at his friend. He had forgotten that the McClarys were aware of the incidents.

"It's worse than you know."

The two men looked at each other for a brief second before Mike tossed the piece of split tree trunk into the bed of the Ram. He turned to Paul, removed his gloves, and spoke two words.

"Tell me."

Paul recounted the events of the last few days as well as the phone call with the Crank as accurately and succinctly as possible. When he mentioned the threats against Lauren, Patrice, and the boys, Mike's eyes narrowed. Paul, who couldn't remember his friend uttering more than a handful of curse words the past few years, was mildly surprised by Mike's comment.

"The son-of-a-bitch."

There was a touch of malice in the delivery.

Mike had no experience utilizing the complicated communications gear and targeting hardware that Paul did, but he was well versed in the use of computers and digital systems. He virtually ran his business from his cell phone.

"And you don't think you can go to the police with this?"

Paul went into more detail on the Miami County Sheriff's Department Incident Report that Crank had texted.

"I don't think there is any doubt that he's inside the systems of law enforcement. I have no idea how. It's like he's some kind of super-hacker. He knew about the body being found in Indiana this morning. I've been checking the sheriff's log from that county every day since Wednesday and I know it hadn't appeared earlier. I'm willing to bet it's still not public knowledge."

He continued.

"The hacking is just part of the equation. Far and away, the biggest problem is his threat to come after my family. I don't think that goes away even if I give him the damn camera."

He stared at Mike.

"I won't let that happen."

There was a tone in those words that got Mike's attention. He supposed he wasn't completely surprised by it. He was aware of enough of Paul's military background that he knew a hard edge must've resided inside. But he had not seen it. He thought he'd just glimpsed a miniscule example of it.

A fleeting thought went through Mike's head. He was pitching for the Indians' Double-A affiliate in Waterbury,

272

Connecticut in 1985. The ballpark, Waterbury Municipal Stadium, was built in 1930 as a dog track, resulting in odd dimensions for baseball. They were playing the last place Reading Phillies. Mike was throwing a shutout, leading 7-0 in the sixth inning. The game was over. It just didn't know it yet.

Mike's roommate Jay Bell was at the plate. Bell was having an excellent season. He would be called up to the big club the following year and enjoy an eighteen year major league career, highlighted by winning a World Series with the 2001 Arizona Diamondbacks. Apparently upset over something that occurred earlier in the season, the Reading pitcher threw three straight pitches up and in, the last catching Bell squarely in the helmet. He had to be carried from the field. The Indians' dugout exploded. The umpires, sensing trouble after the second pitch, were able to get to the foul lines to hold both teams back. Mike watched his roomie being carried through the dugout and down the tunnel to the clubhouse. He was furious.

As he looked away from Bell, Mike's eyes landed on those of his manager, Orlando Gomez. Beginning in 1964, the man had spent thirteen years toiling as a player in the minors. He would go on to coach and manage until 2016. He never spent a day in the major leagues. He had been through the wars of professional baseball and knew what had to be done. He nodded at Mike, who nodded back.

When Mike returned to the mound he would be headhunting. He remembered the feeling and realized it paled in comparison to the look on Paul's face.

"So, what are you thinking?"

The question hung there for a moment.

Paul looked at his friend, took a deep breath, and laid out his plan. He left the part that Mike could assist with intentionally vague.

McClary seized upon it immediately.

"That's where I come in."

Paul hesitated.

"I can't ask you..."

Mike interrupted.

273

"Do you remember my get-together last year after that thing in Bardstown?"

Bardstown, Kentucky, located thirty minutes south of Louisville, was considered by some to be the epicenter of the bourbon industry. The Kentucky Bourbon Trail, now a popular tourist attraction, boasted several stops in and around the town. It was the home of a number of brands known throughout the world as well as a sprinkling of new companies looking for their niche in the market. Jasper Spirits Consulting had several clients in the area.

Paul thought back to the party. He remembered that one of the McClarys' clients had been the victim of ransomware. An outside network had hacked into the company's computer system. They used cryptoviral extortion, encrypting the distillery's files, making them inaccessible, and demanded a ransom payment of forty thousand dollars to decrypt them.

The president of the company had confided in Mike that he quietly had his staff and an outside firm rebuild their system from scratch. It had cost significantly more than forty thousand. Paul remembered with a smile that the president, a self-made man and good old boy from rural Kentucky, had sent a message back to the hackers.

"Go to hell."

The man explained to Mike that there was no guarantee the extortion would not continue into the future even if he paid the initial asking price. He could be out much more than the forty grand. With no realistic chance of ever getting his hands around the hackers' necks, he figured his three-word email was the best he could do.

The story had triggered a discussion about hackers, computer security, and the general state of living in a digital age in the 2020s. Each of the attendees seemed to have recent examples of things that had happened to them.

Some were as simple as receiving scam emails.

Phil and Teresa had received an email that day that read *Your McAfee Subscription has Expired Today, click HERE to renew*. It was from an email address in the United Kingdom that contained the word "Revolutionary."

Paul—a different Paul—and Donna had received one saying *Nicole Rebar has sent you protected messages. We kindly ask that you use the link below to review them.* They knew no one by that name.

Tom and Eileen were in receipt of one that almost comically tried to convey urgency: *Your Account May Be Removed Today! All Devices Are Unprotected!!! LAST REMINDER: Confirmation Needed, Click HERE.*

Mark and Megan were at the party. Mark was a retired Deputy Chief with the Dayton Fire Department. He'd put in thirty years and, in his mid-fifties, had several years remaining to enjoy their three sons and his passion for sports. Like Mike and Paul, he attended a number of Dayton Dragons games and had become a bit of a local celebrity. He sported a fireman's helmet painted Dayton Dragons green at the games. It was topped with a variety of bobblehead figures, baseball cards, and Dragons paraphernalia affixed by glue. Mark could scarcely walk to the beer stand without being asked to be in a photo by another fan.

Megan, a purchasing agent for Reynolds and Reynolds, was used to this and to Mark's love of sports. Their basement was adorned with souvenirs from trips to various Major League Baseball stadiums and National Football League venues.

They had received an email a day or two prior to the party that read, *This is a confirmation email of you recent purchase with us. Invoice 74448156. Please click to review.*

Megan joked that Mark, who was known to sometimes impulsively purchase things online, may have fallen for it and clicked on the supposed invoice if not for the incorrect use of "you" instead of "your" in the body of the email. Many of the attendees smiled, aware that Mark was a notorious and generous gift-giver. A good percentage of his purchases had found there way to some of them in the past.

But some of the stories shared that day were less than humorous. Scott and Ruth owned a business that was at that moment dealing with a computer virus, believed to have infected their system when an employee opened an attachment she thought came from a customer.

Mike continued.

"The point is, I'm just as fed up with these cyber criminals as anyone. I would help go after this guy even if it was a computer thing. But he's coming after your family. How can I help?"

Paul smiled and outlined most of his plan.

Mike stopped him at one point and asked specifics about the camera and the video.

Paul answered.

"I've seen it and I can confirm what it shows, but I don't have it right now. I gave it to another....friend."

McClary grinned.

"Gotta be Gatewood."

Paul's smile confirmed it.

At the end of Paul's delivery, Mike asked a question.

"*Exactly* what can I do to help?"

Paul eyed him.

"How do you feel about putting on a scavenger hunt?"

CHAPTER THIRTY-SEVEN

After laying out the entire proposal to Mike, Paul said he was staying to help load the wood. Mike argued, contending Paul obviously had more pressing tasks, but Paul insisted.

"It will do me some good, help me blow off some steam. Besides, it'll only take a few minutes."

Paul retrieved his own pair of worn leather gloves from under the seat of the Lariat. Fifteen minutes later the bed of the Dodge Ram was filled to capacity. Paul gave Mike one of the Tracfones and the small duffel bag before opening the door to the Lariat.

"Sorry to dump this on you, Mike."

He looked genuinely regretful.

Mike waved him off.

"I'd be upset if you hadn't. Now get out of here. You work on your part. Marge and I will get started on ours."

On his way down the farm lane Paul reflected on the mention of Marge's name.

Another person I care about in the middle of this mess.

He couldn't decide if he should be remorseful for involving his friends, or be happy they were there to help.

He couldn't decide.

So he was both.

The events of the day were wearing on Paul. He tried to clear his mind. As he pulled the Lariat out of the farm lane and onto the country road he noticed a leaf falling from a maple tree across the road. In was not yet September, but the low amount of precipitation that summer had accelerated the process of leaves changing on some deciduous trees.

Paul watched the leaf float downward, riding the air currents. He allowed himself a half smile. Falling leaves reminded him of Wilbur Wright. In 1901, two years before the

First Flight, Wilbur was invited to address the Western Society of Engineers in Chicago. He had become a frequent letter writer to Octave Chanute, a self-taught engineer of some renown who acted as a sort of central data repository of all information on flight. No one had yet attained powered flight. Many were trying. A good number of them, including Wilbur, wrote Chanute with information on their theories and experiments. Chanute compiled this information and disseminated it to others.

Wilbur was a relative unknown. But his wind tunnel experiments told he and Orville that they were on the right track. Glider experiments at Kitty Hawk were proving this correct.

Wilbur hated giving speeches. He once said, "I know of only one bird that talks—the parrot—and it can't fly very high." Yet he accepted Chanute's invitation, traveling by train to Chicago and wearing a suit borrowed from Orville, a more dapper dresser.

His speech, twice as long and much more technical than the engineers in the audience expected, stunned the listeners. Paul was particularly impressed by Wilbur's description of the problem of control when approaching flight. It was simple, yet eloquent. Paul had read it many times.

Holding a piece of paper in the air, Wilbur stated:

> *If I take this piece of paper, and after placing it parallel with the ground, quickly let it fall, it will not settle steadily down as a staid, sensible piece of paper ought to do, but it insists on contravening every recognized rule of decorum, turning over and darting hither and thither in the most erratic manner, much after the style of an untrained horse. Yet this is the style of steed that men must learn to manage before flying can become an everyday sport.*

Paul's smile expanded to both corners of his mouth. He imagined the effect Wilbur's speech must've had on the audience. The organization typically invited engineers as speakers. Men coming from a discipline with a proven set of facts. Many, when finding a prospective flyer would be addressing them, no doubt expected a crank. Instead they witnessed a self-taught intuitive genius.

Paul remembered a time when *he* was an unknown, when expectations of him were limited. It was during his time downrange in Afghanistan, his first time working with Delta. After being inserted by the best helicopter squadron in the world, the 160th Special Operations Aviation Regiment, known as the Night Stalkers, the boys from Delta took down their objective. But they had stirred up a hornet's nest. Taliban fighters swarmed from three sides, pushing in close. They used this tactic to prevent the Americans from calling in air strikes. The closer they got to the Delta troopers, their thinking went, the less chance the Americans would drop ordnance and take a chance of killing their own people.

Harp, a master sergeant, was the senior enlisted man for Delta on the mission. He turned to Paul as the AK-47 rounds cracked through their position.

"What you got, Air Force?"

Paul was wearing a Deltor headset that helped him hear the pilots overhead. He utilized three different radios, including his PRC-117 satellite unit. Four different types of aircraft were overhead, all on different frequencies. All had different loiter times due to differing fuel loads. Each had distinctive weapons and ordnance. Each would need to be employed with a unique, specific method. This had to be done under fire, with friendlies nearby.

Paul made use of FalconView, a moving map program developed at Georgia Tech that tracked every friendly unit in Afghanistan. He employed his SOFLAM target designator.

The precision strikes he called in decimated the Taliban fighters surrounding their position, even at their close proximity. Later, as the assaulters rode the Night Stalker helos back to base, one of the Delta troopers asked Paul how he did it.

Before Paul could speak, Harp answered the man.

"It was FM, pure FM."

The trooper looked at Harp with a questioning look.

Harp elaborated.

"Fucking Magic."

It was nearly 3:30 when Paul arrived home. He was somewhat surprised to see Lauren's Jeep in the garage. He walked into the kitchen and saw her standing at the island, hugging Chappy to her chest with both arms. She turned to him. He saw a mixture of fear and anger in her eyes.

"All of this because a video?"

Her question was laced with indignation. It had a *how dare he* quality.

Paul nodded and stepped toward her. He put one arm around her and scratched Chappy's head with the other.

Lauren returned the embrace with her right arm. As she did, Chappy's lower body slid down her torso. He was pinned between the couple. Only his head and front paws remained suspended above Lauren's left forearm, his wide lower body oozed toward the floor. He looked like a chunky version of the cat in the "Hang in there baby" poster.

Lauren looked down at Chappy and giggled. She couldn't help it.

"This whole situation is just so...ridiculous."

She shook her head as she eased Chappy to the floor. The cat arched its back and rubbed against her leg.

They sat at the table for forty minutes. Lauren asked Paul to fill in the gaps from his call earlier in the day. At the end of the conversation she asked a single question.

"Is there any other way out of this?"

Paul looked at her, shaking his head slowly.

She took a deep breath before nodding.

"Okay, get to work. I'm cooking tonight."

Paul went to the walk-in closet and knelt. The break-in, combined with Lauren's removal of the bins of clothing, left the closet in a bit of disarray, despite the couple's efforts to reorganize it. He spent two minutes groping through and under the hanging clothes before finding what he was searching for.

He pulled out the Ruger 10/22 rifle.

It was a semiautomatic, the carbine version. The stock was light brown and the barrel was just eighteen and a half inches long. It had a box-shaped magazine that held ten rounds. Paul had mounted a four-power scope on the rifle as a teenager. The rifle hadn't been fired in a few years but Paul had cleaned and oiled it after its last use and it still appeared to be in excellent condition.

Paul brought the Ruger out of the closet and laid it on the bed. He went to the nightstand on his side of the bed and opened the top drawer. He fished through shoestrings, a book light, and a dozen odd items before his hand found a small rectangular shape. He pulled out a green and yellow box of Remington .22 Long Rifle ammunition.

Paul opened the box and saw most of the one hundred rounds remained. He reached back in the drawer and seconds later found a second item, an extra magazine for the Ruger. He gathered the items and carried them out to the table.

While Lauren made spaghetti, Paul found latex gloves and a microfiber cloth under the sink and added them to the items on the table. He then disappeared into the garage before returning with a selection of screwdrivers. He put on the gloves and removed one of the .22 rounds from the box.

Paul held it in the light. He had handled thousands of bullets in his life. Most were 5.56 NATO cartridges fired through the M4 he carried on missions. This was the same weapon the Crank claimed to possess. The little .22 seemed almost harmless by comparison.

Paul wiped down the cartridge with the microfiber. He then selected one of the screwdrivers, a small flat-head model, and used it to scratch at the brass exterior of the cartridge. It was difficult to hold the round steady enough to accomplish his task. He reached for a different screwdriver, slightly larger, and tried again. Intent on his task, Paul didn't realize he had an audience.

"You're really sure this part is necessary?"

Paul looked up to see Lauren standing at his right. Chappy had jumped up onto the table and was staring intently at the open box of .22s.

He ran a gloved hand through his hair.

"Who knows? It's a risk, but the potential payoff is huge. It could decide whether we walk away from this..."

He hesitated before finishing.

"...or, I do."

Lauren's eyes narrowed.

"We're in this together. Don't forget that I outrank you, Master Sergeant. You go finish the spaghetti. Give me those gloves."

Paul looked at her with a mixture of surprise and amusement.

"Are you sure?"

"I handle small slides all day, working with microscopes and the analyzer. Plus, I have smaller hands than you."

They traded places. After experimenting with the screwdrivers for less than a minute, Lauren went to the same kitchen drawer that Paul had opened earlier when he accessed the address book. She rummaged through it for a few seconds before producing an X-Acto knife. She turned toward Paul and held it up.

"Gotta use the right tools."

She smiled at Paul. As she did so, something clattered to the floor behind her. Both Lauren and Paul turned toward the table. Chappy was still there. He was watching the .22 cartridge that Lauren had been working on as it rolled between her feet and came to rest in front of Paul.

They looked at each other with raised eyebrows.

Paul couldn't resist.

"It's a one-in-a-million shot that round lands just right and goes off. This whole situation is already convoluted. The only thing that would make it more absurd is being shot by our cat."

Lauren picked up the cartridge and returned to the table.

"I don't think Chappy's out to get us. I think he just wants to help."

She scratched under Chappy's ear. The cat slowly blinked at her. He seemed to be wondering why he was being rewarded for being on the table, a surface that had always been off limits.

When the spaghetti was ready they cleared a space on the island. They sat on stools and ate, mostly in silence, their thoughts to themselves. Afterward they cleaned up together.

Lauren returned to the table to work on the cartridges. Paul joined her long enough to remove the scope from the Ruger. He looked over her shoulder as she finished with one of the rounds.

"You really have a talent for this, maybe you should advertise in some of the shooting magazines, pick up some extra cash."

She smirked.

"I think this skill has a very limited customer base."

Late afternoon faded into early evening as Lauren finished. She had worked on thirty cartridges. Wearing gloves, Paul loaded ten into each magazine, sealing the final ten rounds into a plastic baggie. He handed it to Lauren.

"Maybe put this in the drawer? Someplace Chappy can't get to. Imagine these being spread all over the house after things go down the next day or so."

Lauren, also still wearing her gloves, opened the drawer and placed the baggie and one of the magazines inside. She closed it and exhaled. She hadn't realized she'd been holding her breath. At the table, Paul inserted the other magazine into the rifle.

"Well, that's ready. On to the next thing."

He gathered up the screwdrivers and went back to the garage. He banged around for a short time before returning. In place of the screwdrivers he now held a white plastic bucket, a paintbrush, a wooden paint stirrer, and a handheld garden trowel. He set the paintbrush and stirrer on the kitchen table before sliding open the patio door and walking outside.

Paul moved to the flowerbed just beyond the patio. He knelt between two rose bushes. They still retained some of the blooms from earlier in the summer, pink on Paul's left, red on his right. Lauren's mother, Lisa, had sent several rose bushes to the couple as a housewarming gift. They were a poignant reminder that Lauren's dad had helped select Rose as her middle name. The flowers had thrived in the Ohio climate.

Paul used the trowel to dig between the bushes. He added soil to the bucket until it was a third full then leveled out the low spot he'd created. He returned to the kitchen and sat the bucket inside the sink. He added water to the bucket before using the stirrer to mix it in. He repeated the process two more times until the contents reached the proper consistency.

Lauren had started a load of laundry. She climbed the final steps from the basement in time to see Paul finish.

"Hmmm, you might've discovered a better way to mix pancake batter."

Paul smiled.

"Maybe if I was cooking for an entire assault team."

He walked past her, snatched up the paintbrush, and set the bucket inside the garage. He laid the brush on top of the mixture inside the bucket. He returned, stood near the table, and looked at the ceiling.

"What am I forgetting?"

Lauren thought.

"The phone?"

Paul snapped his fingers.

"That's it!"

He retrieved the fourth Tracfone from the Lariat and spent the next several minutes reviewing its features with Lauren before summarizing.

"Make sure to text, not call, unless it's an emergency...make sure the phone is charged before—"

Lauren held up a hand.

"Paul, for the love of god...I was a Warrant Officer."

CHAPTER THIRTY-EIGHT

Smithson was pissed.

He was pissed *because* he was pissed.

Why had he lost control at Lowe's?

Gotta get a grip. Taking too many chances.

He was driving back to the Airbnb, trying to get there as soon as possible without breaking any traffic laws. He checked his mirrors, looked back to the street in front, and immediately went back to the mirrors.

He reviewed the incident.

That goddamned Bucket-hat guy!

The more Smithson thought about it, the more it made sense. He *had* to get payback. But did he have to completely lose his mind with the Winkler?

He laughed out loud, caught himself, and checked his mirrors again.

If the cops pull me over I'm screwed. Gotta get back to the house.

He continued to review the incident.

There was an older woman walking through the parking lot. I swung the tomahawk at that fucking MENSA sticker and it got stuck at some point. When I was trying to get it loose I looked up and there she was. Was she filming me? Taking my picture?

He concentrated, seeing the replay in his mind's eye.

No! She was on her phone...probably calling 9-1-1.

He checked his mirrors again.

Maybe I dodged a bullet. This whole fiasco is happening because somebody filmed me and I can't wipe the video remotely. If that lady in the parking lot got my image I'd be screwed. There will be store video...Grey can fix that. The lady probably gave the cops a description...that's pretty vague. But she might've seen my plates. Gotta change them pronto.

He was nearing Homeview Drive now and checked his mirrors one more time. No cops.

It's a good thing I wasn't in a Starbucks parking lot. Every fucking person there would have video of me on their phone. I'd be trending in fucking China by now.

The image of the older woman floated back into his head.

Had she been wearing yoga pants?

For Chrissakes.

Smithson made it to the house and pulled up to the garage door. He had access to the garage but hadn't made use of it yet. He asked himself why and couldn't come up with an answer.

Why let the Audi set outside where anyone could see it? Probably should've been parking it inside all along.

He shook his head as he pulled the S8 into the garage and closed the door. He popped the trunk and dug out the Nebraska plates. He found a screwdriver on the workbench and in five minutes had replaced the plates.

He went inside and went through the now-familiar progression of establishing the secure connection with Grey for the purpose of wiping his image from a security system.

This is getting old.

Grey was once again up to the task. It took several minutes, but the Lowe's system was accessed and the recordings for all cameras on the front of the building were eliminated. Smithson believed this was done before they were viewed or forwarded to the Trotwood police.

When the process was completed Smithson let out a breath.

I could use a beer.

He opened the refrigerator and grabbed one of the Warped Wings. He saw the remaining pizza and realized he was starving. He took hold of it and pulled it out. He searched through the cupboards and found a large plate. Half the pizza went onto it before he slid it into the microwave.

Smithson watched through the clear front window of the oven. He took a long pull on the beer.

Had my heart set on McDonalds.

Smithson sat the plate on the table and let it cool as he sipped the beer. The laptop was there so, of course, his hands went to the keyboard. He had no specific task to perform, but like many in the age of computers he started clicking away without knowing quite where he was going.

He started on the pizza. He ate quickly despite the fact that the two-day old banana peppers now added a tang that left the pieces just this side of disagreeable.

He meandered though his email, his bank accounts, and the weather channel. He saw that another hot and humid day was expected again tomorrow but a front was due in Sunday that could bring rain. He went to his favorites and selected *egamersworld.com* where he saw that his favorite team, Evil Geniuses, was kicking ass.

Maybe look again into getting involved with that.

He had checked into esports—organized multi-player video gaming by professional teams—a year earlier and was surprised to find the top teams were valued at four hundred to five hundred million dollars each. Esports had a worldwide audience and was particularly popular in Asia. Smithson had briefly thought about buying a team before he saw the price tag. He didn't have that kind of money—yet—that was mainly because he hadn't really tried to compile massive sums. He had been more interested in inserting himself into the lives of those he extorted, disrupting their worlds. He supposed he could expand Grey's parameters to identify more victims and ratchet up the demands.

Yeah, maybe I'll buy a team...be the star player on it too.

Smithson continued to peruse the *egamer* site and noticed they had picked up a new sponsor. The banner ads read "Quality Toys and Accessories for Adults Try It."

Smithson snorted.

That's about right, adult advertising on the egamer site.

But it got him thinking.

Maybe I should call an escort service, get hooked up with a woman.

The thought hung in his mind for a few seconds before he shook it away.

Dumbass, that's the last thing you need. Lay low. Stay in for the rest of the day. You just went fucking Crazy Horse on a Tesla.

He decided the smarter play was to take it easy with some games.

Maybe some more OVERWATCH 2. This basement setup is sweet. It's not the Lair, but it's pretty sweet.

Before going down to the basement he decided to check on the Hulls. He pulled up the current locations of their phones as well as the Escape and the Jeep. All four were at the Polecat Road location.

Right where they're supposed to be. Probably feeling sorry for themselves.

Smithson closed the Toughbook. He grabbed a second beer and headed for the basement.

At 6:50 p.m. he came up for air.

Wow, I was down there for almost four hours?

He had geeked out on *OVERWATCH 2.* He played for an hour and a half as the character "Winston," a genetically engineered gorilla who utilizes a Tesla Cannon. Smithson appreciated the ironic name of the weapon given the incident he'd been involved in earlier in the day. Winston's other abilities were Jump Pack, which allowed him to jump on enemies to cause damage, Barrier Projector, which permitted him to deploy a protective dome, and Primal Rage, which speaks for itself.

Smithson made full use of this last power.

Word to the wise... do not screw with a pissed off gorilla.

He considered that thought.

That would be a damn good bumper sticker. Considerably better than fucking MENSA.

At around five o'clock he jumped into a game as Reaper. He seemed drawn to this character and the tactic of taking the high ground. He stopped only when he was getting hungry and needed to use the bathroom.

What to do for dinner?

He smiled. There was only one answer. He went to the DoorDash app and ordered his go-to—Big Mac, fries, and a large Diet Coke. He was only somewhat dismayed to see that this simple meal would cost him thirty-two dollars. When it arrived, Smithson was pleasantly surprised with the delivery driver.

No smart-assery at all from that guy. Hunh. Things are looking up.

As he ate, Smithson considered.

This whole thing with the Wrights...smart guys... inventors...tinkerers. They came up with their own ideas, busted their tails working on them...kept at it until their invention came into being. Reminds me of....ME! Grey is my Wright Flyer. What I did was more difficult, of course, but there are some similarities.

It was a cheerful Smithson that returned to the basement for several more hours of *OVERWATCH 2*.

He unconsciously hummed *Whistle While You Work* the entire time.

CHAPTER THIRTY-NINE

Paul finished his preparation for the night as the sun set. He had changed into dark clothes. He wore long black Saucony running pants and a dark red long-sleeve T-shirt. He knew that this shade of red would make him nearly as difficult to see in the dark as black without drawing the same suspicion. Worn Merrell hiking shoes and a dark green Dayton Dragons baseball cap completed his outfit. He also wore his Suunto Core watch. It had been with him for several deployments.

He set the bucket with its mixture and the paintbrush in the bed of the truck. He had removed the front license plate from the Lariat. The state of Ohio now required just a rear plate. A good percentage of drivers still attached them to both the front and rear, many out of habit. Paul fell into this category, seeing no downside to the practice. Tonight, though, he was trying to minimize the chance of being identified.

Back inside the house he made sure one of the magazines was inserted properly into the Ruger, being careful not to get his fingertips anywhere near the cartridge that was visible at the top. He called out to Lauren, who he'd asked to bring a dark blanket from the closet in their bedroom several minutes earlier.

"Hon, I need to get going. Got that blanket?"

Lauren emerged from the bedroom carrying a green Army blanket. That was not what got Paul's attention.

"What do you think *you're* doing?"

She had changed into dark clothes of her own and had a Mets cap in one hand.

"I'm going with you."

Paul waved his hands in front of his chest.

"No....not happening...absolutely not!"

"I'm going. We can stand here and argue if you like, but I'm not changing my mind. You need a driver."

Paul tried to reason with her.

"It's too dangerous. You're just taking a chance that *both* of us get caught."

Lauren stood her ground.

"Look, I already have this stalker guy threatening to shoot me. How could tonight's," she struggled for the right word, "*caper,* be any more dangerous?"

Paul opened his mouth to object then closed it. He had to smile.

"Caper?"

He admitted she had a point. A second person that could act as the driver eliminated some of the risk. Plus, the police would be less likely to pull over a couple without good reason than they would a single male.

"Okay, but I'm in command tonight, Warrant Officer. We do it my way."

Lauren gave him a mock salute.

They took I-75 toward Dayton. Lauren drove. They left their cells at home and brought both Tracfones. Paul said as long as they were together they should first recon a part of the city that would be key the following day. They took Route 4 east for a short time before getting off at Keowee and passing over the Tony Stein Bridge. They worked their way south on city streets. Day Air Ballpark was on their right. Lauren turned to look at it several times.

"In due time my dear, in due time."

Paul tried to use his best Gatewood Dowdell voice but the attempt at humor fell flat. He changed the subject.

"Remember, this is a thirty-five mile per hour zone. There are cameras that snap pictures of speeders."

Lauren nodded as Keowee bent to the right and then formed a "T" at Wayne. Lauren took a left and, as she passed Oak Street, remarked, "Wow, we are really close to the McClarys' place."

Paul nodded and pointed ahead.

"Take a right at that Wendy's. That puts us on Wyoming. Go slow down that street so I can get a good look."

Lauren followed the instructions. They traveled three long blocks down Wyoming, a street with mediocre lighting. If not for the moon, now full, visibility would be iffy.

"Okay, let's take a left on this side street up here, Alberta. It'll take us past the entrance."

Lauren complied, navigating the pickup along a narrow street with cars parked on both sides. They passed the area that Paul mentioned and continued south. Paul had her turn left on Stewart Street and the couple cruised through the University of Dayton campus. Students were returning to school and it appeared Friday night parties were gearing up. Several blocks past the campus they took a left and, now traveling more or less north on Wayne, approached the Wendy's that had marked their first turn.

Lauren broke the silence.

"See anything?"

Paul answered.

"I think so, go down Wyoming again when you get to the Wendy's. There's a little church on the left. Pull to the side of the road directly across from it. I need to get a better look at the area near the church. Put the flashers on. I'll act like I'm checking the left rear tire. This is as good a place as any to do the mud. Can you handle that?"

Lauren smiled and nodded.

"Glad to, it'll be fun."

Lauren pulled the Lariat to the side of the street. There was very little vehicle traffic and no pedestrians. This was not a part of town with shops or restaurants. There was a line of older homes on the north side. The south side featured the small white church and a sprinkling of homes. A chainlink fence topped with barbed wire ran the entire length of the south side, hugging the sidewalk most of the way, snaking behind the church and homes, and returning to the sidewalk again when past the buildings.

Paul knelt at the back tire and peered through the gloom at the church and its surroundings. He could feel the heat of the day radiating up from the black asphalt.

Looks perfect.

He turned to speak to Lauren and...

"*Whap.*"

Paul's head snapped backward as he felt the impact on his face.

"What...?"

He was interrupted by Lauren's giggling.

"Sorry, I thought I'd splatter some across the back of the truck. A big glob flew off at you."

She was holding the paintbrush in her right hand. The bucket was on the street near the curb. Lauren had applied a thick coat of mud on the rear plate to mask their number. She'd then used the brush to dip into the bucket for more and flip it onto the tailgate. Paul took an errant shot in the face.

He couldn't help but laugh.

"Alright Picasso, that looks fine. Let's get moving."

Lauren tossed the bucket and brush into the bed as Paul jumped in the passenger seat. The Ruger was next to him wrapped in the blanket. He unwrapped a corner and used it to clean the mud from his face. Lauren opened the driver's door and got behind the wheel. They both looked at the exposed barrel of the Ruger before Paul spoke.

"On to the target."

They made their way a few blocks north. Paul had reconnoitered the area around the Dragons ballpark earlier in the day. Now, after dark on a Friday night, there was a danger that witnesses could spoil everything. There were a number of bars within a few blocks of Day Air but the fact that there was no home game tonight worked in their favor.

Paul needed to get to an alley that ran south to north and connected to 1st Street, the street that paralleled the first base line of the baseball field. He had identified it earlier in the day after meeting with Gatewood.

The streets south of the ballpark were for the most part in a checkerboard pattern. East-west streets intersected and passed beyond those that ran north-south. Paul had found an exception and it presented an opportunity.

Madison was one of the north-south thoroughfares. It ran in from the south for several blocks on a collision course with the ballpark. But midway between 2nd and 1st streets, less than one hundred yards from the stadium, it veered east and ran parallel to both of them. It terminated at the next north-south street, Sears. Where Madison veered, an alley began and continued toward the ballpark. Day Air was directly across the street from the mouth of the alley, which was crowded with construction equipment.

Buildings were on both sides of the alley, creating shadows. This passage was used as a walkway by fans traveling to and from the ballpark on game nights. That should not be a problem tonight, particularly with the construction equipment parked there.

Paul's original plan was to drive down 2nd Street, turn north at Madison, and follow it a short distance until it made its bend to the right. At that point he would leave the truck running, make his way up the alley, do the deed, and hustle back.

He had to admit it felt better having Lauren waiting for him in the truck. It would draw less attention and make for a quicker exit. They were now cruising slowly west on 2nd. Paul clutched the Ruger, keeping it below the level of the window. It was still wrapped in the blanket.

"Alright, turn right up here just past the catholic church."

Lauren made the right as soon as she got beyond St. Joseph's Catholic Church. She crept north on Madison with the lights of the Lariat turned off. Madison angled to the right and Lauren followed it for twenty feet before coming to a stop behind the church.

Paul exited the door wordlessly and made his way north in the alley. He walked at a leisurely pace, holding the concealed Ruger. His Dragons cap was pulled low over his eyes. He looked right and left as unobtrusively as possible as he picked his way around the construction equipment.

He reached a small crane at the mouth of the alley. It was orange and yellow with the words "JLG ULTRA BOOM" painted on the side. Paul peered across 1st Street from his position in the darkened alley and saw the ballpark less than fifty yards away. He saw the large green, blue, and white, Day Air Ballpark sign at the top of the structure. The exterior of the ballpark was a light brown brick. A line of three-foot high white concrete baseballs bordered the sidewalk. There was a single glass door on this corner of the stadium. It was a standard thirty-six inch width in an aluminum frame. As Paul looked to the right, further down what would be the first base line, he saw two green metal overhead doors. They were closed. All the lights of the ballpark were off.

Paul strained to see or hear anyone in the vicinity. In a perfect world he would lay low for several minutes to make sure he picked the perfect time. But Lauren was waiting back up the alley in an exposed position. A car approached from the right. He ducked behind the crane, checking his six o'clock as he did. The car passed.

Paul quickly unwrapped the Ruger and pulled back the bolt, seating the first of ten rounds in the chamber. His final thought was to assume a position that would guarantee the brass cartridges would be found. Paul shifted to his left and drew a bead on the glass door.

CRACK...CRACK...CRACK

He swung the barrel to the right and took aim at the first overhead door.

CRACK...CRACK...CRACK,CRACK

Paul shifted his aim further right and brought the second overhead door into his front sight.

CRACK,CRACK,CRACK

He moved quickly, not quite at a sprint, rewrapping the rifle as he went. Lauren was watching for him. She was wide-eyed under her Mets cap, shaken by the reports of the rifle as they echoed off the surrounding buildings. Paul jumped into the truck.

"Go, Go.......not too fast!"

Lauren's fingers were white, unintentionally gripping the wheel with all her strength. She reached Sears, continued another block to Webster before turning on the headlights, then turned south and headed for the highway.

CHAPTER FORTY

SATURDAY

Paul woke up at 6:45. He and Lauren had agreed to not set an alarm, reasoning that they would need as much rest as possible for the day ahead. He quietly padded into the kitchen and flipped on the light.

Chappy was crouched on the counter near the coffee maker. Paul sighed.

"Good morning Chappy. You're relentless."

He scooped up the cat and lowered him to the floor.

Chappy stared at Paul for three seconds before jumping back up on the counter.

Paul sighed a second time.

"Okay Chappy, this is not..."

He stopped. He was about to say *this is not the mountain I want to die on today,* a now-common aphorism meaning *I'll fight to the death for some things but this particular battle is not worth fighting.*

Chappy's namesake, John Chapman, *had* actually died on a mountain. Paul felt it inappropriate to use the phrase for something as insignificant as a test of wills with an overweight feline.

"Alright mister, I declare a truce."

He scratched under Chappy's ears before getting started on the coffee.

I'll be on my mountaintop tonight.

Chappy watched him with apparent mild interest.

Paul began to work on omelets, hoping to have them finished by the time Lauren woke up. He turned on one of the stove's burners and retrieved a skillet and a mixing bowl. As he cracked eggs, he thought back to the night before.

They made it safely to the highway after the shooting. Paul was extremely concerned about the response time by the Dayton Police Department. A few years earlier, in 2019, there had been a tragic mass shooting near the entrance of a bar called Ned Peppers in the popular Oregon District of Dayton. The shooter was able to kill a total of nine people and wound seventeen others despite being fatally shot by responding police just thirty-two seconds after the first shot was fired. Paul knew what the DPD knew. A quick response to a shooting is critical.

Lauren was able to keep it together well enough to stay at the speed limit on their exfiltration from the target area. He directed her to exit I-75 a few miles north at Vandalia. They pulled to the berm on the exit ramp and Paul jumped out and cleaned the mud off the rear plate using a towel and a bottle of water. He wanted to eliminate any chance of being pulled over and having the Ruger discovered.

When they reached their house Paul carried the rifle, still wrapped, into the garage and hid it in the corner behind some landscaping tools. Lauren went inside. By the time Paul entered she already had the television on and was scanning channels. Paul had reminded her not to get online to search for news of the shooting. He didn't want Crank to see this and get suspicious. A bit later, on the eleven o'clock broadcast on channel seven, a two-minute piece ran. It showed wide views of the area and featured a short stand-up by a reporter on the scene. At one point a close up was shown of the glass door. Three spider-webbed holes were visible in a small triangular area near the top of the door.

Paul smiled remembering his comment.

"Pretty tight pattern, not bad."

Lauren had looked at him and rolled her eyes.

The fact was, one of the things he was trying to accomplish was to get a feel again for the accuracy of the weapon. After receiving the call from the Crank and conceiving his plan Paul knew he would have to assess the weapon before using it in any direct conflict. He did not feel comfortable firing any rounds on the property behind their house. It would be out of character for him and could be remembered by their neighbors. He knew the shots at Day Air would not be particularly challenging but they would tell him what he needed to know about the weapon.

He had removed the scope from the rifle knowing he would not be shooting in daylight. His lack of night vision equipment meant he would be relying on the iron sights.

A few minutes after entering the house Paul's Tracfone vibrated. He saw a text from Mike.

We've contacted all the usual suspects. They are in for S. Hunt tomorrow.

Paul nodded.

Good man.

Next Paul checked his cellphone. They had both left their phones turned on while they were gone. Paul saw that he had several missed calls from the 765 area code. There were no voicemails. He remembered what the Crank said about blocking calls.

They won't stop trying to reach me. They have a murder to solve.

While Lauren scanned local channels on television, Paul texted back Mike with his Tracfone.

Can you access map on website of the place we discussed today and send me screenshots? In particular, area closest to Wyoming St.?

Paul received a thumbs-up emoji within seconds. Four minutes later the screenshots arrived. Having accomplished all he planned for the day Paul forced himself to get some sleep. It was a skill. Sleeping when he didn't want to was something he learned to do on deployments. It was a damn sight easier than the opposite, staying awake when you were worn to the ground. He headed to the bedroom knowing Lauren needed to decompress at her own pace.

Paul was flipping the omelets when Lauren shuffled into the kitchen.

"Morning Clyde, making me breakfast?"

Paul turned and smiled, catching on.

"Morning Bonnie, I guess we got away with it last night."

He poured two mugs of coffee and handed her one, then held his up.

She clinked it with hers in a mock toast. After taking a sip she eyed Chappy on the counter. She gestured at the cat.

"What's this, new set of ground rules?"

Paul half turned to acknowledge Chappy before looking back at Lauren.

"Let's just say I don't want to fight a two-front war. I'll worry about Chappy when this thing with the hacker is over."

Paul finished the omelets and set two full plates on the island. They discussed the night before as they ate.

Lauren raised a concern.

"What do you think the chances are that we were seen or we're on some security video?"

Paul sipped his coffee.

"Best guess? Fifty-fifty. Cameras are everywhere. There could be one on the stadium pointing at the street. Hard to say. But it was dark and I was concealed. I was more worried about someone calling 9-1-1 with a description of our truck. But I think if that happened we would've had a hard time getting out of town."

"You think they'll find the casings?"

Paul nodded.

"They won't let this slide without a full investigation. That stadium is too important to the city. The police will put some resources into this. They know what they're doing. Ten shell casings outside of a shot-up ballpark? They'll find them. Probably already have."

He took another sip of coffee before continuing.

"No matter what happens tonight, this might be the worst thing I have to do in this whole mess. It was a damn shame but it couldn't be helped."

Lauren, only half kidding, tried to mitigate his guilt.

"I guess you and Mike are going to have to buy a crapload of beers at the ballpark to help the Dragons pay for those doors."

CHAPTER FORTY-ONE

Smithson slept in. It was nearly 9:30 when he got out of bed. He was pleasantly surprised that he didn't have a headache. He'd finished the remainder of the Warped Wings, not quite remembering how many he had. It was past 2 a.m. when he finally pulled himself away from *OVERWATCH 2*.

Kicked some ass with Reaper last night, I remember that.

He decided to shower.

Take a shower every week or so, whether you need it or not.

He chuckled at his wit.

After toweling off he selected his best smelling underwear, hoodie, and shorts and dressed. The selection process was slightly distasteful, even to Smithson. He was hungry but wanted to check with Grey before doing anything further.

There were no new warnings. The Hulls were still at their house. There were no indications that the incident at Lowe's had developed beyond yesterday's status. He checked the Henry County Sheriff's site and saw the discovery of the body was easily the biggest story in that area. The Indianapolis media had picked up on it. The connection to Wilbur Wright's birthplace was mentioned in every story. One Indianapolis TV news outlet had even come up with a banner they ran across the screen on every report on the discovery.

WRIGHT BROTHERS MURDER: BODY IN THE CORNFIELD

It struck Smithson that this was a fantastic hook for the news media. They could really run with a thing like this. It wouldn't surprise him if it became a national story within a day or so.

Biggs will be famous....well, maybe. They still don't know who he is.

He searched for any indication Biggs' car had been discovered and found none.

Well, it can't take much longer...sitting there in the rest stop. Maybe it will still be there tonight. I can wave at it as I drive past on I-70 after taking care of Hull.

Smithson had tentatively decided to leave Dayton immediately after the events that night at Woodland Cemetery. He would pack up everything later in the afternoon and would not need to return to the Airbnb after he took possession of the camera and wrapped things up with Hull.

He closed the Toughbook. It was mid-morning and his stomach was now insistent. He needed to eat and he needed to get moving. He wanted to check out the Huffman Prarie area. He had examined information posted online but wasn't completely sure about access to the area. Technically it was located on an Air Force Base. The open sources didn't give him all the information he sought and he was still leery about hacking into military systems.

Smithson returned to the bedroom to put on his boots. He was in a good mood. All the signs from Grey were positive. He would put this whole mess with the camera in his rearview tonight. He'd put the entire Dayton area in his rearview.

Good riddance.

He was whistling a happy tune as he sat on the bed and reached for the boots.

"What *is* that song?"

He couldn't place it. No matter.

He finished tying his right boot and reached for its mate. They were Salomon Speed Assault 2's. Smithson had noticed they were mentioned in at least two of the books he'd read. It seemed they were preferred by some of America's special operations types.

He remembered thinking, *Well, if the boots are good enough for them...*

The Salomons were mid-height and looked like a cross between an athletic shoe and a hiking boot. He found them on *TacticalGear.com*. The description read "As light, protective and fiercely gripped as its predecessor, the Speed Assault 2 offers more everyday comfort and more technical features. So you'll be equipped for speed and agility in any warm weather and/or wet operation—from desert deployment to jungle training camps." They featured a QuickLace Lacing System, non-reflective ripstop materials, and a ContraGrip TA outsole.

He slipped on the second boot and began to tie.

Smithson hadn't worn them to a desert or jungle but he *had* noticed they gave him excellent grip on fast food restaurant floors that were in need of mopping due to french fry grease. They were jet black, went well with his hoodies and—

Pop.

Smithson looked down.

"Shit Shit SHIT!!!!"

The bootlace had broken.

He was instantly furious. He snatched the boot from his foot and stood, squeezing it in his hand. A microscopic part of his brain tried to urge calm. It was like a small dinghy in a sea of rage.

"QUICKLACE LACING SYSTEM?!? QUICKLACE FUCKING LACING SYSTEM?!?"

He hurled the boot toward the far wall. A low chest of drawers with an attached mirror on top stood there. The boot struck the mirror and shattered it.

Smithson stared at the mirror, his chest heaving. His good mood was a distant memory.

Well...that's a bad omen.

Twenty minutes later Smithson walked into the Dunkin' on Woodman. There were no other customers inside. It was more or less on his way to the Huffman site. The fragrance of fresh donuts greeted him and for a moment he thought the day was back on track, heading in the right direction. Then he saw that the area labeled "Peanut" in the donut display case was empty. This was not totally unexpected. It was nearly eleven in the morning on the weekend and he knew there was a good chance the selection would be picked over. He stood with his arms crossed, a frown on his face.

"Can I help you, sir?"

The cheerful voice seemed to come from another dimension. Smithson turned toward the sound but saw no one.

"Sir? Down here."

He leaned to his left and saw a short Asian woman behind the donut case. She had been rearranging the bottom shelf and was speaking to him while looking through the plexiglass.

He watched as she emerged from behind the case and approached the counter. She wore a brown Dunkin' Donuts apron and visor. Smithson was a head taller than her. He drew himself up to his full height.

"Well, I came here for peanut donuts. I see you're out... again."

The woman appeared to be in her fifties.

"I'm sorry, sir. We've been very busy today."

She spoke without the trace of an accent.

Smithson held his right arm out, turned his palm up, and gestured to the empty store. He turned back to her with his eyebrows arched, not saying a word.

The woman, her nametag read "Veronica," looked back at him with barely concealed contempt. She said one word.

"Earlier."

It came out with the icy tone of a worker who had been on the job for nearly six hours. She stared back at Smithson before speaking again in the same tone.

"Can I interest you in another flavor?"

Smithson closed his eyes and quickly dropped his chin to chest. He shook his head slowly in disgust, and let out a long sigh. He turned to the case in a tortured manner and reviewed the choices.

"Powdered, Toasted Coconut, Plain Stick, Old Fashioned, Lemon Stick, Apple Crumb, Glazed Blueberry... all these choices suck. Is this the stuff you donate to the homeless at the end of the day?"

Veronica crossed her arms and glared at him.

Smithson had standards, but he was also starving. He took an exaggerated breath and exhaled slowly. He swallowed his pride.

"I'll have two Old Fashioned, two Toasted Coconut, and an extra large coffee to go."

Veronica, arms still crossed, nodded. A small smile appeared at the corners of her mouth. She paused for the briefest of seconds before gathering the order.

It was all Smithson could do to resist retrieving the Winkler from his trunk. He stood fuming as Veronica rung up the order.

"That'll be six dollars and eighty-nine cents...would you like to—"

Smithson interrupted loudly, earning back some of his self-respect.

"NO! SCREW RICO!"

CHAPTER FORTY-TWO

Paul wasn't sure of the exact time that Crank would contact him to initiate the night's events. He was convinced that things would culminate in darkness. That meant sometime after 8:30 p.m. If he were a betting man, he would wager the final scene would play out a bit later than that. But Crank had told him he planned to run Paul around for some time before ending at the location designated for the camera drop. It was guesswork trying to determine when this would start.

Paul had no intention of waiting until the last moment to prepare. He slipped on disposable gloves before retrieving the extra magazine and .22 cartridges that Lauren had prepared from the drawer in the kitchen. He brought the Ruger inside from its hiding spot in the garage. While out there he located a coil of thin rope and took it inside as well. He removed the empty magazine then snapped the second one into the rifle. Paul opened the baggie and began to insert these rounds one by one into the first one.

As he worked at this Chappy jumped up on the table. He looked at Paul with passing interest for a second before hunkering down a few inches from the bullets. Chappy was fascinated by the shiny brass.

Paul remembered the first time he had searched for cat videos on his computer. His intention was to show Lauren cute videos of cats playing. They had brought Chappy home just a few weeks earlier. Paul was amused to see that interspersed with these videos were others that were produced for cats to *watch*.

There were animated mice skittering across the screen, fish swimming about in aquariums, and close up footage of bird feeders as a multitude of winged visitors came to eat. Young Chappy was enthralled. He sat and watched some of the videos with the same rapt attention a nervous schoolboy gave a pretty teacher. With others Chappy became more aggressive. His ears pinned back and he swiped frantically at the screen as those damn mice evaded him. Their speed picked up as the video progressed, driving Chappy to higher levels of agitation. Particularly amusing to Paul were Chappy's attempts to find the mice after they disappeared off the edge of the screen. The cat would dart around the side of the computer in an effort to corner the escaping prey, only to be baffled like a member of the audience at a David Copperfield show.

Paul remembered Lauren's comment as Paul watched Chappy.

"I can't tell who's more enthralled, you or Chappy."

Paul reached out and rubbed the cat's forehead with the knuckle of his index finger.

"You're really into these, huh big guy? Maybe when this thing is over I'll drill a hole through one of these cartridges, drain the gunpowder, and hang it on a chain around your neck."

"Oh sure, he'll be the baddest cat in Troy."

Paul turned to see Lauren.

"Do you make it a goal in life to catch me in embarrassing situations with this cat?"

She smirked.

"Shooting fish in a barrel, Paul. Shooting fish in a barrel."

Paul finished loading the second magazine. He would have twenty total rounds. He did not anticipate using even one full magazine but he was determined to be prepared.

If I need more than twenty rounds we are in deep shit. That means I'm in a prolonged gunfight and the police will be alerted.

Paul found the X-Acto knife in its drawer and used it to cut a four-foot length from the rope. The rifle had swiveling sling attachment pieces attached to the wood. One was under the buttstock, the other under the forestock nearer the point where the barrel emerged from the wood. Paul had a sling for the rifle at one time but must've misplaced it over the years. He threaded one end of the rope through the piece near the

308

forestock and tied it off in a tight square knot. He slid the other end of the rope through the buttstock piece. Before tying it off he slung the weapon onto his right shoulder and determined the proper amount of slack. He then tied the second knot before using the X-Acto to cut excess rope from both ends.

He tucked the extra mag into the baggie before heading into the bedroom. He searched for his old cleaning kit, finally finding it at the bottom of the nightstand. He returned to the kitchen to see Chappy pawing at the baggie, apparently in a state of consternation over the disappearance of the bullets.

"Abracadabra, Chappy."

Paul opened the black plastic case and removed three thin aluminum rods. They had threads on each end. He connected them to form one rod roughly thirty inches long. He attached a T-shaped plastic handle to one end and a plastic eyelet to the other. He fished a white gun-cleaning patch from the kit and pushed half of it through the eyelet. He then removed a small orange plastic bottle of Hoppe's Lubricating Oil from the kit and squirted a few drops on the patch. He removed the magazine from the Ruger and opened the bolt. Paul then inserted the patch into the end of the barrel and, gripping the T-shaped handle, pushed the cleaning rod down its length.

Paul could see the now slightly discolored patch when it reached the open bolt. He worked the patch up and down the entire length of the barrel several times before retracting the rod. The patch was now dark grey from gunpowder residue. Paul removed the patch and attached a second one, again dropping a small amount of oil across its length.

Chappy sat watching in fascination. Lauren was across the table, studying the yellow legal pad that featured Paul's notations.

Paul, too, was lost in his thoughts. The smell of gun oil triggered an avalanche of memories from his days as a Combat Controller. Though it was not their prime function when attached to customer units, CCTs had to be expert with their personal weapons. There were different levels of training that they experienced. The most helpful, in Paul's opinion, had

309

been the Special Tactics Advanced Skills Training program, or AST, at Hurlburt Field in Florida. It was also the most demanding. The school was designed to hone the skills of the CCTs, producing mission-ready operators for the United States Special Operations Command. CCTs were expected to hold their own in a gunfight as well as be expert at juggling air assets when working targets.

Once Paul got to his customer units he realized he'd only scratched the surface. The operators with these units were the best in the world at shooting and small unit tactics. They worked at it incessantly. CCTs were expected to work just as hard. Paul had fired so many rounds in training with these men that he couldn't possibly estimate the number. After each session, he cleaned his M4. The gun oil took him back.

"You miss it, don't you?"

Paul was interrupted from his thoughts. He looked across the table to see Lauren staring at him thoughtfully. She continued.

"You went away for a few minutes...you miss those years as Combat Controller, don't you?"

She said it without a hint of accusation.

Paul considered his answer for a few seconds.

"Yeah, I do....sometimes at least. There was some terrible shit mixed into those years but... the guys... I can't describe it."

Lauren nodded.

"I get it. Remember, I knew a lot of those guys...and all the wives and girlfriends. No book or movie will ever capture the bonds that were made."

They looked at each other and smiled.

Lauren broke the moment first, looking down at the legal pad.

"You really came up with all this in less than a half hour? The scouting trips to the ballpark, the other location last night, the bullet casings, the Tracfones?"

Paul nodded.

"I learned from the best."

CHAPTER FORTY-THREE

Smithson was working on his third donut, a Toasted Coconut, when he steered the S8 off of Route 4 East and onto State Route 444. His GPS told him the Huffman Prarie Flying Field Interpretive Center was barely a mile ahead. He was looking for Kauffman Road. As he merged with the traffic on 444 he noticed a large dam to his left, just a few hundred yards from the road.

Hunh...look at that damn dam.

He giggled.

Not nearly as tall as the Hoover Dam back home but pretty DAMN long.

He was still giggling when he spotted a traffic light ahead.

Must be Kauffman.

It was. He turned right. Had he followed Kauffman for another mile he would have reached the northern entrances to the Wright State University campus. Instead, Smithson arrived at Memorial Drive barely five hundred feet after the turn. Memorial began at the bottom of a hill and led up to the right. There was a pull-in area at the base of the hill. He ducked into this area and checked out the signage. The most important fact for Smithson was that the historical site on top of the hill was open from 10 a.m. to just 4 p.m. on Saturdays. A gate at the bottom of the drive was open now but would obviously be closed and locked at four.

Okay, that means this site has marginal value to me for tonight. Can't really send Hull up the hill. I'm sure as hell not coming here with the bolt cutters.

He looked back over his shoulder.

Too much traffic. But I'm here now... what the hell, might as well drive up and check it out.

He manipulated the Audi back in the direction of Memorial and started up. Several hundred feet beyond he saw a single story brick building come into view on his left. To his right, several steps away, stood a tall pinkish stone monument with a bronze face. Smithson cruised past the building and the monument until he came to a parking lot. There was a smattering of vehicles in the lot. About half had Ohio plates.

Don't have a ton of time but might as well check out the monument.

He made his way along a paved stone path that split. The right side led to the building while the left went to the monument. As Smithson chose the left he noticed the door to the building open and a family emerge. A couple in their late twenties walked out. The woman was pushing a stroller. She reached down to adjust something and cooed, apparently at a baby inside. The man was holding the hand of a small boy with blonde hair. The boy had what appeared to be a novelty derby hat on his head, or, as Smithson had learned since reading about the Wrights, a *bowler*. The family crossed Memorial Drive and made for the monument, vectoring in with Smithson.

There was a paved circular area around the monument. Interpretive markers were placed at intervals. The family stopped near the monument as the father posed the boy in front of it. He was intent on getting a picture with the monument in the background. Smithson ambled off to the side. He had no intention of ending up in another video or photograph.

He turned his back on them and began to read the markers. He learned that he was standing on what was known as "Wright Hill." One marker had an arrow on top pointing off in the direction of Huffman Flying Field, where the Wrights perfected their Flyers after the Kitty Hawk years. From this vantage point Smithson could see for miles. He could make out a large flat green area in the direction of the arrow.

That's my next stop.

He shuffled to the next marker, his back to the family. The plaque on this one contained completely unexpected information. The Wright Hill area was the home of Indian burial mounds. Another arrow on top pointed off in a different direction. Smithson strained to see the mounds, a smile on his face.

Bet that pisses off the natives...they would never let this memorial be built up here today.

He shuffled again and came to a marker that featured photographs. One was an overhead shot of the site. It mentioned that the monument at his back was seventeen feet high and consisted of pink granite. It was dedicated on August 19, 1940, Orville Wright's sixty-ninth birthday. The marker also featured a photo of Orville sitting in front of the monument on the day of the dedication. He was sitting beside General Hap Arnold, the commander of the Army Air Corps, the forerunner to the United States Air Force. Arnold had learned to fly as a young man at the Wright Pilot School down there at Huffman Prarie.

Smithson was leaning over to get a better look at Orville in the photo when he was startled.

"Hey mithter, do you like my hat?"

Smithson looked down to see the blonde boy. He had wandered away from his parents as they read one of the plaques. A front tooth was missing and he spoke around it with a lisp.

"It'th called a bowler. The Wright brotherth wore them. My daddy bought it for me. Do you like the Wright brotherth? Who ith your favorite? Mine ith Wilbur."

The boy stopped peppering questions to wipe a runny nose with the back of one hand.

Smithson stared at the boy.

Impertinent little cuss.

"Well Sonny, let me ask *you* a question. Have you ever eaten Boston clam chowder?"

The boy looked at him quizzically.

"Bothton clam chowder?"

"Yeah, Wilbur ate some and it killed him. Gave him typhoid fever. Must've been fucking spoiled. Stay the hell away from Boston clam chowder."

He smiled at the boy before wheeling and walking quickly in the direction of the Audi. He whistled the tune that had been stuck in his head for some time.

Smithson guided the S8 back past the monument. As he passed he saw that the boy wearing the bowler was crying. The father was trying to comfort him. The mother stood next to the stroller with hands on hips, glaring at Smithson.

He decided not to beat himself up about yet another reckless act. No harm had come to him and he was on his way out of the area.

A guy has to have some fun in life.

He laughed all the way down the hill. The Audi came to a stop at Kauffman before turning left. Within seconds Smithson was back on State Route 444 heading east. His GPS directed him to leave 444 in a mile and a half and turn left at Wright-Patterson Air Force Base Gate 16A.

Smithson had been apprehensive about this. He had no desire to interact with Air Force security personnel. His plan was to drive past and assess the gate. If it looked daunting he would be in the wind. He was amazed to see the gate was open wide and there was no indication of security of any kind. In fact the only structure in the area appeared to be the pro shop of a golf course. A nearby sign advertised "Twin Base Golf Course."

Pleased with his discovery he drove past, intending to turn around at the closest opportunity. That next opportunity, however, was another WPAFB gate on his left. This one had several indications of security. Smithson drove on. He found a small surface street on his right and got turned around. He passed the secure gate and made his way back to 16A. He pulled in and eased to a stop, again reading the signs. One caught his attention.

OPEN 7 DAYS A WEEK, 0600-2200

Smithson was pleasantly surprised. Apparently this part of the base was considered a park that was open to the public.

314

This means I can run Hull around here in the dark. Perfect.

He pulled through the gate. There was indeed a golf course pro shop a short distance to his left. He drove on, heading north. There were several vehicles in the golf course parking lot but absolutely none in front of him. According to his GPS he was on Communications Boulevard. He was to follow it until it dead-ended at Hebble Creek Road in a half-mile, turn left, then drive another half-mile to Pylon Road. A right there took him to the heart of Huffman Prarie where he would find historical structures.

Smithson followed the directions but was unable to take the right on Pylon Road. It was blocked by concrete barriers. A sign read simply "Road Closed." Smithson continued west on Hebble Road and was eventually rerouted by his GPS. It took ten minutes of circuitous driving on narrow roads to reach the center of the field. The roads were so narrow they resembled bike paths. One, Marl Road, was lined with trees on both sides for a mile and marked with yellow "Share The Road" signs with icons of bicycles.

When he reached the center of the field Smithson found it to be anticlimactic. There was an old hanger, an odd structure formed by wood rails that were shaped like a pyramid, a bench, and a few interpretive markers. He pulled up as close to one marker as possible and rolled down his window. He squinted. The markers were just far enough off the paved road that he couldn't read them. The heat of the day rolled into the Audi, doing battle with its air conditioning.

Screw it. I'm not walking out there.

Smithson retraced his route back to 444. Despite the let down of the Huffman Prarie site, he was upbeat. The concrete barriers made the area more difficult to navigate. This would be particularly so in the dark. And since the park was open until ten, he could direct Hull inside without breaking any laws or regulations, really screw with him.

The more he could throw Hull off balance, the easier it would be to take him down in the cemetery later that night.

Smithson began to whistle.

CHAPTER FORTY-FOUR

Gatewood Dowdell sat at his desk. He had arrived there at 0600, surprising the Airmen at the gate who hadn't expected him. Roberta made plans for them that afternoon. She wanted to visit nearby Yellow Springs, a small town twenty minutes away. It featured eclectic shops and restaurants and was home to her favorite comedian, Dave Chappelle.

Gatewood hated to disappoint her. He told her something unexpected came up and it required him to go in to base early. She put her hands on her hips, telegraphing to him that he'd better provide more information. In the end, he let on that Paul and Lauren had a serious problem and he was working to help them through "unofficial channels."

"Paul and Lauren?"

There was concern in her voice.

"Well get going Gatewood, Dave Chappelle can wait."

The loose network he'd activated was spread across multiple time zones. Gatewood knew that by working the problem early in the morning he would be able to view any reports sent in at night from the western part of the country as well as early communications from those in the east. He instructed his contacts to send all information and questions to the burner phone.

He had a Keurig single cup coffee maker in his office. By 0730 he'd downed three cups of dark roast and had finished reading all the late responses from west of the Mississippi. He had progressed to texts and voicemails from early risers from the east. His ST-6 and Delta contacts were in Dam Neck, Virginia and Fort Bragg, North Carolina respectively. He knew it was a longshot that these sources would come up with information on a domestic threat like Crank. These guys were manhunters, but they focused on threats outside the borders of the United States.

Still, they were smart and at least as connected as he was. Gatewood held out hope that they could help. He was on the phone with Sluggo, so named because he resembled the character of the same name from the 1950s comic *Nancy and Sluggo,* his contact with Delta, when a call came in to the Tracfone. Gatewood saw that it was a number from the 210 area code.

That'll be Johnny-U from Joint Base San Antonio-Lackland.

"Hey Sluggo, got a call, gotta go. Hit me up with anything you hear."

Sluggo responded with one word before clicking off.

"Check."

Gatewood switched to the second call.

"Woody here. Is that you, Johnny-U?"

"Roger that, Woody, I figured you'd be working that burner early this morning."

Johnny-U was Senior Master Sergeant Juan Yubero. His nickname came from the anglicized version of his first name combined with the phonetic pronunciation of the first syllable of his last name. Johnny-U was the senior enlisted member of his base security force. JBSA was home to the Defense Language Institute as well as Basic Military Training for the United States Space Force.

"Glad to hear from you, Johnny. Do you have something for me?"

"I have a question for you Woody."

Gatewood was intrigued.

"Shoot, what is it?"

Johnny hesitated for a second before proceeding.

"What are your thoughts on me reading Julieta in on this?"

Gatewood answered immediately.

"Absolutely! I should have thought of that. By all means Johnny. Get back to me if you get something."

After ending the call Gatewood touched his fingers to his temples and closed his eyes.

I must be getting old. I should've thought of Julieta from the get go.

Julieta Yubero worked for Interpol. She was on one of their Incident Report Teams. The IRTs were teams of experts deployed to member countries during crisis situations. Julieta's team responded to situations in Central and South America, often related to narco-terrorism.

Gatewood rubbed his eyes before heading to the Keurig for a fourth cup of coffee.

It was over three hours later when Gatewood took a call from a second 210 phone number. He was beginning to think he might not come up with anything relevant for Paul. He picked up.

"Woody here."

The voice was musical.

"Gatewood, this is Julieta Yubero."

Gatewood smiled, remembering her fondly from their one meeting in Arlington, Texas. The couples attended the 2021 Alabama-Notre Dame Rose Bowl game played at AT&T Stadium, better known as Jerry World, named for Jerry Jones. Jones was the owner of the Dallas Cowboys, the regular tenant of the stadium. The Rose Bowl was typically played in Pasadena, California but was moved that year due to the COVID-19 pandemic. The game was not only the Rose Bowl, it was one of the College Football Playoff semifinals. Alabama won and went on to defeat Ohio State for the National Championship. The Dowdells and Yuberos met the night before the game at a military function. They hit it off and had stayed in touch ever since.

"Hey Julieta, so nice to hear from you. Johnny said you might help with this."

Julieta cut to the chase.

"I might have something for you."

Gatewood sat up.

"Do tell."

Julieta responded.

"I'll give you the whole background. This might take a while."

"I pride myself on being a good listener."

Julieta recounted what led to her call.

In May of 2022 Interpol Secretary General Jurgen Stock spoke at the World Econonic Forum in Davos, Switzerland. He revealed that Interpol, the international police organization with 195 member countries, was concerned that state developed cyberweapons would become available on the Dark Net in "a couple of years." He summarized this concern in one comment, saying, "this applies to the digital weapons that, maybe today are used by the military, developed by military, and tomorrow will be available for criminals."

Interpol set up a task force to collect information on crimes that fit into this category. They needed a database. They were aware that fewer than half of cyber crimes committed were ever reported. To broaden their database, they expanded their search, going back several years. A researcher discovered a sixteen-year-old case from Belize, an Interpol member nation.

It seemed a woman had been strangled in an Adults Only resort near Placencia, on the Caribbean coast. Though it was unsolved, the murder itself was not the reason the case drew the attention of the task force. It was the fact that all potential electronic evidence of the crime had been eliminated within hours. Security camera databases had been systematically attacked. Archived images were erased. Computerized guest information had disappeared.

Local police were able to obtain cellphone images from other guests of a potential suspect. He was seen in the background of three images taken at a Tiki bar on the property. The images were of limited value as the suspect was not the main subject of any of the shots. But the victim, a prostitute, was next to him in all three photos.

Within weeks these images disappeared entirely from the computer system used by the Belize National Police Department.

This got the attention of the Interpol task force.

The cyber intruder left no evidence behind. Experts got the impression that the hack was not a long-term process where the perpetrator worked for weeks to crack into the system. It had the feel of something done on impulse, as if the violator had just become aware of the photos and decided to pluck them from the system.

What the hacker apparently did not know was that the Belize National Police Department had a symbiotic relationship with the country's National Security Directorate. The NSD concentrated on threats to the country. These often involved drug cartels. The NSD had copies of the same photos. The hacker either wasn't aware of this or for reasons unknown decided not to penetrate this governmental organization that was connected to the country's military.

"I took your photo and ran it through our facial recognition software. I got a hit. It matched the suspect in the Belize murder with seventy percent probability. That is a very high probability for photos taken sixteen years apart."

Gatewood let out a breath.

"Sure sounds like this is our guy. My man says this guy mentioned killing a woman with his bare hands."

He did not mention Paul by name. He had only revealed Hull's name to two of his contacts. Both had worked with Paul in the past and Gatewood felt they needed to know. The rest of those in his net were assisting solely on the basis of their relationship with Gatewood.

Julieta's tone became more serious.

"This guy is exactly the sort of person the task force is looking for. If he had access to high level or military grade cyber weapons sixteen years ago and he's still out there, we need to take him off the board. It's anybody's guess how far his capabilities have progressed."

Gatewood understood her concern.

She continued, not quite pleading.

"We really need to put out a Red Notice on this suspect and post his picture on the Wanted Persons page of our website."

Gatewood was familiar with Red Notices. They were requests from Interpol to law enforcement worldwide to locate and provisionally arrest a person pending extradition or surrender. He weighed the choices in his head. If a Red Notice went out on the Crank, it could alert the man. He obviously had the resources to discover such an act. He could disappear, only to pop up again and make good on his threats to Paul. The odds of the Crank being tracked and apprehended quickly by Interpol were long.

On the other hand, the scenario that was playing out between the man and Paul should culminate tonight.

I might be asking too much...but Interpol wouldn't have that picture if it weren't for Paul.

"Do me one more favor and wait until Monday morning."

CHAPTER FORTY-FIVE

Paul and Lauren had a late lunch. It was one suited for an Ohio winter, rather than summer. It consisted of grilled cheese sandwiches and tomato soup. It was Lauren's suggestion. She had a growing level of apprehension about the remainder of the day and she associated the meal with her childhood, a time when her mom and dad could keep her safe.

Paul was happy to comply. He had the sandwiches and soup ready in ten minutes. They sat at the table while they ate and reviewed the maps that Mike McClary had texted to Paul's Tracfone. They discussed options and possible backup plans.

Paul tried to relieve some of the tension. He pointed at Lauren's half-eaten sandwich.

"You know, the bread on your sandwich is toasted waaay past the point of your toast. You seem to be enjoying it. Why can't you eat toast that's that dark?"

She tilted her head and looked at him.

"Because this is grilled, not toasted."

She smiled.

"But that doesn't make any sense. They're both just pieces of bread that are heated until they get darker. The—"

Paul's Tracfone vibrated. He looked down to see the caller was Gatewood. He glanced at Lauren, and answered.

"Hey Woody. Lauren's here, let me put you on speaker."

Paul made the adjustment and Gatewood's voice rolled into their kitchen.

"Hello Lauren, how are you holding up?"

He sounded genuinely concerned.

"I'm fine, Woody."

She paused then spoke in a voice that conveyed sincerity.

"We really appreciate you helping with this."

Gatewood spoke in a voice that was more upbeat than he felt.

"I can't let my fellow CCT have all the fun."

Then, more serious, "I have some information for you. It's from an extremely reliable source. I won't tell you who. We should probably keep some level of..."

He searched for a word.

Paul jumped in.

"Deniability?"

Gatewood chuckled.

"Bingo, Sticks, deniability. Let's just say the intel is first rate. It seems this character has been at this game for some time. The image from your camera matched those of a suspected murderer. The crime happened in Belize sixteen years ago. He, uh....strangled a woman."

Paul and Lauren looked at each other. Her eyes were wide.

Paul's eyes narrowed.

Gatewood continued.

"Sorry Lauren, there was no way around it...anyway, this guy, Crank, if it was him, also hacked into some pretty secure computer systems and destroyed evidence. Sounds like it was just chance that there was any trace of his presence left behind. Lord knows what crimes he's committed since then. He's had years to improve his capabilities. My assessment is he can follow through on any threats he's made."

Paul absorbed the information before responding.

"I have to agree with you. He's capable. That's one side of the coin. It's the other side of the coin that I'm more concerned about. He's......"

Gatewood finished for him.

"He's nuts."

"Check."

An hour later a second call came in to Paul's phone. It was Mike.

"Hey Paul, I don't want to bother you....just checking to see if there is anything else you need from us before tonight."

Paul smiled.

"You've already gone above and beyond. Make sure to tell Marge again how much this means to me...and to Lauren. We're sorry to ruin your party."

Mike laughed.

"You kidding, who doesn't love a good scavenger hunt...a nice fire afterwards and a few drinks? This party isn't ruined. Just make sure you two show up."

"Have a bourbon ready for me."

Several concerns and emotions were running through McClary's head. He knew Paul was a capable guy. His background was unfathomable to a civilian. But the challenge he faced tonight was significant. Mike had confidence in Paul, but he was worried. Would this be the last time they spoke? He hesitated, trying to formulate a response that conveyed what he felt. In the end, he kept it simple.

"Count on it."

CHAPTER FORTY-SIX

Smithson drove back into Dayton and entered the downtown area. He wanted to do a quick scout of some of the other Wright brothers sites inside the city. The first two sites were on Monument Street. He found it, not far off of Route 4 and headed west through an area that featured businesses and apartment buildings. He came to a red light a block before what appeared to be a baseball stadium. Looking up, he noticed two large dragon's heads on top of an enormous scoreboard. He was reminded of the dragons in *Century: Age of Ashes.*

Not really a first person shooter game, but fun to play every now and then.

As he waited for the light to change his eyes slid to the left. He could just make out yellow police tape on the other side of the stadium. Two Dayton Police Department cars were parked nose to nose near what appeared to be an alley.

Looks like they had some excitement. I picked the right street. I don't want to run into Johnny Law.

The light changed and he eased past. A few blocks later he cruised past both the Engineers Club, on the left, and the First Baptist Church on his right. Although he viewed both for just seconds he felt he had a good grasp of their locations and layouts.

Nothing too unique about how they're situated....easy access from the street...okay, on to the next two.

The next two were several blocks to the southwest. Smithson congratulated himself for having the upgraded navigation system installed in the Audi. It permitted him to enter multiple locations, allowing him to easily navigate from point to point without resetting the unit. He had spent just five minutes loading the locations before leaving the garage of the

Airbnb earlier. That was immediately after breaking his bootlace.

He unconsciously looked down at his left boot. His eyes were drawn to the knot he'd formed from the two sections of broken lace.

Fuckin' bootlace!

He found the Wright Cycle Shop on Williams Street. He was impressed with the look of the building from the street.

Looks like they've taken good care of this place. Nothing special about access. Hull ought to be able to stop right here in front without drawing attention.

Barely more than a block away was 7 Hawthorn Street, the original site of the Wright family home. Smithson again stayed in his car. He saw a small structure that appeared to be part of a front porch. There was no house. A full size brass replica of a Wright bicycle stood on the sidewalk. Nearby a historical marker stood at the front of the property. It featured a blown up photo of the original house. Smithson saw that the porch replica stood in the exact spot of the original.

He couldn't help it. He giggled.

This is it? A porch? Imagine going out of your way to visit the Wright brothers' house and finding this...a replica porch.

He continued to giggle until a woman in a Sinclair Community College T-shirt jogged past. She gave him a second look. Smithson sunk down a bit in his seat and eased away from the curb.

He skipped over the next location, the Wright Company Factory, since he'd already visited it. The location next in sequence in the system was Carillon Historical Park. He wove his way south past several city blocks that featured residential housing. The temperature was in the eighties again and still climbing.

The park was located near the Great Miami River off a gently curving street, South Patterson Boulevard. Smithson turned through an open gate to Carillon Boulevard, which angled off of South Patterson. He passed a 151 foot tall bell tower named the Deeds Carillon. A parking lot sat in front of a large building, behind which, Smithson had learned, were dozens of structures arranged as if they were a village. Each structure had some historical significance to the Dayton area. One building was dedicated to the Wright brothers.

Smithson saw that the hours to the complex were 9:30 a.m. to 5 p.m. Monday through Saturday. This meant the site would be inaccessible to Hull later that evening. He did a U-turn in the parking lot and came to a stop. He selected the next location on his nav screen and started back toward the entrance. When he approached he saw signs directing him to his left. The exit was a hundred yards in that direction. He adjusted his course and came to the exit.

He paused.

There's no gate here. There is a gate at the entrance. They must lock it at night....but this exit to South Patterson has no gate. I can direct Hull into the parking lot here. What was that old Led Zeppelin album? IN THROUGH THE OUT DOOR!

He giggled again and turned right onto South Patterson. In less than five minutes he found himself in an upscale suburb, Oakwood. Large, well-kept older homes on rolling hills were crowded into an area with a completely different look and feel from the areas of Dayton Smithson had seen so far. He followed the commands of the GPS with two words running through his head.

Old money.

He pulled to the curb at the base of a hill. The address on his screen read *901 Harman Avenue*. Smithson peered up at a magnificent two-story mansion. This was Hawthorn Hill, the Wright brothers' "Success Mansion."

The damn thing looks like the White House. Gotta be a shit-ton of security around here.

Smithson pulled forward until he reached the front drive to the property. He knew the house was open to tours on a very limited basis and those who bought tickets had to park at Carillon Park and ride over in a shuttle bus. That meant there actually might *not* be personnel at the house on a regular basis. He pulled to the curb again and got out of the Audi, surveying the house and grounds.

Hunh, I don't see anyone. The neighbors are pretty close, but—

His train of thought halted as his eyes trailed back down the lane.

"You're shitting me."

There were short metal posts on either side of the drive, perhaps thirty feet in from the street. A single chain ran from one pole to the other, fixed to loops on either end by simple clasps.

That's it?

The remaining location loaded into Smithson's nav system was Wright B Flyer Inc. It was in a hanger several miles south of the city at the small Dayton Wright Brothers Airport. Smithson hadn't researched it very thoroughly. The building housed a small museum and rides were offered for a fee on a Wright Flyer replica. For Smithson's purposes its major benefit was its distance from the other locations. The drive time it would add to Hull's route would help give Smithson ample time to enter the cemetery and get comfortable in his shooting position.

He decided he didn't need to make the drive south. It was now early afternoon and he was getting hungry again. He would pick up some food, head back to the rental, and get ready to contact Hull. He decided it was time for a change in his diet.

Fifteen minutes later he neared Homeview Drive. He sipped on a Diet Coke. The McDonalds bag next to him held a large order of fries and three cheeseburgers.

No Big Mac.

Smithson pulled the Audi S8 into the garage at the rental and closed the door. Inside the house he sat with his food at the table. He munched cheeseburgers and fries while connecting with Grey. The Hulls were still at their house.

Making you sweat.

The story about the body discovery in Indiana had, indeed, begun to break nationally. Grey had culled video reports from various websites. Aerial footage taken from above the Wilbur Wright Birthplace showed a different perspective, but the stories themselves were filled with speculation.

Nothing to worry about.

He was about to move on to his next task but still had half a cheeseburger to finish. He clicked on one more story. It was from a Chicago television station. Near the end of the report the screen filled with images of evidence technicians in a field.

Smithson adjusted the audio.

> *...police are collecting evidence from a location hundreds of feet from the spot the body was discovered. An unnamed law enforcement official told ABC 7 EYEWITNESS NEWS that tire prints found near the site could be matched to the vehicle of any subject apprehended in the future. The source went on to say that Henry County Sheriff's deputies and Indiana State Police continue to develop leads...*

"BULLSHIT! That's complete bullshit! They don't have any leads! I'm in their fucking computers!"

Smithson ended the video. He knew the police had found no specific evidence at the location of the body. Grey had monitored their databases. The mention of the tire tracks, however, got his attention.

Didn't think of that... shit... oh well, what are they gonna do with that? I pop Hull tonight, get the camera, get on the road, go out west and buy new tires...end of problem.

Smithson spent the afternoon playing video games. He took a break around 3:30 to get his gear in order. It took just a few minutes to pack up his clothes and toiletries. He'd decided to wear the same tactical pants tonight that he'd worn Wednesday when he shot Biggs. He changed out of his shorts and into the pants. He went to the garage and organized the gear in the rear seat before opening the trunk.

331

He positioned the M4 for easy access, making sure the magazines were loaded and ready to go. His biggest decision was whether or not to wear the Velocity Systems bulletproof vest. If he wore it with its plates it would have to go over the top of his hoodie. It would be impossible to wear the Colt revolver in its shoulder holster. He would have to decide between the vest and the pistol.

He put off the decision.

I'll think about it while I'm kicking ass with Reaper. Also gotta decide on what site to make Hull start with.

He positioned the vest, revolver, and NVG's for easy access as well and was closing the trunk when he spotted the leather folder with the forged letter.

Fucking Biggs.

Smithson played *OVERWATCH 2* until nearly 5:30. When he stopped he had worked out the sequence he would use with Hull. The games had once again helped simplify a problem. He had the sequence in his head. He picked up his phone and texted Hull.

Leave your house at 7 p.m. Go to Wright B Flyer Inc., 10550 Springboro Pike. Await further instructions. Bring the camera. Your wife stays home. I'll be watching. Text back a reply acknowledging that you received this.

He added a smiley face.

CHAPTER FORTY-SEVEN

At 5 p.m., not knowing when the text would come, Paul suggested they eat dinner. Lauren said she wasn't hungry but Paul insisted.

"You need some fuel. You eat when you need fuel, whether you're hungry or not."

She tilted her head and looked at him.

"Is this like your sleep thing... sleep when you have time, even if you're not tired?"

"Yep. These are old tricks of the trade from Tier One operators."

"Well, you *are* an old Tier One operator, so I guess you'd know."

She helped him put together a salad. They made simple sliced turkey and bagel sandwiches and sat at the island. Paul's cellphone was on the counter between them. They stole looks at it as if it were a ticking bomb. Paul had checked the screen several times throughout the day. There had not been a communication from the Crank since his initial call. Paul noted that there were several more blocked calls from the Henry County area code. There were also three blocked calls from a local number and two from Detective Amos Bunker's cellphone. Paul guessed the local number was the administrative line at the Troy Police Department.

The text came a few minutes after 5:30. Both Paul and Lauren stared at it. A few seconds later the screen began to sparkle. The message was gone within seconds. Lauren looked up at Paul, a look of amazement on her face.

"Oh wow. Just....oh wow!"

Paul nodded.

"Yeah. It's freaky. It's gone now. How the hell am I supposed to text back?"

Lauren reached for the phone. The screen was mostly blank, but the horizontal oval at the bottom of the screen that enclosed the word "iMessage" was still there. She looked at Paul, shrugged, typed *I got it,* and watched as a blue and white arrow appeared, as if it was any other text conversation. She touched the arrow and saw "Message Sent" appear.

Within seconds a two-word response materialized.

Very Good.

Soon this text was also gone.

Paul was the first to talk.

"Damnedest thing I ever saw."

"I was about to say the same thing."

They quickly finished dinner. As they hurriedly tossed plates, bowls, and silverware into the sink, Chappy jumped back up on the counter. Both Paul and Lauren gave him a scratch without a second thought.

They began to work on the remaining preparations for the evening. Both changed clothes, dressing casually. Lauren donned shorts, a mushroom-printed short-sleeve shirt, and sandals. Paul put on the same items he'd worn the previous night—black running pants, a long-sleeve dark red T-shirt, his Merrells, and his Suunto Core watch.

He grabbed a plastic shopping bag and tossed in two Clif Bars, a bottle of water, and, careful not to touch the exposed .22 round, the extra magazine for the rifle. As he did so Lauren reentered the kitchen from the bedroom. She carried the Army blanket they had used to wrap the Ruger. She spread it on the table and Paul once again placed the rifle on top. He folded the blanket over the weapon several times before it was no longer visible then picked it up.

"Might as well get this into the truck."

Paul snagged the shopping bag as he passed the table. He walked into the garage and hit a button on the wall. The overhead door rose upward. When it reached the halfway point Paul ducked under and walked quickly to the Lariat. He opened the door, tossed in the bag, and carefully laid the rifle on the passenger seat. Before closing the door he had a thought.

I can't forget the screwdriver.

He walked back into the garage and opened the top shelf of a tall rolling toolbox. He sorted through the contents before selecting a small screwdriver. It had a short two-inch shank and a standard blade point. He turned back to the truck. He was three steps from the open truck door when crunching gravel caught his attention.

Paul looked toward Polecat Road and saw Detective Amos Bunker coming up the drive in his Miami County Sheriff's Department SUV.

CHAPTER FORTY-EIGHT

It had been a long, frustrating day for Amos Bunker. It began with end of the week paperwork. His Saturdays were supposed to be half-days but this one had spun away from him. Late in the morning he had a call about a stolen motorcycle in Conover. It was located in the northeast corner of the county. By 1 p.m. he was investigating a bad check passed at a landscape equipment distributor outside of Covington on the west side. He had to skip lunch in order to fit in a call concerning possible fentanyl distribution outside of Casstown. This was back on the eastern side of the county.

The fentanyl thing looked like it was going to condense down to a feud between two families, with the amount of actual illegal drugs involved being minimal. Such was the life of a county detective in a rural area. The range of cases was limited to the same ten or twelve incidents over and over again. Today's sampling was a prime example.

Bunker didn't yearn for more excitement, not really. But the repetitive nature of his investigations required significant discipline on his part. It would be easy to lose focus and become lax with follow up. He had seen it happen to a few of the older detectives he'd worked with. He wouldn't allow it to happen to him. Still, something out of the ordinary every now and then would be a welcome change.

Something like that Wilbur Wright murder over in Indiana. It was all over the news now and it appeared to have taken place in an even more rural area than Miami County. Bunker was driving toward the call in Casstown when the dispatcher came across the radio.

"Detective Bunker we have a request from an out-of-state law enforcement organization to speak to you."

Bunker looked at the radio.

"Bunker here. What do you have for me Millie?"

"A Henry County, Indiana deputy called asking about a person in one of your case files. We gave him your cell number. Just giving you a heads up. Expect a call."

Bunker's cell began to ring.

"I think it's coming in right now."

He ended the transmission and took the call. A typically midwestern male voice came through Bunker's Bluetooth enabled car speakers.

"Detective Bunker? This is Deputy Rudy Joseph from the Henry County Sheriff's department over in Indiana."

Bunker was perplexed, and interested.

"You folks have been busy lately. Not sure how you have time to call me with all the reporters you have to deal with."

Joseph allowed himself a short laugh. Bunker thought the man was probably short on patience after the full court press by the news media. He probably wouldn't be in the mood for much more than a short laugh for some time.

"Sounds like you're up to speed on what we're working on over here. We've been trying to reach a possible witness without any success. We contacted your office because he lives in your county. We're told you've had recent dealings with him."

Bunker racked his brain, trying to determine what small-time marijuana grower or burglary suspect could be associated with a case that was now being mentioned several times a day on Fox News and CNN.

Joseph continued.

The man's name is Paul Hull."

Bunker blinked.

Hull?

"You're saying Paul Hull is a witness to the Wright brothers' murder?"

Joseph clarified.

"He called our office on Wednesday to report he was at the site and the doors to the house were open. We sent a deputy to investigate. Our man got in touch with the caretaker and they did a quick walk-through. Nothing was missing and the caretaker promised to check with other employees to see who might've forgotten to lock up. The body wasn't found until yesterday morning. We've been trying to reach Hull ever since."

Bunker thought about Hull. The man seemed like a straight shooter, certainly not a man that he would suspect of being a criminal.

"Is Hull a suspect?"

Joseph didn't hesitate.

"No, at least not at this time. It's hard to figure why he would call our office if he were involved. This crime scene is really in the middle of nowhere. If Hull was involved he could've easily left the area without being discovered. Why call the sheriff? No, we just want to talk to him, and we're having a helluva time getting through on his cell. We can't even leave a voicemail. We thought maybe you could reach out to him and have him call us."

Bunker asked the deputy to text him his cell number and the number of the Henry County office and assured him he would get in touch with Hull before ending the call. He hit the phone control button on his steering wheel and spoke a command.

"Call Paul Hull."

There was one ring before the call was disconnected. He tried again with the same result.

Maybe I'll just stop by his place on the way back into Troy after this Casstown thing. The day is already shot...what difference does a few more minutes make?

Bunker approached the Hull residence on Polecat Road. He glanced at his passenger seat and saw the notes he'd just taken from assorted family members in the Casstown fentanyl case.

What a fiasco. J-Dub accuses Billy Boy, Billy Boy accuses Hoss, Hoss accuses J-Dub.

Bunker shook his head. He checked his watch and saw it was nearly 6:30. The Hulls' lane came into view on his left and seconds later he turned in.

He saw Hull walking from the garage toward a pickup truck on the side of the driveway. As Bunker approached, Hull turned toward him, hesitating for a beat before smiling and waving. Bunker waved back, stopped the SUV, and got out.

"Mr. Hull. Hope you're having a better day than last time I saw you."

Hull continued to the truck. He tossed a small screwdriver onto the front seat before closing the door.

"Well, it would be hard to have a day that was much worse. What brings you out here Detective Bunker? Has there been a break in the case?"

Bunker noted that Hull's question had a hopeful tone, but his face seemed impassive, as if he knew there was no progress in the investigation of the break-ins.

"No, nothing new, at least nothing new on the investigation into the incident here at the house. But the Troy PD interviewed several people near the hospital and there are indications that a black car with out of state plates was seen in the area just before and after your wife's vehicle was entered. They've checked security cameras in the area and found they had issues similar to the one experienced at the hospital. Their people are checking to see what could've caused it. The working theory is a power surge of some kind. But—"

"But you don't believe in coincidences?"

Bunker shrugged.

"I'll hold off on formulating an opinion until we get more information. Anyway, the reason I stopped...I received a call from a deputy in Henry County, Indiana. They've been trying to reach you about an incident you reported to them a few days ago. Sounds like they're having a tough time getting through."

Hull looked back at him for a few seconds, and nodded slowly.

"We've been having some pretty significant phone problems the last couple days....computer too. We're hoping to get that fixed pretty soon."

Hull flicked a glance toward the truck as he said this.

Bunker nodded.

"Well, I have some phone numbers here from the deputy. Can you get in touch with them at your earliest convenience?"

As Bunker handed over a business card with the numbers jotted on the back, the front door to the house opened. Hull's wife Lauren stepped out. She held the doorknob with one hand. She was dressed in nice shorts and a colorful shirt. It appeared she was getting ready for a night out.

"Hello detective, I thought that was you. Everything alright?"

Bunker assured her all was well.

"Yes ma'am. Just dropping off some contact information with your husband. Seems the sheriff's office you folks called in Indiana the other day really wants to talk to you."

She slowly raised her chin as if contemplating.

"Oh, yeah, that was really weird."

Before Bunker could respond she turned to her husband.

"Paul, you have to get ready, we're supposed to leave for the party in a few minutes."

Hull smiled to her. He turned to Bunker and gestured to his running pants and T-shirt.

"I guess this isn't acceptable attire."

Bunker smiled back knowingly and stepped to the door of his SUV.

"No problem Mr. Hull. Don't forget to call Henry County. Looks like this is tied into that murder that's all over the news. If the newspeople find out you have some connection to that thing, well, your life might get very interesting pretty soon."

Bunker disengaged his internal detective switch the moment he closed his door. He was already thinking about the round of golf he would play with a buddy early the next morning. He glanced in his side mirror before pulling away and noticed Hull was nodding.

341

CHAPTER FORTY-NINE

Paul walked to the front door as Bunker pulled away. Lauren waved at the detective and turned to Paul.

"I saw him pull in and knew we didn't have much time. I hope what I did was okay."

Paul put his arm around her.

"Are you kidding? That was perfect. It kind of rushed him along. You're right, we don't have much time, let's get you moving."

They had reviewed phone protocols several times but Paul insisted on going over it once more. They locked the front door and moved to the kitchen. Four phones were on the island. Chappy hunched inches away, watching as if he expected the devices to sprout legs and walk away. There were two Tracfones and two iPhones.

"Your iPhone stays here. He'll see it and hopefully think you're here with it. You take my iPhone. You'll be driving the Escape so he should track both the phone and the vehicle together. Take your burner. The number of my burner is programmed into favorites. Call me if you need to at any time up until it gets dark. After that, text only."

He went on.

"I'll have my burner. If I need to communicate and I think it's safe I'll call you but I'll be practicing noise discipline later and I may only be able to text. Try not to worry if you don't get quick responses from me. I may not be able to respond for long periods. I've loaded a checkmark emoji onto my burner so I can text that to you for short acknowledgements."

Lauren was visibly anxious but smiled when Paul mentioned the emoji.

"You're sure you don't want to use a fist emoji?"

"Check."

They both laughed nervously before Paul continued.

343

"Take the camera and bag. Take some water. And, last thing, try to go to the bathroom before you leave."

She tilted her head.

"Are you kidding?"

Paul shook his head.

"You're going to be nervous and you won't be able to stop at a restroom. Remember, he'll think it's me in that vehicle. If I have to pee, Crank would expect me to unzip and go behind a bush at one of these sites."

Lauren nodded and deadpanned, "Yeah, that does seem pretty true to form. You've perfected that move."

"Off to the bathroom Lauren Rose."

Five minutes later, at 6:57, Lauren emerged from the bathroom and collected her gear from the island. Paul was waiting. He looked at Chappy.

"Wish us luck, big guy."

Lauren scratched the cat under his chin and followed her husband into the garage. She got behind the wheel of the Escape and adjusted the seat and mirrors then punched the address from Crank into the Escape's Sync navigation system. Paul walked just outside the garage and waited for her to pull out. When she was ready Lauren put the SUV in reverse and eased out of the garage. She stopped and rolled down her window. Paul leaned in, gripped her shoulder, and gave her a kiss.

"You'll do great. I love you. See you when this is over."

She reached for his hand and gave it a squeeze.

"I love you too."

She hesitated, looked at him with an expression that seemed to say *do what you have to do,* and spoke two words.

"First there."

Paul smiled and nodded.

"First there."

Lauren turned the wheel and backed the Escape in an arc. She stopped, put the transmission in drive and steered down the lane. Seconds later she was on Polecat, heading west.

She reached the Troy city limits then picked her way through town, passing Kettering Health. She glanced at the east parking lot where her Jeep Grand Cherokee had been parked the day the Crank had broken in.

Well, not broken in, exactly. He must've figured out the door code, hacked it somehow.

She sighed. The world was now run by computers. Most people were able to use them to one extent or another. The equipment she worked with in the lab was highly technical, certainly more advanced than their counterparts from the 1990s when she started in her field. But she and her fellow techs in the lab had evolved with them. They had kept up with the technology.

At least she thought they had. She realized now that the technology was way out ahead of them and they, like most people in the modern world, were trying to hang on as it advanced. This hacker, this Crank, he was out ahead of it. He had figured a way to bend the current computer reality, to make it work for him.

To control it.

She gave a slight shudder as she maneuvered the Escape onto I-75.

I'm lucky to have Paul. He's using his experience to try to avoid this guy's reach.

As she continued south an image of her dad came to her. She wondered if he was watching. She knew if it were possible to reach back into the material world from the afterlife, her dad would put his hands around Crank's neck and choke the life out of him. She imagined the scene.

You screwed with the wrong little girl, you asshole!

Her dad would've given up everything he had to help her in this situation. But he wasn't here.

Maybe dad knew something like this could happen when he made that speech at our wedding.

Lauren's vision clouded with tears.

After passing through Dayton Lauren felt her anxiety level increase. She checked the digital clock of the Escape, looked back at the road in front, and felt her eyes pulled back to the clock. She did this at least a dozen times in a five-mile stretch, occasionally glancing in her mirrors. She realized the screen of the nav system was directing her to get off the highway at exit 41. This was the exit for Austin Landing, a collection of restaurants and retail shops. She had been there a half dozen times over the last few years.

Lauren reached the exit and came to a stop at the top of the ramp. As she waited with her left turn signal blinking she looked to her left and saw the large Field & Stream store east of I-75. The light changed and Lauren passed over the highway and abreast of the store. It appeared to be made completely of timber beams and fieldstone.

I always thought that place looked like a ski lodge.

The nav system directed her to move to the right lane. She did so and, prompted by the system, turned right at the next intersection. She saw ahead on her left what must be her destination. In the center of a line of hangars was one with a large blue silhouette of a Wright Flyer on its left face. The entire right front of the building was covered with fifteen-foot tall painted representations of Wilbur and Orville's heads.

Not much doubt that this is the place.

Lauren pulled into the parking lot in front of the building. She could see a small airfield behind it. Looking closer she noticed the words "FREE MUSEUM, WRIGHT "B" FLYER" were stenciled in black paint under the silhouette of the plane. She checked the clock. It was 7:44 p.m. The sun was low on the horizon to the west. There were no other vehicles in the parking lot.

Now what?

She sat nervously for fifteen seconds before a text appeared on the screen of her iPhone.

Get out of your vehicle, hold up the camera so I can see you brought it, take a selfie with the building in the background. Text it to me.

Lauren sat transfixed, watching the screen shimmer and the text disappear. She felt her adrenaline spike as she quickly grabbed the Tracfone. She fumbled with it for a second before speed dialing her husband.

He picked up immediately, "Yeah?"

Lauren spoke quickly.

"He wants a selfie of you in front of the building!"

CHAPTER FIFTY

Lauren was holding the Tracfone to her ear when she sensed movement to her right. She turned her head quickly and saw a vehicle pull up next to the Escape.

It was Paul.

Smiling, she ended the call and rolled down the passenger side window.

Paul lowered the driver's side window of the Lariat. He smiled back.

"You were right."

It had been Lauren's idea that he follow her to the first few sites, arguing he couldn't get in position at his final location until after dark. His original plan was to drive to a spot near that location and follow her progress over the burner phone until sunset. He would then move in.

"What do I do if he wants a picture with you in it? If I don't send one back he'll know we're not following his rules."

Paul considered this. He knew the entire operation was dependent on several factors beyond their control. The most perplexing was this question of Crank asking for photographic proof that Paul was doing what he was told. There was no way Paul could be with Lauren later. He had to be in position. Why take the chance that Crank was at one of the early locations watching for multiple vehicles?

But Lauren countered that Crank probably wouldn't ask for selfies taken in the dark where backgrounds wouldn't be visible.

"If he asks for pictures, it'll be while it's still light out. He'll want the Wright sites in the pics. We'll just have to take a chance and hope he's not staked out at an early site watching for us. Besides, you can hang back in the truck watching. You only need to come to where I am if he demands a picture."

349

In the end Paul decided to do it her way.

Sometimes the least experienced member of the team has a damn good idea.

Paul got out of the truck.

"Better get it done. I get the impression he's not the patient type."

Lauren snatched Paul's iPhone from the Escape and grabbed the camera bag before joining him and handing over both items.

Paul eyed the hanger and noticed there was a small paved area just to the right.

"Would you look at that...a bowler bench."

He pointed to the brass bench.

"I had no idea one of these was here. Might as well get it in the shot."

He removed the Panasonic DSLR from its bag then pulled up the camera app on the iPhone and reversed the screen. He held up the camera with his left hand while adjusting the position of the iPhone in his right, finally framing a shot that showed him, the camera, the Wright Flyer building, and the bowler bench in the same frame. Just before he took the picture Lauren spoke.

"Don't look too happy. Remember, you're supposed to be pissed."

"I am pissed."

The resulting selfie would bear that out.

Paul sent the photo using the same method Lauren had earlier. They waited for a response while standing in front of the vehicles. Both of them scanned the area looking for any trace of a watcher.

Paul commented.

"If he's out there, we're already screwed."

A tone sounded from the iPhone. Paul held it up.

Wow Paulie, you don't look very happy. Nice bench there in the background. Next stop is the old Wright Company

Factory, 99 Cowart Avenue. Go to the old front gate and pull in. Wait for my next message.

The message began to break up.

Paul looked at Lauren.

"Back into Dayton. I don't know much about that area but I don't think it's the greatest neighborhood. I'll be behind you again for this one."

Lauren nodded. She gathered Paul's iPhone and the Panasonic camera, which was back in its bag. She checked the time on Paul's phone.

"It's two minutes after eight."

They both turned to the setting sun.

It took a bit longer than fifteen minutes to reach the factory site. Lauren led the way, having entered the address into her nav system. She took I-75 back north to U.S. Route 35 East before turning onto surface streets. Lauren noted the neighborhood had its challenges but was heartened to see a modern library building near her last turn. The shadows had lengthened significantly but she was able to make out a low factory complex set several hundred feet back from a fence topped with barbed wire. She pulled off the road and into a drive that funneled her toward a rusted, closed gate. She put the Escape in park. After nervously checking her surroundings she locked her doors.

She swiveled her head, checking for Paul, but he must've turned off his headlights. She knew he was nearby and was again relieved they'd gone with her version of the plan for the early sites. It was uncomfortable sitting here as the sun set. It would've been considerably more so if Paul wasn't nearby.

The text tone sounded. She picked up the phone and saw the message.

Attaboy Paulie. So far, so good. Drive to 2380 Memorial Rd. That's the Huffman Prarie Flying Field Interpretive Center. You've been there before. It will be closed but pull into the drive and wait for instructions...just like you did here.

Lauren picked up her Tracfone and speed dialed Paul as the shimmer effect removed Crank's text.

Paul answered immediately and Lauren talked as she loaded the new address into the Escape's system.

"The Huffman Field Interpretive Museum by Wright State."

She finished with the nav system and looked up. It was 8:29 and the sun was no longer visible. A glow to the west marked the spot where it had disappeared.

"You better get going Paul. He didn't ask for a picture here and I can't believe he'll want more now that it's dark."

Paul was silent for a beat.

"You're right, get going. Keep me up to speed on every text and location."

Then, with resolve, "I'll be ready."

CHAPTER FIFTY-ONE

Smithson was at the rental house in northwest Dayton. All of his gear was packed and, with the exception of the Toughbook laptop, stowed in the Audi in the garage. He sat at the dining room table watching the show on the computer. The red dot of Hull's phone and the blue dot of his SUV were melded together, traveling in tandem across the map displayed on the Toughbook. The wife was doing what wives should do, following orders and sitting at home. The dots representing her iPhone and Jeep Cherokee were at the house on Polecat, now off screen north of Dayton.

Smithson was excited. He was now submerged into a game of his own making. It would get even better in the coming hour or two as it moved from the two dimensional world of the computer screen and assumed three dimensional proportions in the real world. He would be his own character in this game. It wouldn't be virtual reality.

It would be better.

He smiled as he saw Hull's vehicle approach the drive to the Interpretive Center. He glanced at the photo of the man on his phone. He was standing near a bowler bench on Springboro Pike south of Dayton. A mural of the Wright brothers loomed over his shoulder. He held the damn camera in one hand.

Smithson took a long look at the camera.

It was luck, just dumb luck. What were the chances I'd be caught on video in a sea of corn in fucking Indiana? The odds were astronomical. I've done all kinds of shit in the past and was never filmed. Well, if I was, Grey worked his data breach magic and took care of it. That damn camera. Well, not long to wait now.

He hadn't eaten since lunch. He was too hyped. This same thing happened on Wednesday before he and Biggs hit the birthplace site. He had to stop at a McDonalds after getting the hell out of Dodge.

I'll do the same thing tonight. Grab a couple Macs and some fries, jump on the highway, and drive until the juice stops flowing...get a hotel somewhere.

He saw the dots slow at what would be the closed gate at the Huffman Field Interpretive site. He reached for his phone to send the next instruction and again looked at Hull's photo.

Boy, he really looks pissed off.

Smithson giggled.

Several miles to the east Lauren steered the Escape off Kauffman Road and into the mouth of Memorial Road. A locked gate prevented her from going further just as the Crank had mentioned in his now-disintegrated text. She sat at the base of the hill, which rose just west of the Escape. Any lingering traces of the sun were blocked from her view. Lauren noted there was some ambient light. She looked about and saw the moon up and to her left. It was a bit more than three quarters full and reflected light down through the cloudless sky. The slight illumination combined with a fair amount of traffic behind her on Kauffman to make this location much less unsettling than the last one.

Still, she made sure her doors were locked.

She cleared the current location from the navigation system in anticipation of the next message from the Crank. As she waited she glanced up the dark drive. She hadn't visited this site but she knew Paul had been here at least once. He told her it was called Wright Hill, at least at one time.

A corner of her mouth rose as she thought again how thoroughly he became engrossed in certain subjects. Once his interest was triggered by something he pursued it with a passion. She supposed he had been this way on combat deployments, locked in on every detail. She hoped he would find a new long-term interest to occupy the next several years and applied a similar focus. Maybe he would take that position with the McClarys' company. She contemplated.

If we get out of this mess.

The phone dinged, announcing an incoming text. Lauren's attention instantly centered on the device.

Nice job Paulie. Kinda fun steering you around. Go back to 444 and head east. Turn in at gate 16A. Follow the roads back to the Wright flying field. Have fun in the dark. Some roads are blocked.

He again added a smiley face.

Lauren tossed Paul's iPhone onto the passenger seat as the text began to break down. She picked up the Tracfone. Now that it was dark she followed Paul's instruction to text rather than call him. She typed quickly.

Gate 16A. Find the Wright Flying Field?

There was no address to type into the Escape's nav system. The seemingly open-ended instruction from Crank triggered anxiety. Lauren took a deep breath, trying to push it back down as she waited for a response from her husband.

CHAPTER FIFTY-TWO

Paul followed the Escape as Lauren guided it away from the Wright factory. Both vehicles rolled east on Route 35 until they reached I-75. Lauren signaled before merging onto the larger highway. Paul continued past the interchange, watching the Escape's taillights as long as possible.

Good luck, baby.

He snapped his head back to the windshield. His exit was coming up quickly. Barely a minute after passing I-75 he eased to the right lane and took the ramp at Keowee. He continued south for several blocks.

Paul shot a look at the Ruger on the passenger seat, concealed in the blanket. The last few days had run together in his head. It dawned on him that he had been in almost exactly the same position, rifle and all, the night before. Day Air Ballpark was several blocks to the north but it was front and center in Paul's mind for a second.

Well, we'll see if that—what had Lauren called it... caper?— worked.

Paul needed no navigation system to get to his destination. He and Lauren had made this drive many times. He negotiated his way through a series of turns and minutes later found himself on Oak Street. This was in the South Park section of the city. Paul crept slowly down the street. Vehicles were parked on both sides. He scanned for a space and soon found one. It was two hundred feet from a trailer parked ahead on the opposite side. Paul recognized it and grinned.

The Bourbon Trail'r!

He quickly prepared to leave the pickup. He opened a bottle of water and forced down half of it while removing a Clif Bar from the bag and pushing it into the right front pocket of his running pants. He capped the water and left the bottle on the seat then reached under and found his leather gloves. He picked up the small screwdriver and the extra magazine and contorted his body so he could slide them into the left pocket of his pants. Saucony designed the pants with zippered pockets. Paul pulled up the zipper of the left pocket, sealing in the screwdriver and mag.

Paul checked the street, saw a couple more than a block away, and opened his door. He reached back across the steering wheel and grabbed the Tracfone. He stepped onto the street and moved to the passenger door near the curb, pulling on the gloves as he walked and checking the street again. Oak Street ran east to west. The Lariat was parked east of the Bourbon Trail'r, which was directly in front of the McClary house. A car approached from the east and moved in the direction of the Lariat. Paul did not want to be seen by anyone who might recognize him. He nonchalantly went to one knee as the vehicle passed and acted as if he was tying a boot, effective shielding himself behind the Lariat. The car continued down the street and past the trailer.

Paul checked the street again before opening the door and removing the Army blanket containing the Ruger. He locked the truck and slid the key into the right side of his pants beside the energy bar then zippered that pocket as well.

Paul cradled the blanket in his left arm and crossed the street to the south side. He walked quickly in the direction of the McClary's house. Just ahead, several houses from the McClarys', was Cross Street. Paul turned left there and walked normally.

Just a guy trying to get somewhere on a Saturday night.

Paul walked south for a short block before coming to a narrow park that extended to his left and right. There was little artificial light here but moonlight streamed down to give the area a pale hue. He saw a woman walking a small dog some distance to his right. He quickly crossed the park and continued south past two more short blocks of single-family homes. Over seven hundred structures were packed into South Park's twenty-four blocks. The vast majority were two-story houses. A gentrification had occurred the last several years as the homes, many over a century old, were renovated. The McClary house was one such example.

Cross Street ended at Wyoming Street. Paul found himself a few hundred feet from the spot he and Lauren had stopped the pickup the night before. He peered to his right and could make out the white exterior of the Wyoming Street Community Church. He'd taken just a few steps in that direction when his burner phone vibrated in his right hand. He immediately raised it and viewed the screen.

Gate 16A. Find the Wright Flying Field?

Paul looked at the text and realized Lauren needed help finding the specific area of Huffman Prarie where the Wrights made their flights. He had been there but Lauren had not.

Shit. Crank knows I've been there and expects me to find it in the dark.

He searched his memory before removing his right glove and typing.

You turn left into the gate off 444. Pass golf course on left. There is a small wood hangar and what looks like the skeleton of a 15' tall pyramid about ¼ mile ahead of you. No direct road. Follow signs. Make wide arc to left and then back right.

He hit *Send* and stared at the screen, hoping these shorthand directions helped. Seconds later the Tracfone vibrated again.

A checkmark emoji appeared on the screen.

Attagirl!

Paul had been absorbed by the text conversation. He looked up to see a van drive past. The driver didn't give him a second look. There was nothing unusual about a man on the sidewalk staring at his phone.

He picked up the pace, moving more quickly to the west. As he came abreast of the church he checked traffic before stepping across the street. He looked for walkers or joggers and saw no one within a hundred yards.

The church sat back a few feet from the street. A chainlink fence wrapped around the sides and rear of the property before extending down the street. The night before Paul had noticed there was a narrow lane that ran along the left side of the church to the rear of the tract. Anyone down that lane would be virtually impossible to see due to the darkness and the angle from the street. He crossed Wyoming and continued down the lane to the rear of the property.

Paul's actions were smooth. The Tracfone went into his right pocket, which was then zipped. He laid the blanket on the ground and unwrapped the Ruger, looping it over his right shoulder using the rope sling. Next he picked up the blanket and folded it in quarters. The fence was roughly six feet tall with three strands of barbed wire running above it.

Paul stretched his left leg, taking a mental reading of its status. He felt no pain.

Okay, showtime.

Paul held the blanket across his chest with both hands. He charged at the fence from twenty feet away. With his last stride he pushed off with his left leg and leaped. The toe of his right boot found purchase halfway up the fence and he used the momentum to project the blanket to the top of the barbed wire. Paul scrambled up and over the fence before jumping down on the other side. He felt the barbed wire catch his running pants near his upper right thigh but the damage was minimal. The blanket and leather gloves had shielded him from further issues. He grabbed the blanket and tried to extricate it from the barbed wire but it was caught.

Might as well leave it there. It's pretty much invisible from the street and I can use it on the way out.

Paul gathered himself. A tree-studded incline ran to the south from here. He started up. Now that he had scaled the fence his thoughts turned back to Lauren.

Did I give her enough information to find the spot?

These thoughts were interrupted as he reached the top of the incline. He gazed out at uneven terrain. The moonlight revealed tree covered hills and hollows. They were dotted by thousands of monuments.

Paul was inside Woodland Cemetery.

CHAPTER FIFTY-THREE

After directing Hull to the Wright flying field at Huffman Prarie, Smithson carried the Toughbook to the garage and sat it on the passenger seat of the Audi. It was still open. It was no longer connected to the robust signal from the house. It was now locked onto Smithson's personal hot spot. He would be able to watch Hull's progress from the car.

Smithson returned the key to the lockbox. He thought about notifying the owner but decided against it.

Keep them guessing. I have the place rented for several more days. If I don't tell them I'm leaving early they won't come to the place until I'm scheduled out. By then I'll be long gone.

Smithson decided to take Riverside Drive down through the heart of Dayton on his way to Woodland. It was a nice enough drive, he supposed, but he would be happy to leave this place behind. He wound his way down Riverside, passing Knecht Drive. He looked to his right as he drove by and couldn't resist saying it out loud.

"Fucking Biggs."

Smithson drove through the heart of downtown Dayton on the way to Woodland Cemetery. At red lights he stole looks at the laptop's screen, following Hull's progress. He was heartened to see the man appeared to be struggling to find his way through the narrow roads that wove through Huffman Prarie. The speed of the Escape had slowed considerably.

Probably a real pain in the ass creeping around out there in the dark.

Smithson turned onto Woodland Avenue. He drove toward the main gate of the cemetery three blocks away, scanning for a place to park. It took longer than he'd hoped. As he drew within a block of the gate he realized a middle-aged couple was standing beside their idling Honda Accord. Their hands were extended in front of their bodies. They were taking pictures of themselves in front of the cemetery gate.

Well that's weird.

He felt himself growing anxious until five minutes later when he found a spot on Alberta Street a block and a half from the cemetery gate. He turned to the Toughbook and saw that Hull had reached the proper spot at the Flying Field and was sitting motionless.

I'll bet he's sweating bullets sitting out there in the dark.

Smithson picked up his phone and thought for a few seconds before typing his next text.

Sorry to keep you waiting Paulie. Pretty damn dark out there, huh? Next stop is the Engineers Club of Dayton, 110 E. Monument. Rock on.

Smithson watched until the red and blue dots on his screen began to move then shut down the laptop and stored it in its case in the back seat. He checked his surroundings before opening his door and walking to the rear of the Audi. He opened the trunk and looked down at the tightly packed gear. The Pelican case was on top. Back at the Airbnb he had repacked the trunk, sequencing things properly for the night ahead.

The Pelican case had inline wheels that allowed it to be rolled like a suitcase. He had packed it with the suppressed M4, extra magazines, and the bolt cutters. He had no intention of walking down the street carrying an assault rifle so the case was a godsend. He could roll it down the sidewalk looking like a musician taking equipment to a gig at one of the nearby college bars. He removed the case and leaned it on the Audi. He looked down at the next items. He had to make a choice.

The Velocity Systems bulletproof vest was there, as was the Colt revolver in its shoulder rig. He hefted the vest with its internal plates.

DAMN that's heavy.

He remembered the hilly terrain of the cemetery from his visit the day before. The hike from the front gate to the location he'd selected would be a nightmare wearing the weight of the vest on a warm, humid evening.

Fuck that.

He reached for the Colt.

Lauren put the Escape in gear. She'd been sitting for five minutes in the middle of Huffman Prarie, growing increasingly concerned.

Was he just trying to lure Paul here? Is this the ambush site?

She swiveled her head constantly, looking for threats. She saw the wooden hangar that Paul mentioned as well as a contraption that did indeed look like the skeleton of a small pyramid.

I'll have to have Paul explain that to me if... WHEN we get out of this.

She had used Paul's hastily typed directions to follow the narrow roads in the dark. At one point she was sure she was hopelessly lost. She found herself driving down a long tree-lined stretch. The road surface was very narrow.

Am I on a bike path?

She was about to put the SUV in reverse when she noticed a flashing light in the distance. It was moving in her direction.

Is this Crank? Is he coming for the camera?

She decided to take a chance and eased the Escape forward. The light moved closer and Lauren could make out reflective material on a helmet.

A biker?

There was not enough room on the road surface for the SUV and the cyclist to pass each other safely in the dark. Lauren edged to the right as much as she dared without having her tires leave the road surface. She braked to a stop. The rider drew closer and she saw it was a woman. A wave of relief washed over her and she rolled down the window and waved her arm.

"Excuse me! Excuse me!"

The woman slowed to a stop near Lauren's door and braced herself on the side of the vehicle. Before Lauren could speak the woman asked a question.

Are you lost?

Lauren nodded and smiled at the cyclist. She asked for directions to the small wooden hangar. The woman confirmed she was on the right path.

"Go to the end of this road, probably another half mile. When it ends take a right. You'll see the old hangar and the other uh...pointy-topped thingy straight ahead."

Lauren thanked her profusely and despite her time crunch couldn't resist asking.

"Do you ride out here at night a lot?"

The rider nodded.

"Yeah, it's waaay safer than the roads. I work during the day and try to ride out here as much as possible. It's cooler at night and the place is open until ten."

Then she added, as if as an afterthought.

"There's almost no traffic out here."

As she sat waiting for Crank's next text Lauren remembered the woman's expression as she delivered that last line. It seemed to say *I'm exercising...what the hell are YOU doing out here?*

Lauren heard the notification tone on Paul's iPhone. The next set of instructions had arrived.

CHAPTER FIFTY-FOUR

Paul surveyed the cemetery in the moonlight. He had committed the maps that Mike texted him to memory but still thought it best to confirm his course of action by making sure they corresponded to what he saw before him. He crouched behind a tree and removed the Tracfone, quickly pulling up the map that Mike had screen grabbed from the Woodland Cemetery website.

Paul then checked the compass feature of his Suunto watch. He quickly confirmed what he expected. He needed to move east by southeast approximately five hundred yards. He would pick his way through the monuments and stones rather than walk on the roads where he could be spotted more easily. He stepped off in that direction.

As he moved Paul couldn't keep the thought of Lauren from entering his head. The Flying Field would be dark with only the soft light of the moon and stars to help her see things outside of the cone of her headlights. She would have to be virtually on top of the structures before seeing them. How would Crank react if she wandered aimlessly for too long? How freaked out would she be?

Paul couldn't do anything to directly affect her situation. He forced himself to move to a different subject. He thought of the structure that Lauren was searching for. It was the Wrights' catapult tower. They had devised it as a way to launch their planes without benefit of the strong winds available at Kitty Hawk. Weights hung from the top of the structure. A sixty-foot wooden launching rail was laid, starting at the base. Once the propellers of the Flyer were started and the pilot was ready, the weights were dropped and an attached pulley dragged the craft down the rail. Enough speed was achieved to create the lift required to get the plane off the ground.

Paul knew that word of the brothers' flights spread. Daytonians would ride out to Huffman Prarie on the interurban trolley and watch in amazement. Curiously, no press coverage occurred, even though numerous witnesses contacted the local newspapers and raved about the miracle happening right there in their back yard. It was not until January 1 of 1905 that a story was published. Oddly, it was in a magazine about bees, *Gleanings In Bee Culture*. The author, Amos Root, had heard of the Wrights and traveled two hundred miles from Medina, Ohio to watch.

Paul figured he was now roughly halfway to his destination. He stopped and unslung the Ruger. He pulled back the bolt to seat the first round into the chamber before engaging the safety. He began to move forward again, even more cautiously than before. Seconds later the Tracfone vibrated. He crouched behind a large grave marker and removed his right glove, shielding the screen with his left hand to prevent the glare from being visible at any distance. He viewed the screen.

Engineers Club next.

Paul let out a small sigh, relieved that Lauren was leaving the darkness of Huffman Prarie.

He texted back a checkmark emoji.

Smithson emerged from the Audi. He had ducked back in to strap on the shoulder holster after first removing his hoodie. After locking the door he reopened the trunk and removed the Winkler combat axe and fast draw carrier. He attached it to his belt on his right hip. Next he pulled out the ballistic helmet with the PVS-14 night vision monocular attached. He grabbed the handle on top of the Pelican case and began to pull it toward Woodland Avenue. Once he reached it he turned and strode directly toward the front gate a block away. As he drew nearer he looked at a security camera mounted on the chapel. He smirked, knowing Grey had removed it as a threat just as he had with every other camera on the grounds.

People, though, *were* still a threat. He furtively looked back, first over his right shoulder, then his left. There was cross-traffic three blocks behind him on Brown Street. Dozens of establishments that catered to the nearby University of Dayton student body existed there. He saw no possible witnesses.

There were stone towers on either side of the black metal gate. A low row of bushes started at the left tower and ran in a line several yards away from the gate. Smithson walked to these bushes and laid the case in the grass. The case had six press and pull latches. He flipped each of them open and eased back the top cover. He found the bolt cutters and removed them before closing half of the latches. He peeked past the bushes to confirm he was still unnoticed. Verifying this, he walked to the center of the drive and stepped to the gate.

The chain was black steel. It was threaded through openings on both doors. A padlock held the two ends together and hung down like a charm on a necklace. To Smithson's eyes the chain was not particularly heavy.

Why the hell should it be heavy? What are they guarding? Just a bunch of dead people.

He raised the cutters and lined up the blades on either side of one of the links. He squeezed the handles toward each other and, after two seconds of resistance, felt the blades snap together. He repeated the process on the other side of the link and the two ends of the chain fell back against the fence, making a clattering sound. Smithson looked back behind him, remembering the term fighter pilots use to look to their rear.

Check Six.

Seeing no threats Smithson removed the chain. He tried to minimize noise while doing this and was mostly successful. He opened the gate three feet and was encouraged that it barely made a sound. Next he pulled the Pelican case through the opening before closing the gate.

He rearranged the chain so both cut ends draped down on the back side. The damaged link would be invisible from the front. If anyone checked they would have to be within feet of the gate to see the damage in the dark.

Who would?

Smithson carried all of his gear thirty feet into the cemetery and knelt down under an evergreen tree. He fumbled with the helmet and NVGs, finally getting them onto his head with the monocular in front of his right eye. He turned them on and had the off-putting sensation of an illuminated green world streaming into that eye while the left still perceived a world of darkness.

He opened the case and removed the rifle, laying it on the grass. He slipped the bolt cutters inside. Smithson then seated a loaded thirty round magazine into the M4. He grabbed an extra magazine and fitted it into the left thigh pocket of his tactical pants. It fit perfectly. He would have sixty rounds of 5.56 NATO ammunition when he encountered Hull on the hill.

More than enough.

Before setting off he pulled out his phone and checked Hull's progress. The Escape was nearing the downtown area.

I still have some time until he gets to the Engineers Club. I can walk a few minutes then stop and check again. I have plenty of time.

CHAPTER FIFTY-FIVE

Paul was thinking about Psalm 23:4.

He didn't consider himself an overly religious man, but he knew this passage. He thought it would be difficult to come up with a set of circumstances that related to it more closely than his present situation.

He was walking at night between tombstones, looking up at his destination.

If this isn't walking through the valley of the shadow of death I don't know what is.

It had been several minutes since he last stopped. He could make out the surrounding network of roads. He couldn't actually see all of the road surfaces but the absence of monuments in straight lines were a giveaway. He was sure of his position. In front of him the ground rose in a fairly steep gradient. A road ran down from it for two hundred feet before curving away to Paul's right.

That would be Dunbar Road.

If Paul followed Dunbar Road up to the crest of the hill he would be in position to command the entire area. He believed that was where Crank would be. It was not just because it was the high ground, it was due to the fact that the graves of Wilbur and Orville Wright were visible from there.

Paul needed to get close enough to the crest to be in effective range of Crank. He was surveying the trees and monuments on the slope, determining the best course of action, when his burner phone vibrated. He ducked behind a large oak tree and checked the screen.

Leaving Engineers. Routing me past 1st Baptist. On to Cycle Shop, 22 Williams.

Paul removed his right glove. He selected the checkmark emoji and hit send.

He turned his attention back to the hill. He was below its north face. Dunbar Road ran north to south across the hill. Paul could make out a line of mausoleums on the left side of Dunbar at the very top of the hill. He knew the Wright family plot was on the other side of Dunbar, partway down the hill's west slope. He needed to get to a position where he could see the Wright plot. He couldn't remember how far down the hill it was located.

It's been a long time.

In fact, it had been since July 20, 2003.

Paul was the new guy with the 21st STS, his first operational unit. Fresh from the Pipeline, he was anxious to prove himself to his teammates, many of whom had seen combat. They were in Dayton as part of a project being run by the Air Force Research Laboratory's Electrochemistry and Thermal Sciences Branch, based at Wright-Patterson Air Force Base. The goal of the project was to reduce the power system weight carried by Combat Controllers on missions. Before this project the standard weight of batteries carried by a CCT was 35.5 pounds. The project sought to reduce this significantly by using new battery technology.

Paul and his mates were all for this. Batteries were just one of many necessary items that added up to well over a hundred pounds of gear a CCT carried in a standard loadout. Anything the eggheads could do to cut this down would be welcome.

They were also all for a few weeks of relatively easy duty. They worked long hours at the base being fitted with gear, running around putting it through its paces, and giving the techs feedback. They also played hard, sampling a number of the Dayton area bars. They hit the Oregon District the first weekend and then sortied to a half dozen others the next. Then they discovered Flanaghan's Pub on Stewart Street near the University of Dayton.

More specifically, they discovered a group of American Airlines flight attendants doing a layover from Dayton International Airport. The attendants and CCT commandeered a corner of the bar one Saturday night and a good time was had by all. It began when Paul's First Lieutenant, Jay

"Wrought Iron" Gates, spotted a pretty redhead in a group of attractive younger women eating a salad at an outdoor table. Wrought Iron employed one of his standard pickup lines.

"You know...Hitler was a vegetarian."

It had never worked. In his short time with the 21st Paul had witnessed Wrought Iron try this line on three other occasions and he'd barely avoided being slapped each time. But Wrought Iron was undaunted. He was apparently searching for a woman that had the same warped sense of humor as many in special operations.

This time it appeared he found her. The woman, Colleen, snickered. Her friends were mortified, but Wrought Iron didn't care about that. Colleen and Wrought Iron became the central figures in what could've been a scene from a bad movie. Flight attendants and CCT coalesced around them. A good time was had by all, the bar tab was paid, and the two groups agreed to meet back at Flanaghan's the next day for Sunday morning Bloody Marys.

The Controllers arrived at Flanaghan's the next day at the appointed time. It was a pleasant morning so they sat outside on the patio. Two rounds of Bloody Marys and thirty minutes later they came to the realization that the flight attendants were not going to show. Wrought Iron seemed a bit crestfallen. The rest of the team seemed content to sit and enjoy a few more cocktails. Paul was certainly in this group.

Then an odd thing happened. The sound of a low-flying plane came to their ears. This was uncommon in a city, particularly since September 11, 2001. It was the sound of a propeller driven plane, not a jet. The Air Force contingent at the bar searched the sky. One of them, Paul couldn't remember who, pointed to the south at a slow-moving craft. As it drew closer they were surprised to see it was a replica of a Wright Flyer. It flew to a wooded area perhaps a half-mile east of them and began to make long, slow circles.

The Controllers heard a man at a nearby table mention something about a Wright brothers ceremony "over at Woodland." They had no idea what Woodland was. Wrought Iron Gates, now resigned to the fact that the ladies were not coming, announced he was walking over to check things out. He urged the rest of the guys to come along.

"The bar isn't going anywhere, it'll be here when we come back."

With that the Controllers were on their way. They walked across the street and made their way to the front gate of the cemetery. From there it was easy to follow the trail of parked cars. They worked their way to the rear of the property and trooped up a hill until they saw a large group of people in a semi-circle. The crowd stood respectfully around the Wright family plot, in which Wilbur and Orville were interred. The attention of the crowd was on a choir singing *God Bless America*. By the time the Controllers reached the edge of the assemblage an official was speaking. The man finished and introduced the next speaker. Paul was impressed when he heard the name.

It was John Glenn, the man that on February 20, 1962, became the first American in space. In 1996, at the age of seventy-seven, he repeated the feat when he returned to space as a member of the crew of the space shuttle Discovery. Glenn spoke glowingly of the Wrights. The Controllers hadn't realized that 2003 was the one-hundredth year of powered flight until hearing Glenn's words. The former astronaut finished his speech by saying of the Wrights, "Their bodily remains are buried here, but their spirit lives on in every young person who is inspired to dream, to do, and to move the world ahead. Their example is timeless."

Before stepping aside, Glenn told the crowd that exactly thirty-four years earlier, in 1969, the next speaker set foot on the moon. Paul and his teammates looked at each other with wide eyes as Neil Armstrong stepped forward. He too praised the Wrights, saying, "We've lauded the dedication, creativity, and achievements of Orville and Wilbur Wright, but this morning we remember them not for those achievements, but as the kind of men they were: men of honesty, and men of integrity in all they did. That is something for us to honor and emulate."

Paul remembered marveling that the four men, Armstrong, Glenn, and both Wrights, were Ohioans. He remembered descendants of the Wright brothers putting wreaths on the grave of each family member buried in the plot. He remembered a bagpiper playing *Amazing Grace*. And he remembered one of the speakers pointing out recent improvements to the gravesite; a mulched bed of myrtle that had been added around the burial stones, a cobblestone walkway that was laid all the way around the rectangular-shaped plot, and, behind the main headstone with the word "Wright" inscribed on it, the addition of three flagpoles that were being dedicated that day.

Three flagpoles.

After his lone phone conversation with the man he called Crank, Paul came away convinced he knew the location of their meeting place. Crank made it obvious he had a complete history of Paul's visits to Wright brothers sites and he was correct, so far as any man or computer could be after analyzing the data. But the data was incomplete. Crank knew where Paul's vehicle and phone had been for at least the last year, maybe even since they settled in the area three years earlier. But he didn't know Paul had been to the Wrights' graves back in 2003. It was a day he'd never forget.

He couldn't remember the exact location of the plot, but the maps Mike had texted helped fill in the blanks. Still, a two hundred acre cemetery was difficult to navigate in the dark, particularly when you had to avoid marked roads to prevent discovery. Paul needed to first locate the Wright family plot before expanding his reconnaissance to determine Crank's probable shooting hide.

He had no way of knowing if he'd arrived at the cemetery before his adversary. If he had to guess he would put the odds at two to one in his favor. He knew Crank was occupied, directing Lauren all over the Dayton area. He believed the man wouldn't actually penetrate Woodland until some time after dark. Still, he couldn't be sure. He crouched with the Ruger extended, moving deliberately. This is how the operators of his customer units moved at night, stalking their prey, senses heightened. Paul moved slowly up the grade. He was fifty feet left, or east, of Dunbar drive. The line of mausoleums was directly above him, perhaps one hundred and fifty feet away.

That sure looks like a likely spot.

If it was possible, Paul moved even more deliberately. He edged up another ten feet angling to keep stones between him and the mausoleums. He halted behind another tree, one he couldn't identify. He knew the cemetery property was also classified as an arboretum and was home to well over a hundred different tree species. He could tell that it was old. Paul eased around the trunk of the tree and slowly turned his head to the right. Pale reflections from the moon gave the monuments a slight luminous glow. Paul heard the chittering of a small animal and distant traffic from Wyoming Street and Wayne Avenue. He raised himself to his full height, his body pressed to the tree.

He saw the flagpoles.

Well, two of them. From this angle he cold see the center pole, the one that held the United States flag. He remembered that it was slightly taller than the others. There were no lights illuminating the flags. Paul vaguely wondered if the official etiquette about shining a light on a displayed United States flag did not apply in a cemetery. He could just make out the top of the pole furthest from his position. This was the one on the south side. It flew the triangular pennant-shaped swallowtail flag of the state of Ohio, the only non-rectangular U.S. state flag. Paul could not see the third pole, the one closest to him. No matter, he had pinpointed the Wright brothers' gravesite. His eyes moved from the flagpoles at his right oblique to the mausoleum directly above him.

The high ground.

It would be hard to find a better spot to shoot from.

CHAPTER FIFTY-SIX

Lauren was driving west on Monument Avenue, the Great Miami River to her right. She had just passed Day Air Ballpark, the Dragons home, on her left. The excitement that occurred there the previous night barely registered as she concentrated on the task at hand. She was familiar with the area and familiar with the Engineers Club but she didn't know what Crank expected of her. The parking lot of the club was on its south side, behind the building. Was she supposed to go there?

No street parking was available on Monument in front of the club. Lauren slowed as she neared the structure. She looked to her left to view the building and noticed the bowler bench that sat on that side. The bench brought a smile to her face but it was short lived.

What the hell am I supposed to do now?

She couldn't turn left at the next light, Jefferson Street, as it was one-way in the wrong direction. To get behind the building she would have to continue west a few blocks before turning and working her way back. Just then the headlights of a sport utility vehicle came toward her from a narrow exit drive on the left side of the Club. It was barely a car length in front of her. Lauren braked to allow it out onto Monument. She engaged her left turn signal, effectively indicating she wanted to pull into the drive going the wrong way.

The driver of the SUV, a young woman, slowed and looked cautiously at Lauren. She began to ease out of the drive. As she did, Lauren realized the vehicle was a Jeep Renegade. She instinctively raised two fingers of her right hand and moved it from side to side. It was the Jeep Wave. The woman smiled before pulling away. Lauren maneuvered the Escape into the vacated drive and pulled to the parking lot in the rear of the building.

Is it a faux pas to do the Jeep Wave from a Ford?

She sat with the engine running and examined the Engineers Club. It was a large two-story light brown brick structure. Their friends, the McClarys, were members. They had invited Paul and Lauren to attend events there more than once. The interior of the building featured expansive rooms, some with wood covered walls. Paul's favorite room was the library. Its carpeted floor, large curtained windows, fireplace, and floor to ceiling bookshelves holding thousands of volumes, gave it the feel of a study in an old British murder mystery. The McClarys told them the concentration of books, many of which were highly technical, made the library the "Google of its day" to early members.

Lauren's favorite room was a little coffee shop on the second floor. In 1925 the room was installed as a barbershop for members. Orville Wright, a well-groomed and private man, often made use of the shop, getting a trim while looking across the river where, at that time, McCook Army Airfield lay. He could keep tabs on the state of aviation.

The building exuded an air of history. Among the many significant items on display inside was the Wright brothers' third engine. It was built in 1904 and used in stationary tests by Wilbur and Orville until 1906. Legend had it that the brothers painted the aluminum components of the engine with black paint so competitors would think it was made of cast iron and it would be hard to photograph.

Lauren was looking at the building when Paul's iPhone text tone sounded. She picked it up and read the message.

Ola! Next stop is the Wright Cycle Shop, 22 Williams. Pull up across the street. It's barely a mile away. You'll pass 1st Baptist on the way. Site of Orville's funeral...but you knew that. Enjoy.

This text came with a bicycle emoji.

Lauren snapped up the Tracfone and quickly typed a message to her husband.

Leaving Engineers. Routing me past 1st Baptist. On to Cycle Shop, 22 Williams.

Almost immediately a checkmark emoji arrived in return.

376

Lauren shook her head and entered the address into the Sync navigation system. It showed that she was only 1.58 miles away. She checked traffic before pulling out and continuing west on Monument. She had driven just two blocks when she saw the Baptist Church draw near on her right. It was a large structure. Lauren thought it might have been built with the same light brown brick as the Engineers Club. It had five huge gothic windows on its east side, a red tile roof, and a steeple that was pale green. She assumed the material used to construct it had weathered over time. The front steps of the church began a few short steps from Monument.

Orville's funeral, huh? They must've brought the casket right out that door. This street must've been crowded with people.

Lauren had not known that Orville Wright's funeral was held there. If she'd ever heard this it had not registered. Paul obviously must've known for Crank to word his text as he did. She shuddered, recognizing that Crank had intruded into their lives to a degree she could not have imagined before this week. He somehow had put them under a microscope in a very short time.

Three days ago he didn't even know we existed. Now he's moving us around like chess pieces on a board.

She ruminated for a few seconds while following the commands of the nav system, then smiled.

Well, he thinks he's moving ONE of us around the board.

Lauren reached Williams Street and made a left. Slightly ahead and to the left was a short brick wall that held a sign. It read "Dayton Aviation Heritage National Historical Park." There appeared to be a museum several yards behind the sign. She was about to brake and pull to the side of the street but noticed the navigation system was urging her to drive a bit further. She did so and found herself directly in front of the Wright Cycle Shop.

Lauren was aware that the brothers ran their bicycle business from more than one location over the years. She couldn't remember how many. This building certainly fit the image in her mind of a bike shop that was over one hundred years old. It had the look of an old two-story brick house in every way save the windows that covered the front of the structure from the sidewalk up to the second floor. A black sign was positioned above the windows with the name of the business spelled out in gold block letters.

The neighborhood had little street traffic. A restaurant a block away had attracted a number of cars but their inhabitants were now inside. The street itself seemed to be constructed of brick that had been paved over.

She edged the SUV to the curb. Paul, she assumed, would know the history of the locations of the different Wright bike shops. She stared at the building and tried to imagine a world without air travel and two men with no modern resources trying to unlock the secrets of flight. No computers, no internet, no way to easily communicate with colleagues. How—

Paul's text tone brought her back.

Straight 1 block. Left on West 4th. Quick right on Hawthorn. 7 Hawthorn is on left. Wait for instructions. Don't blink, not much there.

The smiley face that came with this text was winking.

Lauren rolled her eyes. She sent a short text to Paul, *7 Hawthorn,* and was driving away as the checkmark response arrived on the screen.

Less than a minute later the Escape idled in front of the site where the Wright brothers grew up. They lived here when they cracked the secrets of controlled powered flight, when they became famous and traveled the world, and when one of them, Wilbur, died. The house was gone. In its place was a small section of porch that had been crafted to look like the original.

Lauren looked out at the forlorn structure standing in the dark.

Hard to admit it but the Crank is right...not much here.

Another tone gave notice of the next set of instructions. Lauren eyed Paul's iPhone.

1000 Carillon Park Blvd. Entry gate will be closed. The exit drive is 500 feet north. Pull in there.

There was no smiley face, no emoji of any kind. The instructions were basic. As Lauren sent the next destination to Paul she wondered if she should read anything into this. She stole a glace at the dashboard clock. It was 9:12.

We must be getting near the end.

Smithson had underestimated the distance from the front gate to the shooting perch he'd chosen. He walked down the center of Woodland Road until it met Central Access Road where he veered right, continuing to walk in the center of the paved drive. At Boy and Dog Road a series of inclines had him breathing hard. He stopped three times to send messages to Hull, directing him to the Cycle Shop, 7 Hawthorn, and to Carillon Park. These sites were within minutes of each other. Smithson needed to keep abreast of Hull's progress so he continually checked his phone.

He found that the monocular aspect of the night vision device made it difficult to view the screen of his cellphone. He had to push the device toward the top of his head when working the phone and then pull it back in front of his eye when he finished. The overall effect was disorienting. He feared he was beginning to develop a slight feeling of vertigo.

Should've practiced with the damn things....should've PRACTICED!

By the time he sent Hull the instructions for Carillon Park he was growing agitated. He still had two hundred yards to cover, most of it uphill. He was sweating in the evening heat and struggling with the NVGs.

Fuck it. I'll go the rest of the way without wearing them.

He removed the apparatus from his head and let it dangle from one hand. He switched the rifle from side to side trying to find a comfortable carrying position. He had planned to play with Hull a bit and thought he'd done a good job of it for most of the evening, but by the time he sent the last text he no longer had the time or inclination to be flippant. After Hull got to Carillon Park there would be just one more site to visit before the big finale.

Maybe I can screw with him a little more after I get settled in.

He gazed up the hill and saw the flags of the Wright plot and, on the crest of the hill above, the top of the Archer Mausoleum.

Maybe have him take one more selfie. It would be a nice souvenir.

CHAPTER FIFTY-SEVEN

Paul tracked Lauren's movements in his mind's eye. He visualized her outside the Engineers Club. Even though she was experiencing what must have been the most stressful day of her life, Paul was willing to bet she thought about the former barbershop on the second floor. When Marge McClary gave them a tour of the building and told of Orville Wright sitting in the room and watching airplanes across the Great Miami River, Lauren smiled. She later told Paul what she was thinking.

"Sounds like something my dad would've done."

Paul imagined her outside of the Wright Cycle Shop on Williams, one of six buildings that housed the brothers' bicycle business. The Wrights began their business in 1892 during the nationwide craze for "safety bikes." These were the modern design, basically still in use today, that replaced the more dangerous "high-wheel" models. The Wrights used profits from their bicycle business to fund their aeronautical experiments.

A story often told is that Wilbur selected an inner tube from the shelf at one of the shops in order to repair a bike for a customer. He supposedly twisted the long, narrow box in which the tube was packaged, bending the two ends in opposite directions. This reshaping of the box produced a eureka moment in which he conceived of wing warping. Paul knew some historians had their doubts about the story. He wasn't sure he believed it either.

What is the word used to described a story like this? One that has iffy authenticity but is widely thought to be true... apocryphal?

Paul imagined Lauren leaving the bicycle shop and driving the short distance to 7 Hawthorn Street. She was now on her way to Carillon Park. He hoped she was holding up as well as her short texts indicated. There couldn't be many more sites. Paul, the former CCT, had a map of the area in his head and he knew Lauren was being drawn toward the cemetery. Paul was becoming increasingly concerned that his theory on Crank's shooting position was not correct.

So far he'd seen no evidence of the man's presence on the hill. Paul knew Crank could be behind any one of a hundred markers in close proximity to the Wright gravesite, but the high ground made too much sense. If Crank didn't show himself soon, Paul would have to consider other options.

At the moment he was crouched behind a large granite marker with the name "Hooven" on two sides. It was roughly the size and shape of the Hulls' refrigerator, if the refrigerator was laid on its side. He was approximately one hundred and fifty feet from a garage-sized mausoleum that topped the slope above, due south of him. From this position he continued to make out two of the three flagpoles at the Wright plot. They were to his right oblique. Due to the sloping ground he could not see the Wrights' graves below the flags.

Paul had made several assumptions. A critical one was his guess that Crank was right-handed. If so, and if he intended to use the mausoleum above for cover, he would probably set up to shoot on the north side. That was the side directly above Paul. If a right-hander fired from the other side the spent brass casings from the M4 would bounce off the nearby wall and deflect back on him. If Crank were left-handed Paul was probably in the wrong position. He made his choice solely on the fact that statistically the man would not be a lefty.

But Crank had demonstrated he was far from the norm in many ways already. Paul's trump card was that he'd made it clear that under no circumstances was Lauren to actually drive up the cemetery roads to the ambush site. She would stay down near the gate. He hoped Crank would expose himself while setting up for his shot. If not, and it became a situation where the men were stalking each other in the dark, Paul would simply have to be better than the hacker. He knew he had all the advantages in training and background. He also knew, or strongly suspected, that the Crank would have a large advantage in equipment and weapons.

It wouldn't be long now. Paul imagined the voice of Gatewood Dowdell in his head.

In due time Sticks. In due time.

The drive from Hawthorn Street to Carillon Historical Park took Lauren five minutes. She tried to make sense of Crank's instructions.

Pull in the exit drive?

She approached the complex from the north on Patterson Boulevard. The navigation system indicated a right turn into the entrance a short distance ahead. She slowed in the right lane and allowed the sparse traffic to pass her. She saw an unmarked drive appear, some distance before the entrance. It did not appear on the screen of the Sync system. It led into the parking lot. Lauren signaled and pulled in. The Crank had been right. There was no gate here. She looked south to the entrance and saw one there. It was closed and, presumably, locked.

How did this guy have these little details?

It was unsettling. The man had been in their house, inside her Jeep. He knew details of their family, of Patrice and the boys. He obviously had extensive knowledge of the Wright brothers and was using that mutual connection with Paul to manipulate them. The seemingly insignificant fact that Crank was aware of this obscure asphalt drive filled her with a sense of dread.

Lauren received the next text less than a minute later.

Very good Paulie! A little fun now. 901 Harman Ave. Hawthorn Hill. Pull in the drive. Get out and unhook chain across drive. Drive up to front of house. Take a selfie with house in background and text to me.

An emoji of a classically styled building with columns appeared at the end.

Lauren stared at the screen, feeling the panic building.

Another selfie?!? What do I do?

She picked up the Tracfone and texted Paul.

Hawthorn Hill next, 901 Harman. He wants a selfie.

While waiting for a response she typed the address into the Sync system. She hit "Go" and saw the destination was just 2.44 miles away. They had less than five minutes to come up with a plan.

CHAPTER FIFTY-EIGHT

Smithson decided to alter his course to the hill's crest. Rather than follow the road in a wide arc that tracked along the right side of the hill before bending left and passing the Archer mausoleum, he decided on a more direct path for the remaining distance. The flags of the Wright burial plot acted as a helpful navigation aid. He knew from his visit the previous day they were more or less directly below the mausoleum. He decided to leave the road and walk toward the flags. His breathing had become ragged and he was sweating freely. Cutting down the distance would be a welcome step.

As he wove through the grave markers on the west face of the hill, Smithson perceived his vision returning to its state before he'd put on the NVGs. He looked at the device in his left hand and frowned.

A damn waste of money. If I can't use them tonight, when the hell can I?

Without the green hue the surroundings had returned to a spookier appearance. Smithson noted it reminded him of *CEMETERY WARRIOR 4,* a first person shooter he often played years earlier.

He reached the lower, western edge of the Wright plot and stared down at the markers. He glanced at Wilbur's then turned to Orville's.

Alright gents, time to check on our boy Hull.

He saw the red and blue icons. They floated into the Carillon parking lot before coming to rest.

Perfect timing. Okay, what to type?

He considered for a few seconds before a sly smile formed on his face.

Very good Paulie! A little fun now. 901 Harman Ave. Hawthorn Hill. Pull in the drive. Get out and unhook chain across drive. Drive up to front of house. Take a selfie with house in background and text to me.

He searched the available emojis on his phone and was surprised to find one that somewhat resembled Hawthorn Hill's front colonnade. He added it to the text and hit send. He looked down again at the markers.

Get ready fellas, Paulie Hull will be coming to see you soon.

He set off up the hill.

Paul continued to scan the high ground above. Without NVGs he was trying to discern movement rather that specific shapes. Anything moving in a cemetery at night, he told himself, was out of place. It was difficult to keep his mind completely focused on the task as he waited for further communication from Lauren.

The Crank had sent her to Carillon Historical Park. Paul knew the connection had to be the significant collection of Wright brothers artifacts that resided there. One of the buildings on the grounds was Wright Hall. It housed the 1905 Wright Flyer, generally recognized as the "first practical airplane" by experts due to its capabilities. Paul grudgingly admitted that the hacker had done his homework.

Paul scanned the hill for threats. It struck him that John Chapman was in a somewhat comparable situation back in March of 2002 in Afghanistan. He had been on elevated terrain facing armed threats. Almost immediately after this thought came to Paul he felt embarrassed about comparing his situation to Chapman's.

Paul was facing a lone killer, albeit one with unprecedented technical capabilities, by himself.

John Chapman had faced dozens of fanatical enemies. He was also alone after confusing nighttime gunfights that resulted in his comrades' withdrawal from the mountain. Believing him to have been killed, his outgunned teammates slid partway down the mountaintop in the pitch black while under fire. Several of them were wounded. It was only determined later that Chapman had been incapacitated by

386

wounds, not killed. He revived as morning came and engaged the enemy for hours by himself. Some of the combat was hand-to-hand.

As a rescue helicopter approached, Chapman charged a machine gun position that was positioned to shoot it down. John Chapman was finally killed. He sustained sixteen gunshot and shrapnel wounds. He was credited with saving the lives of over twenty American servicemen.

Paul's resolve to remove Crank as a threat deepened. He decided the main thing he had in common with Chapman was a conviction to end a threat to others.

If Chappy could do what he did that day, I can sure as hell take on this Crank guy.

Paul's burner phone vibrated. He stopped his scan and ducked back behind the Hooven monument to read the incoming text.

Hawthorn Hill next, 901 Harman. He wants a selfie.

Paul felt the entire plan begin to fall apart.

A selfie?!? Dammit!

He stared at the screen, his mind working. Lauren couldn't sit still. Crank would be monitoring her status. They had to decide on a course of action, and quickly. He held his right index finger over the screen, still unsure how he would respond. Seconds later he began to type.

Go to Hawthorn Hill. Send pic of house. Maybe he will accept.

Paul knew it was a losing strategy as soon as he typed it. Crank obviously wanted Paul in the shot and was almost certainly not going to accept the picture without him in it. He was running out of time. He needed to find the hacker.

Frustrated, he leaned his head around the side of the Hooven monument. The timing was fortuitous. If he had waited another second he would've missed seeing the figure cross Dunbar Drive and disappear behind the far side of the mausoleum.

CHAPTER FIFTY-NINE

Lauren was holding the Tracfone when Paul's return text arrived. Her heart sank when she read it. Like Paul, she believed sending any picture that did not include an image of her husband had very little chance of being accepted by Crank. He would immediately suspect them of scheming in some way. There was no way to predict how he would respond. Her best guess was he would leave the cemetery at once. They would be back in a position of being under threat from the man. So would Patrice and her family.

We'll never find this guy. He can come at us any time he wants.

Lauren looked again at the 2.44 mile distance on the nav screen. Her mind raced as she tried to come up with another course of action.

She covered the distance in a few minutes. Her stress built as she reached the streets of upscale Oakwood. Her mind raced as she tried to think of a solution, some option that would satisfy the Crank.

Maybe quickly scroll through the pics on Paul's phone....find a selfie with a vague background...send him that?

The idea died an almost instantaneous death.

Who am I kidding? Paul doesn't take selfies.

Seconds later Lauren approached the base of a hill. The former home of the Wright brothers looked down at her, grand and luminous in the moonlight. She pulled up to the drive. Crank had been right about the chain. It was little more than a thick wire stretched between poles a couple car lengths up from the street.

How did he know about the chain? We took a tour of the place and I don't remember seeing it.

Lauren thought back to the tour. A guide led the small group from room to room and held up large period photographs that showed the interior during the years Orville, his sister Katharine, and their father Milton lived there. It gave them a perspective that bordered on the eerie. She remembered Paul being fascinated by a picture that showed Charles Lindbergh standing in front of the columned front entrance. It was taken just a month after Lindbergh achieved worldwide fame by flying his plane *Spirit of St. Louis* from New York to Paris. It was the world's first solo, non-stop, transatlantic, flight. He came to Dayton to pay his respects to Orville, one of the pioneers of flight.

Lauren loved hearing the more humanizing stories. She was particularly captivated by stories of Orville's pet dog, Scipio, a Saint Bernard. Scipio had his run of the house. He went almost everywhere with his master, including vacations to Canada. The dog died in 1922 having lived just five years. When Orville passed away twenty-six years later he had just one photo in his wallet. It was of Scipio.

The library was fascinating to both Paul and Lauren. It had been preserved in its exact state on the day Orville died. She remembered his well-worn easy chair in a corner. The inventor, an inveterate tinkerer, had drilled holes in the upholstered arms and attached a bookstand so he didn't have to hold a book.

Stories were shared of Orville, a notorious fast driver, speeding past Oakwood police vehicles on the way to and from his office in Dayton. The officers always looked the other way.

Lauren's mind took comfort in these memories. Her consciousness seemed to take refuge with them, diverting itself from her present situation. That ended abruptly when the tone from Paul's iPhone announced a new text. She snapped back to the present and reached for the phone with a sense of foreboding.

What the hell are you waiting for???

There was no playfulness in the text. Lauren sensed a manic quality to the Crank. But the message had come at the precise instant she was thinking about Orville and the Oakwood cops.

It gave her inspiration. The hacker's message was still shimmering as she began to type.

Oakwood police car parked on street across from me. Officer is watching. Should I wait until he leaves?

Another text appeared in seconds.

Get the hell out of there. Come to Woodland cemetery front gate, 118 Woodland Ave.

Her bluff had worked.

CHAPTER SIXTY

It took Smithson less than one minute to cover the distance from the Wright family plot to Dunbar Drive near the crest of the hill. He crossed the drive and reached the Archer mausoleum. The walk from the front gate had been more of a challenge than he expected. He leaned the M4 against the south exterior of the structure and laid the helmet with the attached NVGs on the grass. He removed his phone from his pocket and watched Hull's progress as he wiped the sweat from his eyes with the sleeves of his hoodie.

Gonna be a lot easier leaving. It'll be mostly downhill.

As he caught his breath Smithson looked at the rifle. The SOPMOD kit he'd procured from the gun dealer contained a number of accessories for the M4. One item was a Trijicon ACOG, or Advanced Combat Optical Gunsight. The reticles are illuminated at night by an internal tritium phosphor. The sight would be beneficial for the nighttime shooting ahead.

But it was still in the SOPMOD case back in the trunk of the Audi.

Smithson had intended to wear his NVGs on the walk up to the mausoleum and keep them on when he made the shot. He wanted to get his money's worth from all his purchases. The SOPMOD kit included a KAC NT-4 sound suppressor, which was attached to the barrel. Smithson told himself that using it for this Op justified the purchase of the kit. By using the NVGs, he rationalized he would be getting a return on that investment as well.

The disorientation he'd experienced when wearing the monocular device made it apparent to Smithson that he would not be utilizing it when Hull came up the hill.

His original plan was to watch Hull walk the camera from Dunbar Drive down to the flagpoles by the Wright graves before taking him out. He had actually paced off the distance during his earlier visit. Now he would be shooting without the benefit of enhanced optics.

Part of Smithson's psyche raged.

I brought two gadgets with me...TWO! An ACOG and NVGs and I end up shooting at night with NEITHER?

Another side of him tried to reason.

It's OK, there's plenty of moonlight. I'll just use the iron sights.

He tried to visualize how it would play out.

I'll have him come up the hill. He'll be on Dunbar, moving left to right.

Smithson had a thought.

Why wait to shoot until he's down with the Wrights? Maybe take him out as soon as he gets out of his vehicle. It'll be a shorter shot. I shouldn't need the gadgets.

Glancing back at his phone he saw the red and blue dots had reached Hawthorn Hill. He kept his eyes on the screen for what seemed an inordinate amount of time.

Come on Hull, send me my selfie. Maybe I get the pic enlarged and mount it on the wall of the Lair.

After another thirty seconds with still no picture Smithson lost his patience.

He texted, *What the hell are you waiting for???*

The answer came back. Smithson read it and felt panic.

The police are on the street. What? And he's asking if he should wait for them to leave? What a dumbass!

He quickly typed another message.

Get the hell out of there. Come to Woodland cemetery front gate, 118 Woodland Ave.

Paul's eyes were locked on the mausoleum above. It had a rough exterior. It appeared to be constructed of large blocks of light-colored stone. He had seen a man walk from Dunbar Road to the far side of the structure. The man was now out of Paul's view. He had seen the figure for fewer than three seconds but it was enough for Paul to recognize he was carrying a rifle.

Paul had seen men carrying weapons in the dark, many times.

Now he waited, trying to sense movement. He realized his left leg was beginning to ache. He'd been crouching behind the monument he was now using for concealment for a few minutes. He changed his body position in order to ease the strain on the leg and to stretch it a bit. He reviewed the situation.

Now I know where he is. I can give him some time...see if he comes to this side to set up for the shot.

His Tracfone vibrated.

Coming to the cemetery. 2 minutes.

Paul was confused.

What happened with the selfie demand? Did she figure a way around it?

Despite burning curiosity to discover the answer, Paul brushed aside the urge to ask for an explanation. He simply selected the checkmark emoji and sent it.

Hopefully he would have the opportunity to discuss it with his wife later.

CHAPTER SIXTY-ONE

It was not quite 9:30 when Lauren approached the cemetery gate. Pedestrian traffic outside the bars and restaurants near the University of Dayton was picking up. Many of the students were preoccupied with their phones. She was careful, trying to anticipate their actions as a few of them crossed the streets with their heads down.

The entrance to Woodland Cemetery was just three short blocks from some of the nightspots. To Lauren it looked as though it was from another century, which, she supposed, in many ways it was. The gates and towers at the front of the property protected a foreboding landscape.

She pulled to the curb fifty feet in front of the gate keeping the Escape running. The beams from its headlights pierced the security of the gates and bathed a distant section of the grounds in artificial light. She saw illuminated tombstones and long shadows. She shuddered.

She knew Paul was in there. He would be on or near the slope where the Wrights were buried. It was up to him now. Paul told her he expected the Crank to expose himself when preparing to shoot. The entire situation was both surreal and outrageous.

This....son of a bitch wants to SHOOT Paul? Over a video I took?

Her eyes were drawn to the camera bag resting on the passenger seat. She began to slowly shake her head when the iPhone lying next to the bag lit up and a tone sounded.

Chain on gate is cut. Remove it. Drive in. Close gate. Follow Woodland Ave. in to Central Access Rd. Turn right, then left on Boy & Dog Rd. (I shit you not, it is named Boy & Dog). Left on Dunbar Road. Park at top of hill. Wright brothers graves will be to your left, below 3 flags. Put camera under U.S. flag.

397

An emoji followed. It was the American flag.

Lauren read the text and sent a short message to Paul on the burner.

Sitting at Woodland gate. He's waiting for me to come up. Good luck. I love you.

She let out a breath. All she could do now was wait for Paul to finish things. They had agreed he would be able to call using his Tracfone at that point. He would go back over the fence and she would drive away from the cemetery. They would meet at the McClary house.

Smithson sat, leaning against the stone south wall of the Archer Mausoleum. He watched the icon representing Hull's Ford Escape approach the cemetery entrance. He'd used the last minute or so composing the text that included directions to the spot a few feet in front of him on Dunbar Road. After the dots stopped moving he sent it.

You ought to thank me Hull, you're finally going to get to see where Wilbur and Orville are buried. Of course it will be the last thing you see, but you get to check one last thing off your bucket list.

He chuckled before standing and reaching for the rifle. He picked it up and chambered a round by pulling back the bolt handle on the left side of the weapon and letting it slide forward. To make sure the round was properly chambered he slapped the forward assist rod on the right side. He stood and brought the rifle to his shoulder while simultaneously crouching in his best first person shooter stance. He sighted down the barrel at monuments in the foreground then swung the barrel toward the flagpoles below.

I feel like Reaper on the high ground!

He was exultant, ready.

Then he had a thought.

Wait, Hull will come up from the left. He'll see me standing here, silhouetted against the light stone wall. I gotta move my stuff to the other side. DAMMIT! How close is he?

Smithson looked to the left, searching for indications of headlights coming up the slope. No illumination was evident.

Where is he?

He checked the map on his phone. The dots hadn't moved from their position near the gate. No longer exultant, Smithson fumed.

What the fuck is he doing?

He typed another message. This one contained a bluff of its own.

If you're not here in three minutes I'm in the wind. Might go straight to Columbus and visit Patrice & the fam. Might even take a trip out to the balloon festival in N.M. and bring your mother in law into this party. Bet your wife would be pissed at you if that happened. 3 MINUTES!!!

Smithson began to gather his gear to move to the other side of the mausoleum.

Down the north slope of the hill Paul was feeling an odd combination of hyper-alertness and embarrassment. The first sensation was familiar. He hadn't experienced it since his days with JSOC, but it was back. The second feeling came upon him when he answered his wife's last text with a checkmark emoji.

The last three words she typed were *I love you.* Ordinarily a pedestrian response like Paul's might be considered insensitive.

Hope she cuts me a break on this one, I—

Paul heard the unmistakable sound of a round being chambered into an M4. It was a sound that was forever locked into his memory bank. He peered up at the mausoleum and, as quietly as possible, raised the Ruger with his gloved hands and eased it into a shooting position on top of the Hooven monument.

Paul was locked and loaded.

CHAPTER SIXTY-TWO

Lauren eyed the text from Crank.

He's threatening my MOM too?!?

She felt furious, frightened.

And helpless.

What the hell do I do now?

She knew that Paul had said she was not to go into the cemetery. It was not a suggestion. It was, she supposed, a command. But Crank was aware she was not moving from the gate and would now be out of their reach in less than three minutes.

Unless it's a bluff.

Lauren deliberated for ten seconds before choosing her course of action. She reached under the front seat and felt for the objects underneath. Her fingers slid over a water bottle and an ice scraper but not what she wanted.

I need a glove, a towel, a cloth......

She opened the console and saw, buried below packs of gum, breath mints, and eye drops, a small stack of paper facemasks. She hadn't seen Paul wear a mask for well over a year. Thankfully he hadn't cleaned these out of the console. She pulled two masks from the stack before opening her door and dashing to the front gate. She put one mask over the fingers of each hand and scrunched them in a claw-like grip. Approaching the fence, Lauren reached up with both hands and grasped the chain. She pulled it from the right door and it snaked out before falling to the pavement with a clank. She then pushed both gates until the opening was wide enough to allow the SUV to pass through.

Lauren rushed back to the Escape and threw the masks inside. She put the transmission in drive and quickly drove through the opening. She rushed back to the gates and eased them shut with her shoulder. She winced as they creaked, hoping they drew no attention to her. She barely checked the street behind her before turning back to the Escape. Lauren couldn't be sure but she thought she hadn't been seen.

No matter, she had to move.

She typed a quick text on the Tracfone.

Driving into cemetery now. Coming up.

Lauren put the SUV in gear and directed it further into the cemetery.

I have to rely on Paul now.

Paul felt his Tracfone vibrate. He hadn't expected any further messages from Lauren. He was completely focused on the target area above. He'd nearly missed Crank's approach to the mausoleum earlier and didn't want to pull his eyes away. The forestock of the Ruger now rested on top of the Hooven monument. Paul was leaning into the stone, left leg bent, right leg extended back and braced against the slope. It was a solid shooting position. He kept his eyes locked on the scene above while reaching for the Tracfone in his pocket with his right hand. He pulled it out, held it near his waist, and angled it to try to lessen the amount of light it would emit from his position. As he did this he could almost hear every Army master sergeant and Navy senior chief he'd ever operated with screaming at him.

WHAT THE HELL ARE YOU DOING, AIR FORCE?!?

He glanced down quickly and was floored by what he read.

She's coming up the hill?!? WHY???

Paul looked up the slope and could see light from their Escape angling upward and illuminating parts of the landscape. He couldn't see the vehicle, just the light as it streamed through the stones and markers, bouncing softly. Fear and dread built in his mind. He felt his heart race.

And then a figure with a rifle scurried from the rear of the mausoleum and crept to the front corner of the north wall. Paul saw him drop some items onto the ground. One was a cellphone, its screen illuminated.

The figure raised its weapon.

402

Smithson had the rifle in his left hand, the NVGs and cellphone in his right. He could clearly see Hull's vehicle coming up Dunbar Drive. The headlight beams were pointed at his left now but in seconds the SUV would follow the curve of the drive in his direction and would light up the markers on the crest of the hill, including the side of the Archer Mausoleum where he stood.

Gotta move!

He walked quickly to the rear of the structure, cut left for a half dozen strides, and went left again. He slowed as he neared the front corner, dropping his phone and NVGs to the ground. He made sure the safety was off and raised the M4.

Hull's Escape was just fifty feet away, moving slowly toward Smithson's position. It was to his left. In seconds it would be directly in front of him. A thought passed through his head.

What would Liam's character do?

He answered himself.

He would go full auto on his target...start just in front of the windshield, hold the trigger down, and empty thirty rounds into it...end of story.

Smithson took aim. He put the iron sight just in front of the driver's backlit head, and squeezed the trigger.

CHAPTER SIXTY-THREE

The suppressed M4 emitted a sharp *"PAP"* before going silent. Smithson flinched slightly but sensed the round went exactly where he aimed, which was two feet in front of the windshield. He swept the barrel over the Escape, still depressing the trigger. He expected a flood of bullets to streak to, and through, the target but it didn't happen. He was confused.

And then he understood.

You fucking idiot! You forgot to flip the selector switch to automatic!

He reached for the switch.

Paul saw Crank turn his body toward the light and take aim. He dropped the Tracfone, snapped the Ruger up at his target, and disengaged the safety.

But he knew he was too late. An image of Lauren's dad, Joe, flashed into his head. *Paul, take care of my girl.*

He saw the suppressed flash of the M4 even as he lined up his own sights on the shooter. Then he realized it had been just a single shot. He saw Crank fumble with the M4's selector switch.

Paul squeezed.

CRACK,CRACK...CRACK,CRACK...CRACK,CRACK.

Smithson's hand had just reached the selector when he felt stinging impacts on his back. He was thrown against the stone wall of the mausoleum. He collapsed, his body folding under itself as if he were a puppet whose strings had been cut. He tried to get up but realized he couldn't move his legs. He was bewildered. Without thinking, he reached for the rifle. It was near his right foot. As his hand gripped the stock of the M4 his eyes slid to his foot.

It was in an unnatural position, twisted in an impossible angle. He realized this was because his knee was bent in a similarly cartoonish manner. He stared at it dumbly.

What the hell? What happened? My legs?

He turned his head slightly to view his left leg and realized it wasn't there. He looked over his shoulder and saw it, contorted and out of place.

Oh shit, that should hurt like hell.

It dawned on him in an instant.

I'm paralyzed?!? What the fuck happened?

Pain receptors in his upper torso began to recover from the shock of the .22 impacts. The bullets had drilled Smithson just below center mass, the first striking him slightly above his right hip. The second round entered Smithson's spine at the L5 vertebrae and blew it out. The lights went out on his lower body. As he collapsed, the weight of his upper body fell upon a lower section that was out of position to absorb the load. Tendons snapped, but he now couldn't feel it. As gravity pulled him down Paul's subsequent rounds smacked into his torso in a nearly straight vertical line.

Smithson began to feel the upper four wounds.

"FUUUUUUCK!!!!"

Paul saw Crank go down and out of his line of sight without firing more shots. A small part of his mind wanted to know why. The operator part of his mind wanted to make sure Crank was no longer a threat. He stepped out from behind the Hooven monument and began to slowly move toward the hacker's last location. He held the Ruger in a firing position. He knew he had four rounds remaining in the rifle and a full magazine of ten more in his pocket. Eighty feet from the mausoleum he made out the top of the man's head. He was crumpled to the ground. Streaks of blood ran up the side of the structure.

He watched as the man screamed an expletive, his face contorted in pain. As the scream echoed through the grounds of the cemetery the hacker gathered up the M4.

Paul looked quickly to the area behind the mausoleum, searching for Lauren. He didn't see her, just the headlight beams from the Escape. He could tell the vehicle was close.

He looked back at his adversary.

Smithson brought the rifle close to his body. His mind fought to make sense of the situation while simultaneously dealing with the pain. A realization came to him.

It had to be Hull!

How in the hell—

He realized it didn't matter how. He was paralyzed, shot up. If he lived he would spend the rest of his life in prison.

In a WHEELCHAIR!

He began to whistle a tune as he manipulated the rifle. It was the same piece that had been stuck in his head all week. He noticed movement. A man was slowly moving up the north slope toward him, picking his way through the gravestones.

Smithson saw that it was Hull. He continued to whistle, wincing through the pain. Hull was barely fifty feet away when Smithson finally recognized the tune. He called out to Paul in a clear voice.

"Hey Paulie...it's *Whistle While You Work!*"

He pressed the suppressed barrel of the carbine against the soft flesh under his chin and squeezed the trigger.

Paul witnessed Crank's actions. He knew the threat was over but still approached cautiously. He reached the body and saw it was in a disjointed heap with equipment strewn about. He made out an iPhone two feet from the body. Its screen weakly reflected the moonlight. It was the most recent model of the phone, several versions newer than both Paul's and Lauren's. Paul shifted the Ruger to his left shoulder and put his gloved right hand over the ejector port. He pointed the barrel at the phone on the ground.

CRACK.

The phone jumped slightly, its screen shattered. Paul trapped the ejected casing against the right side of the Ruger. He carefully tilted the rifle and allowed the casing to settle into his gloved right palm. Turning back toward the Hooven monument, Paul threw the casing as far as he could. He turned back to the body and took note of the gear. He saw the M4 carbine with attached suppressor, tactical pants and boots, a ballistic helmet with a PVS-14 night vision monocular attached, and, comically, a Winkler combat axe on the hacker's belt.

Paul shook his head slowly and said one word before moving in the direction of Lauren and the Escape.

"Amateur."

EPILOGUE

Mike and Marge McClary sat at their back courtyard. Flames leaped from the large square firepit that was the paved areas' central feature. Reflections glimmered off of Mike's Glencairn bourbon glass and Marge's tulip wine glass. Both held their prescribed beverage, but both were untouched. The couple took turns checking the time on their cellphones. Mike had an extra phone, a Tracfone, next to him. He willed it to display a text message, any text message. The phone lay there, dormant, uncooperative.

They were worried. Deeply worried. They knew their friends were in mortal danger. Their party guests were driving around the Dayton area taking selfies next to Dayton landmarks. Paul had told Mike he didn't care what locations he chose as long as some were relevant to the Wright brothers. Paul, though, had insisted that one location be on the list—Woodland Cemetery.

The McClary house on Oak Street was, as the crow flies, barely a quarter mile from the cemetery. This insistence by his friend told Mike it would be a critical location in the night's events. He looked at Marge. She looked back with eyes shimmering with tears. He nodded. He could think of nothing better to do.

They heard the shots, ranging in from the south. There was a deep hollow pop. It was quickly followed by six sharp cracks in three subsets of two. There was silence for most of a minute then another muted deep pop like the first. Finally, thirty seconds later, a last sharp crack.

Mike and Marge turned their heads to the south, straining, both anticipating, and dreading, more shots. There were no more.

Mike replayed the reports in his head.

Those cracks have to be from Paul......have to be.

411

He wanted to believe in his friend's abilities but the uncertainty was extremely unsettling.

He turned to his wife.

"Let's go get ready for them."

Marge took a breath and nodded.

Paul and Lauren exited the area as quickly as Lauren could manage. Paul had her turn off the Escape's headlights so she had to negotiate the narrow curving roads with nothing but the moonlight to show her the way. She began to explain her reasons for going against the plan and driving into the cemetery. Paul cut her off.

"We'll talk about it later."

Then, thinking that had sounded harsh, followed up.

"You did great...fantastic!"

He wanted her to fill in the gaps from her side of the affair, just not right now. He was busy with the screwdriver. The wooden stock of the Ruger was attached to the metal components—the barrel and receiver—by two screws. He pulled out the partially filled magazine before removing the screws. The rifle separated into two halves. One was mostly steel, the other wood.

Paul's original plan was to exit Woodland the same way he came in, by crossing over the exterior fence. He would perform the rifle disassembly while moving in the dark. He wanted to be seen carrying a small bundle after the gunshots, not something the size of a rifle.

They crept the last few yards to the gate. Again activity was evident a few blocks ahead but the small streets nearer to the entrance were quiet. Paul jumped out and pulled open the gates with his gloved hands. He noted the damaged chain on the road below. He hopped back in.

"Go! No sense closing the gate after we pass."

Lauren made her way toward Oak Street, snaking through dark blocks as much as possible. They heard the first hints of sirens less than a minute after emerging from the cemetery.

Before finding a parking space on Oak, Lauren stopped on the street outside of the McClary house. She was adjacent to the Bourbon Trail'r. The trailer was hitched to the Dodge Ram 1500, ready for a quick getaway to Nashville the following morning. Paul approached the bed of the truck and spied what he was looking for, a blue tarp that covered an uneven cube shape. He pulled back the tarp to reveal a four-foot by four-foot stack of the firewood he had helped Mike load outside of Tipp City the previous morning.

He couldn't help smiling. One of Mike's pet peeves was paying what he saw as exorbitant prices for firewood at campgrounds. He took a stand by smuggling in his own, blatantly thumbing his nose at the restrictions against bringing in outside wood.

Paul nonchalantly checked the street before sliding the barrel and receiver of the Ruger into a gap near the bottom of the woodpile. He then pushed in both the partially full magazine as well as the full one from his pocket.

Tomorrow they will be at the bottom of a lake in Tennessee.

They found a spot down the street not far from the Lariat. They exited the SUV and walked to the house. Partway there, Lauren reached for Paul's hand. He turned to her and answered her small smile with one of his own. No words were spoken.

They stepped onto the recently painted front porch and let themselves in. Lauren, dressed for the party, made her way to the kitchen in the rear of the house. She could hear Marge speaking to another woman and realized at least one other couple had filtered in from the scavenger hunt. She walked into the kitchen and saw food, drink, and most important, friends.

Marge greeted her with a tearful hug.

"So glad you could make it."

Paul went directly up the steps to the small second story bathroom. He carried the wooden stock of the Ruger, the rope sling still attached. He saw the small duffel bag he had given to Mike in Tipp City. His party wear was inside. He closed the door and leaned the stock in the corner before peeling off his

413

clothing and turning on the shower. While he waited for the water to reach the proper temperature Paul moved to the vanity and looked in the mirror.

Now I can put down my guns for good.

As he reached for the shower curtain he considered the events of the past few hours. He didn't know what direction the police investigation might take. He could only hope that some of the precautions they put in place would be effective. Would he and Lauren be suspects? How deep would they dig?

Paul knew that if the authorities looked at his phone or vehicle data they would see a similar history as every other couple at the party. They had all driven to various historical sites in and around Dayton.

We just did it the hard way.

He ducked into the shower and scrubbed himself clean, paying particular attention to his arms and upper body to remove gunshot residue. He used the shampoo left for him in one corner. Several minutes later he pulled open the shower curtain and reached for a towel. After rubbing it over his hair and face he opened his eyes.

The rifle stock was missing. There was a glass of bourbon waiting for him on the vanity.

Paul knew the stock was probably being sawed into smaller pieces in the basement that would soon find their way into the firepit.

He reached for the bourbon.

At 8:35 a.m. Sunday Amos Bunker wheeled his Miami County Sheriff's Department SUV onto Woodland Avenue. He saw a uniformed Dayton Police Department officer in front of the open cemetery gates. The officer, a woman, held up her hand to indicate Bunker should stop. He did so and held his badge case out the lowered driver's side window.

The officer looked at the Miami County lettering on the side of the SUV with mild interest.

"Can I help you?"

"Yeah, Detective Amos Bunker from the Miami County Sheriff's Department. I'm supposed to see Detective Calbert?"

He stated it as a question, not a declaration. He thought it might sound more polite that way. He knew the police presence in this area this morning was extensive. He had just driven past a side street and saw evidence technicians working a vehicle parked against the curb. He saw a group of officers just beyond the gate near a large tree. They were viewing a green case of some kind that was on the ground and surrounded by yellow tape. Three police vehicles were parked at various points within a few hundred feet of him. Bunker knew there would be several more inside the grounds. Two local TV vans were down the street taping remotes. The last thing the police needed was an interloper from another jurisdiction.

The officer looked at his badge and nodded.

"Wait one. I'll check with him."

She backed away before getting on her radio.

Bunker reviewed his morning. He was supposed to be golfing right now. He had a 7:55 tee time and, if all went smoothly, he would probably have been hitting his drive from the third tee at Heatherwoode Golf Club south of Dayton right now. Those plans changed when his phone rang a few minutes after 6 a.m. His playing partner, Detective Brooks Calbert of the Dayton PD, was calling to tell him he had to cancel.

"Sorry Amos, we have a bit of a fiasco on our hands. Some kind of a shootout inside Woodland Cemetery."

Calbert's Arkansas twang had stayed with him even though he'd lived in Ohio for nearly twenty years. Calbert and Bunker met in college in Missouri and both ended up in the Buckeye State through a series of twists and turns. Both had been criminal justice majors and had found work in their chosen field. They got together for golf whenever possible.

Calbert continued.

"We have at least two shooters, one DOA, evidence all over the place, and security cameras that were shut down somehow."

This last point got Bunker's attention.

"Mind if I swing by? It could be related to something I'm working on."

415

The officer returned and pointed to the gate.

"You're good to go. Take Woodland here until it ends. Go right on Central Access Road then take a quick left on Boy and Dog."

Bunker stared at her. Before he could ask a question she continued.

"I know, it's a weird name for a road. Just work your way to the back of the cemetery and you'll see a police convention up on a hill. Or look for three flagpoles in a row—that will be the Wright brothers' graves—Detective Calbert should be on the hill just past there."

Bunker nodded and drove through the gate.

The Wright brothers?

He found the area easily. There were at least a half dozen police vehicles strung along the narrow roads as well as a Montgomery County Coroner's Office van. Bunker also saw the three flagpoles.

He parked partway down the hill and began to walk up, feeling a bit foolish in his golf shirt and shorts. He saw that most of the activity was centered around a stone mausoleum on the crest of the hill but there were also uniformed police and forensic technicians sprinkled about the cemetery in small groups.

What the hell?

Calbert, a dark-haired man who stood just over six feet in height, saw him approach and called him over. The men shook hands.

"So what do you have Brooks?"

Bunker left his question open-ended, a technique he usually reserved for dealing with suspects. In this case he thought it would allow Calbert to give a shorthand version of the facts he'd learned in the two-plus hours he'd spent on the scene.

Calbert blew out a breath.

"What the hell *DON'T* we have?"

He began to tick off facts, pointing at different spots on the grounds as he proceeded.

"We have a body up there by the mausoleum with a 5.56 through-and-through round that started under his chin...

416

probably self-inflicted. The reason it's probably self-inflicted is because this bird has a half-dozen .22 holes in him that had to come first. He must've decided to put himself out of his misery."

Bunker began to say something but Calbert stopped him.

"I'm just getting started. The DOA had the 5.56 M4 rifle in his lap. It's a full-auto but was set to fire in semi-auto. He also had a night vision device on a black helmet like you see in the movies and a fancy shoulder holster holding a .357 Colt Python. Oh, and he was wearing a damn *tomahawk* on his belt."

Bunker waited a second before asking, "Is that it?"

"No, no, no, son, still more. We have a green Army blanket draped over the barbed wire down on Wyoming. We have seven empty .22 casings a hundred and fifty feet or so down the hill from the victim. Six rounds hit him center mass, looks like the seventh hit his phone. Ruined it. We won't get anything there. The casings all have an "X" carved in the side. Somebody shot up the Dragon's ballpark the night before last with a .22 and we found similar casings. We figured it for a gang or a vandal....but this shooting here was a helluva lot better than anything I've seen from a gang-banger."

Bunker followed his friend's turns and gestures as the monologue continued.

"There is a hard shell equipment case near the gate with all sorts of military gear and an Audi on the street chock full of more of the same. The keys from this guy's pocket fit the Audi. The car is registered to a bogus name and address. There are extra license plates in the trunk....also lots of cash...it's not counted yet. There was an expensive laptop inside that our tech people seem to be really struggling with."

Calbert stopped to take a breath and Bunker filled the silence.

"Jesus."

"We have bolt cutters down by the gate. The chain there was cut...looks like we'll have some prints from that, but I'm betting they match the victim, not the other shooter. We know the M4 fired another round but we can't find it. Our people are searching down past the .22 casings, figuring he fired at the other shooter. The victim had an assortment of credit cards in his wallet and two I.D.s."

Calbert searched his memory for the names.

"One was for a Glenn Smithson...two N's in Glenn, the other was for an Oliver Haugh. Neither check out. And, oh, get this, our main desk received a call from an unidentified male with a deep voice this morning, this was before any newspeople knew about the shooting....the caller said we need to check with Interpol about the victim. Can you believe it? Goddamned *INTERPOL!* He said the victim is a much bigger fish than we think. The officer on the desk asked the man to identify himself... know what he said?"

Bunker shook his head.

"He said '*In due time, son. In due time.*'"

Bunker nearly laughed. He was about to ask his friend about the security camera outages. They seemed to have much in common with the similar events in Troy a couple days earlier. But Calbert was called back up the hill. The coroner's people were ready to leave with the body.

"Go on up Brooks, I'll wait."

Bunker wandered through the gravestones until his eyes came upon the flagpoles.

Might as well go check out the Wright brothers.

Walking in that direction a thought struck him.

You know, Paul Hull had a little .22 in his closet when we walked through his house after the break-in.

He froze.

Could he have pulled off something here? Could the DOA be the same guy that broke into his house and his wife's vehicle? Hull had books about the Wright brothers near the desk in his office. Coincidence?

Possibilities swam in his head.

Six hits out of seven in the dark, seven out of seven if you count the round that hit the phone. But I just saw Hull last night. He was putting something in his truck......

Bunker's face broke into a smile.

If it was him, we'll never prove it. I'll bet that .22 is long gone.

He walked past the flagpoles and a large monument that displayed a single word, "Wright." He continued for several paces until the stones for both brothers came into view.

Bunker remembered the look on Hull's face in the hospital in Troy when the security man said the cameras on the building had failed. He remembered the Bronze Star certificates in Hull's office.

I was right. He sure as hell IS a capable guy.

Bunker stood on cobblestones, inches from Wilbur's marker. A cold front was moving in and a small pinwheel left near the stone as a momento began to spin. Bunker looked at the markers for each brother and couldn't help marveling at their accomplishments.

His train of thought was broken when the lights began to flash above on the coroners' van. Bunker looked up the hill. The van began to move to the left, pulling away from the other official vehicles.

Well, there goes Glenn Smithson...or Oliver Haugh...or whoever-the-hell he was.

Bunker's eyes trailed back down the hill. He felt a slight breeze at his back coming out of the west. They would get some relief from the heat and humidity today. He looked up at the flags. To his right the pennant-shaped Ohio flag drooped down. The United States flag in the center fluttered slightly. But the flag on the left began to wave. It was navy blue with a white design of some sort in the center. He watched as the flag tilted slightly and opened more fully. He recognized the design.

It was the outline of a Wright Flyer, waving cheerfully in the breeze.

ACKNOWLEDGEMENTS

I owe thanks to a number of people for their assistance with this book. Two depositories of primary source material stand out. The first is the Special Collections and Archives department of the Paul Laurence Dunbar Library on the main campus of Wright State University. The scope of material in their possession pertaining to Wilbur, Orville, and the entire Wright family, is difficult to describe properly. A significant amount of the items under their care can be viewed online at https://libraries.wright.edu/special-collections-and-archives/wright-brothers-collection.

If you are interested in history, treat yourself and pay them a visit. It is best to contact them in advance to request specific files so they can get things ready for you.

The Dayton Room, located on the second floor of the main branch of the Dayton Metro Library, was also an excellent source. The staff, like their counterparts at Wright State, were very helpful. Like Biggs in this book, I could've spent days in each location.

Thanks again to Lauren Reneau for her excellent work creating the book's cover. It has all the right elements to hint at the story inside. Lauren also created the cover of my last book, *Neil Down*. She is two-for-two. Hopefully she gets a shot at a third book sometime in the future.

Gary Schwaiger was once again my "car guy," figuring out the specifics of obscure vehicles with only a few photographs to go by. Thanks Gary.

There were other elements to the story that required specialized knowledge not easily obtained from the internet. Three of these were the world of first person shooter games, specifics of an intense, well-rounded workout program, and the understanding of how one heals after sustaining the kind of career-ending injury Paul Hull had in the story. Fortunately my son Jack was able to answer my questions on all three subjects. He is a Physical Therapist who works out diligently. His home gym is a clone of Paul Hull's. He is also a gamer, though perhaps not to the extent of Smithson. If the story also required information on how to be a great dad to two daughters, Jack could've provided that as well.

Daughter Suzanne Lang took care of the formatting. She also spotted numerous errors in the manuscript, fixing pesky apostrophes and making suggestions on timelines. Though it paled in comparison to her completion of law school, it was no day at the beach. She fit this into narrow windows of her days that are otherwise filled with a number of demands, not the least of which is caring for two young boys, a three year old and a newborn. Like her brother Jack, she is crushing it.

Proofreading is a tedious task. The proofreader gets to see each word in a book before any person other than the author, but doesn't really get to *read* the story. My wife Ann took on this task with *Controlled Flight,* examining each word, comma, and exclamation point. She identified most, if not all, of the errors in the book. I'm responsible for any that remain. Sadly for her, despite thirty-eight years of marriage, she has not been able to correct some of my other errors. I still make her toast too dark. Ann is a medical technologist whose skill and dedication to her work puts even Lauren Hull to shame.

More than one of the people mentioned in the paragraphs above can vouch for the fact that I'm far from a computer person. After assisting me with the most rudimentary tasks on my laptop I suspect they would've put long odds on me writing a book featuring a hacker with uber skills. The specifics in the book pertaining to computer hardware, software, and techniques, are all open source material easily found on the internet. The quote from Interpol Secretary General Jurgen Stock citing concerns about military cyber weapons falling into the hands of hackers is, sadly, factual.

All of the locations in the book, with the exception of the Hulls' house, are real. Many of he Wright brothers' sites are accessible to the public. Some, like Hawthorn Hill, require some effort. Tours are available just two days a week and are limited to twelve people. Tickets are obtained through the Carillon Historical Park. Plan ahead and purchase a combo ticket, which locks in a spot on the tour and gives you full access to the Park.

A visit to any of the sites mentioned in the book could easily include a stop at the Wright family plot in Woodland Cemetery. The specific directions to the gravesites once you're on the grounds are slightly more complicated than I've written them in the book, but look for the flagpoles, you'll find them. FYI, you *do* drive on Boy and Dog Road.

Chappy the cat is the amalgamation of our two real-life cats, Murphy and Mango. Every single trait mentioned in the story comes from one or both of them, right down to the chewing of charger cords.

Chappy the Combat Controller was a real person. John Chapman's story is phenomenal. It was difficult to do it justice in print. The best source for the full story is *Alone at Dawn, Medal of Honor Recipient John Chapman and the Untold Story of the World's Deadliest Special Operations Force,* by Dan Schilling and Lori Chapman Longfritz.

A couple aspects of the story may ring less than believable. Would the Hulls have friends that live just blocks from the cemetery where the final act plays out? Isn't that a bit too convenient? As it turns out Ann and I have friends that live in the exact part of the South Park neighborhood as the fictional McClarys. The real Mike and Marge have a different last name but I have no doubt they would be just as supportive to their friends as their counterparts in the story. You can probably find their house using Google Earth. Look for the large firepit in the back yard.

And what about the odd event that opens the story? A husband and wife stop at a closed historical site in a rural area and discover the doors are unlocked, some left open? Sounds like a scenario dreamed up to start a book like this. In this case it actually happened to Ann and I as we returned from a visit to our son's family in Indiana on Thanksgiving weekend of 2022. Like the Hulls, we called the Henry County Sheriff's Office to report the conditions at the Wilbur Wright

Birthplace. Also like them we were told it would be fine to leave before a deputy arrived. We never found out what happened despite checking online sources for several days.

Add a little imagination and a book idea was born.

ALSO BY

MIKE VAN HORN

NEIL DOWN: A SHOT AT IMMORTALITY

There were two separate parades for astronaut Neil Armstrong in his hometown of Wapakoneta, Ohio. The first was in 1966 after his Gemini 8 mission. The second came in 1969, a few weeks after Apollo 11, when he became the first man to walk on the moon. The first parade was dwarfed and overshadowed by the second. But in "Neil Down," a work of historical fiction, it provides Danny Hitchens critical information he uses to set up the unthinkable. Danny is a teenager growing up in a neighboring town that is even smaller than Wapakoneta. In Botkins, he is insulated from most of the factors that made the sixties turbulent. He grew up playing baseball, questioning religion, and worrying about girls and his future after high school. Danny has a great admiration for those in the space program and the military. This is heightened when his brother joins the Army and deploys to Vietnam. Danny's world is shattered by a series of tragedies. These incidents combine with his issues with religion to turn him dark and vengeful, filled with rage. He lashes out at those he perceives as slighting him. His paybacks escalate until he finds himself, in a decade of high profile assassinations, planning the inconceivable. He will use information obtained during the Gemini 8 Homecoming parade to kill Neil Armstrong.

Available on Amazon

www.ingramcontent.com/pod-product-compliance
Lightning Source LLC
Chambersburg PA
CBHW070347260626
47161CB00001B/48